$+PC$

HILL
PR...

KT-233-654

Paul Doiron is the editor-in-chief of *Down East: The Magazine of Maine*. A native of Maine, he attended Yale University and holds an MFA from Emerson College. His debut, and the first in the Mike Bowditch series of crime novels. *The Poacher's Son* was the winner of the Barry Award, the Strand Award for Best First Novel, and a finalist for the Edgar and Anthony awards. Paul is a registered Maine Guide specialising in fly fishing and outdoor recreation. He lives on a trout stream in coastal Maine with his wife.

For more information, you can visit: www.pauldoiron.com

THE POACHER'S SON

Game warden Mike Bowditch returns home one evening to find an alarming voice from the past on his answering machine: his father, Jack, a hard-drinking womanizer who makes his living from poaching illegal game. An even more frightening call comes the next morning from the police: they are searching for a cop-killer — and Mike's father is their prime suspect. Now, shunned by colleagues who have no sympathy for the suspected killer, Mike must come to terms with his haunted past. He knows first-hand of his father's brutality, but is he capable of murder? Desperate and alone, the only way for Mike to save his father is to find the real culprit . . .

PAUL DOIRON

THE
POACHER'S
SON

Complete and Unabridged

CHARNWOOD
Leicester

First published in Great Britain in 2012 by
C&R Crime, an imprint of
Constable & Robinson, London

First Charnwood Edition
published 2014
by arrangement with
Constable & Robinson, London

A catalogue record for this book is available
from the British Library.

ISBN 978–1–4448–1876–5

Published by
F. A. Thorpe (Publishing)
Anstey, Leicestershire

Set by Words & Graphics Ltd.
Anstey, Leicestershire
Printed and bound in Great Britain by
T. J. International Ltd., Padstow, Cornwall

This book is printed on acid-free paper

For Kristen

Author's Note

This book has its roots in a series of features I wrote for *Down East: The Magazine of Maine*, and I will always be grateful to D. W. Kuhnert, Kit Parker, and the Fernald family for letting me loose on an unsuspecting state. I owe a debt to Warden Specialist Deborah Palman, the late Chief Warden Pilot Jack McPhee (whom I first 'met' in John McPhee's essential 'North of the C.P. Line'), and other past and present employees of the Maine Department of Inland Fisheries and Wildlife who spoke with me on the record and off. The *Maine Warden Service Policy Manual* was my bible during the writing of this book, but I drew also from *Maine Game Wardens* by Eric Wight, *Here If You Need Me* by Kate Braestrup, *Nine Mile Bridge* by Helen Hamlin, and *Spiked Boots* by Robert Pike. I was fortunate to have the help of investigative journalist Roberta Scruggs. Other early readers of the manuscript included Andrew Vietze, Kurtis Clements, Rosemary Herbert, and Cynthia Anderson. For inspiration and information on trapping in chapter 12, I am grateful to Sarah Goodyear for permitting me to excerpt her beautiful essay 'Fur and Steel,' originally published in the April 16, 1998, edition of *Casco Bay Weekly*. Any factual mistakes in the book are mine alone.

 Many of the places in this story don't exist on

the map of Maine (at least not under the names I have given them), but two important exceptions are the townships of Flagstaff and Dead River. In 1950 the Central Maine Power Company built a dam at Long Falls and flooded the Dead River valley northwest of the Bigelow Mountains. Flagstaff and Dead River are gone, but sometimes, when the water is low on Flagstaff Lake, you can take a boat out and peer down at the ruins of what were once two vibrant North Woods villages. To anyone interested in learning more about these lost towns I recommend *There Was a Land*, published by the helpful people of the Dead River Historical Society. I hope that the survivors of Flagstaff and Dead River will see my decision to set this story in their vanished communities as an effort to keep their fading memories alive. I also took the liberty of returning the Somerset County Jail to its former site in downtown Skowhegan.

I will always be grateful to my extraordinary agent, Ann Rittenberg, for showing faith in this book when I had nearly lost my own. I am indebted to the many people at St. Martin's Press who made this process so wonderful: my editor, Charlie Spicer, and his team, Allison Caplin and Yaniv Soha; publisher Andrew Martin; publicity manager Hector DeJean; and marketing manager Tara Cibelli.

Finally and not least, I wish to thank my family, who nurtured my desire to write novels from a young age and always supported me in fulfilling my life's dream. This book would not exist without them.

The heart of another is a dark forest . . .
— Ivan Turgenev

Prologue

When I was nine years old, my father took me deep into the Maine woods to see an old prisoner of war camp. My mom had just announced she was leaving him, this time for good. In a few weeks, she said, the two of us were chucking this sorry, redneck life and moving in with her sister down in Portland. The road trip to the wild country around Spencer Lake was my dad's idea. I guess he saw it as his last chance to win me over to his way of thinking. God knows he didn't really want custody of me. I'd just get in the way of his whiskey and his women. But it mattered to him that I saw his side of things.

And so, one rainy morning, we drove off into the mountains in search of the past.

It was a grueling drive. The logging road was muddy and deeply rutted from the heavy trucks carrying timber out of the clear cuts, and it was all my dad's tired old Ford could do to climb Bear Hill. Pausing at the top, we looked out across the Moose River valley to the forested mountains that marked the border with Canada. I'd lived my entire life in rural Maine, but this was the wildest place I'd ever been. Soon I would be leaving it — and him. Like most small boys I'd always viewed my father as the strongest, bravest man in the world. Now I couldn't understand why he wasn't fighting to

1

keep us all together.

My dad was silent for the first hour of the trip — he was hungover, chain-smoking — but as we drove deeper into the woods he finally started to talk. Not about my leaving, though. Instead he told me how, during World War II, thousands of captured German POWs were brought to the most remote parts of Maine to work in the logging camps. He said the prisoners at Hobbstown Plantation, where we were going, had belonged to Field Marshal Rommel's Afrika Korps. They'd driven panzer tanks through Sahara sandstorms and fought desert battles at Tunisia and El Alamein. The foreign names stirred my imagination, and despite the sadness that was my perpetual condition back then, I found myself leaning forward against the dash.

'Don't expect too much,' he warned. These days, he said, all that was left of the guard towers, barracks, and fences that once made up the Hobbstown POW camp were a few log cabins, hidden among the pines. Trappers sometimes holed up in these old buildings in the wintertime. Otherwise they were just a bunch of ruins rotting into the earth.

Actually, they were less than that. My dad drove by the clearing before he realized it was the place we were looking for. He climbed out of the truck and stood there in disbelief. No cabins were to be seen. There were just a couple of blackened cellar holes covered by tangles of wet raspberry bushes.

I stood beside him in the rain. 'This is it?'

'I guess someone must've burned the cabins down.'

'It's just some holes in the ground.'

'It's still history,' he argued.

Afterward, we drove down to Spencer Lake and parked at the shore, looking down the length of the lake, toward the mist-shrouded Bigelow Mountains. He turned off the engine and lit a cigarette and then, with the rain beating on the roof, he told me a story that has haunted me ever since.

He said that, during the winter of 1944, two Germans escaped from the prison camp. The guards located one right away by following his tracks in the snow. But the other, somehow, eluded capture. Game wardens and state police troopers joined in the search. Guards were put on high alert at the Kennebec River dam in case the Nazi saboteur tried to blow it up. And people in Flagstaff and Jackman slept with loaded shotguns under their beds. It was the biggest manhunt in Maine history — and they never found him. The prisoner just vanished into the wild and was never seen again, alive or dead.

'You'll find some loggers who say he's still out there,' my dad said, 'holed up in some cave, not knowing the war's over.'

I looked hard into his eyes. 'You're lying,' I said.

But he wasn't lying. Years later, after my dad and I had settled into a life pattern of long estrangements punctuated by awkward visits, I read about the incident in a book. A German POW really had escaped from Hobbstown and was never seen again. And I didn't know what disturbed me more: that I had doubted my father reflexively, or the wistful look that came into his eyes as he told that story, as if his own greatest wish was to vanish into the woods and never return.

1

A black bear had gotten into a pigpen out on the Beechwood Road, and it had run off with a pig. There were bear tracks in the mud outside the broken fence and drag marks that led through the weeds into the second-growth timber behind the farm. The man who owned the pig stood behind me as I shined my flashlight on the empty pen. He had called me out of bed to drive over here, and his voice over the phone had been thin and breathless, as if he'd just run up a hill.

'Warden Bowditch,' he said, 'I never seen nothing like it.'

His graying hair was wet from the rain that had just stopped falling. He wore an old undershirt stretched tight over his swollen belly and a pair of wash-faded jeans that hugged his hips and exposed an inch of white skin above the waistband. He carried a .22 caliber rifle over his shoulder, and he was holding a sixteen-ounce can of Miller High Life. His eyes were as red as a couple of smashed grapes.

It was a hot, humid night in early August. The thunderstorm that had just finished drenching midcoast Maine, five hours north of Boston, was moving quickly out to sea. A quarter moon kept appearing and disappearing behind raggedy, fast-moving clouds that trailed behind the storm like the tail of a kite. Crickets chirruped by the hundreds from the wet grass, and far off in the pines I heard a great horned owl.

The bear had clawed apart the plank fence as if it were a doll-house, leaving a pile of splintered boards where the gate had been.

'Tell me what happened, Mr. Thompson,' I said, moving the beam of the flashlight over the puddled ground.

'Call me Bud.'

'What happened, Bud?'

'That bear just scooped him up like he was a rag doll.'

I shined the light against the farmhouse. It was a clapboard frame building with a broken-backed barn that looked about to collapse and a chicken coop and toolshed out back. Behind the house was a dense stand of second-growth birch and alder with pine woods beyond. The bear had only to cross thirty feet of open field to get to the pigpen.

'You said you saw the bear attack him?'

'Heard it first. I was inside watching the TV when Pork Chop started screaming. I mean squealing. But you know it *sounded* like screaming.' He slapped a mosquito on his neck. 'Anyhow, I looked out the window, but it was raining, and I couldn't see a damned thing on account of how dark it was. Then I heard wood snapping and Pork Chop screaming and I grabbed my gun and came running out here in the rain. That's when I seen it.'

Now that I was close to him I could smell the heavy surge of beer on his breath. 'Go on.'

'Well, it was a bear. A big one. I didn't know there were bears that big around here. It was reaching over the fence with its paw, leaning on the fence, and the boards were just snapping under its weight. And poor Pork Chop was back in the corner, trying to get away, but it wasn't any use. The bear just hooked him with its claws and pulled him in.'

'How come you didn't shoot it?'

'That's the thing of it. I did, but I must have forgot to load the gun.' He rubbed his hand across his wet eyes and shifted his weight from one foot to the other. 'It wouldn't have really attacked me, would it?'

'I doubt it.' There are no recorded reports of fatal black bear attacks on humans in the state of Maine, but I'd read of fatalities in Ontario and Quebec, and it was probably only a matter of time until something happened here. 'You were right not to provoke it, though. If you'd shot the bear with a .22 you probably wouldn't have killed it, and there's nothing more dangerous than a wounded animal.'

Except a drunk with a gun, said a voice in my head.

'I loved that pig.' He swung the rifle off his shoulder and held it up by the strap. 'I wish I'd shot that son of a bitch.'

'You shouldn't handle a firearm when you've been drinking, Bud.'

'He was the smartest pig I ever had!'

I raised my flashlight so the beam caught him in the eyes. 'Do you live alone here?'

Whether it was the light or the question that sobered him I don't know, but he blinked and ran his tongue along his cracked lower lip and looked at me with renewed attention.

'My wife's moved out for a while,' he said. 'But she'll be back before too long.' His expression turned pleading. 'You don't need to talk to her, do you?'

'No. I just wondered if anyone else saw what happened.'

He scratched the mosquito bite on his neck. 'I got an old dog inside. But he's deaf and just about blind.'

'I meant another person. You said you hadn't seen the bear around here before. Is that right?'

'I didn't even know there were bears this near the coast. You don't think it'll come back here, do you?'

'Probably not, since you don't have another pig. But I see you keep some hens.' I gestured with my flashlight toward the chicken coop, using the beam to draw his attention. 'The bear might come back for the hens, although I doubt it will. Why don't you go inside and put that gun away. I want to take a look in the woods.'

He glanced at the trees and shivered. 'Be careful!'

I watched him shuffle away into the house, head hanging, beer in hand. No wonder his wife left him, I thought. Then I remembered my own empty bed back home and I stopped feeling so superior. Sarah had been gone exactly fifty-five days. Earlier, I'd gone to bed thinking that it would be fifty-six days when I woke up, but that was before Thompson called. So here it was fifty-five days again.

I got to work measuring the paw prints in the

mud. They resembled the tracks a barefoot person might leave walking along a beach. Judging by the distance between the front and hind feet, I figured it was a medium-sized bear, two hundred pounds or so.

I followed the drag marks through the field, and the rainwater that clung to the weeds soaked through my pants legs. The trail disappeared into the low bushes — scrub birch and speckled alder and sumac — that grew along the edge of the forest. I directed my light into the wet mass of leaves, half-expecting to see the beam reflected back by the eye shine of the bear's retinas.

Thompson's description suggested a curious young bear expanding its diet from berries and beechnuts to the other white meat. Probably the animal was miles away by now, having gorged itself on Thompson's beloved pig. Still, I found myself listening for anything to indicate the bear might be nearby. A mosquito whined in my ear. Ahead of me and all around, I heard trees dripping in the darkness. Switching the flashlight from my right hand to my left, I reached down to touch the grip of my sidearm. It was a heavy SIG SAUER P226 .357 Magnum that I had never fired except at a practice range.

I pushed my way into the forest. Beaded rainwater spilled off the leaves onto my shoulders and face. I was drenched in an instant.

After a few steps, I was through the green wall of bushes and saplings at the edge of the wood. Beneath the trees the air was still and heavy with the smell of growing things — as humid as a hot-house. I made an arc with the bull's-eyed flashlight beam along the forest floor, looking for drag marks. But the soft carpet of moss and pine needles had absorbed all traces of the bear's passing, and I saw no more blood drops. I wandered deeper into the woods, searching.

I found the pig a hundred yards in.

It lay on its side in a puddle of congealing blood. Its throat had been torn out, and its haunches had been chewed to a red pulp. The bear had not attempted to bury the carcass or cover it with leaves. It was possible it had heard me coming.

I switched off the flashlight and stood under the dripping trees, listening. I knew retired game wardens and ancient trappers who could hear the rustle a buck made passing through alders across a stream. Men who were so at one with the woods that they didn't fully exist among other human beings but were only truly themselves outdoors. Maybe someday I'd be one of those old woodsmen. But for the moment I was still a twenty-four-year-old rookie, less than a year on the job, and my senses told me nothing about where the bear was.

I turned the flashlight back on. Then I went up to the house to tell poor Bud Thompson what I had found.

* * *

By the time I got home it was well past midnight. I'd left the light on outside the screen door and moths were swirling about, butting themselves stupidly against the glass.

As I stepped inside, I was surprised again by my empty house. Sarah had taken most of the furniture with her when she moved out. It always startled me, coming home, to see how little I actually owned. Stacks of books and newspapers, a steel gun cabinet, fallen antlers I had collected in the snow.

Moonlight shined in through the windows, bright enough to see by, so I left the lights off as I moved through the house, shedding my damp shirt and boots as I went. I unbuckled my gun belt and put it away, then wandered into the kitchen. Frosty light spilled out of the refrigerator when I swung the door open. I found a bottle of beer and pressed it against my forehead as I made my way out into the living room.

I cracked open the beer and toasted Bud Thompson and Mike Bowditch — two women-less men dousing our loneliness with alcohol. Except that unlike Thompson, I had chosen to be alone. An empty house was what I'd wanted all along, even if it had taken Sarah years to realize it.

She'd hung in there with me from Colby College, where we'd met, through the Maine Criminal Justice Academy and the Advanced Warden Academy and my long weeks of field training. She'd toughed it out, thinking it was a phase I was going through, that eventually I'd go to law school like we'd talked about and become a prosecutor and maybe someday a judge. But it wasn't a phase, and it was only after I had gotten posted in coastal Knox County that she realized that being a game

11

warden was a twenty-four-hour-a-day, seven-days-a-week way of life, and for reasons neither of us fully understood, I'd chosen it over her.

So she left.

And I missed her — and counted the days since she'd gone away. But I was relieved, too. Relieved that I no longer had to justify my emotions to anyone else. I could spend the night alone in the woods searching for a dead pig and be content in a way that made absolutely no sense to anyone who wasn't a game warden. With Sarah gone, I could love this solitary and morbid profession without excuses and not have to look too deeply into the dark of myself.

That was when I noticed a small blinking light across the room.

It hadn't occurred to me to check my answering machine. I'd been gone only an hour and a half, and most everyone I knew had my pager number if they needed to get a hold of me. My first thought was that it had something to do with the bear. Maybe someone else had seen it outside their house, or maybe it had gotten into another pigpen.

When I pushed play there was the raspy sound of breathing on the other end for a while before a man finally spoke: 'Mike? Hello? Pick up if you're there.' There was a long pause. Then, in the background, came a woman's voice: 'Is he there?' The man said: 'No, goddamn it! He's not home!' Followed by a disconnect.

I didn't recognize the woman, but the other voice was deep and monotone, just like mine, and hearing it again after two years was enough to start my pulse racing. Why was my father calling after all this time? What could he possibly want from me now?

I stood still in the dark while the tape rewound.

2

My father made his living in the Maine North Woods. In the cold-weather months he cut birches and maples for logging companies, snapped the boughs off fir trees to make Christmas wreaths, and ran a trap line for beaver, muskrat, and mink. In the spring and summer he did some guiding for a hunting and fishing camp up at Rum Pond near the Canadian border. All told, I doubted he earned more than twenty grand a year — not counting whatever he brought in poaching. But it was the life he'd chosen for himself and, ultimately, none of my business.

He'd grown up in the remote logging town of Flagstaff, the son of a U.S. Border Patrol agent and his Quebec-born wife, and from what I heard he was a gifted student and promising athlete. Vietnam changed all that. After boot camp, he joined the Seventy-fifth Ranger Regiment and did two tours in the jungle with a long-range recon patrol unit. Then an NVA grenade sent him home with shrapnel scars across his back and shoulders. In Maine, the Purple Heart qualified him as a hero, but people in Flagstaff said they no longer recognized him as the same sweet and shy Jack Bowditch he'd once been.

After the war he held down jobs at paper mills and trucking companies, never for very long, but long enough to convince my mother he had prospects he never really had. She left him after nine on-and-off years of marriage, moved south with me in tow, and got remarried to a better man than my father could ever be.

What her leaving did to him, I can only guess. For years he'd functioned more or less as part of society, but after my grandparents died and my mom left, his drinking got worse and his impatience with the failings of other human beings hardened into something like contempt. Now he tended to live as far from people as possible, wherever the trees were thick.

★   ★   ★

The last time I saw him, I got my face smashed in a backwoods bar fight.

It was the summer after Colby. My dad didn't show up for graduation, which was just as well, because I knew there'd be an argument if my stepfather was around, and I didn't want them making a scene. But a few weeks later Sarah and I decided to drive to Rangeley to do some fly-fishing. She'd always wanted to meet my dad, and since he was living at Rum Pond, which was more or less on the way, I couldn't think of a way to squirm out of it. So I gave him a call, and we arranged to get together for beers at a place called the Dead River Inn near Flagstaff.

It turned out to be a northwoodsy sort of tavern — cedar logs, deer heads — attached to an old hotel. It wasn't as seedy as most of my father's watering holes, but it was a Saturday night, there were a dozen motorcycles outside, and the stares that followed Sarah through the door made me think of broken bottles and bloody fists.

My father sat at the end of the bar with a shot of whiskey and a long-necked beer in front of him. He wore a flannel shirt and Carhartt work pants, and his boots were caked with mud. His thickly muscled body — a solid fifty pounds heavier than my own — seemed too big for the stool on which he was balanced. As always, his hair and beard were wild as if they never knew a comb. But every woman I knew seemed to find him dashingly handsome.

'Dad,' I said. 'This is Sarah Harris.'

The way he looked her up and down, it was as if he were trying to breathe her in. Not that I could blame him. Sarah was wearing a sleeveless top and hiking shorts that showed off her tanned legs. Her short blonde hair was swept back behind her ears, and her heart-shaped face was shining from days in the sun.

'Mike's told me a lot about you,' she lied.

'Don't believe a word of it,' he said, taking her small hand in his rough paws.

We found a seat at a round oak table in a dark corner of the bar. There was a little oil lamp in the center with a dancing flame that gave all our faces a golden cast. My father ordered us beers and another shot of Jim Beam for himself.

'You want one?' he asked.

'I'm driving.'

He snorted. He didn't think it was much of an excuse.

Sarah glanced back and forth between us with a big smile. 'I see where Mike gets his blue eyes.'

'I guess the kid turned out OK,' he said with a wink. 'But he didn't get all his old man's best parts.'

'Mike says you work at a sporting lodge,' she said.

'I do some guiding over to Rum Pond. I don't suppose you like to fish.'

'We're headed over to Rangeley tonight,' I said.

'Yeah?' He looked over my head into the crowd.

'We're going to start at the Kennebago and then fish the Magalloway.'

'Sounds good,' he said absently.

Sarah and I turned around in our seats to see what he was looking at. At the bar a stumpy man with a shaved head and a bushy black goatee was staring at us. He wore a camouflage T-shirt stretched tight across his thick chest. There was a strange smile — almost a smirk — on his face. He raised a glass of beer in our direction.

My father pushed his chair away from the table and stood up. 'I'll be right back.'

We watched him shoulder his way through a group of tie-dyed Appalachian Trail hikers waiting to be served beer. He stepped right up to the man with the shaved head and put a hand on his shoulder and said something. The man's smile vanished. After half a minute or so with my father in his face, he put down his glass and left the room.

'Who's your dad talking to?' asked Sarah.

17

'I have no idea.'

'Your dad looks a little like Paul Newman — if he hadn't had a bath in a while. He's got that beautiful wild man quality. I bet there are a lot of women who want to tame him.'

I didn't know how to respond to her. I liked to think I had no illusions about my father, but it always annoyed me whenever anyone else criticized him. He could be crude and petty, but I also believed that he was a better man than anyone gave him credit for being. I knew he'd been badly scarred by the war, and so I made allowances for his drinking and his silences, consoling myself with the knowledge that I alone understood him.

My father returned with our drinks. He'd brought me a whiskey despite what I'd said.

'Who's that guy you were talking to?' I asked. 'The one with the shaved head?'

'Nobody.' He downed half his whiskey in a gulp. 'Just a paranoid militia freak. So, you got a job lined up or what?'

For the past few weeks, ever since I knew we were coming here, I'd imagined him asking that question and I'd imagined myself answering it. I put my beer bottle down and took a deep breath. 'I'm applying to the Maine Warden Service.'

He looked me full in the face, his eyes glassy from the liquor. 'You're fucking kidding.'

'No,' I said. 'I'm not.'

He threw back his head and gave a loud laugh. 'They're not going to take *you*.'

'Why not?'

'You're too smart. Why do you want to waste

your education on those pricks?'

Sarah said, 'He'll probably apply to law school after a few years.'

I stared at her, but she avoided my eyes. Sarah still hadn't come to terms with the financial ramifications of my decision. Her dad, back in Connecticut, had lost a fortune when the dotcom bubble burst. One of her great fears in life was remaining poor while all our college friends became successful doctors, lawyers, and bankers.

'Law school,' my father said. 'Now there's an idea. We need a lawyer in this fucked-up family.' He reached in his shirt pocket for a pack of cigarettes. He offered one to Sarah, but she waved her hand at it as if it were a hornet.

'You can't smoke in here,' I said, but he ignored me.

'What about you, honey, you taking a vow of poverty, too?'

She stiffened in her chair. It hadn't taken my dad long to find her tender spot. 'I'm getting a master's in education at the University of Maine while I teach at a private school.'

'A teacher.' He lit the cigarette with a shiny Zippo lighter like the one he brought back from Vietnam. 'Wish I had one as pretty as you when I was a kid.'

Sarah excused herself to use the bathroom. We both watched her walk away. When he turned back to me, he was grinning again and shaking his head. 'A game warden, huh?'

'That's right.'

'Well, it's your life, I guess.' He finished his

beer. 'What's your mom say about this?'

'I haven't told her yet.'

'You're afraid she'll be pissed. I'm glad I didn't pay for your college, is all I can say. So how's my buddy Neil?' He said my stepfather's name like it was a ridiculous word. My parents had been divorced for more than a decade, but somehow my father, who'd probably gone through dozens of women himself in the interval, was still jealous.

'The same, I guess.'

'So that Sarah is a good-looking girl. How serious are you two?'

'Pretty serious.'

'Do you love her?'

'Yeah,' I said. 'I think I do.'

'You *think* you do? That's a pussy answer. What I'm asking is, would you die for her?'

Now it was my turn to be dumbfounded. 'What kind of question is that?'

'It's the *only* question.'

I would have asked him what the hell he meant, but across the crowded bar I saw Sarah waiting to use the ladies' room. Three guys in leather jackets and denim were standing around, but she was ignoring them.

My father turned to see what I was looking at. 'You better go over there.'

'She can take care of herself.'

'So you're just going to let them talk to her like that?'

'Like what?'

He leaned back in his chair, appraising me. In his mind there could be only one reason for not going over there: He thought I was afraid.

I downed the whiskey, feeling the liquor scald the back of my throat. Slowly I rose to my feet.

I felt him watching me as I crossed the room.

Sarah was next in line for the bathroom. The three bikers had closed partially around her, and now she was speaking with them. Two were huge, fat in the gut, with arms as thick around as my calves. But it was the smallest one, half a foot shorter than me, who saw me coming. He had a blond beard and a red bandanna knotted around his head and he was wearing sunglasses despite the hour and darkness of the room. I knew it was the short ones who always have something to prove.

'You all right?' I asked Sarah.

'I'm fine,' she said.

'Doesn't look that way.'

Her eyes blazed at me. 'Sit down, Mike. I'll be right there.'

I couldn't believe she was pissed off at me for trying to rescue her, but she was.

'Yeah, *Mike*,' said the short one, tilting his head up at me. 'Go have a seat.'

I saw my face distorted in the dark mirrors of his sunglasses. The jukebox was blasting Guns N' Roses's 'Sweet Child O' Mine.' I felt the thudding bass line shake the wood floor beneath my feet.

'OK, guys, that's enough,' said Sarah. But they weren't listening to her anymore.

'Let's go, Sarah.' I reached out to take her arm, but the short one knocked it aside.

'Don't touch her,' he said.

21

'Fuck you,' I said.

Out of the corner of my eye I saw one of the big bikers swing a beer bottle up fast and felt it break against the side of my skull. My knees buckled and the next thing I knew I was down on the floor, being kicked in the face. I remember the iron taste of blood and the smell of spilled beer and the distinct sound of Sarah screaming.

Then the music died, the lights came on, and I was flat on the floor, looking up into a kaleidoscope. My vision was blurred as if I had Vaseline in my eyes.

Above me loomed my father. He had an arm wrapped around the short biker's neck and was pressing the edge of a hunting knife against his throat. A crowd of faces, a wall of bodies circled us. The short man knew better than to fight. He let his body go limp. My father tightened his grip.

I tried to rise, but the muscles had dissolved in my arms and legs.

'Put it down, Jack!' It was the bartender, a lean, silver-haired woman with a deeply tanned face. She had a pump shotgun trained on my dad's chest.

I saw his eyes flick sideways, taking it in.

The bartender racked a shell into the chamber. 'I said, 'Drop it!''

With one motion my father shoved the biker away and dropped the knife. The man fell to his knees beside me, gasping for breath, one hand clamped to his bleeding throat.

'They attacked my kid, Sally,' said my father.

'Tell it to the cops.'

Five minutes later a sheriff's deputy arrived with his gun drawn. The deputy, a soft-looking guy with a face that made him look like an evil baby, made my father kneel on the broken glass. He twisted his arms behind him while he put on the handcuffs. But my father just grinned. He was having the time of his life.

More police arrived — a state trooper and an old game warden pilot I knew named Charley Stevens. They arrested my father and the three bikers on assault charges. Everyone wanted me to go in an ambulance to the hospital in Farmington, but I refused. The result was a scar on my forehead, right at the hairline, that I'd almost forgotten about until the Warden Service gave me a crew cut.

'He was just trying to help me,' I told Charley Stevens.

'That may be,' said the old game warden. 'But he could have killed that man.'

'I'll bail you out,' I told my father.

He shook his head. 'I'll be out before morning. It's a bullshit charge and they know it.'

They led him away in handcuffs, and the next day when we went to the county jail in Skowhegan, we learned the charges had indeed been dropped against him, just as he'd predicted. I tried to phone him afterward at Rum Pond to say thanks, but he never did return my calls.

★   ★   ★

23

Until now. I didn't know why my father had called me, but if he was coming back into my life after two silent years, trouble was sure to be close behind.

3

A few hours later I awoke to the cackling of crows. At dawn, a gang of them took over the pines around my house, and their harsh quarreling voices roused me from sleep.

The house I was renting bordered a tidal creek that flowed through a field of green spartina grass down to the Segocket River. As the tide went out, the creek would shrink to a bed of sour-smelling mud, and great clouds of mosquitoes would rise off the salt pannes. But at high tide I could slide my canoe down into the stream and follow the water all the way to the sea.

The house was a single-story ranch that Sarah and I managed to rent cheap on account of its ramshackle condition. A lobsterman had built the place without a blueprint, making improvements and repairs as necessity dictated and his bank account allowed. When he gave us the keys, he also gave us a hammer and a roll of duct tape, saying, 'Expect you'll need these from time to time.'

He was right. Each rainstorm seemed to reveal a new leak in the roof. Sarah had hated the place from the start, but she refused to stoop to renting a mobile home, and on my piss-poor salary and her school stipend, it was the best we could do. Still, I always liked the old place. From the window above the kitchen sink I could watch herons and egrets hunting in the tidal creek, and at first light there was always the good smell of the sea, miles downstream.

This morning, though, I didn't hang around to enjoy the quiet. I took a quick shower, put on a clean uniform, and made a call to my supervisor, Sergeant Kathy Frost, at her home.

Kathy was an eighteen-year veteran of the Maine Warden Service and one of the first women in the agency's history, back before affirmative action opened things up. She'd had to pass the same physical fitness test as a man to get in — bench press, sit-ups, push-ups, running, and swimming. Now, in addition to being one of three sergeants supervising wardens in Division B, she oversaw the K-9 unit and was odds-on favorite to replace Lieutenant Malcomb when he retired.

This morning she sounded like she was coming down with a cold, her husky voice even huskier than usual. 'I don't know if you've seen the news, but a cop got killed last night.'

I felt as if I'd been punched in the gut. 'Who?'

'A Somerset County deputy named Bill Brodeur.'

'Oh, shit.'

'You knew him?'

'We were at the academy together. What happened?'

'It was a double homicide — Brodeur and a guy from Wendigo Timber. They were shot up in Dead River Plantation.'

'Dead River?' I closed my eyes and saw my father's bearded face, like the after-image of a bright light, flash across the inside of my eyelids.

26

When I opened them, the room seemed out of focus. 'Did they get the shooter?'

'Not yet.'

'So does CID have any suspects?'

'Only two hundred or so pissed-off lease holders. You know the big controversy they've got going up there? How Wendigo bought up all that timberland and is planning to kick out the camp owners? Well, there was some sort of public meeting last night, and I guess it got pretty hot. Brodeur was there as a bodyguard to this guy Shipman from Wendigo, driving him over to Sugarloaf for the night, and someone opened fire on their cruiser.'

'Was Brodeur married?'

'No, but the Wendigo guy had a wife and two little boys.'

It had been years since a cop was murdered in Maine. Even so, it was something you always carried with you. The possibility of it, I mean. I glanced at the answering machine. The little red light wasn't blinking anymore; my father's voice was gone, erased. What had he wanted to tell me last night?

'Mike? You still there?'

'I got this weird message on my answering machine last night. It was from my dad. He lives up near Dead River.'

There was a pause on the other end. 'Weird in what way?'

'Well, we haven't spoken in a couple years.'

'Maybe he heard what happened and was concerned about you, being a law officer and all.'

I laughed, a single sharp laugh.

27

'Or maybe not,' she said. 'You said he owns a camp up there?'

'Not exactly. Last I heard he was working for Russell Pelletier over at Rum Pond Sporting Camps. Wendigo owns all that land now. If they sell it, Pelletier will lose his business.'

'You think that's why he called you?'

The suspicion in her voice made me uneasy, as if I'd somehow given her the wrong idea. 'It's probably nothing. He gets drinking late at night.'

'My brother's like that.' She paused long enough for me to hear a dog barking in the background. 'So did you talk to him?'

'I was out on a call.' I told her about my evening with Bud Thompson. 'I think I know the bear that got his pig. The one I'm thinking of has a thing for greasy barbecue grills. Last month it was up on a patio licking some guy's hibachi.'

'Sounds kinky. You want me to bring over a culvert trap?'

'What about Dick Roberge?' I said, referring to the local animal damage-control agent who assisted us trapping nuisance wildlife.

'Dick's getting his knee replaced.'

'You don't mind bringing over a trap?'

'I'm headed to Division B, anyway. Where do you want to meet?'

'How about that place where we caught that night hunter last month?'

'Give me a couple hours.' We were both about to hang up when she came back on the line.

'Maybe in the meantime you should give your old man a ring. Just a suggestion, but if it were my dad and I hadn't heard from him in years, I'd be a little curious about the timing.'

★ ★ ★

In the few months we'd been working together I'd learned to follow Kathy's advice. Better to make the call than spend the day wondering what my dad was mixed up in.

My father didn't have a phone himself at his cabin but relied on the owner at Rum Pond Sporting Camps to take messages for him. The lodge itself was so remote no phone lines connected it with the outside world, and the surrounding mountains made cell-phone reception iffy at best. Instead, the owner, Russell Pelletier, used an old radio phone to make and receive calls. When no one picked up, I tried the in-town answering service and got an earful of static until the machine came on.

'Hey, you've reached Rum Pond Sporting Camps, and if we ain't here, we're probably out fishing.' When I was sixteen, I'd spent half a summer washing dishes at the camps. The only woman there had been Pelletier's chain-smoking wife, but this pretty voice definitely didn't belong to Doreen.

The machine started to record. 'This is Mike Bowditch,' I said. 'Jack's son. I don't know if he's still working there — Charley Stevens told me he was, but we haven't talked in a while — I mean, my dad and I haven't talked. Anyway, I got a call from him last night. I'm not sure what it's about. Can you tell him I called?' I rattled off my cell-phone and pager numbers and hung up, embarrassed at my stammering incoherence.

How come everything to do with my father left me feeling like I was nine years old?

★　★　★

The sun had risen over the pines and the day was shaping up to be another steam bath. I had two hours to kill before Kathy showed up with the culvert trap, so I decided to stop in town for breakfast. I desperately wanted to see a newspaper.

The Square Deal Diner, in Sennebec Center, was owned by a plump and hyperactive widow named Dot Libby who also ran a motel and gift shop out on the highway, served as chair of the school board, organized the municipal Fourth of July picnic, and played the organ every Sunday morning at the Congregational Church. She was the mother of six (four living) and grandmother of twenty-two. I knew all this within five minutes of meeting her. Dot liked to talk. Her late husband had passed away several years earlier from prostate cancer, but the joke around town — probably started by Dot herself — was that he died of exhaustion from trying to keep up with her all those years. She kept a photo of him on the wall of the diner, where he continued to stare down at her with sad, hound-dog eyes.

' 'Morning, Mike!' she shouted as I came through the door.

Every head in the room turned to look at me. I felt blood rush to my cheeks. I've always

30

blushed easily. 'Hey, Dot.'

'So what are you gonna do about that bear?'

'News travels fast.'

'Heard it over the scanner.' She poured me a cup of coffee. 'You gonna shoot it?'

'Hope I don't have to.'

This early, the crowd consisted mostly of locals: carpenters, fishermen, auto-body mechanics, road crew workers. All males. Dot and her youngest daughter Ruth, who waited on the booths, were the only females in the place.

'Can I have the bear meat if you get it?' Dot had red blossoms on her cheeks and laugh-wrinkles around her eyes. Her face sometimes reminded me of a talking apple.

'You ain't adding bear to the menu, are you, Dot?' said a prematurely bald young man I didn't know at the end of the counter.

'It's for the shelter, Stanley.'

From a booth behind me another voice said, 'You're not going to waste good bear meat on those dogs.'

I swiveled around to see who was speaking and saw Hank Varnum, the lanky proprietor of the town grocery. He was sitting with a clamdigger I recognized but whose name escaped me. As a newcomer to the area, I was still having trouble connecting names and faces, and since my position as district warden ensured everyone knew who I was, I often found myself pretending to recognize people who recognized me.

Dot made a face. 'Bear's too stringy for my taste.'

'You can make a decent chili with it,' said bald

31

Stanley at the end of the counter. I noticed he had a newspaper spread out under his plate of pancakes.

'Or a good hash,' offered someone else.

'How big did Bud say it was?' asked Varnum's clamdigger friend.

'He didn't get a great look at it,' I said.

'And knowing Bud, I bet he was drunk off his ass. I bet he shit himself when he seen that bear eat his pig.'

'I'd thank you not to use profanity in my restaurant,' said Dot.

The clamdigger looked down at his ketchup-smeared plate and began scraping up the last shreds of scrambled eggs.

'I'll let you know about the bear, Dot,' I said. 'I'm hoping we won't have to shoot it at all.'

'Oh, you'll shoot it,' she said confidently. 'You won't have any choice in the matter.'

'I hope you're wrong.' I gestured at Stanley Whatever-his-name-was at the other end of the counter. 'You mind if I take a look at that newspaper?'

'You gonna arrest me if I say no?' He gave a grimace that passed for a smile and shoved the paper down my way. Half of the pages slid off the counter. What was the deal with this asshole?

'You hear about that shooting last night, Mike?' asked Hank Varnum.

'Yeah, I heard about it.' I retrieved the sheets of newsprint from the floor. I found the front page and spread it out in front of me. The headline read:

TWO GUNNED DOWN IN
NORTH WOODS AMBUSH

There was an old file photograph of the Dead River Inn, where the public meeting had taken place that led up to the shooting. It looked the same as I remembered it from the bar fight two years earlier.

The article didn't say much beyond what Kathy had already told me over the phone: Somerset County Sheriff's Deputy William Brodeur, and Wendigo Timberlands, LLC, spokesman, Jonathan Shipman, had been leaving the inn by a back road, driving to the Sugarloaf resort from Dead River, when a person or persons opened fire on the police cruiser.

'It was only a matter of time,' said Dot.

I glanced up.

She gestured at the paper. 'Until something like that happened.'

I hadn't followed the Wendigo land purchase all that closely, being so preoccupied, first with my new job and then with Sarah's growing unhappiness. I knew the company had recently bought something like half a million acres of forestland in the northern part of the state, including scores of privately owned camps and sporting lodges. These were largely lake- and stream-front cabins built on sites leased from Atlantic Pulp & Paper, the local company that had previously owned all that timberland. It was the way Maine paper mills used to reward their longtime employees, by granting them leases to build rustic vacation camps on company property. Many of these leases had been in the same families for generations.

'People up there are madder than hell,' said Dot, 'and I don't blame them. They were promised that land, and now this *Canadian* company comes in and says, 'Sorry, we're ripping up your contract, get out.' I'm not excusing what happened, understand. I'm just saying you could have predicted things might turn ugly.'

I thought of my father and Russell Pelletier and all the other people I had met up that way whose future was now in the hands of Wendigo Timber. 'I hadn't heard they were going to evict all those leaseholders.'

Hank Varnum, six foot six with a mug like Abe Lincoln, came over to the counter to pay his bill at the cash register. 'They're not really evicting them,' he said. 'Not outright, anyway. What they're doing is offering to sell them the land their camps are on.'

'For hundreds of thousands of dollars,' said Dot. 'Who can afford to pay that kind of money?'

'They have the choice of moving the buildings somewhere else,' said Varnum.

'You ever try to move a fifty-year-old log cabin?'

'I thought you were a believer in free enterprise, Dot.'

'I am.'

'Wendigo bought that land legally. It belongs to them, and by law they can do whatever they want with it.'

Dot's face glowed red. 'You know what they're going to do, don't you? They're going to sell that forestland to rich out-of-staters, and it's all going to get developed. They've already put up a bunch of gates. It used to be you could hunt or fish or snowmobile wherever you wanted up there. Now it's all going to be off-limits. Is that what you want to see happen?'

Varnum said, 'You can't fight progress, Dot.'

'It's not progress,' I said.

The sound of my voice seemed to surprise everyone, myself included. I almost never weighed in with a personal opinion at the Square Deal, just answered questions and made polite conversation. It had something to do with wearing the uniform, holding myself in check. But it pissed me off to think of the North Woods gated and turned into a private playland for the rich.

'Mike's right,' said Dot. 'And if I was one of them leaseholders, you can bet I would have been at that meeting last night, screaming my lungs out.'

'I'm sure you would,' said Varnum.

After he had left, Dot said, 'I'm sorry, Mike. What can I get you? You want a molasses doughnut?'

'That would be great.' Truth was, I didn't have much of an appetite.

'The one I feel sorry for is that deputy,' she said. 'I wonder if he had a family.'

Of course, he did. We all do.

35

4

A number of years ago, some Hollywood producers made a movie about a man-eating crocodile that had somehow taken up residence in the frigid waters of a northern Maine lake. The hero of this motion picture was supposed to be a Maine game warden. Prior to filming, the actor who had been chosen to play the part of the warden took a look at the summer uniform we wear — dark green, short-sleeved shirt and pants tucked into combat boots, white undershirt, black baseball cap with a green pine tree and the words *Maine Game Warden* stitched around it in red — and refused to put it on. He said we looked like the Brazilian militia. Instead, the actor opted for a more casual outfit of khaki shirt and blue jeans, the better to combat the killer croc and romance Bridget Fonda.

So much for realism.

In my experience, the profession of game warden was misunderstood enough by the public without Hollywood drawing another caricature. Many people — urban and suburban people, especially — didn't recognize the uniform or understand what it signified. Hikers would come up to me in the woods and say, 'Oh, are you a forest ranger? How's the fire danger today?' Others would say, 'I'd really love to work with animals,' not realizing that most of the animals I saw were dead or seriously wounded or sick with rabies or brain worm.

What I tried to explain to these nice people was that I was a cop, and the forest was my beat. The statute that created the Maine Warden Service in 1880 gave the governor the authority to appoint wardens 'whose duty it shall be to enforce the provisions of all laws relating to game and the fisheries, arrest any person violating such laws, and prosecute for all offenses against the same that may come to their knowledge.' That legal description was accurate, but it didn't remotely describe my job.

For one thing, the duties change from season to season. Winter means game wardens must deal with ice fishing and rabbit hunting and hunting bobcats with hounds. It also means snowmobiling accidents, one of the fastest-growing law enforcement issues in the Northeast. In mud season — which is what Mainers have instead of spring — open-water fishing gets underway and dipping for smelts by night. Dogs chasing deer become a problem. And wardens begin enforcing boating laws on Maine's 5,782 lakes and ponds, as well as all navigable rivers and streams. Canoes overturn; swimmers drown. Summertime brings ATV accidents in the woods. Wardens stumble upon secret marijuana gardens. And poaching — a year-round problem — gets worse as hunting season nears. Autumn is just plain crazy. Hunting and trapping of all sorts — bird, bear, raccoon, duck, moose, deer — keep wardens busy day and night. Investigating hunting accidents in Maine is the special responsibility

37

of the Warden Service. Then there are the four-season emergencies: deer-car and moose-car collisions, tracking escaped convicts, rescuing injured mountain climbers, searching for people lost in the woods.

It's a physically demanding job. A warden must be able to manhandle a dead moose into the back of a pickup truck using nothing but a come-along or be able to hike up a mountain in the night to rescue a camper struck by lightning. Mostly, it means spending a lot of time outdoors, alone, in all sorts of weather conditions.

As a district warden, I didn't report to division headquarters in the morning. Instead, I worked out of my house, setting my own schedule and assisting other wardens in neighboring districts on an as-needed basis. Most days, I patrolled my district by truck, boat, or snowmobile, issuing warnings, handing out summonses, and making arrests. Wherever I went in the woods, I traveled with the heart-heavy knowledge that I was alone and without backup, that the most apparently casual encounter could turn bad on me if I let down my guard, and that if I ran into trouble, I should probably not expect help any time soon.

★   ★   ★

After leaving the Square Deal, I decided to drive north along Indian Pond. I swung past a couple of roadside turnouts — shady places along the bank of the pond where you could cast out into the weed beds for smallmouth or pickerel — but no one was fishing this early. Across the pond, though, I got a glimpse of the public boat launch. Someone in a black SUV was backing a big powerboat on a trailer down the ramp into the water. I decided to say hello.

By the time I arrived at the ramp, the powerboat was already in the water. A boy who looked to be about nine years old stood on the shore, holding a nylon rope that kept the boat from floating off across the pond. The sport-utility vehicle, a new-looking Chevy Suburban with so much chrome it reflected the sun like a mirror, had pulled up the road to park. As my truck rolled to a stop at the top of the ramp, the boy gave a quick look in the direction of the SUV.

I saw right off that there were no registration stickers on the bow of the boat. 'Good morning,' I said.

The boy didn't answer or make eye contact. He was a scrawny, dark-haired kid, dressed in a T-shirt and a baggy bathing suit.

I took a step toward him. 'That's a sharp boat you've got.'

The boy glanced again up the road. Out of the corner of my eye I saw a man climb from the Suburban.

I tried a new approach. 'You going fishing this morning?'

The boy nodded, almost imperceptibly.

'Hey!' The driver of the SUV came walking up fast, holding a pair of spinning rods, one in each fist. He was dressed in a lavender polo shirt and white tennis shorts, and he wore a gold chain around one tanned wrist. His shoulders, neck, and chest were corded with muscle as if from lifting weights in a gym, but his legs looked like they belonged to a skinny teenager. 'What's going on here?'

'Your son and I were just talking about fishing.'

'Is that so?' The man approached within a few feet of me, his eyes on a level with my own. An invisible, aromatic cloud of after-shave hung around his head.

'You two headed out for the day?' I asked.

'That's right.'

'You'll find some good-sized smallmouth at the south end of the lake where the creek flows in.'

He didn't answer at first. 'You wanna see my fishing license, right?'

It wasn't the way I'd wanted the conversation to go, but so be it. 'Thank you. Yes, I would.'

He transferred both of the rods into one hand and reached into his back pocket. He handed me a folded piece of paper. It was a fifteen-day, nonresident fishing license issued to an Anthony DeSalle, of Revere, Massachusetts. In the summertime it seemed that the entire population of Greater Boston participated in a mass invasion of the Maine coast. You could sit along Route 1, watching the traffic crawl north to Bar Harbor and Acadia National Park, and for minutes at a time you wouldn't see a Maine license plate. Tourism was the lifeblood of the local economy, and so it was probably inevitable that these summer people — with their flashy cars and fat wallets — provoked equal amounts of love and hate among my neighbors in Sennebec.

'And your registration for the boat, too, please,' I said.

'You gotta be kidding.'

'No, sir. I'm not. You have no registration stickers on your boat.'

'I just got them yesterday.'

'You need to put them on.'

'I haven't even gone out onto the fucking water yet!'

The little boy was watching us with wide eyes.

'Watch your language, please,' I said.

'My language? Jesus Christ.' He rummaged in his pocket for his registration. Then, realizing he didn't have it on him, he dropped the spinning rods at my feet and turned and stormed off toward the Suburban.

'Mr. DeSalle?' I called after him.

'It's in the car!'

I watched him throw open the door and begin rummaging around inside the vehicle.

I glanced over at the boy, who was now standing ankle-deep in the water, tightly clutching the boat line. His whole body seemed as taut as the rope.

A moment later DeSalle came walking back. He waved a piece of paper at me. 'Here it is, OK? My goddamned registration.'

He thrust the paper with the attached validation stickers into my face.

'Sir,' I said, 'your son is watching us. You might think about the example you're setting for him here.'

'How I raise my son is my own fucking business, buddy.'

'You need to cool down, Mr. DeSalle.'

A sheen of sweat glistened along his forehead. 'I'm renting a house on this lake, you know. Fifteen hundred bucks a week!'

I glanced down at the registration. Then I handed him his papers back. 'I hope you have an enjoyable vacation.'

He jammed both documents into the front pocket of his shorts. 'Yeah, I bet you do.' He brushed past me and waded out toward the floating boat, grabbing the rope away from the boy. 'Pick up those fishing poles.'

The boy approached me cautiously, with one eye on the gun at my side. I bent down and picked up the rods and handed them one by one to him. 'Here you go. I hope you catch a big one.'

'Come on, let's go!' DeSalle stuck the new registration stickers onto the bow of the boat.

The boy hurried out into the water. His father grabbed the rods away and threw them into the powerboat. The boy tried to scramble over the gunwale, but he lost his footing and fell back with a splash into the water. DeSalle glowered. The boy stood up quickly, his rear end soaking wet. He grabbed the gunwale and pulled himself into the boat. I could see him blinking back tears.

'Don't you cry,' said his father.

I took a step toward them. 'May I see your flotation devices, please?'

DeSalle spun around. 'My what?'

'Your flotation devices.'

'This is harassment!' He glared at me fiercely, and then, when I didn't budge, he reached over the gunnel and held up an orange life jacket. 'Here it is, OK?'

'You're required to have two personal flotation devices, Mr. DeSalle. Do you have another one?'

He searched the boat with his eyes. The boy followed his gaze, as if wanting to help him find what he was looking for, but his father paid no attention to him.

Finally, DeSalle turned back to me. 'No. That's it. So write your fucking ticket and get it over with.'

'I need to see your driver's license, Mr. DeSalle.'

For a second, I think he expected me to wade out to get it, but when I didn't budge, he splashed back to the boat ramp. I summonsed him for having insufficient personal flotation devices, wrote down the date he would need to appear at the District Court in Rockland if he wanted to contest the fine, and handed him the ticket to sign. Throughout it all, he managed to keep his mouth shut, and I began to think he had smartened up, but as he thrust my pen back at me, he said, 'So what happened? Did you wash out of real cop school or something?'

'Mr. DeSalle, you better think carefully before you say another word.'

I tore off the summons and handed it to him, and he crumpled it into his fist. For an instant I thought he might toss the paper into the pond, but instead he shoved it deep into his pocket.

'You're going to have to find another PFD before I can let you onto the water,' I said.

'You're fucking kidding.'

'No, sir. And I asked you to watch your language.'

We stared at each other a long moment, his eyes looking redder and redder, and then he snapped his head around to face the boy. 'Get out of the boat.'

'Dad?' the boy said.

'Get out of the boat! Ranger Rick says we can't go fishing.' DeSalle swung back around on me. 'Thanks for ruining my kid's day.'

'Don't push your luck, sir.'

I expected him to have a smart-mouthed answer for that, but instead he just strode off toward the parked SUV.

The boy was standing knee-deep in the water, holding the boat line again in his fists. His mouth was clenched and his eyes were fierce. Whether his anger was directed at me, at his father, or at himself, I couldn't say. Probably it was all three. Then the Suburban came roaring in reverse down the ramp, pushing the trailer expertly into the water.

DeSalle hopped out of the cab of the vehicle, leaving the door open and the engine running. 'Stay out of the way,' he told his son, snatching the nylon line from the boy's hands.

From the top of the ramp I watched while DeSalle winched the powerboat onto the trailer. It took him a few minutes to secure it in place. As he worked, he kept his eyes from drifting in my direction. He had made a decision to pretend

44

I was no longer there. Maybe he realized how close he was dancing to the edge.

My last look at the boy was through the window of the SUV as they pulled onto the road. DeSalle was talking to him — I could see his mouth moving, a flash of teeth. The boy was pressed down in his seat, chin tucked close to his chest, shoulders hunched against the barrage of his father's words. It wasn't hard for me to imagine what the rest of the day was going to be like for that kid.

5

Half an hour later I was parked along an ATV trail in the woods near Bud Thompson's farm. I was waiting for Kathy Frost to show up with the culvert trap, but all I could think about was that asshole DeSalle. Every time I pictured his kid's frightened face, I just got madder.

My cell phone rang. It was the state police dispatch in Augusta.

The dispatcher told me a woman had just reported a nuisance bear, this time on the Bog Road, on the far side of the Catawamkeg Bog from where I was parked. 'She sounded pretty worked up about it,' said the dispatcher. 'She wanted me to call in the National Guard.'

Kathy was 10–76, or en route, when I caught up with her by phone. I told her to meet me at the address the dispatcher had just given me. She didn't apologize for being late.

The Catawamkeg Bog was a nearly trackless expanse of woods and wetlands, maybe ten miles in diameter, surrounded by some of the most prime real estate on the midcoast. Most people I met didn't even know this little postage stamp of wilderness existed — which was just fine by me if discovery meant trees being cut down and new subdivisions going up. There was no direct route across the bog, except by ATV or snowmobile, so it took me longer than I'd hoped to circle around to the far side and find the address.

It was a neat and tidy little place that reminded me of a bluebird house. White trim and shutters, bright flower beds of chrysanthemums and geraniums kept alive in the heat by the regular application of generous amounts of tap water, a perfectly edged brick walkway leading up to the front door. No one seemed to be home. The windows were all closed; the shades were drawn. And no sign of a bear anywhere.

I knocked at the door.

No one answered.

I knocked again.

'Who's there?' whispered a woman's voice.

'Game warden,' I said. 'You called about a bear?'

Slowly the door opened a crack. A chain was stretched across the opening. Through it I saw half of a very small woman's face and the darkened interior of her house.

'It's about time! I called nearly an hour ago.' She looked past me in the direction of my truck. 'They only sent one of you?'

'Yes, ma'am.'

'But it's still out there! The bear!'

'Tell me what happened, Mrs. — ?'

'Hersom.' She looked to be in her late fifties, a pale, sinewy woman, with deep-set eyes and hair like a rusted Brillo pad. She closed the door, unfastened the chain, and swung the door open again. 'Come in, quick!'

I stepped inside. Mrs. Hersom closed and locked the door behind me.

'You don't need to do that, Mrs. Hersom. The

47

bear's not going to try to get in.'

'Ha!' Mrs. Hersom literally threw her head back when she laughed, like the villain in a Hollywood B movie. 'That's what you think. Well, take a look at this.'

She spun around and hurried off down a darkened little hall. The inside of the house looked as spic-and-span as the outside, not a hint of dust or disorder anywhere. But an acrid odor — like burnt bacon — hung in the air.

The smell was stronger in the kitchen where Mrs. Hersom stood waiting for me. She thrust her arm out, index finger extended at the back door.

I didn't notice anything.

'Open it,' she said. 'But be careful!'

I unbolted the door and opened it. Beyond was an aluminum-frame screen door, nearly yanked off its hinges. The metal was bent, the screen shredded. 'The bear did this?'

Mrs. Hersom crossed her arms across her narrow breasts. 'No, I did it. Of course the bear did it.'

I straightened up. 'Tell me what happened, Mrs. Hersom.'

'I was cooking breakfast. I had the door open and that window there.' She pointed her chin at the window. 'And suddenly I heard this noise behind me. It sounded like a knock and I thought it might be the little boy who lives down the street. He comes over for lemonade. So I said, 'Who's there?' Then I heard another noise, and I turned around. And there was this huge black bear leaning against the screen door, trying

48

to come in. I just about fainted!'

She didn't strike me as the fainting type. 'Then what happened?'

'I shut the door. What do you think I did? Invited it in?'

'And the bear clawed the screen?'

'Not at first. First it came around to that window. It stood up and stuck its head inside, like it wanted to climb in, but it couldn't, so it went back around to the screen door and started tearing it apart. I thought I was going to have a heart attack.'

'What happened next?'

'Well, my daughter had left this thing outside — what do you call it? — a Thighmaster.'

'A Thighmaster?'

'You know, one of those exercise thingies you squeeze between your thighs. She had left it in the backyard. I looked out the window and the bear had the Thighmaster in its teeth. It was chewing on it and clawing at it and tossing it in the air.' Mrs. Hersom's eyes grew wide. 'I kept thinking, 'That Thighmaster could be me!''

'How long ago did this all happen?'

'Forty-five, fifty minutes. If you hadn't taken so long to get here, you might have been in time to shoot it. Why do you let those things run around wild?'

'I'm sure you were scared, Mrs. Hersom, but black bears rarely harm human beings.'

'Don't patronize me. That thing was danger-ous. If I'd had a gun, I would have shot it. My daughter has a gun, and I'm going to borrow it.'

'That's not a good idea, Mrs. Hersom. Believe

me, you did the right thing in calling the police.'

My pager buzzed on my belt. Kathy's cell number showed on the display. 'Excuse me. My sergeant is trying to reach me.'

'You're going to shoot it, right?'

'No, ma'am. Not unless I have to.'

'Well, what if it comes back?'

'Excuse me just one second.'

Kathy's voice was full of merriment. 'Guess what just ran across the road in front of me?'

'You're kidding?'

'I'm at the corner of Bog and Tolman. Get over here.'

I said, 'I need to go, Mrs. Hersom. The bear was just seen up the road.'

'What about me?'

I backed out of the kitchen. 'I'll come back. Close your doors and windows for now, and you'll be OK.'

She followed me down the hall. 'Who's going to pay for my screen door?'

'I need to go, Mrs. Hersom.'

She called after me down the walk, 'If you see that bear, shoot it!'

★ ★ ★

I found Kathy's new GMC parked in the shade of some trees, a mile up the road. The trailer with the culvert trap was hitched to the back of it. Kathy was nowhere to be seen, but a ticked-off red squirrel was chattering in the beeches at the side of the road.

I pushed through some dusty roadside

50

raspberries and found my sergeant standing underneath an old beech, looking up at the squirrel perched on a limb above her head. The little animal was scolding her as if she had given it offense.

'I hate to tell you,' I said, 'but that's not a bear.'

'And I was just thinking we could have used a smaller trap.'

'So where did it go?'

'Over there. Into the bog.'

Kathy Frost was a tall, sun-freckled woman with a bob of sandy hair and the toned arms and legs of a basketball player. Her uniform had a huge stain over her right breast.

She noticed where I was looking. 'Breakfast burrito,' she confessed sheepishly.

'Actually, I was checking you out.'

'In your dreams.'

We spread out a topo map of the area across the hood of my truck and put our heads together. Kathy's bug repellent of choice was Avon Skin So Soft, a perfumed lotion that gave her a feminine scent that seemed at odds with her mannish body language. Sarah had used that same lotion whenever we went hiking. In spite of myself, I found myself losing focus on what Kathy was now telling me.

She guessed that the bear was ranging out from a cedar swamp, roughly midway between Bud Thompson's farm and the Bog Road. 'In the winter,' she said, 'that swamp's a primo deer yard. They really bunch up under those cedars to get out of the snow. I could see your bear using it for cover from the heat.'

On my map a dotted line indicated an old logging trail that led from the road down into the heart of the swamp. That road seemed to offer the best access into the bear's territory.

Getting down it with the trailer was another story. About fifty yards in, we came across a fallen tree — a storm-toppled spruce — that we had to winch out of the way before we could drive any farther. Then Kathy nearly got her truck stuck in a dry rivulet that had been carved in the road during the spring runoff.

A few hundred yards in we found the remains of a burned house. It was just a weed- and bottle-filled cellar hole today, but once, maybe a hundred years ago, someone had built himself a house there and chopped down the cedars and hemlocks to clear a yard. Now the forest had closed back in around the foundation, and wild rhubarb and sumac grew thick and tangled around the blackened stone walls. It was as if the place had somehow managed to slide backward into the past.

Kathy stopped her truck in front of me and got out. 'Did you see those fresh claw marks on that beech back there?'

'I guess I missed them.'

'Let's have a look around. I think this just might be the spot.'

★ ★ ★

Does a bear shit in the woods? You'd better believe it. Kathy found scat in the road beyond

52

the cellar hole. She crouched down and broke the black turd apart with a stick.

'It looks like dog shit,' I said.

'That's because he's eating meat. If he was eating berries, it would be gloppier — like a cow patty.'

'Gloppier?'

'See how the grass is still green under the scat? That means it's fresh. Now you see what I mean when I say a warden really needs to know his shit.'

I groaned.

Her knees cracked as she straightened up again. 'Let's set that trap, Grasshopper.'

The trap itself was a barrel-shaped tube — identical to the metal culverts that run beneath roads — three feet in diameter and about seven feet long, perforated with holes the size of tennis balls. The culvert was welded sled-like to a pair of angle-iron runners that attached to the trailer. One end of the tube was closed with a heavy grate; the other consisted of a steel door that could be propped open and then triggered to fall shut when a bear upset the bait pan inside.

'Bears are funny,' said Kathy as we propped open the gate. 'Sometimes you'll catch one in five minutes. Other times they'll figure out a way to steal the bait without ever throwing the trap.'

'Dick Roberge told me he once trapped the same bear three times. He'd release him miles away and he'd keep coming back.'

'I know that bear,' she said with a laugh. 'We called him Homer.'

Kathy had brought along jelly doughnuts and bacon to use as bait. 'Now, your bear has a taste for pig,' she explained. 'Which is why I brought along the bacon. But in the past I've used lobster shells and bananas, cat food and strawberry jam, suet smeared with molasses. Anything fatty and stinky, basically.'

We dropped a trail of doughnuts and bacon strips leading to the mouth of the trap. I told her about Mrs. Hersom and the Thighmaster, and she laughed and said that at least the bear was well aerobicized now. Then, as if continuing the same light conversation, she said: 'Did you end up calling your old man?'

At first I didn't know what she meant — I'd done such a thorough job of focusing on the job at hand — then it all came back to me like a remembered bout of nausea. 'I tried. He wasn't around.' I shivered as I stepped out of the sun into the shadows. I was sweating from the heat and the exertion, but a chill was rising from the forest floor. An odor of decomposition drifted up from the shadowed stretch of road leading down into the swamp. 'You hear anything more about the investigation up there?'

'Just that it's got priority over everything else. I guess the attorney general wanted to see the crime scene himself. They have Soctomah running the investigation for State Police CID. You know him?'

'By reputation. He's supposed to be good.'

'Best in the state.'

'Good,' I said, throwing the last doughnut into the bushes. 'I hope he nails the son of a bitch.'

She was quiet a long time, her eyes on mine. I had no idea what was going through her head. But her silence made me uncomfortable.

'Should we put up the signs now?' I asked.

'Sure,' she said.

The signs were bright yellow squares of plastic that we were required to tack to the trees surrounding the trap. On them was written: DANGER. BEAR TRAP. DO NOT APPROACH. When we had finished posting the last sign, we leaned against the fender of my truck and shared a bottle of warm, plastic-flavored water.

From the front seat of my truck came the trill of my cell phone ringing. We both looked at each other. The phone trilled again. I opened the door and picked it up.

'Mike? This is Russ Pelletier. From Rum Pond.'

A shiver went through me. 'Yes,' I said. 'Hello, Russ.'

As a teenager I had spent a nightmare summer living in my dad's cabin and working for Pelletier and his alcoholic wife at Rum Pond. The experience had not ended well.

'It's been a long time,' he said.

'Eight years.'

'That long? Shit, I'm getting old. Your dad says you're a game warden now.'

'That's right. Down on the midcoast.'

He paused. I got the impression he was smoking a cigarette. 'Actually, your dad is the reason I'm calling. You left a message here this morning saying you wanted to talk with him. I suppose you heard about what happened up here last night — the shootings?'

'Yes?'

'Well, the cops were just here looking for your dad.' He paused again to take another drag on the cigarette. 'They arrested him, Mike. I don't know how else to say it.'

6

The speedometer read seventy miles per hour, dangerously fast for this country road. Every so often I would catch myself and slow down, then minutes later I'd find myself flirting with seventy again.

The cedar swamp lay miles behind me. An hour had passed since I'd crossed out of my district, headed first west and now northwest, toward the distant jail in Skowhegan where my father was being taken in handcuffs. But in my mind I was still standing under the cedars, the cell phone pressed against my ear, hearing Russell Pelletier say:

'They arrested him, Mike. I don't know how else to say it.'

I felt the ground slide suddenly beneath my feet. 'Arrested? For what?'

Pelletier said: 'A deputy came out here this morning wanting to question him, and your dad lost it. I wasn't around when it happened. But I guess there was a fight and your dad was Maced. Anyway, they're taking him to the jail in Skowhegan. I'd drive down myself, but I've got a camp full of sports. Maybe you should call over there, find out what's up.'

'The police think he killed those men? Is that what you're saying?'

Pelletier took his time answering. 'They seem to think he knows something.'

'But that's not why they arrested him? Not for murder. It was because he struck an officer, right?'

'Like I said, I wasn't there when it happened, so I can't say. I just heard about it when I got back from fishing. I think you should call over to Skowhegan. Get it all sorted out.'

'It doesn't make any sense.'

'I'm sorry for the bad news, kid,' Russell Pelletier said as he signed off.

⋆ ⋆ ⋆

I told Kathy my father had just been arrested, but she had gathered as much from overhearing my end of the call.

'They think he shot Brodeur?' she asked.

'I don't know. I guess a deputy drove out to Rum Pond to question him, and something happened. They're taking him to the Somerset County Jail right now. I don't know what the charge is.'

Kathy came around the front of the truck and held out her hand. 'Give me your phone.'

'Why?'

She punched in a number and brought the phone to her ear, waiting for a response. 'If they were going to arrest your father for killing a cop, they wouldn't send a single deputy to do it.' Someone must have picked up on the other end, because suddenly she was no longer speaking to me. 'It's Sergeant Frost with the Warden Service. I heard one of your deputies just arrested a man named Bowditch. He's the father of one of my

58

wardens. I wonder what you can tell me at this point.'

Her conversation was brief and hard for me to follow without hearing the other end. Mostly it consisted of Kathy trying to convince someone to tell her what was going on and him refusing. Two minutes later she handed me back the phone with a defeated look on her face.

'The sheriff's office won't say what happened,' she said, 'but it's pretty clear the deputy wasn't authorized to arrest your dad. I get the sense that he went out to Rum Pond on his own to ask some questions, and tempers flared.'

'So they're not charging him with murder?'

'I don't know, Mike. I don't know what they're charging him with.'

'My dad's a prick,' I said, 'but he's not a cop killer.'

Kathy was silent. She crossed her freckled arms.

I reached into my pocket for my keys. 'I've got to get up there.' I climbed into the truck and slammed the door shut. The noise was like a gunshot. 'You've got to cover my shift for me.'

'Mike.' She sighed.

'Please, Kath,' I said. 'If it were your father, what would you do?'

★　★　★

Kathy didn't answer my question, but then again, why should she? Her father was a retired Presbyterian minister, and chief of the volunteer

59

fire department. Not some saloon-brawling logger with a rap sheet of misdemeanors and the public persona of a Tasmanian devil. How could Kathy Frost understand what it was like to grow up with such a man?

It seemed like I'd spent my whole life either embarrassed by him or trying to win his approval. I even became a law officer because of him — to make amends, if that was possible, for the petty crimes he'd committed against society and against his own family. That night at the Dead River Inn, when I told him about my plans to join the Warden Service, was supposed to be my declaration of independence. I wanted him to see me — and himself — in a new way. But all he did was laugh.

So why was I rushing to his rescue now? I guess I was still waiting for the day when he decided he needed me.

That day was today, but instead of being pleased, I was pissed off. I didn't for an instant think he was capable of cold-blooded murder. But was he capable of waking up with a hangover and punching out a sheriff's deputy who got in his face? Yes, he was. Self-incrimination was my father's stock and trade. And now, for all I knew, he had both the State Police Criminal Investigation Division and the Somerset County Sheriff's Department believing he was a cop killer. Jack Bowditch: the State of Maine's Public Enemy Number One.

The stupid prick.

I drove fast along a newly paved stretch of forest road. It was a miracle I didn't run my truck headfirst into a telephone pole. On the dashboard, the speedometer was back up to seventy.

7

The last time I'd visited the Somerset County Jail had been the morning after the bar fight in Dead River. Now, here I was rushing to his rescue again. It hardly felt as if two years had passed.

The jail was a brick fortress, next door to the old courthouse in downtown Skowhegan. It was a spooky building that always brought to mind a story my dad told me as a kid. Years ago, a prisoner wrapped his hands in towels and scaled the razor-wire fence that surrounded the exercise yard. He thought he could escape by swimming across the flood-swollen Kennebec River. Big mistake. A week later searchers found his broken body stuck in the dam downstream.

Now my father was a prisoner in the same jail.

I opened the glass door leading to an office. Seated behind a high counter, a lone dispatcher was taking a call, jotting down a note on a pink message slip. A police radio chattered beside him.

'Ma'am, you did the right thing,' the dispatcher said without glancing up at me. He was a harried-looking guy with wire-frame glasses and auburn hair combed and sprayed over a bald spot. Behind him was a wall of wood-partitioned cubbyholes stuffed with more pink slips. 'We'll be glad to check it out for you. I'll send someone down as soon as I can.'

On the counter was a clipboard holding the week's pink incident reports, left out for reporters who covered the crime beat. I leafed through them, looking for the name Bowditch. I saw nothing, but I knew how paperwork lagged in these offices. Chances were that my father was still being booked downstairs in the jail, having his mugshot and fingerprints taken.

'No, I can't say when exactly,' the dispatcher continued into the receiver. 'A deputy will be there as soon as possible. No, I really can't say when.' He put down the phone and gave me a blank, shell-shocked expression. 'What an effing morning,' he said.

Effing? 'I'd like to see Sheriff Hatch, please.'

Before the dispatcher could respond, a busty woman in uniform — the redness in her eyes showed how much crying she'd done that day — appeared in the door behind me.

'Heard anything from Pete?' she said.

'I still can't raise him,' said the dispatcher.

The woman seemed to notice me for the first time. 'Can I help you?'

Her wrinkled lips were painted a metallic pink, the color of a Mary Kay Cadillac. Like the dispatcher, she was wearing a black ribbon pinned to her uniform shirt, a reminder of their murdered deputy.

'One of your deputies just brought in a prisoner,' I said.

The phone started ringing again, but the dispatcher didn't answer it right away. The woman's eyes directed themselves to the little name plate on my uniform.

63

'I believe it's my father,' I said.

'Stay right here,' she said, and darted through the door. Through the glass wall I watched her enter the sheriff's office.

The dispatcher answered the phone. 'Sheriff's office,' he said, keeping his eyes on me as if I might suddenly break and run

The raccoon-eyed woman returned. 'It turns out the sheriff wants to see you, too,' she said to me.

★　★　★

Sheriff Joe Hatch sat across from me behind a dark-stained oak desk, his big-knuckled hands folded on the blotter. He had mustard-brown hair going white about the temples, a brush mustache, and the shoulders of a retired defensive tackle. Pinned to his lapel was that same black ribbon everyone else was wearing.

'I'm sorry about Deputy Brodeur,' I said.

He nodded.

'I was at the criminal justice academy with Bill,' I continued. 'He was a good man.'

The metal springs in his chair creaked as he shifted his considerable weight. 'What can I do for you, Warden?'

'One of your deputies just arrested my father — his name is Jack Bowditch — up near Rum Pond, and I heard he was being brought here.'

'Who told you this?'

'I got a call from Russell Pelletier. He owns Rum Pond Camps.'

I waited for him to respond, but he didn't.

One of my legs began twitching.

'Look, I don't know what my father did — ' I began.

'He assaulted an officer!'

'Russell Pelletier seems to think he's a suspect in the Brodeur homicide.'

He smoothed his mustache. 'The state police are running that investigation.'

This wasn't going the way I'd imagined, not that I had much of a plan coming in. 'I don't know what happened to your deputy today — and I'm not making excuses for my father. I just feel like there's the potential for a misunderstanding here, and I don't want the CID investigation wasting time.'

'What are you trying to say?'

'I'd like to speak with my father, please.'

There was a tentative knock at the door. 'Come in!' barked the sheriff.

It was his secretary again. Her mascara looked even more smeared than before. 'They found him.'

Without another word, the sheriff rose to his feet and left the room. I remained seated, staring at the closed door. In the silence I could hear the rumble of traffic passing along the street outside. What was going on here? Who had they found?

They left me alone in that room for close to ten minutes.

★   ★   ★

When the sheriff returned, the first thing he did was remove his jacket and toss it onto a chair.

65

His big body was throwing off a lot of heat. I could feel it across the desk and smell it in the sharpness of his Old Spice deodorant working overtime. 'Tell me about your father. When was the last time you spoke with him?'

'Last night.'

'Hold on.' He reached into a desk drawer and removed a tape recorder. He set it on the blotter between us. 'You said you spoke with him last night.'

'Not exactly. He left a message on my answering machine.' I cleared my throat. 'What's with the tape recorder?'

He gave me the biggest, falsest smile I'd seen in an ages. 'We just need to clear a few things up.'

That was a line investigators fed to suspects, not fellow officers. 'What's going on here, Sheriff?'

'You say your father's being falsely implicated in the homicide. I thought I'd give you a chance to set things straight. What was the message?'

'It wasn't anything really. He just sort of wondered aloud where I was and then hung up.'

'And where were you?'

'On a call.'

'Did you erase the message?'

I looked out the window. Something — a fast-moving shadow — had spooked the pigeons off the next roof. I watched them scatter in a hundred directions.

'I didn't realize it was important,' I said.

He was still all smiles, but the strain was showing in the tightness of his jaw. 'So you erased it?'

'Has my father asked for a lawyer?'

His smile gave way like a dam bursting. He leaned across the desk at me. 'Let me tell you something about your *father*' — he practically spit the word — 'your father is accused of killing a cop. If I were you, I'd answer my question.'

'I didn't come here to incriminate him.'

'I called your lieutenant. He's on his way here.'

'Lieutenant Malcomb?'

'What do you think he's going to say when I tell him you're refusing to cooperate in a murder investigation?'

'I *am* cooperating.'

'You destroyed evidence when you erased that message.'

Everything seemed to be spinning out of control. 'Maybe we should wait for Lieutenant Malcomb to get here. I feel uncomfortable saying anything else right now.'

'You feel uncomfortable?' He grabbed the tape recorder and clicked it off. 'One of my men is dead and another's on his way to the hospital. So I don't really give a damn how you feel.'

'The hospital? What are you talking about?'

'We lost radio contact with a deputy of mine named Pete Twombley half an hour ago. I've had men looking for him ever since. I just got a call that his cruiser was found off Route 144. They found Twombley beat up and handcuffed to a tree. I don't know how your father overpowered him, but right now every law enforcement officer in western Maine is out there hunting for him. Maybe you should rethink the attitude and get on the right side of this. Because, the way it's looking, the next time you see him is going to be at his funeral.'

8

I sat alone in the lobby outside the dispatch office waiting for my division commander, Lieutenant Timothy Malcomb, to come through the door. The sheriff had gone off to supervise the manhunt. I felt like a kid waiting for his mom to pick him up outside the vice principal's office.

The enormity of what was happening was more than I could wrap my mind around. At this moment state troopers, deputies, and game wardens were hunting for my father in the woods along the Dead River. The FBI had been called in from Boston. TV news crews were probably rushing to the scene. By tomorrow morning the entire State of Maine would know the name of Jack Bowditch.

When I applied to join the Warden Service, I worried a lot about my father's criminal record and how it might affect my application. I remembered sitting in a room with leaded windows and flaking green brick walls while two interviewers peppered me with questions about my past. It was wintertime, but the room was as hot as a greenhouse thanks to an old steam radiator that hissed at us throughout the interview. I was a sweating mess waiting for the moment when they would produce a folder with my father's rap sheet — his mug shots taken over the years, his inked fingerprints, his list of drunk driving offenses and simple assaults and night hunting citations — but that moment never came.

I left that interview believing I'd shaken off the past. But the moment had only been postponed. From this day forward I would be remembered as the son of a cop killer.

So why was I more convinced than ever of his innocence? Whoever ambushed Jonathan Shipman and Bill Brodeur hoped to scare off Wendigo Timber by making a statement in blood. I knew my dad was capable of violence. But the cold-blooded murder of two men, including a police officer, for quasi-political reasons? He was a bar brawler, not a terrorist.

If that was the case, then why had he fled? And how had he managed to overpower Deputy Twombley and crash the cruiser? The message on my answering machine seemed central to the mystery. Why had he called me last night and who was the woman with him?

My greatest fear was that the searchers would corner my father in the woods and there would be a standoff ending in gunfire. In a few hours the case might be closed forever and I would live the rest of my life knowing I did nothing to save him.

Screw it, I thought, rising to my feet. Let them bust me for insubordination.

★ ★ ★

Heat was curling off the car tops when I crossed the parking lot, and the inside of my truck was like a Dutch oven. I started the engine, glanced in the rearview mirror, and my heart just about stopped. Lieutenant Malcomb was striding toward me across the asphalt. I rolled down my window.

'What's going on, Bowditch?'

I knew bullshitting was useless at this point. 'I was on my way to the incident scene.'

'My instructions were for you to wait here.' As always, he sounded like he had gravel in his voice box.

'I know that. I'm sorry.'

'I don't want an apology, Warden.'

'I couldn't just sit here, Lieutenant — not knowing what's going on up there.'

'The state has rules. They exist for a reason. You can't be involved in this investigation, and you know it.'

'I'm already involved,' I said. 'Please, Lieutenant. It's my father they're looking for. I've got to be part of this. If something happens — maybe I can talk to him, get him to surrender. He'll listen to me.'

He was wearing mirrored sunglasses that made reading his expression just about impossible, and he was already one of the stoniest-faced guys I'd ever met, like a walking granite statue in a green uniform. But when he spoke again I got the sense of something softening in him. 'This isn't a situation you can control, Bowditch.'

'I know.'

'He's the one making all the bad choices.'

'I understand that.'

'He'll be given every opportunity, but it's up

to him what happens next.'

'Sir, all I'm asking is a chance to be present. I want to be able to tell my mother that I did everything I could.'

After a moment of silence, he said, 'Get out of the truck, Bowditch.'

My heart sank, but I did as I was told. The lieutenant waited for me to lock the door and then he started off across the lot. At first, I thought we were headed back into the sheriff's office, but he kept walking toward the street, and that was when I saw his truck parked around the corner.

'Lieutenant?'

'You're right. It's better that you're there. But only as an observer.'

★ ★ ★

Maybe it was because my father was accused of killing a cop, and he wanted me there as a warning to all the other cops that revenge was not an option. Or maybe he was bringing me along as a witness who could testify that every attempt at a peaceful resolution was made and the use of deadly force was warranted. Maybe he just understood a son's anguish. I didn't know why Lieutenant Malcomb brought me along with him, but the truth was, I didn't care, either.

On the road we didn't speak for the longest time, both of us listening intently to the police radio. Troopers, deputies, and wardens called in their locations. K-9 units were en route. The Northern Maine Violent Crimes Task Force had taken over a local fish hatchery as its command post. There hadn't been a manhunt like this in Maine in years.

Lieutenant Malcomb scarcely acknowledged me as we drove. He smelled strongly of cigarettes. Kathy Frost had told me he'd started smoking again after his wife died last fall.

'I got a phone call this morning you should know about,' he said. 'A man says you harassed him and his son this morning on Indian Pond.'

'Anthony DeSalle,' I said.

'Tell me what happened.'

I straightened up in my seat. 'He was putting in a boat at the public landing with his son. I checked his license and registration. I cited him for not having adequate PFDs. He didn't appreciate being cited. That's about it.'

'He claims you were verbally threatening.'

'Excuse me, Lieutenant, but that's bullshit.' I tried unsuccessfully to keep the resentment out of my voice. 'I think I displayed considerable restraint with Mr. DeSalle. He swore at me repeatedly in front of his little boy. I thought he might take a swing at me at one point. It doesn't surprise me he made a complaint. I think Mr. DeSalle has problems with anger management.'

I waited for the lieutenant to speak.

'That's my assessment, too,' he said at last. 'The guy's choice of language didn't win any points with me, either. Maybe that kind of talk works down in Massachusetts.'

'So what happens now?'

'I'm not inclined to do anything for the moment, but if this DeSalle makes a complaint

73

in writing, we'll have to do some sort of investigation. The colonel wants us to make internal affairs a priority these days. We can't appear to be covering anything up.'

The day was increasingly become surreal. In the context of what was going on, this thing with DeSalle was almost comical — almost. Unfounded or not, a citizen complaint could dog me for months. I didn't need any more distractions.

'Do you know anything about Deputy Twombley's condition?' I asked.

'Just some cuts and bruises,' he said.

'The sheriff didn't tell me what happened.'

'A trooper found the cruiser off the road. It had gone off into a pretty deep ditch. That fool Twombley was handcuffed with his arms around a tree. He said your father attacked him, forced them off the road.'

'Wasn't my dad handcuffed? How did he get loose?'

'Good question.'

'He can't have gone far on foot,' I said.

'The trooper who found the crash saw a blood trail. Twombley says your dad was injured. He says your dad stole his shotgun and sidearm.'

So my father was armed, bleeding, and on the run. Was there an outcome to this situation that wasn't bad?

The lieutenant's cell phone rang. The person on the other end was the colonel of the Maine Warden Service — that much I could figure out. But the lieutenant was so monosyllabic, I couldn't follow the rest of the conversation at all.

Not until my name came up. 'I've got Mike Bowditch with me,' he said There was a long pause. 'Yes, sir. I will.'

Will what? I thought. Will take responsibility for him? Will keep him out of trouble?

After he finished with the colonel, the lieutenant checked in with the state police and Division B. I watched our speed increase with each new conversation. But we were still too far away from the scene — a solid half hour, at least — for blue lights and sirens.

'They're calling in the reinforcements,' he said at last. 'I guess they've got Charley Stevens up there in his plane already. You know Charley?'

'Yes, sir,' I said uneasily.

Charley Stevens was the retired warden pilot who showed up at the Dead River Inn on the night of my father's arrest two years earlier. He was something of a legendary character in the history of the Maine Warden Service — one of those people who is always smaller in person than you expect, given the size of his reputation. I knew he'd retired up around Flagstaff Pond and still helped out the department with his Super Cub, searching for missing hikers, doing overflight moose surveys, that sort of thing. So it was no surprise he was assisting with the manhunt.

What I didn't tell the lieutenant was that Charley Stevens and my dad had a long history together, or that the retired pilot, more than anyone, was probably responsible for my joining the Warden Service. It was a long story and a bad memory, especially under the circumstances.

Lieutenant Malcomb reached into his breast pocket for a piece of gum but didn't offer me any. I watched him pop it out of its foil packet and stuff it in his cheek.

My mouth was very dry. 'You don't have an extra stick of that, do you?'

He smiled at me, the first time that day. 'It's nicotine.'

'I don't care,' I said.

9

The State of Maine is the largest in New England, roughly as big as all the others combined. From Portland, on the coast, you can drive to New York City in five hours, but it takes more than six to reach the town of Madawaska, where Aroostook County juts up into Canada. These distances can make it hard for newcomers to get their bearings — everything seems farther away than it should be. As a result, most people never travel beyond the lower third of the state. They cling to the coast, with its lighthouses and beaches and picture-postcard fishing harbors. Relatively few travelers venture into the state's northwestern mountains, but that was where Lieutenant Malcomb and I were now headed.

It was a familiar road. As a child I had once lived along Route 144 before my mother stole me away to southern Maine. The two-lane forest road forks off the busier Carrabassett highway and curves roughly northwest, through the backwoods townships of Dead River Plantation and Flagstaff, before reconnecting with the highway again near the Canadian border at Coburn Gore. It is the gateway to one of western Maine's last remote regions, a wedge-shaped section of forested mountains and moose bogs between the Kennebec River and eastern Quebec. Deep in the heart of that wild land, accessible only by logging road or floatplane, is Rum Pond.

We weren't going that far, thankfully. The search zone, according to Lieutenant Malcomb, was concentrated between the highway and the Dead River, a circle twenty miles in diameter. Even so, it was a forsaken stretch of woods. There were some newer split-level homes and spiffed-up old farmhouses back near the Carrabassett River, but as we traveled north, farmhouses gave way to mobile homes, which in turn gave way to cabins with yards full of junk cars and barking dogs chained to posts. The sight of these shacks filled me with a sort of gut-sick nostalgia. I'd spent the first part of my life holed up in identical white trash mansions — just my mother and father and me. It was a childhood straight out of the Brothers Grimm, and I hated anything that reminded me of it. Which was just about everything at the moment.

This was my father's country. He used to brag that you could drop him, blindfolded, anywhere in the woods between Rangeley and Jackman and in five minutes he'd deduce his location. It wasn't an idle boast. He'd hiked hundreds of miles through these mountains with a rifle slung over his shoulder, needing no compass to guide him home. Maybe a man couldn't actually disappear here anymore, not in this age of heat-sensing helicopters and GPS trackers. There were too many roads, too many people. But if anyone could vanish into these North Woods, it was my dad. I wondered if the searchers knew what they were chasing.

We ran into the first roadblock in a barely settled area of industrial timber south of the Dead River and east of the Bigelow Mountains. Two state police cruisers had angled themselves across both lanes, blocking traffic. There were a handful of cars and campers and pickup trucks pulled off to the side of the road, waiting to be let through the outer perimeter.

A state trooper approached Malcomb's window. 'The command post is set up at the Otter Brook hatchery,' he told us.

'Who's the OIC?' asked Lieutenant Malcomb.

'The sheriff, sir. But Major Carter is en route.' In other words, the sheriff was temporarily the officer in charge until the state police tactical team arrived.

'Are the K-9 units here?'

'Not yet, sir.'

Which meant the grid search, as such, hadn't begun. I checked my watch. By my crude reckoning, my father had already been on the run for close to two hours.

★ ★ ★

There was another roadblock set up at the ditch where Deputy Twombley had careened off the road. Half a dozen police officers, most in body armor and carrying semiautomatic weapons or shot-guns, were clustered around their vehicles, waiting for something to happen. I'd never participated in a hunt for an

79

armed fugitive, but I'd taken part in grid searches for an Alzheimer's patient, missing hunters, and a couple of lost children. Hurry-up-and-wait was the way these operations usually worked.

Yellow police tape marked the spot where the cruiser had crashed off the road. The car had plunged twenty or so feet down, ripping off alder branches and evergreen boughs before landing sideways in a couple of feet of marshy muck. This was the manhunt's inner perimeter, the zone where searchers would concentrate their efforts and expand out.

I tried to make sense of what I was seeing. Earlier this morning, Pete Twombley drove out alone to Rum Pond on his own authority, but to do what? Accuse my dad of murder? Twombley should have called for backup after things turned ugly, but instead he'd proceeded with my father toward the jail in Skowhegan. From Rum Pond, traveling along logging roads, it would have taken them at least an hour to reach this spot, at which point the cruiser went off the road. And Twombley was incapacitated long enough for my dad to take his weapons. Or so the deputy claimed.

My father had been arrested before; he knew when a bogus charge wouldn't stick. Did he think he was being set up? Again I came back to the question: If he was innocent, why had he fled?

★ ★ ★

As the nearest government building with working phone lines, the Otter Brook Fish Hatchery was the logical site for a command post. It occupied a cluster of white clapboard buildings arranged around a long row of roofed spillways and tanks. The compound stank like a chicken farm from the meal pellets they fed the trout.

In front of the old office loomed the State Police Mobile Crime Unit, an enormous white-and-blue motor coach nearly the size of the building itself. An ambulance, state police cruisers, patrol cars from Somerset and Franklin counties, warden trucks, and unmarked Dodge Chargers were gathered in the gravel lot.

We went inside. There must have been twenty uniformed officers crowded into that dimly lit space. But the one I zeroed in on was Sheriff Hatch. He was leaning over a topo map spread out across a table, the center of attention. The room smelled of too-warm bodies and coffee brewing.

Dim as it was, I kept my shades on, not wanting to make eye contact.

The sheriff glanced up at me and scowled. 'What's he doing here?'

'You want to step outside for a minute, Bowditch,' said the lieutenant.

'No problem.'

Why was I so surprised by their reactions? As a family member of a suspected cop killer, I should by all rights have been barred from the scene — would have been barred if not for the lieutenant. Uniform or not, I was the son of the

81

fugitive they were all hunting. My loyalties were necessarily suspect.

I drifted over to the nearest spillway. A slanting roof covered the sluice. Beneath the rippling surface of the water the blurred shapes of rainbow trout flashed like silver coins at the bottom of a fountain. I closed my eyes and imagined myself on the Kennebago River casting an emerger over a quiet stream, caddis flies rising around me, the sun hot on my neck.

'Mike Bowditch?'

I turned around. It was a man I'd never seen before. He was a muscular guy — a weekend weight lifter, by the looks of him — maybe forty years old, with a graying crew cut and close-set brown eyes. He wore a short-sleeved dress shirt and a navy tie still tightly knotted despite the heat of the day. There was a holster and a badge clipped to his belt.

He held out his hand for me to shake. 'I'm Wayne Soctomah.'

'You're investigating the homicides.'

'Detective Menario and I are. The sheriff told me you spoke with your father last night.'

'Not exactly. He left a message on my answering machine.'

'You mind if I ask you a few questions about it?'

'No.'

I expected him to pull out a tape recorder, just like the sheriff did, but he didn't even take notes. He asked exactly what I'd heard on my answering machine, and I told him, word for word.

'Do you have any idea who the woman was with him?'

'A girlfriend, I'd imagine. My dad is something of a ladies' man.' I nearly said *lady-killer.*

'No one in particular?'

'Not that I know about. But we haven't spoken in years.'

'Do you remember him ever mentioning Wendigo Timber?'

'No. The last time I saw him, this was still APP land.' I decided to see how far I could push my luck. 'Look, I know your investigation is ongoing, but can you tell me anything about what happened up here last night? I read in the paper about the meeting at the Dead River Inn. Do you think it was connected to the homicides?'

He grinned, amused at my brashness. 'In other words, what do we know about how and why those two men were killed?' He considered this for a moment. 'I'm not going to say anything to compromise the investigation, but I can tell you that Jonathan Shipman and Deputy Brodeur were gunned down last night about five minutes after they left the Dead River Inn. They were trying to slip away from the crowd by driving down a logging road instead of going out the front way, and it appears that someone was waiting for them and opened fire on the deputy's cruiser. I won't say there's a direct connection between the meeting and the homicides.'

'But it goes to reason, right? You think someone who was upset about the Wendigo deal snuck out of the meeting to set up an ambush.'

'I really can't speculate. And I've already said too much.'

'I appreciate the courtesy.' Actually, I was surprised by the detective's willingness to say anything at all, considering what was happening with my father. Maybe he was the straight shooter Kathy said he was.

Soctomah smiled again. 'I'd be asking the same questions if I were in your place. You want to help your father, so you need to know exactly what's going on.'

I started to say, yes, but caught myself. Was he suggesting that I'd cover up for my dad to protect him? 'I just don't want you guys wasting your time on a dead end,' I said.

'That's the last thing we want, too. We're fortunate to have your help in this.' He glanced up at the sky. 'Man, it's like a sauna out here. What say we get out of the sun?' He gestured toward the mobile crime unit parked across the lot.

This guy is pretty slick, I thought.

★   ★   ★

Sure enough, when we'd settled down inside the motor coach and he'd grabbed us a couple of bottled waters, out came the tape recorder. 'You understand about this, right?'

'Yeah,' I said.

We went back over the subject of the answering machine message again, this time for the record, and then moved on to my father's

84

views on corporate ownership of the North Woods, his marksmanship with high-powered rifles, and general proclivities for violence. Midway through the conversation another detective appeared, a spark plug with a snub nose and a do-it-yourself buzz cut, who sat in the back of the vehicle, watching me with a sullen expression. Detective Menario, I presumed.

'How would you describe your relationship with your father?' asked Soctomah.

'What do you mean?'

'Were you close? Distant?'

'I lived with him, on and off, until I was nine years old. But after my parents got divorced, I only saw him occasionally. I spent a couple of months with him at Rum Pond when I was sixteen, working at the camp, washing dishes, that kind of thing, but it didn't work out.'

'What happened?'

'I was a kid. I had unrealistic expectations.'

'About what?'

'About everything,' I said. 'He had his own lifestyle, and I didn't fit in.'

'Does he have any friends in this general vicinity? Someone he might turn to if he got himself into trouble?'

'I don't know. The only friends of his I met were Russell Pelletier and a guide named Truman Dellis. That's a guy you should definitely talk to. He's violent and alcoholic, and I wouldn't put it past him to shoot a cop.'

The detective ignored my suggestion. 'Anyone else?'

'There was another guy. I'm not sure he was a

friend exactly. I saw my dad talking to him at the Dead River Inn. He had a shaved head and a goatee. My dad called him a 'paranoid militia freak.''

'Would your mother know about your father's acquaintances?'

The possibility hadn't occurred to me before. 'You're not going to drag her into this.'

'Where does she live?' asked the agitated detective, Menario.

'Scarborough. She's remarried. And she has a different name now, Marie Turner.' I gave them her phone number. 'She's going to freak out when you call her.'

'Why's that?'

'She's got a new life, a new family. She doesn't like to be associated with my dad anymore. It was a bad time in her life, and she'd rather forget it.'

'She's an ex-wife.' Soctomah gave a knowing smile. 'Mike, I understand how difficult this situation must be for you. You've dedicated your life to enforcing the law, and now your father's a fugitive. But I don't have to tell you that your dad's a lot better off if we can find him quickly and get him to surrender. So if there's anything else you can think of, any other piece of information that might help us, we need to know about it.'

'Only this,' I said. 'He didn't murder those men.'

Soctomah blinked, clearly taken aback. 'Why do you say that?'

'Because I know what's in his nature. He may

be a son-of-a-bitch — I know that better than anybody — but he's too smart to kill a cop. I don't expect you to believe that. But the man you're looking for is some sort of terrorist kook. He killed that V.P. from Wendigo to send a message. My father wouldn't do that.'

'So if he's innocent,' asked Menario, 'then why'd he run?'

'I don't know.'

A look came into Soctomah's eyes that I didn't recognize at first. Then I realized: He was embarrassed for me. He thought I was deluding myself, and he felt pity.

'I know it looks bad,' I said. 'But you're mistaken about him.'

Soctomah stood up in such a way as to make me stand up, too. 'Thanks for taking the time to talk with us, Mike,' he said, escorting me to the door. 'We'll keep you posted.'

'You know where to find me,' I said, putting on my sunglasses to face the daylight again.

10

The search got under way and I had nothing to do. Lieutenant Malcomb said I'd be an observer, and that's exactly what I was: a spectator forced to watch while a platoon of heavily armed officers was deployed into the wooded hills east of the Bigelow Mountains.

When I was a teenager I used to have nightmares about being a ghost. In my dreams I'd float around like a phantom watching my family and friends, unable to speak to them, unable to interact. It was the worst thing I could imagine, and it was exactly how I felt now. Stuck in a crowded room, forced to follow the search on topographic maps, hearing the bloodhounds only in my imagination.

The dogs had picked up my dad's trail easily enough at the crash scene. But my father was a professional trapper, and he knew about scents and how not to leave them. His boots were always rubber-bottomed because leather and canvas leave a human odor. And he knew how to zigzag across streams and find paths of bare stone more or less impervious to smell. He scrambled through bogs so choked with fallen trees — spiked branches everywhere — that the dogs cut their pads to shreds trying to follow. He knew he probably couldn't outwit the hounds, but he could definitely exhaust their handlers and gain himself some time.

The reports came back by radio. Trail lost. Trail found again.

The tension got to people in different ways. I drank coffee until my stomach burned. The officer in charge, Major Carter, of the state police tactical team, kept checking his watch. The sheriff left the room every fifteen minutes to piss. Lieutenant Malcomb found a pack of Lucky Strikes on a desk and stepped outside.

I found him behind the building, standing beside a bubbling spillway, lighting a cigarette. 'Lieutenant,' I said. 'I know what we talked about before, but I'd like to be posted into the field. Let me direct traffic or something. I can't just stand around like this, waiting.'

'We're all waiting.'

'But you need more men out there.'

'The governor's got the National Guard on standby.' He dropped the cigarette and crushed it beneath his boot. 'I think we can spare you, Bowditch.'

There was nothing to say to that. Overhead I heard a faint drone and then saw a small airplane flash in the sun. It banked and swung westward into the deepening shadows beneath Little Bigelow and disappeared from view.

'That's Charley Stevens,' said the lieutenant, as if identifying a species of bird. He left me staring up at the darkening peaks. In the mountains you really do run out of daylight early.

★　★　★

89

The Bigelows were named for Major Timothy Bigelow, who came through here with Colonel Benedict Arnold on his march to Quebec in 1775. It was a chapter of the Revolutionary War nobody talks about much anymore, but I remembered how jazzed I was as a kid to learn that my hometown was near a site of historic significance. My dad told me that Arnold brought a thousand men from the sea up the Kennebec River in leaky bateaux, portaging the heavy boats over Pleasant Ridge to the Dead River, then along the Chain of Ponds, heading overland again across the Height of Land that fences the border with Canada, and finally down the Chaudiere to storm the ramparts of Quebec. It was a daring plan and a complete disaster. Hundreds of soldiers deserted, drowned, starved, or froze to death along that long march. More died on the Plains of Abraham in the snow beneath of the walls of the city. It was the first major defeat of the revolution, but I was captivated by the story anyway — the courage of the men fighting their way through a wilderness of impassable forests and wild rivers — and I remembered how crestfallen I was to hear afterward about Arnold's treason at West Point. How could my hero have become a traitor?

I watched the sun dip below the summit — the colors changed in an instant as it dropped from view — and I thought about all the lessons we fail to learn from history.

★   ★   ★

I was still outside half an hour later when officers came pouring out of the command post. Suddenly the parking lot was awash in blue lights and sirens. The sheriff made a beeline for me. Behind him were Lieutenant Malcomb and Major Carter, who was fastening on a Kevlar vest.

'We've got a situation,' growled the sheriff. 'Your father's gone barricade.'

'He's taken a hostage,' explained the lieutenant.

He motioned me to come with him in his truck, and I did.

'Who's the hostage?'

The lieutenant cranked the engine. 'An old recluse named Bickford. The dogs tracked the scent to his cabin. And when troopers approached the door, they were fired at.'

'Shit.'

'I hope we can talk your old man out of there, Bowditch.'

He's dead if we don't, I thought.

★　★　★

It was like a high-speed caravan. As we raced through the woods, our emergency lights turned the roadside trees blue and red — carnival colors that had no place in the natural world.

My father had traveled far since morning, more miles than seemed possible for an injured man on foot, and not in the direction anyone expected, either. Instead of making for the major roads, he'd gone north, turning away from the village of Dead River and moving deeper into the industrial forest now owned by Wendigo Timber.

The state police tactical team had thrown up a perimeter at the end of a dirt road, beyond rifle range of the cabin. This was their show now, and if the troopers couldn't induce my dad to give up his hostage and surrender, they would go in with tear gas and automatic weapons.

The sheriff and the others were waiting behind an improvised barricade of police cruisers.

'What's the situation?' asked the lieutenant.

'One shot fired.'

'Anybody hurt?'

'No.'

'Is he contained?'

'Completely.'

The cabin was a sorry-looking structure fashioned of red-painted boards and plywood, with silver Typar holding it all together like so much duct tape. There was only one crooked window in front, a cockeyed angle on the world. A rusty Nissan pickup was parked beneath some pines. A rutted ATV track ran up the hill into the woods.

'How do you know my father's in there?' I asked.

'The dogs were indicating all over the place when they got here,' said Major Carter. 'There's no exiting scent trail, as far as we can tell.'

An FBI agent I hadn't met stepped forward. He was African-American, which immediately set him apart from all the white faces around us. 'What do we know about the hostage?'

'He's a local hermit named Wallace Bickford,'

said the sheriff. 'I'm told he's retarded.'

'He's brain injured,' said Lieutenant Malcomb. 'A tree fell on him ten years ago, and he lives off Social Security and worker's comp.'

The FBI man was jotting notes onto a pad. 'He's disabled?'

'Yeah, but it doesn't stop him from poaching deer. He baits them in close to his cabin and then potshots them through an open window. Charley Stevens and I pinched him a few times over the years.'

'Are we sure it's just the one hostage?' I asked.

'We can't get close enough to the window to see.'

Word came that the tactical team had moved into position around the cabin. Snipers with nightscopes had all the doors and the window in their sites and were prepared to breach the building on command. Major Carter announced that he would act as tactical negotiator.

'Do we have a phone line in there?'

'No.'

'I hate these goddamned bullhorns,' said the major. He grabbed the microphone from the cruiser and snapped on the loudspeaker switch. There was an electronic crackle, and then his voice boomed out into the dusk: 'John Bowditch. This is Major Jeffrey Carter. I'm with the Maine State Police. I'd like to talk to you. We are not planning an assault. You are in no danger. I repeat: We are not planning an assault.'

We waited, but there was no reply. The only sound was the static and pop of police radios from the dozen parked cruisers. A line came

93

back to me from a video we watched at the academy: 'A hostage situation is a homicide in progress.' 'Call him Jack,' I said.

'What?'

'Jack, not John. He hates the name John.'

He switched on the mic again. 'Jack, this is Jeff Carter again. It's imperative that we have a conversation right now.'

I whispered to the lieutenant, 'Why isn't he asking about the hostage? Shouldn't we find out if he's OK in there?'

'He doesn't want the H.T. to think the hostage has any bargaining value.'

'H.T.?'

'Hostage taker.'

The major's voice came back over the speaker: 'What I'd like to do, Jack, is give you a cell phone. That way, we won't have to shout at each other.' He made a hand gesture to a trooper in full-combat armor to start forward. 'I have a man bringing you a cell phone. This is not an assault. He's just bringing you a phone so we can talk.'

The trooper began creeping forward, using the cover of the pines to draw close to the building.

Then came a muffled shout: 'Don't come up here!'

The trooper froze in place.

There was something about the voice that raised the hairs along my neck.

'OK, Jack,' answered the major. 'Whatever you say.'

Slowly the trooper backed away from the cabin.

I grabbed the major's shoulder. 'It's not him.'

He swung around on me. 'What?'

'That's not my father,' I said. 'I don't know who it is, but it's not him.'

'Are you sure?'

'Positive.'

'Could it be Bickford?' asked the FBI agent.

For the first time in hours I felt something like real hopefulness. 'What if he's not in there?'

'Somebody shot at my men,' snapped the sheriff.

'What if it's just Bickford?'

'The dogs tracked him here, for Christ's sake.'

Suddenly the strange voice shouted again: 'I hear them outside the walls! Don't come in here!'

Major Carter switched on the loudspeaker again: 'Nobody's coming in, Jack. You have my word on that. Jack, we've got your son, Mike, here.'

I knew I was there to help negotiate, but the thought of actually talking my dad into surrendering left me wondering if the major knew what he was doing.

The FBI agent wondered, too. 'You can't put a family member on the horn.'

'Under normal circumstances, I'd agree,' said the major. 'But Bowditch called his son last night. We have reason to believe he trusts Mike to get him out of the situation.'

'I think it's a big mistake,' the FBI agent said.

The major started to hand me the mic but held it back a moment. 'Talk slowly and normally. You're going to tell him that you're here, and he's in no danger. You can vouch for that.'

'I can?'

'Yes, you can. You're going to say that he should let us give him a phone. That's all. Don't mention the hostage, don't make any promises. Our only goal right now is to convince him to take the phone. Staying on the loudspeaker like this, forcing him to shout, just ratchets up everybody's adrenaline. We need to take this situation down a notch.'

'What if he's not in there? What if this is just some sort of mistake?'

'You're going to help us find that out.'

I took up the microphone. 'Dad, this is Mike. You need to take the telephone, OK?' The major motioned to me: Slow it down. 'It's just a cell phone. Will you let them bring it to you?'

The trooper inched his way up the path, looking as unthreatening as a man in full-body armor can look.

OK, I thought. Throw the phone.

But the trooper kept going. I heard one of the hounds whining behind me, then a whispered hush from the dog's handler.

The window was totally dark. If someone inside was looking out, I couldn't see him.

Just throw the damned phone.

The trooper was now no more than ten yards from the porch. Slowly he lowered the hand with the phone in it, getting ready to pitch it underhand in front of the door. The placement had to be perfect. If my dad was inside, he'd probably make Bickford reach for the phone, but he couldn't risk having his hostage escape.

Three things happened next. The trooper lofted the phone and it landed, too high, with a smack against the bottom of the door. At the same time the dog that had been whining before let out a sharp yelp. And just as suddenly a gunshot exploded the cabin's window.

The trooper dived to the ground and rolled for cover behind the tail bed of the pickup truck.

The first shot had come from inside the cabin, but the next one came from the woods to my left.

Through the loudspeaker the major shouted: 'Hold your fire! Hold your fire!'

I wasn't even aware of rising, but suddenly I was sprinting forward up the dirt road. I heard the lieutenant shout my name, but I kept going until I stood at the foot of the porch, holding my arms up for all to see. Another shotgun blast splintered the boards near my head. 'Stop firing!'

'Hold your goddamned fire!' Carter shouted.

I waved my arms. 'Stop shooting!'

But there were no more shots. The smell of gunpowder drifted in the night air.

A weak voice came from inside the cabin. 'Help.'

'Dad?'

The door creaked open. I took a step toward it — and was tackled by the trooper who'd been crouching behind the pickup truck. He pinned me to the ground with the weight of his armored body. Around me I was aware of a rush of feet moving past — tac officers storming the cabin, weapons pointed.

Dust was in my eyes, and I couldn't see a damned thing. Inside the cabin I heard the SWAT officers shouting commands: 'Get down! Don't move!'

I tried to push with my arms and knees. The trooper shoved my head into the dirt. 'Stay down.'

Inside the cabin I heard shouts that the building was secure.

The trooper on top of me repositioned his weight, and I used a wrestling move to roll him off. In an instant I was on my feet, leaping up the porch steps and through the door.

On the floor writhed a little old man, dressed in canvas coveralls, with a kind of white man's Afro. A trooper, in battle gear, knelt on his back. The man's face, pressed to the floor, was smeared with blood as if he'd run nose-first into a plate-glass window. More blood was spattered on the cigarette-burned carpet. I saw a rifle lying across the room. The cluttered, bottle-strewn room smelled of something noxious — a sour, musky odor like stale urine, only stronger.

'I'm dying,' said the old man again. 'I'm dying.'

Two troopers threw me against a paneled wall and held me there with the weight of their bodies as I tried to surge forward. 'Where is he?'

'There's no one else in here,' I heard a trooper report into his throat mic.

'Where's Bowditch?'

'Where is he?' I shouted. 'Where's my father?'

Wallace Bickford raised his bloody head and gave out a wail. 'Gone,' he said. 'He's gone.'

11

It turned out Bickford wasn't seriously wounded at all. He'd just suffered a lot of small facial cuts when he shot out the window. The little man was now perched on an ambulance bumper while a paramedic daubed his face with antiseptic. His hair was really something else — a frizzled gray brush that looked like he'd plugged his finger into an electrical socket.

The sheriff folded his arms. 'You're saying the gun went off by accident — twice?'

'Yeah! I never meant no harm.' He spoke as if his tongue were swollen, but I got the sense it was a permanent speech impediment.

'Oh, I bet you didn't,' the sheriff said. 'So where did Bowditch go?'

'Otter Brook Bog, like I said. He said he needed my ATV.'

'And you gave it to him. Because you're such a generous and giving individual.'

Bickford looked at the sheriff like he'd just asked him something in Swahili. 'No, because of the moose.'

Then, for the second time in ten minutes, he laid out his story. Jack Bowditch, he said, had arrived at his cabin an hour before nightfall saying he'd shot a moose at Otter Brook Bog and needed an ATV to haul it out before the wardens caught him. 'He said he'd give me half the meat if I let him borrow it,' the old man said. 'He said if I didn't let him take it, he'd tell the wardens the deer meat in my freezer was from poaching — which is a lie.'

'So Bowditch took the ATV.' Major Carter removed his helmet and tucked it under his arm; sweat shined along his high forehead. 'But I still don't understand how he got through the perimeter. The dogs scented no exit trail leaving the cabin. Even if he was riding an ATV, the dogs should have winded him.'

'The smell,' I said. 'That bad smell inside the house. Didn't you notice it?'

'I thought that was just Mr. Bickford's natural aroma,' said the sheriff.

'It's deer lure,' I said. 'Hunters make it out of the urine and tarsal glands of bucks. It's used to cover human odors and bring deer into a tree stand.'

'He doused himself with it,' said Lieutenant Malcomb.

'You smelled how strong that stuff can be,' I said. 'He knew it would cover his scent and throw off the dogs. He must have known Bickford had some of the stuff. That's why he headed this way.'

'So we'll just key the dogs in to the deer lure,' said the sheriff. 'And they'll follow the new scent. All it does is delay us a little.'

'Do you know how many deer are in these woods?'

'Is there any way we can track the ATV tonight?' asked the FBI agent.

'Unless one of our planes spotted him from above, I don't see how,' said the lieutenant.

'There's almost as many ATVs on these logging roads out there as deer. He might be ten miles away by now, and with a full tank he might get thirty more miles before he runs out of gas. We'll take tire prints to match if we can, but unless someone spotted him, I don't see how we follow him tonight.'

'So why the hell did you start shooting when the troopers arrived?' the sheriff demanded of Bickford. 'Do you have a death wish?'

'I was scared,' said the old man. 'I looked out my window and all I see are soldiers. You didn't give me no chance to explain myself. I figured you was going to burn me out — like Waco. This is my property, and the Constitution says I have the Second Amendment.'

'This isn't your property,' said the sheriff. 'This property belongs to Wendigo Timber. You're squatting here illegally.'

His eyes blazed. 'It's my home! They can't take it. I won't let them.'

'So you agree with what Bowditch did — killing that man from Wendigo Timber? Maybe you helped him do it.'

Bickford paused, mouth open. Then he wiped his runny nose and looked away. 'I didn't do nothing. It was an accident. Just like I said.'

⋆　⋆　⋆

'What's going to happen to him?' I asked Lieutenant Malcomb. The adrenaline had left me and I was crashing fast — I felt like the blood in my arms and legs was transmuting to lead.

101

'It's up to the attorney general, but I'd say he's facing a mess of charges — misdemeanor and felony — from obstruction of justice to accessory to homicide after the fact. Plus we're going to have a look in his freezer as soon as Hatch is done taking tire tracks, so that's not counting poaching violations.'

I shivered. 'It doesn't seem like he knows what he's saying. The guy's clearly brain injured.'

'Don't be fooled,' said the lieutenant. 'He knows right from wrong. Anyway, that's not for us to decide.'

'Does the major know which officer fired at the cabin?'

'One of the sheriff's men.'

'That second shot nearly hit me.'

He looked at me hard. 'What you did, Mike — running up like that — was the stupidest thing I've seen in a long time. I'd be even more pissed except for the fact you probably saved that man's life.'

I didn't feel particularly noble. I'd been trying to save my father, not Wallace Bickford. I looked up at the cabin, which was lit up now from the inside as the state police evidence technicians searched it for signs of my father having been there. 'I didn't exactly follow what the sheriff was saying about Bickford being a squatter.'

'He built this cabin without permission a decade ago, but APP never made him move it.'

'You mean they just let him squat here.'

'Bickford used to work for APP. Letting him stay here was cheaper than a lawsuit. Whose fault do you think it was that a tree fell on that poor man's head?'

And now Wendigo Timber had bought the land from Atlantic Pulp & Paper, and like all the legal leaseholders, Wallace Bickford was facing eviction from his home. Was it possible that he killed Shipman and Brodeur for just that reason? And what did it say about my father that he sought out this brain-damaged man and basically stole his four-wheeler? It certainly didn't look good that he'd put Bickford at risk. On the other hand, I told myself, being desperate didn't necessarily make him a murderer. He did what he needed to do to escape.

'I'm going to see how they're doing with those tire tracks,' said the lieutenant.

I started to follow him, but Malcomb held up his hand. 'Sorry, Bowditch. It's a crime scene now and it's off limits for you. Why don't you take my truck back to the hatchery?'

★ ★ ★

There was a different mood at the command post. The faces were longer, the energy had drained out of most of the bodies, but still the search continued. In his plane Charley Stevens called in locations where he saw headlights, but this was August in the Maine woods and ATV riders were commonplace across the region. Unless the task force got lucky, there was no way to pick him out. It was only a matter of time until the search was suspended, at least for the night. I sat in the corner and ate a ham sandwich.

I wondered what kind of luck Kathy was having with our bear trap. She'd probably just checked it for the first time or would be checking it soon. I considered calling her, but I didn't have the heart to face her questions.

'Hey, Bowditch.' I looked up into a cherub face atop a deputy's paunchy body. He had a big bandage on his forehead and a cut on his lip. The name tag above his belly said TWOMBLEY. For some reason he was now handing me a cell phone. 'It's your lieutenant.'

I pressed the phone to my ear. 'Sir?'

'I want you to go home, Bowditch. I spoke with Carter and there's nothing more for you to do here tonight. The sheriff said one of his men will give you a ride back to Skowhegan.'

'I'd prefer to stay.'

'If anything breaks, we'll get you back up here. But we're looking at a new timetable for this thing now. We'll talk again in the morning.'

'Lieutenant — '

The cherubic deputy held out his hand for his phone. 'Let's go,' he said.

★　★　★

I followed Twombley to a patrol car and we got going. 'I heard what happened, this morning,' I said. 'How are you holding up?'

'How the fuck do you think I'm holding up?'

I knew then that I was in for a long ride back to Showhegan.

104

After what Twombley had been through, I was surprised the sheriff hadn't sent him home earlier — or at least to the hospital. I could only assume that he'd insisted on taking part in the manhunt in order to repair his damaged reputation. At the command post I'd heard more than one officer laughing about the embarrassing predicament my dad had left him in. He already had a new nickname: Treehugger.

I studied the deputy's battered profile. There was something familiar about it. 'So why did you drive out to Rum Pond?' I asked.

'What?'

'The sheriff said you went out there on your own authority. What evidence did you have on my dad?'

He glanced over at me for the first time. 'Go fuck yourself.'

Outside the roadblock TV news vans were drawn up. I saw spotlights trained on reporters' incandescent faces. Cameras turned in our direction as we made our way through the gauntlet of stopped traffic. Reflexively I raised my hand to conceal my face.

What would I tell my mother? I'd scarcely thought of her at all. But Detective Soctomah would be calling her soon, and she was guaranteed to freak out, afraid my dad was going to drag her reputation through the mud. If they gunned him down tomorrow, her first concern would be that her friends would see her name in the newspapers. How could she bear her neighbors knowing that she'd once been poor white trash, married to such a violent man?

I leaned my head against the glass.

Some time later I was awakened by gunshots. I sat up with a start. Twombley was looking over at me, smirking. I'd been dreaming. We were cruising past the brightly lit shopping plazas outside of Skowhegan. That was when I remembered that pink face. Twombley was the deputy who had arrested my dad two years ago at the Dead River Inn, the one who made him kneel in broken glass. So they had a history together. He'd pegged my father as a likely murderer and decided to bring him in without proof.

I could imagine what had happened next. 'So what did he do — taunt you from the backseat? Is that how you ran off the road?'

He kept his eyes on the road, as if he hadn't heard me.

I continued: 'What happened next? You went around to drag him out of the car, and he knocked you down? How did he get your gun away from you?'

'Fuck you.'

I noticed his holster was still empty, but now that I thought about it, I remembered seeing him at the standoff — that evil baby face. He'd been carrying a shotgun. 'I bet you're the one who fired, too. Back at Bickford's cabin.'

His answer was another smirk.

'A little trigger happy, aren't you?'

We pulled into the parking lot of the Somerset County Jail. My truck shined green beneath the streetlights.

'Ride's over,' he said.

I got out and started walking away.

He shouted at me through his window: 'You better hope someone finds him before I do.'

* * *

Afterward, driving home to Sennebec, I stopped to remove a dead porcupine from the middle of the road. I parked my truck so that the spotlight illuminated the animal, turned on my flashing blue lights, and got out. Using a pair of heavy gloves I kept in my truck for occasions like this one, I lifted the carcass carefully, avoiding the barbed quills and dripping blood. I set the porcupine in the bed of my truck to dispose of later in an old sandpit near my house — a place that had become, in the eight months since I'd finished my training period and been assigned to this district, a mass grave for porcupines, skunks, crows, gulls, woodchucks, raccoons, foxes, vultures, and deer.

Quills stuck in the heavy canvas and leather of my gloves, and the palms were black and sticky with blood. I sat behind the wheel of my truck a moment, the window rolled down, the engine silent, and found that when I removed the gloves, my hands were shaking uncontrollably. I thought about all the dead animals I saw in the course of a day: a dead porcupine lying in a darkened road, dead trout in a fisherman's creel, a dead deer lashed to the luggage rack of a late-model Chevrolet. Why had I chosen to spend so much time in the company of death?

Headlights approached from the opposite

direction, coming fast at first, then slowing almost to a crawl as they drew near. As the car passed me, I saw a man behind the wheel, a woman next to him, kids up late in the backseat. They all had their eyes focused on the red smear in the road. They wanted to know what had died there. They were curious, and they couldn't help themselves.

I couldn't fault them. It was human nature.

12

As a kid, I probably ate more deer meat than I did hamburger. For the first part of my life, I lived with my mom and sometimes my dad in a series of house trailers and backwoods shacks in the hardscrabble farmland of western Maine. We moved a lot, every year or so. Sometimes more often than that. My father would get fired from a job at a sawmill or a well-drilling company, and then we would have to move again. We lived under power lines that hummed in the night and beside stinking landfills of old automobile tires. Each trailer seemed a little shabbier than the one we rented before. My mother used to say we were 'downwardly mobile.'

She was a reckless, dark-eyed beauty, the youngest of five kids, who'd grown up as the center of attention in her household and lived life without ever taking precautions against possible misfortune.

Six months after my dad got her pregnant, they were married in a big Catholic wedding down in Madison, where she insisted on wearing white. The wedding pictures only showed her from the chest up. She looked happy enough, though.

I don't know whether she ever loved him. God knows he didn't make it easy for her. My impression of my father during that time is of a fatalistic young guy, wounded in body and soul, who couldn't believe the good luck that had come his way in the form of this gorgeous girl, who knew from having been to war that good luck never lasts, and so went about sort of preemptively destroying his luck before it could go bad on him.

Somehow their marriage lasted nine whole years. It survived a couple of miscarriages and lots of 2 a.m. visits by the police. By the end, which is when my memories are sharpest, they were fighting constantly. My mom knew she wanted a better life — she was educating herself, taking adult ed classes at the high school and reading constantly — and she was sick of being broke all the time. They argued about not having money to buy groceries or heating oil, about my dad's binge drinking, about how he disappeared for days without telling her where he was going or where he'd been.

He never struck her, no matter how much she screamed or spat or slapped at him, but this only seemed to make her all the madder. As it was, his face during those battles just about glowed red with rage. If he had come home drunk one night and cut our throats with a kitchen knife and set fire to the trailer and shot himself in the temple with his .22 pistol, it probably wouldn't have surprised any of our neighbors. Those sorts of domestic holocausts are regular enough occurrences in isolated north-country towns as to be almost predictable.

The forest was his escape. Whenever things got too hot at home, he disappeared into the woods with a rifle or a fly rod and we wouldn't see him again for days. Then he'd return with a skipper buck he'd shot for the freezer or a knapsack full of trout. Peace offerings.

My dad said he was a poacher out of necessity; he took game whenever and wherever the opportunity presented itself because he was too proud to accept food stamps. That's what he said, anyway.

During the legal deer season in November he would spend days following the hoofprints of a big buck along oak ridges and down into dark valleys where icy creeks ran fast through thickets of cedar and tamarack. He never fired until he had the best possible shot on the biggest buck he was likely to see that year. Then he would spend hours dragging his gutted, 200-pound trophy out of the forest.

I can't remember a single Thanksgiving when we didn't have a dead buck hanging in the trees outside our trailer, within view of the road. My dad said he hung the carcass outside to age the deer meat and give it a rich, gamey taste. But I knew he did it to prove to the men who lived in the neighboring houses — the same rough-and-tumble crowd he worked with at the sawmill and drank with at the Red Stallion in Carrabassett — that he was a better hunter than they were and, therefore, to his way of thinking, and mine, more of a man. A dead deer in a tree was just the way he chose to advertise himself.

★ ★ ★

The last year my father lived with us — before my mother packed me up for good to live with her sister in Portland — he kept a trapping shed behind the trailer we had rented near the town of Dead River. Steel traps hung from my mom's clotheslines. Other traps were piled high inside the rickety shed. Also back there was a fifty-gallon barrel filled to the brim with a foul-smelling liquid he used to dye the traps to better conceal them in the brush. My mother forbade me from entering the shed or touching any of his equipment, but I spent many hours watching him while he waxed his traps outside with paraffin.

One December morning my mom drove into Farmington to take her Dale Carnegie course. Normally, she was reluctant to leave my dad to babysit me. She knew he was likely to go out suddenly, abandoning me alone in the trailer. This morning, however, I was tucked in bed with a pretty bad chest cold, which meant she couldn't pawn me off on the neighbors.

After she'd gone, he came into my darkened bedroom and flicked on the light. He wore a faded flannel shirt stretched tight across his big chest and stained wool pants tucked into rubber hip boots. His long hair was slicked back behind his ears. His beard needed trimming.

'Hey,' he said. 'How'd you like to go trapping? It'll be our secret from your mom.'

'But I'm sick,' I told him.

'You've got a cold. It won't kill you to get outside. You said you wanted to go. I'm giving you the chance. So quit whining and get up.'

112

I got up. Over my pajamas I put on a bulky snowmobile suit, the one that made me look like a pint-sized version of the Michelin man. Outside, I could hear the clanging noise of my father loading the back of his Ford pickup. I hurried outside, nearly tripping over my too-big boots.

It was a bitterly cold morning. Little snow had fallen so far that year. What there was of it lay in hard blue patches in the shadows of the pines. But the ground was frozen solid, and the frigid air stung my cheeks and made my eyes water.

The cab of my father's pickup smelled of pungent animal odors: musk and urine. I turned my face to the crack in the window and tried to breathe in the clean, cold air that whistled through.

My father grinned. 'You'll get used to it.'

Beneath my feet was a wooden crate filled with Mason jars containing glands afloat in murky fluids. Scents and lures. To make some of them he put animal parts in a blender.

My nose began to run. I wiped it with my sleeve, leaving a slimy trail on the fabric.

'How's that cold?'

'OK.'

He winked at me. 'You're a tough little guy, aren't you?'

I smiled. 'How do you know where to trap, Dad?'

'That depends,' he said. 'For foxes, you want a mix of fields and wood. Maybe some trails coming in. For mink, the best places are the streams that lead from pond to pond. After that, it's trial and error. Here's a place for coons,' he said, pulling over beside a thicket of brambles. 'I got a coon trap back in there. Come see.'

I followed him as best I could through the dense puckerbrush. Branches scratched at my face, and I had to cover my eyes with my arm to keep from getting switched. A hundred or so yards from the road, I caught up with him. He stood beside a little stream. The water of the stream was black and so quickly moving that it hadn't yet frozen, although there was ice crusted along the edges.

'Look,' he said, and pointed.

At the base of a tree on the bank of the stream was a big raccoon. It clung stiffly to the trunk. The steel trap grasped one of its black hind paws firmly, and the chain that held the trap was twisted around the trunk. After having been caught, the raccoon had tried to climb the tree to safety. But the trap had him pinned.

While I watched, my father drew his .22 pistol out of the pocket of his drab army coat and leveled it at the raccoon's head. The sound of the shot made me jump.

I hadn't realized the raccoon was still alive.

It jerked and let go of the tree. My father put away his gun and waited for the quivering to stop. Then he approached the dead animal and released it and set it on the bank. He straightened out the chain and reset the trap, hiding the jaws with dead leaves so they were all but invisible.

'Here,' he said, giving me the raccoon to carry by the ringed tail back to the truck.

But the body was too heavy, and even using both hands I didn't get very far with it. My father watched me struggle with my burden for a while before finally taking it away from me. He slung the raccoon over his shoulder, holding it by the tail. It swung back and forth along his back as he walked. Its eyes were open and on a level with my own as I followed behind him.

The cold had frozen the snot inside my nostrils, and I began to cough. When we got back inside the truck, my father reached under his seat and pulled out a bottle of whiskey. He held it between his legs while he drove, taking sips when there were no other cars on the road to see.

At the next stop, I followed him down a hill. The grass was brittle from the cold and made a crunching noise beneath our boots, like a person eating potato chips. At the bottom was a frozen pond, filled with standing dead trees like sharpened poles. There was an area of open water at one end of the pond where a stream flowed out. A muskrat was struggling in the water, near a hummock of grass and dead branches where the trap had been set. My dad waded out into the knee-deep water until he stood over the small, writhing animal and shot it with his pistol.

My father tossed the wet little carcass back at me so that I had to jump out of the way. Lying on the reed bank, the muskrat seemed very small. Its teeth were bared yellow, and its fur was slicked like it had been dipped in motor oil. I was wracked suddenly by a fit of coughing.

My father was going on about prices. Muskrats, he said, brought in just a buck apiece, scarcely worth trapping. Raccoons could go as high as twelve dollars, if you skinned them out carefully. While he reset the trap, he rattled off the current prices he got for each of the species of animals he took. Others, he said, got the best prices — as much as forty-two dollars for an otterskin.

'There's a hole in my boot,' I said softly.

'What do you want me to do about it?'

'My sock is wet.'

His eyes bored into mine, forcing me to look away. 'You want me to take you home?'

'No.'

'Then don't be such a baby.'

We made more stops along the trap line. Sometimes there were animals in the traps, and sometimes the sets were empty. As the day wore on, I began to cough steadily, bringing up gobs of green phlegm that I spit out into a mitten. My left foot, encased in its leaky boot, became soaked and numb. After a while, it was as if I were sleepwalking through a barren dreamland of skeletal trees, gravel pits, sunken meadows, and standing water, limping along, trying in vain to keep up with my father, who seemed only intermittently aware of my presence.

He tuned the radio to a country music station, and he tapped his fingers along the steering wheel in time to the songs that were all about heartbreak, booze, and betrayal.

'Dale Carnegie,' he said with a snort. 'Can you believe that shit? There's probably some guy down there in that class that she likes. We should go down there and check up on her. Wouldn't she be surprised? She doesn't know what I'd do for her. That's her problem.'

We forged on, checking more sets, wading through rushing streams and clambering up steep banks. I wanted to stop, wanted to go home, but I didn't dare say so.

'What does she want me to do?' my father said, but I don't think he was talking to me at this point. 'Does she want me to cut my fucking heart out and serve it to her on a golden platter? Is that what it's going to take?'

I can scarcely remember crossing the withered cornfield where we found the fox. All I remember is standing at the edge of a field beneath an overcast sky, clouds pressing down overhead and the smell of snow in the air, while my father advanced on the trapped animal with a crowbar.

The fox was a rust-orange blur. It jumped and jerked at the end of its chain, the trap digging deep into its leg as my dad came up. Torn between fight and flight, it growled and snapped at us. Then it bounded away, leaping high into the air, only to be pulled violently to earth by the chain. That was when my father stepped in with the crowbar. He tapped the animal once, sharply, above the muzzle. And the fox flipped onto its side, shaking and foaming at the mouth as if gripped by a seizure. Then, in disbelief, I watched my dad kneel on its spine and grip its nose with one big hand. Firmly, he pulled the head back until there was a loud snap and the fox stopped moving.

As we walked back across the frozen cornfield, I turned my head so I didn't have to see him cradling the beautiful, limp body.

'Dad, why didn't you just shoot it?'

'A bloodstain will ruin a fox fur,' he explained. 'You have to kill it with your hands. There's no other way.'

My eyes were wet, so I squeezed them shut. 'I wish you'd shot it.'

I could feel him looking hard at me. 'You asked to come along,' he said. 'This is the last time I take you trapping with me.'

For the rest of that day I remained in the frigid cab of the pickup while my father ventured down embankments and off into stands of second-growth spruce and tamarack. My body ached, and I was colder than I'd ever been. I curled up into a ball on the cracked vinyl seat.

★　★　★

I was awakened by my dad shaking my shoulder roughly. Darkness had fallen and snow was swirling in the headlights. We were back home, outside the trailer, and my mom was standing in the dooryard in front of the truck. She was lit up by the glow of the headlights. Snow dusted the top of her hair.

I remember my mom gathering me up in her arms. I remember drifting through the long ride to the hospital in Skowhegan. Then the bright lights of the examination room, a nurse taking my temperature. I don't remember anyone ever

118

telling me I had pneumonia, but that's what it was.

My next memory is of waking up in the night to find my father seated beside my hospital bed, watching me in the half-dark. In my memory his bearded face looms over me like a grotesque mask of itself. Tears are streaming down his cheeks — the first tears I've ever seen him shed. I ask him where I am and what has happened to me, but he just turns his head away so I won't see him cry. After a minute he gets up and leaves, and I am alone again in my strange bed.

13

I came home to a bunch of messages. There were the usual game warden calls: questions about obscure boating regulations and which fishing spots I'd recommend. And a message from Kathy Frost telling me she checked the culvert trap earlier that evening and it was empty. She'd check it again in the morning unless she heard from me. Bud Thompson called, drunk, wanting to know about the 'status of my investigation concerning the bear.'

And then there was a message from Sarah. I was startled to hear her voice after weeks of not hearing it at all. 'Mike, I heard about your dad — it's so horrible, I still can't believe it. I don't know if you want to talk about it. But I was thinking of you there alone and . . . it's all right to call me, if you want.'

I did want to, very much. But what was I going to say? That I missed her more than I'd ever imagined? She'd probably come over, if I asked. But what kind of prick would I be to take advantage of her kindheartedness — or pity or whatever it was — just because I was feeling so damned lonely? If we started up again, she'd just end up heartbroken like before. A month from now, I'd still be the same unresponsive bastard I'd always been and she'd be the one feeling lonesome.

I crawled into my empty bed and was asleep in minutes.

★ ★ ★

When I opened my eyes the next morning, I caught a glimpse of perfect blue sky — like an antique bottle held up to the sun. For half a minute I had that peaceful amnesia you feel when you first wake up. Then I remembered my father.

Before anything else, I called Kathy Frost.

'I just got off the phone with the lieutenant,' she told me. 'He said they suspended the search after dark. They'll be starting again soon, but everything's been scaled back. Charley Stevens volunteered to go up again in his Super Cub, but I can't say anyone's feeling hopeful about finding your dad.'

'I've got to get back up there.'

'Forget about it. The lieutenant wants you back at work. Either that or take a sick day and stay home. The sheriff doesn't want you at the incident scene.'

'What if they find him? You weren't up there, Kathy. Those Somerset guys are trigger-happy.'

'He killed a cop, Mike. What the hell do you expect?'

'Nobody's proved he did it.'

There was a silence on the other end. When she spoke again, her tone was hard-edged. 'He beat up Twombley and took off. That's pretty close to an admission of guilt, in my book. Do you want me to check that trap for you or not?'

121

'No.'

'OK, then. Call me if you catch a bear.'

★   ★   ★

Half an hour later I pulled into the parking lot of the Square Deal Diner. I dropped some coins into the newspaper machine outside the door. Then I retreated to my truck and spread the pages across the steering wheel to read in the sunshine.

Just about the entire front page of *The Bangor Daily News* was devoted to the story.

POLICE HUNT FOR SUSPECT IN NORTH WOODS SLAYINGS

Below was a grainy color photograph of the crash scene where Twombley's cruiser had gone off the road. There was also a picture of my father. It was the mug shot they'd taken the night of the bar fight two years ago. He looked drunk and defiant, like a man capable of violence.

The article identified Jack Bowditch as a fugitive wanted for assaulting a police officer and named him as the chief suspect in the murders of Deputy Sheriff Bill Brodeur and Wendigo Timberlands Director of Environmental Affairs Jonathan Shipman. There wasn't a whole lot else I didn't already know. Wendigo had announced a reward of fifty thousand dollars for information leading to the arrest and conviction of the killer. The article never mentioned Wallace Bickford or

122

the standoff at his cabin.

Deeper in the newspaper was a companion piece to the lead article:

PUBLIC MEETING PRELUDE TO MURDER

A photograph, taken at the meeting, showed a stocky man with a shaved head and a goatee — identified in the caption as Vernon Tripp of Flagstaff — standing in a crowded room shaking his fist at some unseen person.

It was the man from the Dead River Inn, the one my father spoke with the night the bikers beat the shit out of me. What had my dad called him — a 'paranoid militia freak'? The paper reported he'd been thrown out of the public meeting after he threatened Shipman.

Tripp was identified in the article as the owner of the Natanis Trading Post. 'We have someone from outside trying to dictate our lives and businesses,' he was quoted as saying. 'Everything we do now is controlled by them.' The article noted that he was facing charges of criminal trespass and theft of services for protesting a Wendigo checkpoint earlier in the summer.

As I looked closer at the photo, I noticed something else. Seated in the background was another face I knew. It was pretty blurry, but I definitely recognized the bowl haircut and dragoon mustache of Russell Pelletier, the man who ran Rum Pond Sporting Camps. Pelletier never mentioned that he'd been at that public meeting. As a leaseholder facing eviction, it made sense he was there, but still, seeing him in the photograph raised goose bumps along the back of my neck.

'You people think you can draw an iron curtain across the Maine North Woods,' Tripp said before he was evicted from the meeting. 'You're about to learn a hard lesson. Just wait and see.'

No wonder they threw him out. I felt a surge of hopefulness. Surely, the detectives had looked at Tripp as a possible suspect. I reached for my cell phone to call Soctomah.

There was a tapping at my window that made me jump. It was apple-faced Dot Libby in her waitress outfit. 'Ain't you coming in, Mike?'

'Not today, Dot.'

She looked at me with surprise, as if we were actors in a theatrical performance and I'd just ad-libbed my lines. 'No breakfast?'

'I just wanted to see the paper.'

The look of concern hadn't left Dot's face. 'We're all sorry about your father.'

So the word was out in Sennebec about my connection to the cop killer. Why was I surprised? 'Thanks,' I said, starting the engine. 'I appreciate it. I should probably get going.'

'Wait a sec,' she said, and hurried back inside before I could say a word.

I sat there with the engine idling, not sure what to do. In the diner windows I could see faces looking out at me through the sunfaded curtains.

A moment later Dot returned. She clutched something in a napkin. She pressed it to me through the open window. 'You be sure to stop in for lunch,' she said.

I told her that I would.

As I drove away, I wondered why I'd promised to return for lunch when I had no idea what the day would bring. Was it just to reassure Dot? In a small town like Sennebec, routine is such a precious thing — it's how people get to know and trust one another. I'd only been in town for eight months, but I was already becoming somewhat predictable to my neighbors. It was the first step to becoming one of them, part of their community. Maybe that was what I was afraid of happening.

Inside the napkin was one of Dot's homemade molasses doughnuts. My favorite.

★ ★ ★

On my radio I called in to the dispatcher to tell her I was 10–8, on duty and available to respond. Then I tried Detective Soctomah.

'What can I do for you, Mike?' he said, polite but not friendly.

'Remember I told you about that bald guy my dad knew at the Dead River Inn two years ago? Well, I just saw the Bangor paper and there was a picture from the public meeting. It's him, Vernon Tripp.'

'We spoke with Mr. Tripp yesterday.'

'So he's also a suspect?'

In his silence I sensed his disapproval as clearly as if I'd seen his face. 'We'll keep you up to date, Mike — as events warrant.' I thought he was going to hang up on me then, but instead he said, 'Does the name Brenda Dean mean anything to you?'

'I don't think so. Who is she?'

'She works at Rum Pond Sporting Camps. She's says she's your dad's girlfriend.'

'That's what she thinks. She's probably one of ten.' I tried to sound lighthearted, but Soctomah wasn't in the mood for humor.

'Your father never mentioned her?'

'No. Do you think she's the woman I heard on my message machine?'

There was silence on the other end.

'Detective?' I said.

'We're all set here, Mike.'

'I know the sheriff doesn't want me up there, but — '

'You don't have to call me again,' said Soctomah. 'Not unless you remember something else important that you left out of your statement.'

'I understand.'

'Good,' said the detective.

$$\star \quad \star \quad \star$$

To occupy myself I decided to check the culvert trap. I followed the rutted dirt road down through the hemlocks and cedars to the old cellar hole at the edge of the swamp. As I neared the trailer, I saw that the trapdoor had fallen shut. Because of the liquid shadows beneath the trees I couldn't see what, if anything, might be caught inside.

The sound of an animal thrashing about was

the first thing I heard when I got out. I moved slowly, but the animal heard me coming and fell silent at once. Slowly I circled around to the gate-end of the trap to have a look.

'For Christ's sake,' I said aloud.

Inside the trap was the fattest raccoon I'd ever seen. Fat like a furred basketball. A stomach swollen with doughnuts and bacon. Heavy enough to trigger the door when it clawed at the bait bag.

I opened the door and stood aside, waiting for the raccoon to come out, but it seemed content to huddle at the gate-end, as if it had decided to take up residency inside the trap. Finally, I had to go around to the opposite end and poke a stick at it through the grate to get it to move. The gluttonous animal edged out of the culvert and plopped heavily to earth.

I came around the side of the trailer. The coon glanced over its shoulder with an expression that showed its disdain for me and then waddled down the dirt road toward the swamp. As it wobbled away, I was reminded of a very drunk man making a last shaky effort to preserve what remained of his battered dignity. I knew exactly how it felt.

14

The only thing I could do was work, so that's what I did. I patrolled my district from end to end. I checked fishing licenses and boating registrations. I responded to a call about a possibly rabid fox that had disappeared into some cattails by the time I arrived on the scene. The day got hotter and hotter until every road was shimmering with mirages.

Somehow I managed to miss lunch at the Square Deal.

The call finally came late in the afternoon. It was Lieutenant Malcomb. I pulled over onto a sand shoulder to speak with him. He said, 'They found the ATV. It was hidden outside a camp in Eustis. The owner claims the place was broken into sometime last night. She says lots of stuff was missing — camping supplies, food, a rifle. She says your dad stole a car, too.'

'So he could be anywhere,' I said, trying not to sound relieved.

'We have an APB out on the vehicle. The Canadians say he hasn't tried to cross the border today, but I doubt he'd try Coburn Gore or Jackman. He'd cross on foot in the woods.'

'Are they still holding Wally Bickford?'

'Yeah, they've got him over at Skowhegan, awaiting a bail hearing.'

I didn't answer.

'Stay away from this, Bowditch,' he said.

'You've got the sheriff pissed off enough as it is. Understood?'

'Yes sir.'

'Focus on doing your job. It'll get you through this. It always does.'

*　*　*

His advice was easier said than done. The rest of the afternoon was a blur. I chased my thoughts down every back road in the district and accomplished exactly nothing.

If I were my dad, where would I run? He'd already managed to slip past the roadblocks, and with the kind of head start he'd had, he might be in New Hampshire, Vermont, or even Massachusetts by now. The town of Eustis was less than thirty miles from Canada, but there was no chance he'd risk the official border crossing at Coburn Gore. He'd ditch the car soon, knowing it would be reported stolen. Which meant he'd have to find another vehicle or at least a secure hiding place.

By the time I turned toward home, the light had softened to a shade of almost purple, and the fireflies had begun their slow dance in the fields along the road. I switched on my headlights for the drive back to my rented house on the tidal creek.

Sarah was waiting for me when I got there. Coming up the dirt drive through the pines, I saw her little red Subaru parked beside my Jeep. It was all I could do not to pull a U-turn.

On the June day when Sarah moved out we'd

both told ourselves it was for the best. She was on the edge of tears that whole rainy afternoon, and if her sister Amy hadn't come along to help, she might even have changed her mind. But Amy was resolute. She was convinced her gorgeous little sister could do better than a loner like me. And she was certainly right.

Now, after nearly two months of giving Sarah the space she'd said she wanted, I found her sitting on the back steps of the house we'd once shared. She was looking out at the tidal creek slowly dissolving into the dusk. She was wearing shorts and a baggy green T-shirt, and she'd taken off her sandals and set them beside her bare feet.

She slapped her leg, flattening a blood-swollen mosquito. She looked at her hand in disgust. 'One thing I certainly don't miss about this place is the bugs.'

'Just let them bite you. That's what I do.'

'Always the stoic.' She stood up, appraising me, uncertain at first whether to attempt a hug and then deciding no. 'You weren't going to call me, were you?'

'No.'

'That's what I figured.' Her short blonde hair was cut even shorter since the last time I'd last seen her. 'Have you heard anything about your dad?'

'They're still looking for him.'

I motioned to the door. 'Do you want a beer or something?'

A big smile broke over her face. 'God, yes.'

We went inside and sat down at the kitchen table. She glanced around at dust-covered countertops, and the bare walls stripped of all those bright paintings she loved. 'This place looks worse than I imagined,' she said. 'It's pretty pathetic, even for you.'

'Let's not get into my cleaning habits.'

'All right. I thought you were going to offer me a beer.'

I opened a bottle for her, then excused myself to go change clothes. She called after me: 'You're really strict about that, aren't you? Not drinking in uniform, I mean.'

'It's the law.'

'You're in your own house!'

I came back, barefoot, wearing jeans and a T-shirt. 'How's summer school?'

'They're little monsters, but I love them.'

Sitting across the table, she studied me as she sipped her beer. 'You look tired.'

'Yesterday was a long day.'

'When I saw your dad's face on the news I felt like somebody had punched me. It still doesn't seem real.' She leaned forward across the table. 'Mike, what the hell is going on?'

Sarah never made a secret of her curiosity; she thought nothing of asking total strangers the most direct, personal questions. Usually, during our conversations, she acted the role of irresistible force. I was the immovable object.

'A deputy named Twombley went out to Rum Pond yesterday morning to talk to my dad. I don't know what information he had, but there was a fight, and Twombley arrested him. On the way back to Skowhegan, the cruiser went off the road and my dad escaped.'

131

'The search — what they showed of it on TV — looked like a military operation.'

'I was up there last night until late, but they sent me home.'

'What for?'

'Because I'm the fugitive's son and they don't want me fucking up the investigation.'

'But you're a game warden.'

'I've also been telling people my dad's innocent.'

'Oh.' She began chewing on a troublesome cuticle. 'Why do you think that?'

'My dad's no terrorist. You met him. Can you picture him getting involved in some plot to murder a police officer and intimidate Wendigo Timber?'

She looked doubtful. 'You have to admit he's violent.'

'He's a bar brawler. He doesn't care about politics. All he cares about is drinking and hunting and getting laid.'

'Do you have any idea where he is?'

'None whatsoever. And I don't really care, either.' I felt my face warm with blood. 'I'm just trying to do my job and go on with my life.'

'I don't believe that for a second.'

'So don't. I don't even know why you came over here. It's hard enough seeing you again.'

'How do you think I feel?'

'You're the one who left, Sarah.'

She took a breath and put her palms flat on the table. 'I didn't come over here to fight with you.'

'So why did you then? Morbid curiosity?'

132

'Maybe I was lonely,' she said. 'Did that ever occur to you? I was thinking a lot about you even before this. And with your dad in the news now — it made me scared for you.'

'Scared?'

'It's your dad, Mike. You can pretend like he's just some stranger, but you can't fool me. I know what that man did to you.'

'What are you talking about? He didn't do anything to me.'

She made a face. 'He abandoned you. He broke up your family.'

'My mom did that.'

'But you blame him.' Sarah wasn't crazy about my mom — she thought she was way too concerned about appearances and material possessions, ironically enough, considering her own tastes in shoes — but she liked my dad even less. After Sarah met him, she was convinced he was responsible for everything bad that had happened in their marriage.

'I think I'd rather fight with you than have you psychoanalyze me.'

'Do you want me to go?'

'If you're going to lecture me, yes.'

From the tightness of her jaw, I could see she was fighting to keep her emotions in check. After a long silence she said, 'Do you mind if I use your bathroom first?'

'You know where it is.'

After she left, I noticed how dusk was seeping into the house. The kitchen was practically dark. I got up and snapped on the light, but it was too bright, so I shut it off again. I didn't really want her to leave, but I didn't want her to think she could just breeze back like nothing had changed.

When she came back from the bathroom she said, 'I'm sorry, Mike. I don't know why I'm lecturing you. It's just really weird being back here. It feels familiar and strange at the same time.'

'I know what you mean.'

She lifted her beer bottle, but it was empty. 'Do you want to go get some dinner? We could go to the Square Deal.'

'I'll cook something.'

She grinned, a certain, mischievous grin I only ever saw when we were alone. 'You'll cook something?'

'I'll make us some sandwiches,' I admitted.

★   ★   ★

We sat around in the dark eating roast beef sandwiches and drinking beer and talking about our college years. It seemed the safest subject. After a while we moved to the scratchy sofa in the living room. She had three beers, which was one more than her limit, but I didn't even think to stop her. I just watched her body loosen and a smile settle across her lips. I was trying to convince myself that we were back in the past, when she was still the happiest person I knew.

'Do you remember that outing club trip to Great Pond?' she asked, her voice a little too loud.

'The one where Ted and Lisa hooked up?'

'And they rolled around in poison ivy.'

134

We both started laughing. 'I'm surprised that never happened to us.'

'I need another beer,' she said.

'I'll get you one.'

We both stood up at the same time. She laughed, and I laughed, and then I kissed her. She pulled away at first, but I leaned my body against her and wrapped my arm around her waist. Suddenly she started kissing me back. Her hair smelled of faded perfume and of hours spent in the August sun. When we stopped kissing, she maintained eye contact.

'We shouldn't do this,' she said, but there was no certainty in her voice.

'I've missed you.'

'I've missed you, too.'

I reached my hands up under her T-shirt and felt the warmth and softness of her skin and then I unfastened her bra and she leaned back to pull the shirt over her head. I cupped her breasts in my hand, first one, then the other, and pushed my head forward to kiss each nipple, feeling each one harden in my mouth.

She stood up then and unbuttoned her shorts and stepped out of them and her underwear, too. Standing before me, she pulled my T-shirt over my head, and I kissed her flat stomach above the dark golden triangle of hair. She took my head in her hands and tilted it back and kissed me again, hard. I stood up, kissing her all the time, and felt her fumbling with the button of my pants.

She pressed me naked back onto the couch cushions. Then she straddled me and guided me inside her. I felt the warmth of her and the surprising wetness and I trembled and groaned so loud it surprised us both. She smiled and gripped the back of the sofa and leaned forward so that her hair was in my face. As she moved, her breathing became audible, and her back became slick beneath my hands. She lifted her eyes and kissed me again with her mouth wide open, and I slid my hands beneath her thighs and stood up from the couch.

With her legs wrapped around me, I carried her into the bedroom and laid her down on the bed. I was above her now and lunging into her. She put her arms out for me to hold. She wanted me to pin her to the bed, and I did. Her eyes were closed tight now, and she was biting her lip, and I felt the muscles of her body tensing and tensing, and I pressed on harder until a shudder ran first through her, then me.

Afterward, she curled herself against me, pressing a hand flat on my chest, with a leg thrown over mine. We didn't speak. I thought that I would surely fall asleep first, exhausted as I was, but soon her breathing slowed, and I knew she was fast asleep.

The moon was out now, and the light through the open window made Sarah's blonde hair appear to be touched with frost. I watched her for a long time and thought how beautiful she looked lying there and I wondered what the hell was wrong with me that I'd let her slip out of my life. The smell of pine needles drifted in through the window screen, and outside I heard the orchestrations of the crickets in the cordgrass of the salt marsh. After a while, I rolled over and shut my eyes and tried to sleep. But it was no good. In the morning she'd just end up regretting everything she had done when she was drunk. What we'd done tonight would just make it harder for both of us to say good-bye again.

* * *

The phone rang just after midnight. Sarah moaned but didn't wake. I padded out into the living room and just managed to pick up before the answering machine did.

'Hello?'

'I need you to do something,' said my father's voice.

My heart began to flutter. 'Dad, where are you?'

'Canada.' The fuzz of static told me he was speaking on a cell phone.

'How'd you get across?'

'Never mind that.' He paused, as if listening to something on his end. But I didn't hear anything. 'I'm being set up, Mike. They're trying to pin it on me, but I wasn't anywhere near that place. You ask Brenda.'

'Brenda Dean?'

'Yeah. She'll tell you I was with her the whole time.'

'Who's setting you up? Is it that guy Tripp?'

'Maybe. Him and somebody else. I've got my suspicions.' There was a silence on the other end. 'Is your phone clear?'

'What?'

'I thought I heard a click. Jesus, are they

tapping your phone?'

'You've got to give yourself up, Dad.'

'I didn't do anything! They set me up!' He was terrified. I'd never heard fear in his voice before.

'You assaulted that deputy, Twombley.'

'He attacked me.'

'Your face is all over the news. You have hundreds of police officers looking for you, and they all think you're a cop killer. They're not going to take you in alive. You've got to give yourself up. If you're innocent, you don't have any reason to be afraid — '

'I *am* innocent! Talk to Brenda.'

'We'll find you a lawyer.'

'A lawyer.' He practically spat out the word. 'Yeah, right.' Then he hung up.

Moonlight had leeched the color out of everything inside the room: the walls, the furniture, the floors. Even the skin of my hands looked gray. It was as if I had woken up inside an old black-and-white movie, a film noir.

Except that this was no dream. I crossed into the kitchen and snapped on the overhead light. The sudden brightness made me wince. At the sink, I splashed cold water on my face and rubbed it along the back of my neck until the hairs stood on end. I filled my mouth with water and spat it out. Then I braced myself against the countertop and faced my reflection in the window above the sink.

What should I do? I had a legal and ethical duty to report this conversation to the state police. If I didn't, I'd be acting as an accessory to homicide after the fact. I could go to jail. But if I

138

told the authorities about my dad being in Canada — and how was I to know he was really there? — I'd be betraying his trust. And beneath the anger he'd sounded so terrified. If I couldn't get Sarah to believe he was innocent, what hope did I have of convincing anyone else?

I wandered back out into the living room and sat there in the dark for a while, looking at the telephone. But I couldn't bring myself to pick it up.

★ ★ ★

Sarah rolled over when I came back to bed and half-opened her eyes. Her breath smelled of beer. 'I thought I heard you talking to someone.'

'I was on the phone.'

'Who was it?'

'Nobody,' I said. 'Somebody thought they spotted a bear I'm looking for.'

15

When I awoke the next morning, I found Sarah already sitting up beside me, propped against two pillows. I had the feeling she'd been studying me while I slept.

'How long have you been awake?' I asked.

'Not long.'

'You fell asleep pretty fast.'

She gave me a weak smile. 'I thought I heard an owl last night.'

'Oh, yeah?'

'It sounded like an owl. It was in the pines right outside the house.'

'Did it keep you awake?'

'No.'

I slid up beside her.

'Mike,' she began. 'I don't know what happened last night.'

'I got you drunk and took advantage of you.'

She rolled her eyes. 'Give me a little credit. I was the one who came over here. You don't think I figured this might happen?'

'You figured right.'

She rested her head on my shoulder. 'This is so confusing.'

'No, it's not.'

'What do you mean?'

'It means this was a one-time thing. We both know it. So let's quit pretending.'

She sat up. 'Why are you being such a jerk all of a sudden?'

I had no excuse for myself — except that in my messed-up logic, hurting her now seemed kinder than hurting her later. And I would hurt her later. I'd already proven that.

'I'm just being honest about the situation.'

'What the hell does that mean?'

'It means I'm not going to quit my job.'

'I never asked you to.'

'When you were living here, all you did was complain about being lonely and poor. You kept harping on how little money we'd ever have and how we'd never be able to travel abroad or have a nice house like Amy's. And you're right. We'll never have those things. Maybe you should just find yourself a corporate lawyer to marry, like my mom did.'

She stood up. She looked blowsy and bed-headed and absolutely beautiful in the morning sunlight. 'Fuck you.'

Outside I heard tires rustling on dry leaves, a vehicle coming down the dirt drive.

'Someone's here.' I scrambled out of bed and lifted the curtain.

A green patrol truck came to a stop behind mine. Kathy Frost climbed out. From her expression I couldn't tell whether she was bringing me bad news or good.

'Who is it?' Sarah asked, wiping tears from her eyes.

I pulled on a T-shirt and a pair of boxers and hurried out of the room.

Kathy did a double take when I yanked open

141

the door. She looked me up and down, a smile spreading across her face at the spectacle of me in my underwear.

'What's going on?' I asked.

'Good morning to you, too. Isn't that Sarah's Subaru?'

'She's here. So what?'

She cocked an eyebrow. 'Didn't mean to interrupt.'

I stepped outside quickly, forcing her to move back. Then I shut the door behind me. 'What's going on, Kathy?'

'I just wanted to let you know I checked our trap this morning.'

'You what?'

'Yeah, I was up early. So I decided to drive over and have a look. No luck, though.'

'I didn't ask you to do that,' I snapped.

'What's the big deal?'

'It's my fucking responsibility.'

'Cool down, Undershorts. I just figured you had enough on your mind without having to worry about a stupid bear. I thought I'd help you out.'

The door opened behind me, and Sarah came out. She'd dressed quickly and hadn't even bothered to put on her sandals but clutched them tightly to her chest. 'Sergeant.'

'Hi, Sarah. I didn't know you were here.'

'It's all right. I have to leave, anyway.'

'Sarah,' I said.

She brushed past me. 'I've got to get out of here,' she said, climbing inside her car. 'I should never have come back.'

'Don't leave like this.'

She started the engine and put the car in reverse. She backed up so fast I thought she was going to clip Kathy's fender. I watched the dust rise behind her as she disappeared down the drive.

'Ouch,' said Kathy.

She was still standing there when I closed the door.

★ ★ ★

I waited until I heard her truck leave before I sat down next to the telephone. I punched in the number and waited. The phone rang for a good two minutes before a man finally picked up. 'Rum Pond,' he said.

'Brenda Dean, please.'

'Who's this?' It was Russell Pelletier. I recognized the smoke-strained voice.

'It's Mike Bowditch.'

'Mike,' he said. 'How are you holding up, kid?'

'Is Brenda there, Mr. Pelletier?'

'Afraid not. The police wanted to talk with her, so she went in to Flagstaff first thing this morning.'

'She's with the police?'

'Yeah. They sent a car out for her. Left me to wash all the fucking dishes.'

So Detective Soctomah had brought her in for questioning. Presumably she'd given my dad an alibi for the night of the murders. But unless she had proof, there was zero chance of them believing her. In fact, based upon my testimony about that message my dad left on my machine, the one with the woman's voice on it, they probably viewed her as an accessory.

Pelletier broke the silence: 'Your old man really fucked up this time.'

'How come you didn't tell me you were at that meeting at the Dead River Inn?'

'How's that?'

'I saw your picture in the paper. You didn't tell me you were there.'

'The whole town was there. What the hell are you implying?'

'Maybe you know what really happened that night,' I said.

'I've got dishes to wash.' He hung up before I could say another word.

★　★　★

Was Russell Pelletier one of the men my father suspected? I had no way of knowing. It was true that I'd always disliked the sporting camp owner with his drooping mustache and perpetual cigarette. And he certainly had cause to want Wendigo chased off — more cause than my father did, at least on the surface. He was facing the loss of his business, his way of life. He definitely had a motive to murder.

Not that he would admit anything to me. Why had I provoked him? Any chance I might have had to get information out of Pelletier was gone now, and with Brenda Dean in police custody I was at a definite dead end. If I drove up there, Lieutenant Malcomb would have my badge, and

144

without that, what good would I be to my dad?

I had no choice but to go out on patrol. And hope that something happened that would map out my next move.

* * *

Maine used to be famous for its cool summers. Now it seemed that every August came with an actual heat wave. Hello, global warming.

This day was another scorcher, ninety degrees in the shade, which meant no fish biting on the lakes, which meant fewer fishermen to check but lots more recreational boaters. I drove around to the various public landings with the air-conditioning at full power and the police radio turned loud, listening for anything that might indicate a break in my dad's case. And I did my best not to dwell on Sarah's expression as she drove off this morning.

Then, in the afternoon, I stopped at the municipal boat launch at Indian Pond and there was Anthony DeSalle's black Suburban in the parking lot.

Through my binoculars I saw his big powerboat floating on the water. I should've known I might run into him again. He'd said he was renting a house on Indian Pond, and it was only logical to conclude that he intended to make use of his boat again while he was on vacation. Sooner or later we were bound to cross paths.

Maybe he figured he'd scared me off by filing a complaint. Maybe he figured I would leave him alone now.

Fat chance.

I nosed my truck into a parking space facing the water, rolled down the window, and waited. The smell of the lake drifted in, a languorous odor of algae blooms and gasoline from outboard motors.

When I finally saw DeSalle's boat headed in, I felt a surge of adrenaline. I climbed out of the truck and walked to the end of the ramp.

DeSalle was at the helm, and his son was with him. There was another man in the boat this time, dark haired and deeply tanned. He had a thick chest, big arms, and spindly little legs, all shiny with suntan oil, and he wore a red bathing suit and a gold chain around his neck. The little boy, I noticed, wasn't wearing a personal flotation device.

'Maine game warden. I need to inspect your boat, please.'

'I don't believe this bullshit,' said DeSalle.

The other man hopped over the gunwale into knee-deep water and splashed ahead of the boat, guiding it with his hand into the shallows. He came right toward me, but I held my ground at the base of the ramp.

'What's your problem?' he said. His eyes were so brown they were almost black, and his breath smelled of gin.

'I need to inspect your boat, please.'

'We saw you watching us,' said DeSalle.

'You've been waiting here for us to come in.'

'Just doing my job, Mr. DeSalle.'

'The hell you are.'

DeSalle pointed his finger at me. 'This is fucking harrassment.'

'If you have a problem with me, Mr. DeSalle, you can make another complaint.'

'Screw you,' said the other man.

'What's your name? I want to see some I.D.'

He threw back his head and laughed. 'You want to see some I.D.? Here it is.' He grabbed the crotch of his bathing suit and squeezed.

I took a half step forward.

'Knock it off, Frank,' said DeSalle. He nodded his head in the direction of the parking lot.

A car had pulled up without my hearing it, and a man and a woman were busy removing a pair of river kayaks from its roof.

'You want to inspect my boat, Officer?' said Anthony DeSalle in a loud voice, loud enough for the couple to hear, 'Go right ahead. Be my guest.'

'I want to see your I.D. first,' I said to the man he'd called Frank.

'Sure thing, *Officer*.'

He reached over the gunwale to pick up a flowered shirt. His wallet was in the pocket. The name on the driver's license was Frank Nappi, of Saugus, Massachusetts. He also had a valid fifteen-day Maine fishing license.

DeSalle held up a piece of paper. 'Here's my registration — which you've already seen

147

— unless it expired since two days ago.'

The registration was in order, of course. There were sufficient PFDs in the boat now, and the fire extinguisher was approved and fully charged. There were three fishing rods in the stern, but no indication that they'd caught any fish or used illegal tackle.

When I looked up, DeSalle was leaning against the dashboard with his arms crossed and a smug smile on his face. 'I talked with your lieutenant. You're in a shitload of trouble.'

'How old is your son, Mr. DeSalle?'

The smile left his face. 'He's ten. Why?'

'He doesn't need a fishing license,' said Frank Nappi.

'You're right, Mr. Nappi. He doesn't. But he is required by law to wear at least a Type III personal flotation device while on board a watercraft.' I removed my citation book from my pocket and stepped back from the boat. 'I'm citing you, Mr. DeSalle, for operating a watercraft without proper safety equipment.'

'You think you're pretty tough, don't you, fucker?' said Nappi.

'I've heard enough out of you, Mr. Nappi.'

'Warden?' The voice came from the top of the ramp where the couple with the kayaks were waiting for us to move so they could put in. I had only glanced at them before, but now I recognized the young woman as Dot Libby's youngest daughter, Ruth, the pudgy waitress from the Square Deal Diner. 'Mike? Are you all right?'

Seeing her did something to me; all at once the fire seemed to go out in my brain. Just the sound of a woman's voice did it.

Suddenly it was over.

Nappi seemed to know it, too. When he turned back to me, he was still sneering, but the muscles in his arms and neck seemed to relax.

'I'm fine, Ruth,' I said, keeping my eyes on Nappi. 'Thank you.' Over my shoulder, I said to DeSalle. 'Your driver's license, please, Mr. DeSalle.'

This time he gave it to me. I wrote up the ticket and held it out for him. He grabbed the paper from me and said in a soft voice, 'Your career is over, asshole.'

I climbed to the top of the boat ramp and stood beside Ruth Libby and her boyfriend while DeSalle and Nappi loaded the powerboat onto the trailer. All the while, the boy, forgotten by his father, watched me. I couldn't tell from his expression what he was thinking. Maybe he wanted me to rescue him, maybe he wanted to kill me. The blood was still pounding in my ears, very loud. I knew my face was red with it, too.

'Those guys were rude,' whispered Ruth's boyfriend.

'They're pricks,' said Ruth. 'We missed you the last few days at the diner, Mike.'

My mouth tasted of the dirt-dry parking lot. 'I've been busy. Tell your mom I'll be around one of these days.'

'Tell her yourself,' she said.

* ★ ★

My pager went off as I was sitting in my
parked patrol truck, trying to get my
paperwork together while I cooled down. I
didn't recognize the phone number that came
up, but I dialed it, anyway. The department
didn't reimburse us for cell phone calls, even
when they were made for job-related reasons,
but most of the wardens I knew continued to
carry personal cells and pay for the privilege
out of their own pockets.

'This is Mike Bowditch with the Maine
Warden Service. You just paged me.'

'Thanks for returning my call. My name's Rob
Post, and I'm a writer with *The Portland Press
Herald*. I'd like to speak with you about your
father.'

'I'm on duty, sir.'

'Your father is the suspect in a double
homicide and the subject of an international
manhunt. Can't you take five minutes to talk
with me? I think your family should be given an
opportunity to respond to the things being said
about him.'

I closed my eyes and leaned back against the
seat. 'I have nothing to say.'

'It will help your father if you talk to me,
Mike,' said Post.

I laughed.

He knew he was losing me. 'I understand you
were present at the search scene last night. How
did it feel being a warden involved in hunting for
your own father?'

'Don't call me again, Mr. Post.'

'Do you think he killed those men?' he asked before I hung up.

I looked out through the windshield at the mirror surface of Indian Pond, the pearl-gray sky above. My brain could scarcely form a thought — it felt like it was wrapped in cotton batting. I drove back to my empty home.

16

I heard the phone ringing inside the house. The sound carried through the screen to the back porch, where I'd gone to watch the sunset. I couldn't have told you how long I'd been sitting there, but mosquitoes had raised welts along both my arms. The phone summoned me back to myself from a faraway place. I got up and went inside and picked up the receiver.

'I shot it!' said a man's slurred voice. 'I shot it!'

'Mr. Thompson?'

'I shot the bear!'

'It came back to your farm?'

'Yeah, it came back. Came back just now.' I could practically smell the liquor on his breath through the phone.

'And you say you killed it?'

'Hell, yes.'

'You're sure it's dead?'

'Come see for yourself.'

I picked up my gunbelt from the tabletop where it lay beside Sarah's empty beer bottles. Then I went out into the last minutes of daylight.

★ ★ ★

I drove fast along the Beechwood Road, feeling the frustration inside me building to anger. All

152

the hours I'd put into trapping the bear had been for nothing. The animal was dead, and I didn't even know why I was speeding.

The sun had just disappeared behind the ridge as I came up on Bud Thompson's farm. I saw the dirty clapboard house, the broken-backed barn, the rickety chicken coop. It seemed ages since I'd last visited this place. I was startled to realize it had only been three nights earlier.

Bud Thompson was nowhere to be seen. I'd expected him to be waiting for me on his front porch or at least to come running when my truck pulled into the driveway. Most of the windows were dark, but deep within the house I saw a faint light, like a dying ember.

I circled around the house to the backyard. Thompson hadn't bothered to repair the pigpen; the pieces of the broken fence still lay scattered where the bear had tossed them.

I looked back at the house. The mudroom door was wide open.

'Mr. Thompson?'

There was no answer. I heard the chickens scratching about in the coop. A car rushed past the house and down the hill.

'Mr. Thompson? It's Mike Bowditch with the Warden Service.'

The inside of the house smelled of stale beer and mothballs. I flicked on the kitchen light. Thompson's .22 rifle lay on the table amid a bunch of empty beer cans and stock car racing magazines. There was a smear of blood on the cracked linoleum floor leading down the hall.

'Mr. Thompson?'

I heard a whimper. The bathroom door was ajar, light spilling out through the crack. Inside, Thompson was seated on the toilet. He had rolled up his pant leg and was clutching a bloody towel to his calf. He looked up at me with red, tear-filled eyes and shuddered. He smelled like he had showered in malt liquor.

'What happened?'

'I thought I killed it.'

'It bit you?'

'I went out to have another look. I must've only stunned it.' He shook his head sadly. 'I hit it in the head. I thought I killed it.'

'Let me see your leg.'

'It's bleeding pretty heavy.'

He peeled back the towel. Blood began pumping out from the torn flesh. The bear had torn an egg-sized chunk of meat from the muscle of his calf.

'It's bad, isn't it?' he asked.

'You're going to need some stitches, but you'll be all right. Keep pressing hard against the wound.'

He nodded and shuddered again.

'What happened to the bear?'

'It went off into the woods.'

'Great,' I said.

I left Thompson and went back to my truck to request an ambulance. With the sun down, the sky was turning violet and shadows were creeping out from beneath the trees at the edge of the forest. I didn't have much time. I removed my Mossberg 12-gauge from its locked holder and ejected the buckshot shells from the chamber and magazine. Then I loaded the shotgun with heavy deer slugs and hooked my Maglite on my gunbelt.

When I came back inside the house, I found that Thompson had dragged himself out to the kitchen. He was seated at the table, with a new towel knotted around his leg, and he was gulping down a can of beer like a man dying of thirst.

I reached out to take the beer can away from him, but it was already empty. 'If you move around, you're just going to make it bleed more. The ambulance should be here in twenty minutes or so. Stay still and keep applying pressure to the wound. And lay off the beer.'

He looked at the shotgun in my hand. 'Where are you going?'

'To find that bear.'

He turned his head in the direction of the window. 'It's too dark.'

'I'm not going to leave it out there all night suffering on account of your stupidity. Where did you last see it?'

'Back behind the pigpen.'

'Where was it shot?'

'Back behind the pigpen.'

'No, I meant where was it injured?'

'In the head. I must have just stunned it.'

I glanced at the rifle on the table; it looked like a child's toy. 'I told you you'd have a hard time killing a bear with a .22. You're lucky it didn't maul you just now.'

'I thought I got it through the eye.'

Under the fluorescent kitchen light I could see the feathery blue veins in his cheeks and along

155

his nose. I doubted if he was even fifty, but he looked like a man twenty years older. 'A deputy will probably arrive before the ambulance does,' I said. 'Tell him where I've gone, but let him know that he shouldn't come after me. I don't want anyone else in the woods right now.'

'Don't go out there.'

'You won't bleed to death, if that's what you're worried about.'

His eyes filled with tears again. 'I'm sorry.'

'I don't want to hear it,' I said.

★   ★   ★

On the doorstep I paused and drew a deep breath. Darkness was coming fast. The sky in the west had turned the color of a bruise, and overhead I saw Vega, the first star of evening. I had only minutes to find the bear before it became too dark to hunt.

I crossed the yard to the pen, searching for the spot where Thompson had brought down the animal with his gun. I found it easily enough: a patch of trampled weeds and claw-scratched dirt near the place where we had buried the pig. Dust-coated pearls of blood clung to the grass there.

Why did the bear come back here?

I crouched down and touched two fingers to the spoor, smelling the ferrous, rusty smell of fresh blood and feeling a quickening of my pulse as I scanned the edge of the forest. The animal might or might not be dying. I knew that when a heavy bear is shot, the thick fat beneath the skin

156

can plug up the wound. This one had probably found a hollow under the cover of some nearby spruce to hide and rest. All I knew for certain was that a wounded black bear was capable of killing me now if I stumbled upon it suddenly in the darkness beneath the trees. I might get a shot off, but not before it crushed me beneath its weight and fastened its jaws around my skull.

I wiped my hand in the dirt and rose to my feet. Even in the weakening light the blood trail showed clearly in the weeds leading back across the field. A wind was blowing at my back, just the faintest of sea breezes, really, but it would be enough to carry my scent to the bear where it was hiding in the timber. Bad luck for me.

I followed the track through the wall of sumacs and alder, ducking my head against the leaves to enter the forest. Here the wind diminished, but I could still feel its breath against the back of my neck, and when I set down my feet on the dry leaves, the sound was sharp and brittle. The trunks of the trees crowded close about me, the paper birches glowing ghost-white in the shadows. Every spruce seemed large enough to conceal a bear beneath its dark, shaggy boughs.

I tried to remain still.

There were no crickets, no sound whatsoever beyond the whisper of wind in the treetops.

After a minute, my eyes had adjusted themselves to the gloom as much as they were likely to do, given the lateness of the hour. I figured I'd have to look hard to find the trail again. But I didn't. At my feet there was a small, starry splatter of blood on some moss.

I followed the spoor down the hillside. The bear, bleeding hard, had gone fast at first. I could see where his claws had gouged the pine-needled floor of the forest, and even where there was no blood, the crushed ferns and snapped branches of alders showed the violence of his passing.

Then he found his way into a dense stand of black spruce trees that had bristling boughs like pipe cleaners. The trunks of the trees grew very close together here, and I could not push my way through without going blindly, noisily, with the breeze driving my scent ahead of me. I figured the bear had hidden himself somewhere deep inside the thicket, crouched down there amid the darkening shadows, waiting for night to come to make him safe. He could be lying inside those spruces, and I would not see him until I was only a few feet away. By then it would be too late.

I knelt down and rested the butt of the Mossberg on the ground. I wished again that I had a dog to help me track. My better judgment told me to call Kathy Frost and ask her to bring her dog, Pluto. With a K-9, we could find the bear, even in pitch darkness. But I seemed to be disregarding my better judgment as a matter of course these days. To hell with being careful, a voice said in my head. Be a fucking man and get the job done.

I eased myself through the nearest spruces putting my foot down as quietly as I could, heel first and then toe. Dead spruce branches scraped the skin of my face and bare arms, then sprang back into place behind me, making a whipping sound. Almost instantly I realized that I would never be able to track the bear here. It was too dense, too dark.

That was when I heard the crash. Maybe twenty yards off to my right, at the edge of the spruce thicket, came a sound like a big tree falling, and I knew it was the bear running. He went crashing clear of the spruces. Branches snapped as he bulled his way through.

I followed as best I could. Keeping my head down to avoid being jabbed in the eye by a sharp branch, I shouldered through the boughs. Then I was back outside the densest part of the thicket. My heart was beating so loud I could no longer hear the bear, but I caught a glimpse of movement through the timber, and I went after it at a dead run. I let gravity carry me down the slope.

The bear turned on me at the bottom of the hill. He'd run himself into a streambed that cut like a ravine between this slope and the next, and he didn't have the energy to climb out. He turned and lowered his head beneath the hump of his shoulders and bared his teeth.

I had to slide on the dead leaves to stop my momentum. I fell backward, onto my ass, and suddenly found myself sitting upright on the ground, like a toddler surprised at having lost his balance, not twenty yards from the bear. For a split second neither of us moved. In the twilight the bear looked immense. I saw that one of its eyes was a bright red mess. Then, suddenly, the bear charged. He was halfway to me before I could even blink, and I was swinging the shotgun barrel up. I don't remember pulling the trigger, but the explosion brought stars to my eyes, and when I could see again, the bear lay motionless five yards in front me.

I had a hard time getting to my feet. I heard a strange sound and then realized it was my own raspy breathing. My eyes were wet and stung as if I had dust in them.

Keeping the shotgun trained on his head, I approached the bear. But he was already dead. The slug had torn a big hole through the front of his skull, blowing away a chunk of bone, lifting a flap of skin and thick hair. The smell of the animal was strong, all sour musk and blood, and standing over it, I saw that I'd been wrong about his size. Stretched out on the ground, dead, he was only about as big as a medium-sized man. He even looked a little like a man wearing a bear suit.

The breeze blew again, and the sudden chill made me realize that my undershirt and shirt were soaked with sweat. I shivered and clicked on the shotgun safety and took a seat on a big, moss-covered stump. My tailbone ached from where I'd hit the ground. The bear was too big to drag out of there on my own; I would need to get help. I glanced back up the wooded hillside. From this angle, it looked as sheer as a cliff and about a mile high.

'Shit,' I said.

★ ★ ★

All the way up that hill, I cursed Bud Thompson. I'd known from the start that I might have to kill the bear. Dot Libby had even said so. Killing wounded and nuisance animals was part of what I did for a living as a game warden. Death was part of nature, a fact of life.

But seeing that bear stretched lifeless on the ground and knowing that maybe a mile away my culvert trap was sitting empty filled me with an almost unbearable sense of waste. The bear's death felt absolutely unnecessary, and the thing that bothered me most was that I couldn't understand why the bear had returned to this farm when there was no longer a pig here.

It took me at least fifteen minutes to hike back to Thompson's farm, and even before I reached the hilltop I saw blue and red lights flashing through the trees. A sheriff's cruiser and an ambulance were parked in Thompson's driveway and there was another Maine Warden Service patrol truck, beside my own, pulled up on the lawn.

Kathy Frost was waiting for me outside the pigpen. 'I was on the road and I heard the call come over the radio.' Her forehead was furrowed with concern. 'Your face is all scraped.'

I touched my cheek; my fingertips came away red.

'What happened?' she asked. 'Where's the bear?'

'It's dead. About a quarter mile down that hill.'

'Shit. That's a long way to haul it out.'

161

'It would have died, anyway,' I said. 'It had lost a lot of blood.' I glanced up at the house. The first-floor windows were all alight. 'Where's Thompson?'

'Inside. The EMTs are trying to convince him to go to the hospital. You should have stayed with him, Mike. You should have waited for us to bring a dog in.'

'I was pissed off,' I said. 'So why the hell did the bear come back here? It doesn't make sense'

'He was baiting it.'

'What?'

'He was putting out food for it.' She motioned for me to follow her around the pigpen. Inside the fence was a heap of trash. I saw an empty tin for a canned ham and a Dunkin' Donuts box and other refuse that I hadn't noticed before.

I stood there gazing at it. 'Son of a bitch.'

Kathy came up behind me. 'There's something else we need to talk about, Mike. The reason I was out this way was because we got another call from Anthony DeSalle. Have you lost your mind? You know better than to have contact with someone who's made a complaint against you.'

There was a buzzing sound in my head and I was having a hard time hearing her. It was the sound of the flies amplified about a hundred times.

'It comes across as a pattern of harassment,' she said. 'Mike, are you listening to me?'

'He was trying to lure it in,' I said.

'What? Who?'

'Thompson. He knew I had a trap out there, but he was trying to lure it in so he could shoot it himself.'

'The bear killed the man's pig,' she said. 'Cut him some slack.'

'That was three days ago.'

'He's allowed to shoot a wild animal destroying his property.'

'Not three days later he's not.' I turned and started walking in the direction of the house. 'He baited that bear and he shot it illegally. He broke the law.'

Two medics came out of the kitchen door carrying Thompson on a stretcher. His pant leg had been scissored off, and his wound was wrapped in a new white bandage.

I stepped in front of the EMTs, blocking their way. Thompson gave me a confused, boozy smile. 'Is it dead?'

'It's dead.'

'You shot it?'

'Yes.'

'Can I have the skin? I always wanted a bearskin rug.'

It was all I could do not to punch him. 'You didn't tell me you were putting bait out. That's illegal, you know.'

His smile drooped at the corners. 'It killed my pig.'

'I don't care.'

'It was self-defense.'

'The hell it was. You baited that bear.'

'Excuse me, Warden,' said one of the medics. 'Can we continue this conversation later?'

'Get out of the way, Mike,' said Kathy Frost from behind me.

'The man needs to go to the hospital,' said the other EMT.

I pointed my finger at Thompson's nose. His eyes bounced back and forth from my face to the shotgun in my other hand. 'You broke the law, Thompson, and after they stitch up your leg, I'm taking you to jail.'

'No, you're not,' said Kathy in her hardest voice. 'Come on, Mike. Let these men do their jobs.' Her fingers dug like talons into my shoulder. 'Let these men do their jobs.'

I stopped resisting and let her pull me back a step.

We watched the EMTs carry Thompson to the ambulance. When they'd closed the back door and started the engine, Kathy released my shoulder. 'You were out of line back there.'

'Sorry,' I said. 'Drunks just piss me off.'

'You're off duty. As of now.'

'What? I said I was sorry.'

'Fine. I accept your apology, but I still want you to go home. You're on vacation as of tonight.'

'What the hell does that mean? Are you suspending me?'

'Only if you force me.'

I opened my mouth to speak.

She held up her long, callused hand. 'We're not discussing this. You're going home, and you're going to get some rest. You have tomorrow off, and then you're on vacation for a week. We'll talk about the DeSalle complaint

164

when you get back. Maybe by then you'll have your head together.'

'What the hell does that mean?'

'It means we're all sorry about your father, and we understand how freaked out you must be about it. But if the situation's screwing up your judgment, then it's better if you're out of uniform for the time being.'

'What about the bear?'

'I'll take care of it.' She gestured at my truck. 'Go home, Mike. I mean it.'

Her expression was unflinching. I knew I'd crossed some sort of line with her, and I wasn't sure how it had happened.

Halfway across the lawn I turned and said, with half a smile, 'You wouldn't really suspend me?'

But the look on my sergeant's face gave me no comfort.

★   ★   ★

That night I got really drunk for the first time since I'd become a game warden. I took out a half-empty fifth of Jack Daniels a college friend had left behind the last time he'd rolled through town, and I sat on the porch. A mist was rising off the marsh, and the smell of tidal mud and sea salt was thick in the air. A killdeer kept flying back and forth along the creek making a hysterical cry as if it had lost something irreplaceable.

When I awoke the next morning, I found myself inside, lying facedown on the couch. The phone was ringing, and it took everything in me to stumble across the room to answer it. Sunlight, flooding through the windows, burned my eyes.

'Hello?'

'I need to see you,' said my mother.

17

The town of Scarborough is where I'd spent the second half of my childhood after my parents divorced and where my mom and stepfather still lived. It is only a two-hour drive south along the coast, but it always feels longer because the land changes so much with every passing mile. These days, southern Maine is just an extension of the Boston suburbs.

When we first moved to Scarborough, right after the divorce, there were still cornfields and thick oak forests that stretched for miles. Then the houses really began to sprout, first along the country roads heading down to the beaches, and then in vast subdivisions wherever there was enough land for building. Soon the weedy fields where I'd caught garter snakes became a grid of neocolonial homes and impossibly green lawns. Woods where Wabanaki Indians had once hunted deer were cleared to make way for 'Indian Woods Estates.'

As a teenager, I fought the future as best I could. Rather than taking up soccer or skateboarding, I cast for striped bass in the Spurwink River. Instead of playing video games I read *The Last of the Mohicans*. I watched the pavement spread under my feet and dreamed of moving to the North Woods and becoming a game warden. As if you can ever really escape what's coming.

★　★　★

My mother had received a call from my father, and she was in a panic. She didn't want to go into the details over the phone. 'I need you here,' she said.

It was a brilliant morning. The blue of the sky and the green of the leaves looked like colors from a child's picture book. After two hours on the road, I pulled into the driveway of my mother's beautiful new house. Next door, a rainbow haze drifted across the lawn from the neighbor's sprinkler system.

I rang the bell and waited. After a while, I had the sense of someone on the other side of the door, studying me through the peep-hole, and then it opened and there was my stepfather. Neil Turner was a tall, flat-stomached man with a full head of dark hair going silver at the temples. He wore a lime-colored polo shirt and khakis and was clutching his cell phone. He smiled awkwardly and extended a hand for me to shake. 'You really didn't have to drive all the way down here.'

'It's OK,' I said.

'Is that Michael?' my mother called from the second floor.

'It's me,' I said.

She appeared at the top of the steps. She was barefoot, and she was wearing white shorts and a striped blue cotton shirt. A small gold crucifix hung at the base of her throat. She hurried downstairs to embrace me. 'It's so good to see you.'

I smelled shampoo in her hair as she hugged me. 'It's good to see you, too, Mom.'

She held me at arm's length. There were dark circles under her eyes. As she studied me, her forehead became wrinkled, the only lines in an otherwise perfect oval face. She touched my cheek. 'Michael, what happened to your chin?'

'I scratched myself going through some bushes. I want to hear about the call you got from Dad.'

She glanced at Neil, who was now standing against the relocked door.

'Why don't we go out into the living room,' he said.

They sat together on a couch holding hands, and I sat across from them. It was a cream-colored room with Scandinavian furniture, and sheer curtains that let in some gauzy sunlight. On the coffee table was a book of Matisse paintings and a framed picture of Neil with his daughter from his previous marriage. They'd redecorated since Sarah and I were last here at Christmastime.

'I shouldn't have called you,' said my mother. 'Neil told me not to, but I was in a panic.' The slight French-Canadian accent in her speech seemed more pronounced than usual: a sign of stress I'd learned to recognize.

'Tell me about the phone call,' I said.

She glanced at Neil, and he squeezed her hand. 'He called early. It must have been eight o'clock. It sounded like he was on a cell phone. There was a lot of static.'

'What did he say?'

'He said he didn't kill those men. He said he'd asked for your help, but that you wouldn't help him.'

I felt a tightening in my chest. 'Did he say where he was?'

'Canada somewhere. He wanted to talk with Neil.'

I met my stepfather's eyes. 'About what?'

'He wanted me to represent him.' Neil smiled a mirthless smile and shook his head. 'Can you believe that? I'm a tax attorney.'

When I'd suggested my dad find a lawyer, he'd laughed at me. I guess he'd had a change of heart. But did he really want Neil's legal advice? The two men hated each other. Then again, how many lawyers did my dad know? 'So what did you say?'

'I hung up on him, of course, and I called the police. I spoke with that detective — Soctomah.'

'What if he wanted to surrender? How do you know he wasn't looking to give himself up?'

'The man's a murderer,' said Neil.

'He was asking for your help,' I said.

Neil laughed sharply. 'It was probably some sort of ploy to find out if we were home. When I heard his voice, I was scared for my life.'

'What the hell are you talking about?'

Neil looked at me as if he could not believe how slow-witted I was. 'I thought he might come here. If he killed those two men, who knows what else he might do.'

'We don't know he killed anybody. He says he's been framed.'

Neil waved his hand as if to drive off a bad

170

smell. 'The evidence — '

'What evidence? Did Soctomah tell you what proof they have?'

'I was worried for your mother's safety.'

I was about to interject something about his selfless concern for my mother's welfare, but she spoke first. 'He wouldn't hurt me,' she said, shaking her head.

Neil said, 'You don't know that, Marie.'

'He wouldn't hurt me,' she said again.

'Well, there's nothing to stop him from hurting *me*. He threatened to kill me once. Or have you forgotten?'

My mom glanced at the window as if she hadn't heard him.

Neil was looking at me now. 'It was after your mother and I got engaged. He was waiting for me one night in the parking lot outside my office. He was drunk. He told me he would kill me unless I broke it off.'

'He wouldn't have killed you,' said my mother softly.

'He showed me the gun!'

'Jack says things when he gets drunk,' said my mother. 'It's just talk.'

'Why are you still making excuses for him?' He glanced back at me again. 'The man's a murderer. I'm sorry, but it's the truth.'

'You don't know the first thing about him,' I said.

'I know the type of man he is.' Neil rose to his feet, smoothing the front of his shirt. 'I can't believe how naive you both are. He's still manipulating you, and you don't even see it. I'm going to finish packing.'

He left us there in that sunlit room. 'Why is he packing?'

'We're going to Long Beach — to visit Jessica. Neil's afraid of Jack showing up here. We've had reporters calling. I just want to forget all this has happened. It's like a nightmare.' She removed a wadded tissue from her pocket and dabbed it at her eyes.

So that was it. They were getting out of Dodge, leaving my dad to his fate. And if he had been thinking of giving himself up, Neil's reaction would almost certainly have made him think twice about contacting another lawyer. 'I can't believe the bastard hung up on him.'

'Michael!'

I knew I was being too hard on Neil, who had been a decent guardian to me for much of my life. It was all so perverse. Until four days ago, I'd pretty much stopped even thinking of my real dad, and yet now that he was back in my life, I felt compelled to side with him. 'I still don't understand why he called you after all this time. It doesn't make any sense.'

'He still calls me,' she said. 'He never stopped over all these years.'

The admission shocked me. 'What do you mean he still calls you?'

'When he's been drinking.'

'But Neil — '

'Neil doesn't know. It's my secret.'

It was a revelation that left me just about speechless. I had been certain my parents never communicated except through me. 'What do you

— what do you say to each other?'

'We just talk. I know he can be horrible, cruel, when he's drinking, but there's another side to him that people don't see. He's a lonely man who needs a woman in his life. He's very passionate, and without a woman, he becomes lost. But his heart is good. When I heard that he was a suspect in those murders, I didn't know what to think. Everybody's so sure he did it. But I couldn't make myself believe it. I just went to bed and cried.'

I went around to the sofa and sat beside her. 'You could have called me.'

'Thank you.' She patted my hand, but I could tell that she never even considered it.

I cleared my throat. 'When was the last time you spoke with him? Before this morning, I mean.'

'It's been a while. He stopped calling about two years ago.'

'Did he ever mention a woman named Brenda?'

She looked up, and for an instant I thought I saw a spark in her eye — a little of the old fire from her trailer trash days. 'Who is she?'

'Soctomah says she's his girlfriend up at Rum Pond. The state police are holding her as a material witness.'

'I don't know the woman.'

'Was there anything else about your conversation? Maybe just something you sensed?'

'He's frightened. You father would never admit to being scared. But I could always tell. Michael, you have to help him. You're in law enforcement.

Can't you tell people he's innocent?'

In her mind, it was as simple as that: If I said he was innocent, they'd believe me. 'He has to give himself up.'

'He doesn't trust anybody.'

'Well, he's going to have to start.'

She pinched the gold cross around her neck between her thumb and forefinger. 'It's too late.'

With that she rose to her feet above me. She wiped the corner of her eye again and then smiled and took my face in her hands. 'How are you, Michael? You don't look well.'

'I'm fine. I've just had an exhausting week.'

'But you still like your job?'

'Yeah, I do.'

'Do you still think about applying to law school?'

'No.'

She nodded. 'How's Sarah?'

I'd never told them about Sarah moving out. In the two months since she'd been gone, it had never once occurred to me to tell my mother about it. That's how estranged we'd become. Part of me was tempted to tell her the truth now — she'd been so candid with me — but instead I heard myself say, 'She's fine.'

She studied my eyes, and I wondered if she could detect my lie. 'I'm sorry we never get up to see you two.'

'We all have busy lives.'

'Seeing you reminds me of so many things, Michael. You look so much like your father.'

I was beginning to realize that my mom — the rebellious Catholic schoolgirl who had gone from life in a backwoods trailer to suburban affluence — had depths to her heart I'd never be able to fathom.

18

When I was sixteen I told my mother I wanted to spend the summer with my dad. She tried to talk me out of it. She said I didn't know what he was really like. I said, 'That's the reason I want to go.' Eventually, she gave in. She knew I hadn't spent any significant stretch of time with him since the divorce, and I think she realized that the experience was something I needed to get out of my system. And I'm sure she didn't mind being rid of me for three months during the tennis season.

'It would be great to see you!' my father said when I finally reached him over the radio phone that was Rum Pond Sporting Camps' only connection to the outside world. 'The only thing is, I don't have space for you at my cabin. And I doubt Pelletier would give you a room.'

I said I would camp outside all summer in a tent, if need be.

'Let me think about it a bit and get back to you.'

But he never did. So I kept calling. I said I was willing to do whatever needed to be done at Rum Pond — washing dishes, splitting firewood, anything — in exchange for food.

'I guess we can find work for you,' he said. 'But you know I'll be busy, too. I don't want you to expect too much.'

I said that wouldn't be a problem.

Two days after school let out in June, I was on the bus from Portland to Waterville. My dad had said he would pick me up at the station, but there was no one there when I arrived. I waited and waited. When I finally got through to Rum Pond, Russell Pelletier said my father was off somewhere in the woods, and I'd just have to hitchhike the eighty or so miles up Route 201 to The Forks and from there find my way down a logging road — another twenty miles — to camp. If I was lucky, he said, I might be able to catch a ride into the woods with one of the pulp trucks. 'Otherwise you're looking at the longest walk of your life,' he said with undisguised amusement.

I wandered out into the parking lot, feeling the sudden weight of the packed clothes and books in my backpack. What the hell had I gotten myself into?

I started through Waterville in what I hoped was a northerly direction, looking for the road to Skowhegan. I walked maybe half a mile before I became aware of a pickup creeping along behind me. It was an old Ford, and it was moving at scarcely more than an idle, ten or so yards back. A flutter of fear announced itself down in the bottom of my stomach.

Suddenly I heard the truck's engine rev and out of the corner of my eye saw it gunning toward me. I stumbled onto the shoulder and fell over on my ass. The truck squealed to a stop beside me, and the passenger door opened.

Inside sat a dusky-skinned man with a case of Budweiser on his lap and a broken-toothed grin on his face. My father was behind the wheel.

'Hey, pretty boy, want a lift?' he said.

'I think he's having a heart attack,' said the other man, speaking with a singsong accent I didn't recognize. He looked to be about my father's age, but not as healthy; there was a flabby look to his arms and chest. He had bowl-cut black hair and a face that was as round as a pie. 'We got him, I think.'

'Yeah, you got me.' I stood up. 'That's real funny.'

'Lighten up, Mike,' said my father. 'We're just yanking your chain.'

'Mr. Pelletier told me you were off in the woods somewhere.'

'We told him to say that!' said the other man. 'We wanted to see what you'd do.'

'This is Truman Dellis,' said my father.

'Howdy,' he said.

'There's not enough room up front. You'll have to ride in back,' said my father.

I wriggled out of my backpack and tossed it into the truck bed, then climbed in, trying to find a spot to settle down between the junk. There were a couple of chainsaws back there, two spare tires, and another four cases of beer. The bed was heavily rusted and wet with oil, and as we headed north, I felt it soaking through the seat of my new jeans.

It was a long, spine-rattling ride. Every pothole jolted me into the air or caused my teeth to clack against one another. Through the back

178

window of the truck cab I watched my father drinking beer while he drove. Every now and again, Truman would turn around and wave at me through the glass and laugh. The wind ruffled my hair and poked its cold fingers into my ears. Once I caught the faintest hint of Truman singing along to Garth Brooks on the radio.

Meanwhile the country streamed by. The rolling agricultural lands around Waterville and Skowhegan gave way to the dark forested river valley of the Kennebec. Green-hazed mountains appeared in the west, and the houses became fewer and fewer along the highway — just the occasional old clapboard homestead lost amid the maples and spruce. North of The Forks, where the Dead River rushes into the Kennebec, we turned onto a rutted logging road and followed the setting sun up into the hill country. Dust, raised by the logging trucks, powdered the trees along the road, and one time a big truck, loaded with trees the length of telephone poles, came barreling out of the woods as if intent on flattening us like an insect against its grill. My father played chicken with it before dodging aside at the absolute last second. The truck rushed by, horn blaring, pulling a hurricane of dust behind it that left me choking, half-blind, and spitting mud.

I was dirt-covered and sunburned when we reached the last forest gate that blocked the road down to Rum Pond. Truman scurried out of the truck and unlocked the chain gate so we could pass. Soon we were burrowing through old-growth pines, taller than any trees I had ever seen. I peered over the top of the cab and saw a flash of blue ahead through the pine needles and then suddenly we were stopped in a compound of buildings made of hemlock logs and pine planks.

My father lay on the horn, and Truman leaned his head out the window and shouted, 'This is it!'

A man with a drooping black mustache appeared in the door of one of the log buildings. He had a cigarette clenched between his fingers. 'Is this the new serf?' he asked, pointing at me with the lit end of the cigarette.

'Yep,' said my father. 'What do you think?'

'Kind of scrawny.'

'But he's a hard worker — just like his old man.'

'I thought he was *your* son.'

'Fuck you,' said my father. 'This is Russ Pelletier. He owns this dump.'

'You want me to give him the ten-cent tour?' Pelletier asked my father.

Truman was unloading the cases of liquor and lugging them into the back of what I assumed was the main lodge.

'Go ahead,' said my father. 'Send him over to my camp when you're done.'

'What about my stuff?' I asked.

'I'll take care of it. Damn, it's good to see you, Mike.' He clapped me on the shoulder so hard it hurt, but the gesture made me happier than anything in a long time.

For the next half hour Pelletier showed me around.

The sporting camp consisted of a main lodge, four guest cabins, an open-sided woodshed, toolshed, and boathouse, all built on the shore of a long lake carved between mountains. There didn't appear to be a single other building on the lake, just miles and miles of spruce and maples sloping down from talus cliffs to the water's edge.

'This was originally a logging operation,' Pelletier said. 'Built back in the eighteen nineties. You see that building over there by the lake? That used to be a post office. It served as the central location for distribution of mail for this whole area — from Flagstaff all the way up to Jackman.'

Black flies had descended in a buzzing cloud around my head as we stood looking at the lake. 'Where's your nearest neighbor?'

'That depends,' said Pelletier, oblivious of the biting insects. 'There's another sporting camp over to Spencer Lake, but you'd have to hike over those mountains there to get to it. We have to drive down to Flagstaff or out to The Forks to get our mail and everything else we need.'

I waved my hand near my face, but the bugs kept biting me.

Pelletier looked at me with a sly smile. 'I guess they like your blood,' he said. 'Come on, let's go inside.'

★   ★   ★

Inside the kitchen of the main lodge, a skinny little girl was chopping onions for a stew pot. Truman was leaning against the sink eating a raw onion as if it were an apple.

'Howdy,' he said.

'This is Truman's girl, B.J.,' said Pelletier. 'She and my wife, Doreen, do all the cooking around here.'

'And I'm the chief bottle washer!' said Truman.

The girl glanced up at me and quickly looked away. She couldn't have been older than twelve. Except for a single long braid that trailed halfway down her back, I might have mistaken her for a boy. She had a bony face with eyes the same almond shape as Truman's.

'Hello,' I said.

'Doreen lives up at our house in Flagstaff during the week,' said Pelletier. 'That makes B.J. here the only full-time female at Rum Pond. Isn't that right, B.J.?'

'I guess,' she said without looking up from her cutting board.

'She's shy,' said Truman.

Pelletier escorted me into the lodge's great room, where a towering fieldstone fireplace rose up to a smoke-blackened ceiling. A shabby-looking moose head stared down from the mantel, and old upholstered chairs and wicker rockers were arranged around the hearth. In the dining room were two long tables with benches where the 'sports' — as Pelletier called his guests — ate their meals family style. A big picture window showed twilight descending on the hills and the first canoe returning across the lake. Pelletier poured himself a mug of coffee without offering me one and lighted a new cigarette and leaned back against the serving counter.

'Your dad says I should put you to work,' he said.

'Yes, sir.'

'Do you know what a serf is?'

'It's a Russian peasant — sort of an indentured servant.'

'I wasn't really joking when I called you one before. You're going to work hard here if you plan on eating my food. And don't think you're going to be guiding fly fishermen. You'll be washing dishes and cleaning cabins.'

'Yes, sir.'

He gestured through the window at a stretch of heavily wooded shoreline a hundred yards or so down the lake. 'Your dad's camp is down in those trees. Go settle in but be ready to wash dishes after supper.'

I was about to leave when he called me back. 'One more thing.'

'Yes?'

'Your dad works for me, understand? What that means is that I'm the boss here. Your dad does what I say and that means you do, too.'

'I understand.'

'Just so we're clear, kid.'

★ ★ ★

My father's camp was set back amid the pines on the hillside above the lake. It consisted of three separate log cabins — one for sleeping, another with a fireplace and table for playing cards, and a third with a kitchen — all of which opened onto a plank deck with cedar rails. The whole affair was raised on stilts above the floor of the forest, and a steep set of stairs tumbled down the hill to the gravel beach below. There was no electricity, only propane gas for the lights, stove, and fridge, and no plumbing, just a two-seater out-house behind the woodpile.

My 'room' was the middle cabin. A plastic-coated mattress, taken apparently from a child's bunk bed, had been laid out in a corner, but aside from that, my father hadn't made any effort to clean up for me. Empty beer cans lay scattered about the floor, amid water-warped issues of *Fur, Fish, and Game*. The roof, I later learned, leaked just about everywhere.

What Pelletier had told me about my role as camp serf proved to be an understatement. When I wasn't washing dishes, I was sweeping out cabins or splitting firewood or clearing brush. Enviously I watched the fly fishermen, affluent men and sometimes women from Massachusetts and Manhattan outfitted with the best Sage rods and Simms waders, head out in canoes in the morning. In the evening, I had the privilege of filleting the trout they had caught for lousy dollar tips. Groups of them came and went, but to me they were always the same insufferable rich people.

My father didn't seem particularly interested in spending time with me, either, as it turned out. In fact, I saw more of Russell Pelletier and even his wife, Doreen — a hard-faced, unhappy woman who was only at the camp on weekends — than I did my dad, who always seemed to be off somewhere in the woods or running errands out to Flagstaff.

The person I spent the most time with was Truman's daughter, B.J., who worked in the kitchen with me. She was a strange, silent girl. From Pelletier, I learned that her mom had died of alcohol poisoning some years earlier. The two of them — Truman and B.J. — had lived in the same cabin at Rum Pond ever since, spending each winter with relatives on the reservation at Indian Island in Old Town.

The fact that Truman and B.J. were actual Penobscot Indians seemed exotic at first. After a while, though, I found myself disliking both of them, and I began to wonder whether that made me a racist. Truman was an obnoxious fool, and B.J. was just weird. But then, I also disliked Pelletier, for his chain-smoking bossiness. I probably would have disliked his wife, too, if she'd ever noticed me.

Every day that passed at Rum Pond I felt more and more disillusioned and lonely. I don't know what I had expected — something out of Hemingway's Nick Adams stories, maybe. I thought I'd have some free time to canoe or fish or hike. And I did have time, but I was almost always too exhausted to make use of it. All I wanted to do was sleep, but even that was impossible since my father and Truman stayed up just about every night past midnight, drinking.

185

After dinner, I would walk back to my father's camp in the half-light, bone-weary and stinking of sweat from my day's work, and I'd find them there on the porch or in front of the fire. I tried to ignore them and just go to sleep, but they wouldn't let me. The more they drank, the more they wanted me to join them.

★   ★   ★

'Do you know what I think?' said Truman one evening — it must have been three weeks or so after I arrived, sometime in early July. It was a cool night and therefore not so buggy, and we were all sitting in Adirondack chairs on the deck. I wanted to go to sleep, but I knew their laughter and loud conversation would keep me up, so I was doing my best to humor them by having a beer. I guess I also thought that this was what my father expected of me, and I hadn't yet given up trying to please him.

'I think Mike has a secret admirer,' said Truman.

'And who would that be?' asked my father.

'He knows who.'

'No, I don't,' I said.

'Is it you, Truman?' asked my father. 'Come on, you can confess your true feelings.'

'Me!' He threw back his head and let out a laugh so loud it stirred up one of the loons out on the lake. 'No. B.J.! I think she has a crush.'

My father lighted a cigarette and shook out the match. 'Hey, Mike, you know what that stands for — B.J.?'

'She's just a little girl!' I said.

Even Truman made a displeased, grumbling noise. 'That's not funny.'

'You're a prissy one, aren't you?' My father took a sip of his beer. 'How's your mother, anyway?'

He had asked me this question ten times since I arrived here, always when drunk. 'You know how she is.'

'How's my buddy Neil?'

'The same.'

'Fucking lawyer. Drives a Volvo.'

'Yuppie,' said Truman with disgust.

'So what do you think of Rum Pond?' my dad asked me for the umpteenth time. He always fell back on the question when he could think of nothing else to talk with me about.

'It's all right.'

'Did I ever tell you about the Nazi who escaped from the POW camp?' He gestured with his cigarette in the general direction of Hobbstown.

'You told me when we went on that trip to Spencer Lake, remember?'

I became aware of a soft sound, a faint almost insect-like buzz. It grew louder and louder. In the purple sky above the hills I saw the red lights of a very small airplane, equipped with pontoons instead of wheels, flying lower than any plane I had ever seen.

'Son of a bitch,' said my father.

'Who's that?'

'Game warden. Charley Stevens.'

Truman spit over the rail. The airplane darted

across the lake and then turned and disappeared over a hill.

'You know why he's doing that, don't you?' asked my father. 'He wants to let us know he's watching us. Like he's daring us to try something.'

'He's a game warden and a pilot?' I said.

'Yeah.'

'And he flies at night?'

'You just saw him.'

'Must be pretty dangerous.'

My father sat up in his chair and pointed a finger at me. 'You ever meet a warden?'

'No.'

'I didn't think so. They're arrogant bastards, is what they are. You won't think they're so cool when they take you to jail.'

I finished the last foam in my beer. 'I'm going to bed.'

'Who's stopping you?'

Inside my cabin I undressed down to my undershorts and climbed into my sleeping bag. As always, my feet overhung the end of the child's mattress. I could smell their cigarettes through the screen and heard them talking for a while in unusually hushed tones. After a while, I heard the Ford truck start up and saw the white head-lights cutting through the unchinked slats between the logs of my cabin. Then they were gone, and all I heard was the wind moving through the tops of the pines and, every now and again, one of the loons calling out on the lake.

I dozed fitfully, whether because of the single beer I had drunk or because I sensed that my father and Truman had gone off to make trouble of some kind.

But several hours later — it might actually have been less — I was awakened by the sound of the Ford returning. At first I was disoriented because there were no headlights shining into my cabin. Then I realized that they'd driven up with the lights off. I heard the doors slam and the pickup gate thrown open and harsh whispers and grunts and Truman breaking into a fit of giggling. Heavy boots sounded on the deck. As their shadows passed my screen I saw that they were dragging something big into the kitchen cabin.

I pulled on a T-shirt and jeans and went barefoot outside. A propane lamp fizzled on in the kitchen, throwing light onto the deck. Through the screen door I saw the carcass of a big deer, a doe, spread across the table and my father and Truman standing over it drinking thirstily from cans of beer.

'Where did you get it?' I asked.

They both jumped at the sound of my voice.

'Christ,' said my father.

'Where did you get that deer?'

'Hit it with the truck.'

'You did not.'

My father threw away his empty beer can. It clattered off one wall. 'Come inside and shut that door.'

I stepped in and pulled the door shut behind me. 'You jacked that deer. That's against the law.'

My father and Truman looked at each other and started laughing.

'Kid,' my dad said. 'You don't know how funny you are. Come on. I'm going to show you how to butcher a deer.'

I remembered all those solemn lectures my father used to give me on poaching — how he only took illegal game out of necessity, that it shamed him to have to do it, but he had a hungry family to think of. Now here he was laughing about it.

I glanced at the window. 'What about the warden?'

'Screw him.' He removed his hunting knife from his belt. 'Grab that old blanket. We'll need it to catch the blood.'

I watched my father slit open the deer. He spread the doe on her back along our breakfast table and inserted the blade down below her rib cage and began working backward, using his fingers to open the cavity. Then he tied off her anus and vagina with a pigging string and, climbing up on the table and straddling the deer's leg, pulled out the entrails. As a child, I remembered watching my father field dress a deer but never with this kind of speed. My father did all the cutting while Truman caught the organs in a five-gallon pail.

'Here,' said my father, tossing something at me suddenly.

I caught a small piece of metal in my hand. It was the mushroomed bullet that he'd dug out of the doe's heart. For some reason I didn't drop it but instead squeezed it tight in my fist.

Truman cocked his head. 'Oh, shit,' he said.

That was when I heard the plane.

It was flying in low across the lake getting louder and louder until we heard the splash of the pontoons setting down on the water's surface. I glanced through the window.

'It's coming up to the beach!'

My father blew out the gas lamp, plunging the cabin into darkness. 'Go down there,' he said to me. 'Don't let him come up here.'

'What am I going to say?'

'Just stall him.'

I slipped outside and paused for a moment on the plank deck looking down at the small floatplane as it taxied into the shallows. The door popped open and a man dressed in a darkish uniform climbed out and stood on one of the floats. Then he splashed into the water and waded to shore. It was my first look at Charley Stevens.

'Hey!' I said, and jumped barefoot down the plank steps to meet him.

He squinted up at the dark figure hurtling toward him. 'Good evening.'

'Hi!' I said. 'Hello.'

'Now who might you be?'

'Mike Bowditch.'

'Bowditch, you say? You're Jack's son, then.'

'Yes, sir.'

'Could you tell him that Charley Stevens would like a word.'

'He's busy.'

He paused and gave me an appraising look up and down. 'Mike,' he said finally, 'I'm going to ask you a question, and I'd like you to answer with the truth. If I go up to that cabin there, what am I going to find?'

A jacklighted deer, I wanted to blurt out. The words were literally at the tip of my tongue. But when I spoke, it came out as, 'Nothing.'

He shook his head and let out a sigh, and I realized the expression on his face wasn't displeasure so much as disappointment. Even though we had never met, he had expected better of me. 'I'm afraid I'll have to have a look, anyway.'

He brushed past me and had taken two steps up the stairs when my father's voice sounded above us in the darkness: 'Kind of late for flying, isn't it?'

Charley squinted up at the moonlit silhouette looming at the top of the stairs. 'Is that you, Jack?'

'What's going on?'

'I thought we might sit down and have a cup of coffee.'

'I'm all out of coffee, Charley.'

The warden smiled. 'Maybe you can help me with some detective work.'

My father laughed. 'Is that so?'

'You see, I've been flying tonight and — maybe you saw my plane earlier?'

'I saw it.'

'The thing of it is, we've had a bad problem with night hunters out this way. So I thought I'd fly around a bit, what with the moon so bright, and see what I could see. And wouldn't you know about a half hour ago I saw a pair of headlights over on the King and Bartlett Road. The funny thing about them, though, was that they weren't moving. In fact, it looked to me like maybe what was going on was that somebody was jacking a deer over there. You know what also gave me that impression? The minute I swung over in that direction, those lights just snapped off all of a sudden.'

'What does that have to do with me?'

'Well,' said Charley. 'The coincidence is that the truck I saw bore a resemblance to that old Ford you drive.'

'That's quite a coincidence.'

'It occurred to me it might actually be your truck, in fact.'

'I've been here all night. Ask the boy.'

The warden looked at me. 'Is that true, son?'

I nodded.

'You mind if I have a look at your truck, anyway? Just so in the future I can learn to tell it from the other one.'

'How about showing me a warrant first?'

'What do you say I just have a look around so we can clear up any misunderstanding.' The warden took another step up.

'Don't come up here!' said another voice.

Charley froze. I saw his hand drop down near his holstered side-arm. 'Now who would that be?'

'Truman Dellis,' I said.

'I'd like a look around, Jack,' Charley said. There was a new hard edge to the warden's voice.

'Not without a warrant,' said my father.

'Go away!' shouted Truman.

193

I heard my father hiss, 'Put it down. What's wrong with you?'

'What's going on up there, Jack?'

'Nothing. It's just too late for this bullshit, Charley. Why don't you just get out of here?'

'Please.' I wasn't even aware that I had spoken, but Charley Stevens turned to me. Something in my eyes must have told him of the danger he was in.

'All right,' he said after a long moment. 'I'll come back in the morning.'

'Bring a warrant!' shouted Truman.

Charley smiled but didn't answer him. Instead, he turned to me. 'I'll see you later, Mike.'

Standing rigid as a statue, I watched the warden pilot descend the remaining stairs and wade back out into the shallows to his plane. He tapped his forehead, a gesture of good-bye to me, and then climbed into the tiny cockpit. Moments later, the propeller began to turn and the plane taxied off to deeper water. I watched it take off until its shadow passed across the moon.

Only then did I realize that I had been holding the bullet the whole time. I opened my fist and saw it gleaming there in the moonlight. Quick as I could, I tossed it into the lake.

★   ★   ★

Later I learned that Truman Dellis had been aiming a rifle at Charley Stevens while he stood on the stairs.

My father chewed him out about it. 'What

194

were you going to do? Kill him over a damned deer, you fucking idiot? What the hell's wrong with you?'

I was unimpressed by this sudden show of conscience or rationality or whatever it was, especially since we spent the rest of the night getting rid of the deer parts. Truman and my father carted the meat and bones away to bury in some secret spot in the forest while I scrubbed the kitchen clean.

The next morning, while I was working at the sporting camp, Charley Stevens returned with another game warden to inspect my father's camp and truck. Russell Pelletier was pissed about it, but he told me they didn't find so much as a deer hair. Truman Dellis spent the next day with a smug grin on his face, but I knew my father had been humiliated by having the wardens search his cabin. And he hadn't even been able to keep the deer.

A few days later, I told him that I wanted to go home.

'It's about the other night, isn't it?'

'No.'

'That Truman is a crazy son of a bitch when he's drinking. I don't know what the hell got into him.'

'That's not it.'

Color rose to his face. 'So what is it, then?'

'This isn't what I expected it would be.'

'I'm not driving you to Waterville.'

'That's all right. I'll hitchhike.'

He thought it over a bit, then said, 'Pelletier's

going to Augusta tomorrow. Maybe you can get a ride out with him.'

'I'd appreciate it.'

'I never promised you anything,' he said.

'No,' I said. 'You didn't.'

19

Driving home from my mother's house, I remembered that the funeral of Deputy Bill Brodeur was scheduled for sometime that afternoon at the Colby College gymnasium in Waterville. On my cell phone I punched in Kathy Frost's number. 'I want to apologize for last night.'

'Save it, Mike.'

'So what did you do with the bear?'

'I sent the head to Augusta for a rabies test and buried the rest just to be safe. Look, I can't talk now. We're all getting ready for Brodeur's memorial service.'

'What time is that, anyway?'

'Noon.' There was a pause on her end. 'I hope you're not thinking of showing up. Malcomb would throw a shit fit if he saw you there.'

'I just want to pay my respects.'

'Then stay home. Nobody wants to see you there, Mike. You might not like it, but that's just the way it is.'

'I'll think about it,' I said, hanging up and turning off my phone before she could slip another word in.

If I hurried, I might still make the service. I stopped at a gas station and bought a razor and shaved quickly in the restroom, cleaning myself up as best I could. Then I put on the spare field uniform I kept in my Jeep for emergencies.

When Kathy first told me about the Flagstaff homicides, I'd assumed I'd be part of the formal retinue of uniformed officers — game wardens, municipal and state police, sheriff's deputies, firefighters — who always attend the memorial services of a fallen law officer in Maine. But after my father lit out for the hills with a target on his back, it became clear that my presence at Brodeur's funeral would be unwelcome. Now that I was unofficially suspended, I found myself unconcerned about such matters. If I really believed in my dad's innocence, I had no reason to hide my face.

Road construction kept me from getting anywhere fast. Sunlight angled through the driver-side window as if through a magnifying glass. I blasted the air-conditioning until a mist formed on the inside of the windshield and goose bumps rose along my neck. The dashboard clock clicked off the minutes toward noon and I was still too many miles away. I thought of my fellow wardens gathering at Division B, all of them solemn and quiet in their red-and-green dress uniforms. In my mind I saw a parade of green patrol vehicles heading north in a procession up the interstate while I approached alone in my Jeep.

I hadn't been back to the Colby campus since graduation. As I negotiated my way through downtown Waterville, heading up Mayflower Hill, I felt a nervous excitement, as if I were returning to a new year at school. I saw brick buildings rising against a blue sky, and green lawns where summer students sprawled reading

198

books and listening to music. I saw Miller Library with its white bell tower. Sarah and I once enjoyed a quickie in one of its darkened classrooms.

The funeral was well under way by the time I arrived. The parking lots between Seaverns Field and the gym were jam-packed with civilian vehicles and police cruisers. But my eyes went immediately to the green trucks bearing the emblem of the Maine Department of Inland Fisheries and Wildlife that were scattered among the other vehicles.

There was no room in any of the near lots. Finally, after driving around for ten minutes I found a space halfway across campus. Then I had to jog.

When I reached the gym, I found the foyer empty, but I could sense the proximity of a crowd in the next room. A large group of people gives off an energy like the buzzing of a hive of bees. Still, I was unprepared for what I saw. There must have been close to a thousand people seated in that gym. Rows of folding chairs, holding dozens of law enforcement officers in their multicolored uniforms, were arranged on the parquet floor, and still more officers occupied the lower bleachers. Civilians sat above them with only the highest benches on either side unoccupied. Basketballs hoops had been folded up to the ceiling to give everyone a better view.

Brodeur's flag-draped coffin rested on a platform surrounded by flowers at the front of the auditorium, and hanging behind it were other flags and banners. A podium and microphone stood nearby, and Sheriff Hatch, dressed in his uniform today instead of a sport coat, was reading from a prepared speech.

I hung inside the doorway at the top of the stairs and listened.

'Bill was what you might call soft-spoken,' Hatch was saying. 'But as they say, still waters run deep. Even though he was new to the department, I believe he was becoming a role model for other officers to follow. You can never accurately predict a man's potential, but I believe Bill Brodeur had as bright a future as any deputy I have seen in thirty years of law enforcement.'

The sheriff cleared his throat and then took a long moment trying to find the place in the text where he'd left off. 'Bill gave his life in defense of another human being. Too often certain actions of law officers are called heroic by the media when really they are just part of doing our job. That's the way Bill felt about it. If he heard you call him a hero, I'm sure he'd just look over his shoulder to see who you were referring to because he surely wouldn't recognize himself in that word. We, however, can recognize Bill's valor for what it was, an act of sacrifice and courage. William Brodeur was a genuine hero, and it was my privilege to know him for all too short a time.'

On the floor of the auditorium I was able to pick out the red dress jackets of Lieutenant Malcomb, Kathy Frost, and dozens of wardens I knew seated together in a row. Among the police officers on the dais I saw Deputy Twombley. His dress uniform was as tight around his middle as a sausage casing. His cherub cheeks were shining with tears.

The next speaker was Father Richard Pepin, a thin, bespectacled guy with a French accent, who identified himself as Brodeur's parish priest. He recalled the deputy in the sort of vague terms that made me think he knew the family well but the young man not at all. He asked that everyone remember the other man killed that night, Jonathan Shipman, of Wendigo Timber, whose family must also be grieving, and he ended with a prayer for the assembled law enforcement officers, asking God to 'protect these brave men and women, grant them your almighty protection, unite them safely with their families after duty has ended. Amen.'

'Amen,' we all said.

The service went on like that. Family and coworkers of the dead man talked emotionally about him, but the shapeless anecdotes they told — of his love of snowmobiling and NASCAR — left me without a sense of who Brodeur had been as a man. I realized, too, that no one had mentioned a girlfriend. The picture that emerged was of a quiet, responsible, yet unremarkable young man. His death seemed senseless and unlucky — he truly was in the wrong place at the wrong time.

The service drew to a close. While a bugle and bagpipes played taps, the pallbearers lifted the flag from the coffin and folded it in military fashion into a tight triangle and presented it to

201

Brodeur's mother. She clutched it to her breast. Then, along the aisle, an honor guard formed a corridor of uniformed bodies. Everyone stood as the dead man's coffin floated on the shoulders of the pall-bearers down the aisle and outside into the sunshine.

I watched the auditorium empty. I knew that Brodeur would be given a twenty-one-gun salute as his coffin was loaded into the hearse. Then uniformed officers would line the roadway down Mayflower Hill. Outside, afterward, there would be a crowd of familiar faces. My gut felt like a knot of worms.

'Warden Bowditch!'

I hadn't realized anyone was behind me. I spun around and came face-to-face with a wiry old man in an ill-fitting black suit. He had a hawk nose and fierce green eyes that held my own without blinking. I almost didn't recognize him without his warden's uniform.

'Warden Stevens,' I said.

He held out his hand for me to shake. 'Call me Charley.' He held my hand a long moment, looking straight into my eyes. His grip was like a blacksmith's vise. 'You going outside?'

I nodded, hesitantly. 'Yes.'

'I'll come with you then, if you don't mind the company.'

It had been a while since we'd seen each other; I knew that he and his wife lived somewhere near Flagstaff. I wondered if he'd driven the two hours to get here or whether he had flown his airplane across the miles of forests and lakes. According to Lieutenant Malcomb,

202

Charley Stevens never drove anywhere when he could fly.

Outside, I fumbled for my sunglasses. Charley just turned his face to the sun and smiled. He must have been in his late sixties, but he had the vitality and physique of a backwoods farmer: strong hands, flat stomach, and no chest to speak of. His grizzled hair stood up like the bristles of a horse brush.

The honor guard was preparing to fire their rifles in the field across the parking lot.

'Didn't expect to see you here,' he said casually.

'No?'

'Your dad isn't the most popular feller around now, is he?'

I felt my skin flush red. 'I guess not.'

'I told your lieutenant he'd give us the slip in those woods. I said Jack Bowditch is as woods-smart as they come.'

Twenty-one rifles fired within seconds of each other. I felt my heart stop and resume beating. Silence rushed in to fill the vacuum created by the bullets.

Charley said: 'Did you know Deputy Brodeur?'

'We were at the academy together.'

'So you were friends?'

'Not really.'

'Did he strike you as a good cop?'

'Yeah, sure. I mean, the man is dead. I'm not going to speak ill of him.'

The crowd began breaking up. Other uniformed officers were moving their vehicles to line the procession route.

Charley squinted over my shoulder. 'There's a familiar face. Hey, Russell!'

Russell Pelletier stood alone smoking a cigarette. He wore a corduroy jacket, too heavy for the weather, and a loud tie that didn't match his plaid shirt.

'How's it going, Charley?' Pelletier's voice was like a public service warning for throat cancer.

'It's a sad day. I guess I didn't realize you were acquainted with Deputy Brodeur.'

'I saw him around. You know how it is.'

Charley placed his big hand on my shoulder. 'Do you remember this young man?'

'I remember.' Pelletier didn't offer to shake hands. After our last phone conversation, where I practically accused him of framing my dad for murder, that was no surprise. He looked at Charley. 'Any word about Jack?'

'We're still looking,' said the old pilot. 'The FBI thinks he's in Canada.'

'But you don't?'

The pilot shrugged his shoulders.

'It's a damned tragedy,' said Pelletier. 'That son of a bitch really screwed up this time.'

'So you think he's guilty then?' I said.

'He beat the snot out of Pete Twombley. Of course he's guilty.'

What Charley said next took me by surprise: 'I can't figure what his motive would be, though.'

It was the first time anyone involved with the investigation had voiced even a little doubt about my father's guilt, and I didn't know what to make of it.

Pelletier blew out a mouthful of smoke. 'Jack was just pissed off about what was happening with Wendigo and the leaseholders. He was already angry about the thought of me losing the camp and him out of a job. And he was drunk as always.'

'What about Brenda Dean?' I asked.

'What about her?'

'Detective Soctomah thinks she's my dad's accomplice.'

'I wouldn't put it past her.'

'So I guess you're not bailing her out, then?' said Charley.

Pelletier laughed, but his eyes were dead serious. 'As far as I'm concerned, that little bitch is on her own. I'm already looking for another cook.'

'She's still in jail?' I wondered what Brenda had done to make him hate her this way.

'Far as I know.'

Charley pulled on his long chin, probably considering how much to tell us. 'Soctomah thinks she knows more than she's saying. But they don't have anything to hold her on, really. I expect they'll be letting her go today or tomorrow.'

'I just hope the damn fool gives himself up soon.' Pelletier finished his cigarette, dropped it to the ground, and squashed it like a bug. 'There's been enough killing already.'

He didn't say good-bye, just walked away.

Charley looked at me. 'Old Russ has never been much for the social graces.'

'I worked for him, remember?'

'I guess you think your dad has been falsely accused.'

'What I think doesn't much matter. Does it?'

He smiled and nodded, but I couldn't tell what the hell he was thinking. 'Look,' he said, lifting his chin. 'There's your lieutenant.'

Lieutenant Malcomb was coming toward us fast across the lawn. A mob of Somerset deputies hung back, waiting to see what would happen next. I saw Kathy Frost there, too.

'Look who I found,' said Charley.

'So I see. Can you excuse Warden Bowditch and me, Charley?'

'Sure thing. Take care, young man.'

'Good to see you again,' I said.

'Same here!'

Malcomb waited until the old pilot had wandered away before he got in my face. 'What the hell are you doing here? Didn't Frost tell you to stay home?'

'I just wanted to pay my respects.'

'That's bullshit. You're not even in your dress uniform. Remove your sunglasses, Warden. Look me in the eye.'

I did so.

He stepped even closer. His breath smelled of tobacco poorly masked by breath mints. 'I've been blaming your bad decisions lately on what's going on with your father. And maybe I never should have brought you up to Dead River. But with every new, fucked-up thing you do, I've started to wonder about your judgment in general. Kathy told me about your behavior yesterday. What the hell were you thinking,

206

confronting DeSalle again? And that crap with the bear? I'm surprised she didn't suspend you on the spot.'

'If you'll just let me explain.'

He tapped my chest with his index finger. 'I don't want to hear it, Bowditch. Not now. But tomorrow morning you're going to come to my office, and you and I are going to have a conversation about your future as a Maine game warden. You might want to think about your answers beforehand — you've got a lot riding on them.'

'Yes, sir.'

'I'll see you in my office at eleven sharp. Now get the hell out of here before the entire Somerset County Sheriff's Department comes over to kick your ass.'

He waited for me to cross the parking lot, his presence serving as a deterrent from any ass kicking on the part of the Somerset deputies. I tried to remember where I'd parked my vehicle, but all the patrol trucks looked the same until I looked at the license plates. It took me a full minute to remember that I had come in my own Jeep and that it was parked halfway across campus.

20

I spent the rest of the day of Brodeur's memorial
service washing my patrol truck and completing
the last of the paperwork I still owed the Warden
Service. In the morning I would report to
Lieutenant Malcomb's office, and unless I
convinced him otherwise, he would almost
certainly suspend me until a disciplinary hearing
could be held concerning my recent behavior.
Between the incidents with DeSalle, my
confrontation with Bud Thompson, and my
attendance at the funeral, I'd pretty well pushed
the boundaries of acceptable conduct by an
officer as far as they could go. If I still wanted a
career as a Maine game warden, I'd need to
throw myself on the lieutenant's mercy and hope
for the best.

I said a prayer and turned in early.

But just after I dozed off, I awoke with the
terrified conviction that the escaped Nazi
POW was standing over my bed in the pitch
blackness. Heart hammering, I fumbled for the
lamp. But, of course, no one was there.

★　★　★

The phone rang while I was getting dressed for
my meeting with Lieutenant Malcomb. I expected
it might be Kathy Frost, warning me not to be
late, but instead it was Detective Soctomah.

208

'Mike, we need you to come up to Flagstaff and talk with your father's girlfriend, Brenda Dean.'

'Me? What for?'

'We've been holding her as a material witness, but the A.G. says we don't have enough evidence to make anything stick, so we're kicking her loose. She claims she was with your father at Rum Pond at the time of the shootings and says she doesn't know anything about his current whereabouts.'

'But you think she's lying?'

'Pretty much.'

I'd been looking for some way, any way, to participate in the investigation, and now, out of the blue, Soctomah was offering me exactly what I'd wished for. There had to be some sort of catch. 'What makes you think she'll talk to me?'

'She says she trusts you.'

'But I don't even know her.'

'That's not the way she makes it sound.'

Did Soctomah think I was lying, too? If he suspected me now, I wondered what he'd think if he learned of the phone call my dad made to me. In all likelihood that clandestine conversation would be the final nail in the coffin I was building for my career.

His offer raised another problem. If I went to Flagstaff, there would be no way I could make my mandatory meeting with Lieutenant Malcomb at eleven. So this was the decision before me: Meet with Malcomb and lose my last opportunity to help my father before some hotheaded deputy gunned him down, or go to

Flagstaff and kiss my career good-bye.

I made my choice.

'I'll do it,' I said to Soctomah. 'But it's going to take me four hours to drive up there.'

There was a pause on the other end, and I heard murmuring in the background. After a few seconds Soctomah came back on: 'Charley Stevens says he'll fly down to get you.'

'Can I speak with him?'

I waited for the phone to be passed along. 'Hello, there!' said the old pilot.

'You don't have to fly all the way down here.'

'It's no trouble,' he said. 'Besides, I thought you and I might have a chance to catch up a bit on the ride up. Now where should I meet you?'

'What about the Owl's Head airport?'

'Don't need an airport. All I need is a little calm water to put her down. Where might that be in relation to you?'

'There's the public boat landing over at Indian Pond.'

'And I'll have you back in time for supper.' He paused, and I heard more background whispering. 'Seems the detective wants another word.'

Soctomah came back on the phone. 'Mike? There's one more thing. Don't wear your uniform. We want Brenda Dean to feel like she's talking to a friend, not an officer of the law.'

As I hung up, I wondered how many opportunities I'd have after today to wear the warden's green.

★ ★ ★

210

An hour later I was standing at the public boat landing at Indian Pond wondering if Anthony DeSalle and his muscle-bound buddy were going to drive up when I heard a faint drone that grew louder and louder. Suddenly, a white-and-red floatplane appeared over the trees. It banked hard and began a tight circle over the pond. Two canoe paddles were lashed to its pontoon cross braces. The plane appeared to be the same little Piper Super Cub I had seen Charley Stevens set down on Rum Pond eight summers ago.

The airplane sent spray shooting off the lake as it touched down on the water. I watched it turn and taxi in my direction. Then the propeller sputtered to a stop, and the plane drifted in the rest of the way to the ramp. The door swung open, and Charley Stevens stepped onto a pontoon. Being retired, he wasn't wearing a warden's uniform, but his outfit still gave him a semiofficial authority — he had on a pair of green Dickies and a matching T-shirt. Cocked at an angle on his head was a green baseball cap with the Maine Inland Fisheries and Wildlife logo.

'I heard somebody here needed a ride,' he said.

'That would be me.'

'Then climb aboard, young man.' He jumped off into the shallow water and turned the plane slightly so its nose was facing deeper water. Then he held it steady by one of the braces like a groom holding the reins of a horse.

Using a strut to pull myself up, I climbed onto the pontoon. The Super Cub was a little two-seater — about seven feet tall by twenty feet long — and it seemed about as rugged as a child's kite.

'What's this thing made out of — balsa wood?'

Charley laughed. 'Might as well be.'

I ducked my head and climbed into the cockpit's cramped rear seat. As I fastened the shoulder harness, I wondered what possible good it would do in a crash.

Charley waded around to the rear of the plane and gave it a shove toward deep water. Then he leaped after it, landed on the pontoon, and walked on it like a river driver walking on a log. He swung into the cockpit and belted himself in, saying over his shoulder, 'It gets kind of noisy in here with the engine going, so you'll need to use that intercom to talk.'

As we skittered along the calm surface of the pond, I watched the wall of trees along the far shore draw nearer and nearer. Then, as if a balloon were inflating inside me, I experienced the lift of the wings via a sudden lightness in my stomach, and we were airborne. I looked down at the jagged treetops and wondered how we'd missed clipping them.

Charley was right about the noise. Between the sound of the throttle and the rush of wind outside the cockpit I was half-deaf. I put on the intercom headset.

'Keep your eyes on the horizon if you get to feeling green about the gills,' said Charley. 'There should be a bucket back there, too, if you need it.'

'I'll be all right.'

'That's what they all say!'

Beneath the plane the midcoast was spread out in a quilt of blue and green. Behind us were the indigo waters of Penobscot Bay, with its islands scattered about like puzzle pieces. Ahead stretched miles of broadleaf forest and blueberry barrens and pocket farmland, all crosshatched with roads.

To the south I saw the muddy coils of the Segocket River and my own little tidal creek. I glimpsed the Square Deal Diner and the Sennebec Market. But what really struck me, from above, was all the new development — whole neighborhoods being carved out of wooded hilltops, luxury houses sprouting up in lawns of mud. It was a domesticated landscape, growing even more so, and the thought of a few fugitive bears hiding out along the ridgetops and in the remaining cedar hollows filled me with a melancholy ambivalence.

'Jerky?' Charley asked through the intercom.

'No, I'm fine.'

He held up a plug of what looked like withered shoe leather. 'I meant moose jerky. The Boss made it.'

'The Boss?'

'My wife, Ora.'

'I'll pass,' I said.

Charley began gnawing at the plug of dried meat. For some reason my eyes kept focusing on the white line above the tan of his neck where his hair had recently been barbered. In the close quarters of the cockpit the hickory smell of the jerky was pungent.

He said, 'So why did you join the Warden Service, if you don't mind me asking?'

The shuddering motion of the plane was beginning to get to me. 'Because it's all changing.'

'What's changing?'

'The woods. The state. Everything. More and more people keep coming up here, up to Maine, and they don't understand what's special about this place. They have these distorted ideas about nature that comes from growing up in a city or a suburb. Kids think meat comes from a supermarket. They're disconnected — the whole country is — and I didn't want to live that way. I thought that if I joined the Warden Service maybe I wouldn't have to, and maybe I could help a few people see things differently. It sounds stupid to say it.'

'No, I wouldn't say that. But it does sound like you're mighty attached to the past for a young man.'

'I just wish I could've seen the woods back when you were starting out.'

'Back in the Stone Age, huh?' He chuckled. 'Well, it was changing even then. Oh, there were still the river drives, but people forget how sick those rivers were not so long ago. Why, back in the sixties the Androscoggin used to light on fire from time to time on account of all the pollution from the paper mills. And we didn't have near as many moose or deer back then. Of course there weren't all the logging roads — which meant people had a harder time getting into the woods.' He tapped some dial on the control panel. 'I guess my philosophy is that time moves on, and you better move with it. If you live in the past, you just miss out on the present.'

I didn't answer. I was beginning to feel nauseated.

'Being a warden isn't for everybody,' said Charley. 'The pay's poor and the benefits are slim. I've known a few young wardens who had second thoughts and decided to get out and no one thought the worse of them.'

So this was why he wanted to talk with me. The old fart wanted to determine for himself whether I had the right stuff to be a warden. Well, the joke was on him because, by blowing off my meeting with Lieutenant Malcomb, I was likely shitcanning my career, anyway.

'You can't be angry all the time and do the job well,' Charley continued. 'I take it your lieutenant wasn't happy to see you yesterday.'

'I made an error in judgment.'

'That's natural. You know, the night you and I first met, over at Rum Pond, I could see you were a different sort of character from your dad. Still, it surprised me when I heard that you'd applied to become a warden.'

'It surprised my father more.'

'I'll bet it did,' he said. 'Tell me something. What would've happened if I'd gone up those stairs that night? What would I have found?'

'A deer, just like you thought. But you never would have made it up the stairs.'

'Why's that?'

'Because Truman Dellis would have shot you.'

Charley laughed. 'Old Truman's a mean shot,

all right, drunk or sober. I was grateful you helped me out that night.'

'But I didn't help you.'

'Sure, you did. You told me not to push my luck. Maybe you didn't say it, but I could read that look in your eyes.'

'I was a stupid, scared kid.'

'Don't be so hard on yourself. Most of the brave men I've met used to be scared kids. Hell, you can't even be brave without first being afraid.'

'You sound like a fortune cookie.'

Over the intercom Charley said, 'Yeah, the Boss says I'm getting to be a gasbag. But when you get to my age, you figure everyone expects you to be wise.'

My forehead had grown clammy with sweat. I began wishing I'd skipped breakfast.

'Soctomah tells me you think your father's innocent,' Charley said suddenly.

'It just doesn't make any sense that he would want to kill that Wendigo guy, Shipman. If they close Rum Pond Camps and put Russell Pelletier out of business, so what? My father's had other jobs. He'll survive. He always does.'

'Maybe he had a different motive.'

'Like what?'

'Could be somebody paid him to do it.'

That was something I'd never considered. I took a minute to think it over and look out the window. We'd already crossed more miles than I would have imagined possible in such a short time — heading north and west above the hardscrabble farms and glacial bogs of central

216

Maine. Looking down at the ant-line of cars moving along the roads didn't help my airsickness any. I pressed my hand to my stomach.

'You know they found tire tracks,' he said.

I wasn't sure I'd heard him. 'What's that?'

'They found tire tracks near the crime scene that matched your dad's old Ford. They also got a partial boot print that matched your dad's size based upon ones in his cabin.'

A bad taste had risen in my throat. 'Did they find the boot?'

'Nope,' said Charley. 'There were no spent cartridges. And the dogs didn't pick up his scent. But then a woods-smart man like your dad knows how to throw them off.'

I began to salivate. 'Why are you telling me this?'

'If it were my old man, I'd want to know. Your dad's in a mess of trouble.'

I felt like I was going to throw up.

★　★　★

Charley left me alone for a while after that. I heard him talking on the radio — presumably to Soctomah, giving him our estimated arrival time — but I couldn't focus on what he was saying. The hour was approaching when I was expected to report to Lieutenant Malcomb's office, and very soon it would become clear that I wasn't going to show. What would happen then? I wondered. Would he send Kathy Frost to my home to drag me in, or just start dismissal

217

proceedings? At the moment, I couldn't recall what the policy manual said on the subject of unexplained absences from duty.

When I could finally bring myself to look out the window again, the land had changed. No longer were we flying over patchwork fields and house lots. Instead, a mixed evergreen and hardwood forest extended out to the horizon, a lush green expanse broken only by ponds and rocky hills.

This was the wild country I'd dreamed of as a boy — what Ernest Hemingway had called 'the last good country' of big maples and hemlocks — but it had been a false dream then, and it was a false dream now. The last of the old-growth stands had been cleared half a century ago. Swaths of razed ground opened up like ragged wounds on the hillsides. Slashings littered the edges of these man-made barrens and a network of dirt-and-shale logging roads connected them to one another.

'Look at all these new roads,' I said.

'They keep building them. Used to be they'd leave the cedars and birches standing. But these days, you know, they can find a use for every tree. I swear they have saws now that can cut a straight board from a crooked tree.'

Old clear-cuts and plantations of new saplings showed themselves as pale green patches against the darker green of the second-growth woods. From the air the forest looked like the commercial crop that it was.

But still there was a *wildness* here — at least in the speed with which the forest healed its scars. I saw deer browsing in a clear-cut, a big bull moose using a logging road as a short cut from one bog to another. Nature will forgive humankind just about anything, and what it won't forgive I hope never to witness.

We passed a ribbon of road that must have been Route 144, but I didn't see any of the landmarks — the fish hatchery or Wally Bickford's cabin — to orient myself. Over to the right I thought I spotted the Dead River, creasing the tops of the trees. The Bigelows loomed ahead.

'Is this the Wendigo land?'

'Part of it,' said Charley. 'Did you see the new gate and checkpoint back there?'

'Where's Rum Pond?'

'Over there.' He gestured off to the right. 'It's way behind those mountains, so you can't see it. But that little lake up ahead is Flagstaff Pond. Back in the forties a power company was going to dam the Dead River and flood this whole valley — until people got up in arms about it. Just like they're doing now. It's always something.'

As we drew nearer and began turning for our descent, I could see a little downtown between the Dead River and marshy Flagstaff Pond. I saw clapboard houses and a Mason hall and not a whole lot else. As the plane touched down on the lake, I was beginning to think that I'd just made the worst mistake of my life by coming here.

'The evidence you mentioned,' I said as we floated, motionless, beside a dock. 'None of it's incontrovertible. It could be someone planted it to set him up.'

Charley didn't respond directly but instead asked a question of his own. 'Where do *you* think he ran off to?'

'The last I heard he was across the border in Canada. That's what he told my mom yesterday.'

'But you don't believe it.'

'No.'

'Nor do I,' said Charley Stevens, opening the door.

Climbing out, I glanced again at my watch. It was 11:05 a.m. And I was officially AWOL from the Maine Warden Service.

21

We left the plane tied to the dock and walked into the village. It was a short walk, not more than a quarter mile or so, but hard going because of the heat. The sun was burning a hole in the sky above Jim Eaton Hill, and the air was suffocating even in the shadows of the pines. We passed some cabins for rent near the lake and then a row of farmhouses with blistered paint and gardens all gone to seed. Grasshoppers sprang up at our every step, the only signs of life around. The entire population of Flagstaff — all hundred-and-something people — seemed to be taking a collective siesta.

A sheriff's patrol car and an unmarked state police cruiser were parked outside the clapboard town hall. Charley and I went inside.

Detectives Soctomah and Menario were waiting for us in the clerk's office. They were both wearing dress shirts and ties they refused to loosen despite the heat. We exchanged sweaty hand-shakes all around.

'Thanks for coming, Mike,' said Soctomah. 'You look a little green. Charley didn't show you any of his stunt-flying tricks.'

'Just one. I think he called it a death spiral.'

The detective smiled. Charley threw back his head and laughed like this was the funniest joke he'd ever heard.

Soctomah motioned to a chair beside the

clerk's desk. 'Have a seat.'

'So where's Brenda Dean?'

'Downstairs.'

'I thought she was getting out of jail today.'

Menario's face was brick red under his gray buzzcut. 'We told her we'd give her a ride back to Rum Pond. We didn't tell her about the pit stop.'

'Does she know I'm coming?'

'No,' said Soctomah, 'but she indicated earlier that she's willing to speak with you.'

'I don't know why.'

'That's what you keep saying,' said Menario, tugging on an ear-lobe.

Soctomah leaned against the desk. He looked shrunken since the last time I'd seen him — as if the investigation had forced him to miss a few visits to the weight room. 'There's something else we want to talk with you about, Mike. Before we bring you downstairs.' Something about the way he said these words made me uneasy. 'We understand your father called your mother yesterday.'

I nodded. 'Neil — my stepfather — said he spoke to you about it.'

'Your father claimed to be in Canada.'

'That's right. Did you try tracing the call?'

'We couldn't verify his location,' said Soctomah.

'It's kind of unusual, him calling his ex-wife like that,' said Menario.

'What are you getting at?'

'How long did you say your parents have been divorced?'

'Fifteen years.'

Soctomah said, 'It was our understanding from talking with you that they no longer had a relationship. You even asked us not to interview her.'

'I didn't realize they've kept in touch. You're not accusing her of complicity?' The back of my T-shirt stuck wetly to the chair as I leaned forward. 'The fact that she reported my dad's call — you don't tell the police something like that if you're acting as an accomplice.'

'So why did he call her?' asked Menario

'Because Neil's a lawyer. I don't know. It's not like he has a lot of people to turn to now.'

'He's got you,' said Menario.

'What's that supposed to mean?'

'You're his biggest defender. Seems like he'd be in touch again.'

I was beginning to wonder whether getting me up here, asking me to speak with Brenda Dean, was just a pretext to interrogate me. Was she really downstairs, or was this all just a trap?

'You told us he left that message the night of the murder,' said Soctomah, looking me dead in the eyes.

'That's right.' I tried to keep outwardly calm, but my thoughts were racing. Did they know about the conversation I'd had with Dad three nights earlier? Had they been tapping my phone?

'We would have expected him to contact you again,' said Soctomah. 'You're a law enforcement officer and his son. It seems like he would have asked for your help before he called his ex-wife. You're sure you haven't spoken with him?'

Everything I'd learned at the Criminal Justice Academy about detecting a lie flashed through my head. Liars rub their eyes. They cover their ears. They touch their lips and look away, usually upward and to the left, trying to conjure a plausible falsehood out of their imaginations. I'd learned that all but the most pathological of liars will give themselves away through certain microexpressions. An experienced interrogator — a decorated sergeant with the Maine State Police, for instance — can detect a lie nine times out of ten.

'No,' I lied. 'I haven't spoken with him. And I resent the suggestion that I would withhold evidence from a murder investigation.' I didn't know how much to push my luck, but I tried to muster a little indignation. 'I thought you brought me up here to talk with Brenda Dean, not make cheap shots at my expense.'

In the window an electric fan moved the hot air around a little. I became aware of Charley Stevens watching me carefully from across the room.

'OK,' said Soctomah at last. 'We're just trying to cover all the bases. Let's talk about Brenda.'

'What do you want me to ask her?'

'Just get her talking about your father. Show you're concerned about him.'

'I *am* concerned about him.'

'Then you won't have any trouble convincing her to trust you.'

'I'm no lawyer,' I said, 'but it seems like you're going to have admissibility problems with anything she says to me. Did you talk to the A.G. about this?'

Soctomah put up his hands, a halting sort of gesture 'We're not looking to make a case against her. That's not why we brought you here.'

'We want to find out where that son of a bitch is hiding,' said Menario.

I leaned back, and the old chair gave a creak like it might break. 'You think she knows where my dad is?'

'If anyone does, she does,' said Soctomah.

'Or you,' said Menario.

It was hard working up any anger over Menario's accusation when I felt so complicit, anyway. My dad wanted me to talk with Brenda Dean, and the detectives, unwittingly, were giving me the opportunity. But what if Brenda really did know where he was hiding? What the hell would I tell them then?

'You're putting the young man in a tight spot here,' said Charley Stevens.

'We realize that,' said Soctomah. 'But what's the alternative? The longer his dad is on the run, the more likely it becomes that he — or somebody else — gets hurt. Do you want that on your conscience, Mike? Or are you willing to step up here and help us resolve this situation today?'

'I'll talk to her,' I said, as if I weren't desperate to do so, anyway.

★   ★   ★

225

We descended a flight of warped wooden stairs and then passed through a darkened hallway lit only by a glowing red EXIT sign. My buddy, Deputy Twombley, was standing outside a door at the end. When he saw me, his lips pulled back from his teeth like a chimp mimicking a human smile.

'How's she doing?' Soctomah asked him.

'She keeps bitching about going to Rum Pond.'

The door opened, and at first I thought no one was there. Then I saw a barefoot young woman sitting on the floor with her back against the wall and her knees drawn up in front of her. Her face was dark-eyed and angular, all cheekbones and jawline, and she was wearing blue jeans and a sleeveless top that showed her lean, brown arms. A pair of work boots lay on the floorboards beside three cans of Diet Pepsi.

'Mike?' she said.

'B.J.?'

I felt like I'd been sucker punched. The last time I'd seen Truman Dellis's daughter she'd been a shy little twelve-year-old chopping carrots for soup in the kitchen at Rum Pond. Now she was a woman, and an attractive one, too.

'I didn't know your name was Brenda,' I stammered.

'Brenda Jo.' I could see she had just been crying. 'Who were you expecting?'

Soctomah loomed over my shoulder. 'What's going on, Mike? You said you didn't know her.'

'We worked in the kitchen together at Rum

Pond when we were kids. I thought her last name was Dellis.'

She rose to her feet, pushing against the wall to get there. 'That's my old man's name. I use my mom's.'

Suddenly I made the connection. 'You're my dad's girlfriend?'

She lowered her eyes and nodded yes.

How old was she now? Twenty? Twenty-one? I'd seen my father charm some younger women, but none as young as this. The idea made me queasy. 'He never told me.'

'So you two have a history after all,' said Menario, not even bothering to hide his animosity. In his mind we were all covering up for a murderer.

Brenda glared up at the detectives with tear-reddened eyes. 'This is a pretty cute trick. I should've figured a ride home from jail was too good to be true.' She raised her chin in Soctomah's direction. 'You jerks are still going to bring me to Rum Pond, right?'

'That's what we agreed,' said Soctomah.

'We'll leave you two to get reacquainted,' said Menario.

When he closed the door, it seemed to suck all the air out of the room. I heard muffled conversation from the hall, a harsh laugh, then echoing footsteps moving away.

There was a single, cobwebbed window at ground level, above her head. It let in a little dusty light that left most of the room in shadows. There were filing cabinets and bookshelves with heavy ancient volumes gathering dust. Brenda and I studied each other.

'So I guess they haven't found Jack yet,' she said.

'Why do you say that?'

'You wouldn't be here otherwise.' She gave me a smile that was more sad than happy. Her front teeth were slightly crooked. 'I can't believe you didn't know who I was. That's pretty funny.'

'Hilarious,' I said. 'When did you stop using 'B.J.'?'

'When I figured out why men liked saying it so much.'

That made sense. I'd heard more dirty jokes at Rum Pond than anywhere else in my life. 'So now it's Brenda.'

'It's always been Brenda. My mother never called me B.J. It was my old man who started that.'

I pictured Truman Dellis's pie-dough face, eyes that went from dopey to dangerous in a heartbeat. 'How is Truman?'

She ignored the question. 'You don't have a cigarette, do you?'

'I don't smoke. Soctomah said you had something to tell me.'

She started to tear up again. 'This is all so fucked up. First, Jack being accused of killing those guys, and then the cops coming after me. They put me in jail, and I didn't even do anything. I never heard of a material witness before.'

'They can't hold you anymore,' I said. 'Not without evidence.'

'So what am I doing here?'

'They were just delaying you until I arrived. They thought if we spoke it might clear some things up. That's why I'm here. It's the best way to help yourself — and my dad.'

She rubbed the back of her neck and glanced longingly at the dirty window. 'Can't we talk outside? It's like an oven in here.'

'We can talk here.'

'They probably got this room bugged.'

'It's not bugged, B.J.'

'Brenda!' For an instant her face was contorted with anger, and then, just as quickly, became mild again.

'I'm sorry,' I said, ashamed at my own clumsiness. The truth was that I found the whole situation disorienting, the idea of this good-looking woman being the skinny girl I once knew, and the realization that she now shared a bed with my father. 'It's hot, and I'm tired and not thinking straight. Let's just talk for a while, and then I'll get you a ride back to Rum Pond.'

'So you're on their side then?'

I almost laughed out loud at the absurdity of it all. She thought I was on the side of the cops, and the cops thought I was on my father's side. In reality I was just the rope in a tug-of-war.

'It's not funny,' she said. 'You don't care about him.'

'Of course I do. He's my father.'

'Then why are you trying to help them catch him?'

'Because if I don't, some cop is going to shoot him. As long as he's on the run, he's in danger. I've spent the past five days trying to protect

229

him. As far I can tell, I'm the only person in the state who thinks he's innocent.'

'He *is* innocent.'

'Do you have proof?'

'I was with him that night at Rum Pond. He wasn't near Dead River or that meeting.'

'You already told the detectives that. They think you're lying. They say they have evidence that puts him at the scene.'

'What evidence?'

I knew I probably shouldn't tell her what Charley had confided in me, but I wanted to hear how she explained it. 'Tire tracks from his pickup. And a boot print. There's also the fact that he assaulted a police officer and is now a fugitive from justice.'

She reached down for the can of Diet Pepsi on the floor, pretending like she hadn't heard me. 'He had no reason to kill that paper company man.'

'Soctomah thinks he was pissed off. Wendigo was closing down Rum Pond Camps and kicking him out of his cabin. He wanted to scare them, make them think twice.'

'That's stupid. He doesn't give a shit about Rum Pond or that cabin.'

'Maybe someone put him up to it. Someone like Pelletier?'

'Jack wouldn't piss on Russ Pelletier if he was on fire.'

This was news to me. Pelletier had been brusque at the funeral, but I figured he was just mad at me. 'I thought they were friends.'

'Friends.' She said the word as if it carried a

230

bad taste. 'Where have you been?'

'Living my life — until this happened.'

And now that life might be over. I'd sacrificed my relationship with Sarah for my career as a warden, and now that career was in shambles. What would I do if I lost my job?

Brenda leaned back against the cinder-block wall and looked at me through half-closed eyelids. 'You're mad at him.'

'Of course, I'm mad. Who wouldn't be? He's made my life miserable, but I keep trying to help him. And all it gets me is more aggravation.'

'Poor Mike.'

'This is a waste of time.' I turned toward the door. 'They're going to charge you with hindering apprehension, *B.J.* When you're both in prison, you can write love letters to each other back and forth.'

'Screw you!'

'You're a fool,' I said. 'And I'm a bigger fool for saying I'd talk to you. He said you'd give him an alibi.' The words were out of my mouth before I knew what I was saying.

'You spoke with him?'

I froze with my hand on the doorknob. What had I just admitted? I tried to change the subject. 'Look, it's clear you're not interested in helping him.'

'When did you speak with him?' She sensed the change in me, and she knew. If the detectives found out that I'd spoken with my dad and not told them — I was facing an accessory charge, no different from Brenda. 'He called you, didn't he? Is he OK? What did he say?'

231

There was no use in denying it even if it gave her a weapon against me. 'He said someone was trying to frame him.'

'Did he say who?'

'He suspected someone, but he wouldn't say who it was.'

Her eyes were so dark they looked black, but behind them something was going on. She was tougher and smarter than she seemed. And I was definitely dumber.

'I know who it was,' she said at last.

I waited. 'Well?'

'My old man.'

'Truman? I don't believe it.'

'He changed since you knew him. He had a bad accident in the woods, lost an eye. Then he moved to town. He didn't want to be near your dad anymore. They had — what do you call it? — a falling-out.'

'Over you?'

She lowered her eyes again as if the subject shamed her. 'Me — and other things.'

'What other things?'

'It doesn't matter. What matters is he turned mean, even meaner than before. He rents a room over Vernon Tripp's barn. You know the Natanis Trading Post on Route 144? 'There's a big wooden Indian out front and another one up in the barn.' That's Tripp's joke.'

Tripp was the guy the police originally suspected, the bald one from the Dead River Inn. 'Was Vernon Tripp in on it? My dad seemed to think there might be more than one person involved. Some sort of conspiracy.' In spite of myself, I felt a surging hopefulness.

'Maybe. All I know is he hates Wendigo.'

'But why would Truman want to kill Jonathan Shipman?'

'His accident happened when he was working for Atlantic Pulp & Paper. He couldn't work for a while. Then, when he could work again, Wendigo bought the land and they wouldn't hire him on account of his disability.'

'That's no reason to kill one of their vice presidents. Not to mention a sheriff's deputy.'

'Money's a reason.'

'So who hired him, then?'

'Pelletier.'

'Russell Pelletier's not that stupid. He knew killing Jonathan Shipman wasn't going to stop Wendigo from evicting the lease holders. There's nothing gained by it.'

'What else could he do? They're taking his whole life.'

Sweat rolled down into my eyes. The room was insufferably hot, and I was having a hard time processing all the details. Brenda didn't seem sharp enough to spin such an elaborate lie. And yet I distrusted any theory that dovetailed so neatly with my own hopes. 'I want to believe you, Brenda. But the detectives can't make a case without proof.'

'All I know is my old man hasn't been out to Rum Pond in three years, and then the day before the murder I looked out the kitchen window and saw him behind the boathouse talking to Pelletier. If they weren't planning something, what was he doing all the way out

233

there in the woods?'

'If you think Pelletier is a murderer, then why the hell are you going back there?'

'I need to get my stuff.'

'You said my father had a beef with Pelletier. They used to be buddies. What happened between them?'

'A few years ago, Russ started coming on to me pretty regular. It was after him and his wife separated. One night he got drunk and tried to do something. Jack beat the shit out of him. He said if Russ didn't leave me alone, he'd kill him. After that, Pelletier's been too scared to fire him. He's left us alone, though.'

'How old were you?'

'Seventeen.'

She wasn't a whole lot older now. I couldn't exactly view my father's behavior in chivalrous terms, even if she did see him as Sir Lancelot. 'And my dad waited until you turned eighteen? Is that it?'

Once again her face was distorted with anger — it happened in a heartbeat — but this time her eyes shined with tears. 'Who are you to judge my life? You didn't grow up with a bunch of disgusting creeps calling you names. Jack's the only real man I've ever known.'

It made sense that my dad wanted to protect her, but did she really need protecting, or was Brenda Dean a lot wilier than she let on? 'So what you're saying is that Pelletier and Truman conspired to kill Jonathan Shipman and Deputy Brodeur and frame my dad.'

'Yes.'

'Why didn't you tell Detective Soctomah this story?'

'It's not a story.'

'Why didn't you tell him?'

'He wouldn't have believed me. Besides, Jack told me not to. They'd just cover it up, he said. If I told you, maybe you could convince the cops to look into it, being a warden and all.'

Not for long, I thought. Not the way things were going.

She looked up, her eyes still shining. She was genuinely gorgeous, I thought, when the hardness passed from her expression. Under the circumstances, it made me uncomfortable to find her so attractive.

'You've got to do something,' she said. 'I'm afraid the cops are going to kill him if they get the chance.'

'Not if he gives himself up. He told me he was in Canada. Did he ever take you anywhere remote up in Quebec, someplace he might use as a hideout?'

'No,' she said with such firmness I suspected she was lying.

'All right,' I said. 'There's just one more thing I don't understand. If Pelletier nearly raped you, why did you stay there at the camp, working for him all these years? It doesn't make sense.'

She shrugged. 'Where else would I go? Rum Pond's the only home I've ever had since my mom died. Besides, with Jack I felt safe. He wouldn't let anyone hurt me anymore.'

I was still trying to process that remark when I heard the echoing sound of footsteps coming

235

quickly along the hall. The door opened behind me. Menario stood there, his face aglow. 'Hey, Bowditch. Your sergeant is on the phone, and she's ripshit. How come you didn't tell us you were suspended?'

22

I followed Menario back up the creaking stairs to the clerk's office. In the corner of the room, Charley Stevens was perched on a desk, sipping from a styrofoam cup of hot coffee, of all things. Soctomah, brow furrowed with annoyance, was holding a wireless phone to his ear. 'He's here,' he said to the person on the other end. He handed me the phone. It was slick from his sweaty hand.

'Kathy?' I said.

'You stupid piece of shit.'

'I guess I deserve that.'

'You are officially suspended. Appeal it with your union rep, if you want, but as of this moment you are prohibited from acting in any capacity as a warden until further notice.' The static on the line told me she was using her cell.

'How did you track me down?'

'I went over to your house and when you weren't there, I called Sarah. She didn't know where you were, so I figured maybe you'd mixed yourself up with the homicide investigation again.' She was quiet for a moment. 'Jesus Christ, Mike. What the hell's happened to you?'

'It's my dad, Kathy. I have to do this.'

'So you're just flushing your career down the shitter?'

'That's for the lieutenant to decide.'

'Don't put this on Malcomb. He was just

237

going to send you to a counselor, give you time to get your head together. I can't believe you would just blow him off like that.'

I didn't have an answer that would satisfy her, so I didn't bother responding. 'So what happens now?'

'I'm driving up there.'

'What? Why?'

'Because I'm your friend as well as your supervisor, and I'm not going to let you do this to yourself. You're a good warden, or at least you used to be. Besides, I've invested too much time training you. You'll plead temporary insanity to Malcomb. Maybe we can still get you off with a suspension.'

I listened to my sergeant with mixed emotions. On the one hand I felt like I didn't deserve the support she was giving me. On the other, I resented her meddling in my personal life. 'You spoke with Sarah?'

'Yeah, and she's even more pissed with you than I am, if that's possible.'

'You shouldn't have called her.'

'Cry me a river. I'm on the road now. I should be there in a few hours. If you're not there, I'm going to hunt you down and cut your balls off.' And with that, she hung up.

As I handed Soctomah his phone back, he said, 'You should have told us you had a meeting with Lieutenant Malcomb.'

'If I had, you never would have brought me up here. And frankly, what's going on with my job isn't any of your business. Now do you want to hear what Brenda had to tell me or not?'

My boldness seemed to take him back a little. 'Go ahead.'

I told them everything Brenda had said — almost everything. I left out the part about my dad's secret midnight phone call and my being an accessory to his escape after the fact. Other than that, I related the entire conversation. 'A lot of what she said makes sense,' I concluded.

Menario snorted. Soctomah was gazing abstractedly at the window fan, the blades spinning round.

'All your evidence is circumstantial,' I said, glancing across the room at Charley Stevens. 'A tire track and a boot print? You can't get a conviction on that, and you know it.'

If Soctomah was pissed off at the old warden for spilling the beans on an active investigation, he certainly didn't show it. He was as composed as ever.

Not Menario, though. 'Goddamn it, Charley.'

'I thought the young man deserved to know.'

His face was purple, his neck swollen. He looked like a man who was in the process of being strangled by his own shirt. 'It's an active investigation.'

'From what Charley says, you don't even have enough to go to trial,' I said.

'The guy's a fugitive. If he's so innocent, why'd he flee to Canada?'

'My dad knew you wouldn't believe him, given his record. Brenda says he was scared that Truman and Pelletier might try something against him.'

'He wasn't afraid,' Charley Stevens said softly.

'What's that, Charley?'

'Jack Bowditch wasn't afraid of those two. No way.'

Soctomah scratched his chin contemplatively. Then he leveled his eyes at me. 'Well, this was a waste of time.'

I was dumbfounded. I'm sure my jaw dropped. 'Aren't you going to check out her story? Talk to Dellis and Pelletier?'

'We've already conducted interviews with both of those individuals,' he said in the same flat, impersonal voice I'd heard him use on television when briefing the press.

'But what about my father?'

'At the moment, he's still the chief suspect.'

'Thanks for coming in,' Menario said in his most sarcastic tone.

'If anything breaks, we'll let you know,' said Soctomah. 'Your sergeant has asked us to keep you here until she arrives, but we need to get going. I promised to bring Brenda Dean back to Rum Pond, and I'm not going to break my word.'

I was speechless.

Soctomah looked at Charley Stevens. 'Can you stay with Mike until Sergeant Frost arrives?'

'Oh, sure,' said the old pilot. 'I'll take care of him.'

★ ★ ★

They took Brenda Dean out the front, and as she passed, we made eye contact. She looked terrified. Through the window I watched the

240

unmarked cruiser and Twombley's patrol car pull away from the curb. 'This is bullshit!' I said to Charley. 'They're just going to blow this off. It doesn't matter what she says.'

He shrugged. 'The girl's not exactly trustworthy.'

'Then they should prove she's lying.'

'Soctomah knows what he's doing. You should have faith in him.'

'I'm not just going to go back home with Kathy Frost and forget about this. No fucking way.'

'So just what exactly are you going to do?' Charley looked at me with an expression that seemed to combine fascination and annoyance.

'I'm going to talk to Truman Dellis.'

'I've been asked to babysit you until Sergeant Frost arrives.'

'You can't keep me here, Charley, and you know it. I'm not under arrest for anything. And you have no authority with the Warden Service anymore.'

'So you're just going to walk over to the Natanis Trading Post.'

'That's right.'

'It's ten miles down the road.'

'I'll hitch a ride.' I was beginning to get a sense of how foolish I sounded, like a rebellious teenager. 'Look, I appreciate your bringing me up here, I really do. But I can take care of myself.'

He was silent for a long moment, then his weathered face split into a wide smile. 'Fair enough. But before we part ways, I could do with a bit of lunch. How about you?'

'I'm not hungry.'

'Sure you are! Tell you what, Flint's Garage is right up the road. You're going to need a car to get down to Dead River. If you'll have lunch with me, I'll drive you wherever you want to go today. We can borrow one of Flint's old beaters.'

'Soctomah isn't going to appreciate me fucking around with his investigation, and Kathy's going to be ripshit when she finds I'm not here. I don't want to get you in trouble, too.'

'I've been in trouble since before you were born.'

I remembered that Lieutenant Malcomb had said the same thing about his old friend. 'You don't have to do this, Charley.'

'I got nothing else scheduled. That's the nice thing about being an old geezer.'

Part of me wanted to be alone, but another part thought he might be helpful when I confronted Truman. There was no question in my mind that this offer was just his way of keeping an eye on me. I wondered whether I was in danger of selling Charley Stevens short. How much of his jolliness was genuine and how much was a put-on? 'I'm really not hungry, though.'

He clapped me hard on the back. 'Then you can watch me eat!'

⋆ ⋆ ⋆

Ten minutes later, Charley emerged from the darkened bay of H. B. Flint's Garage, jangling a set of car keys. I followed him around the

242

building to a weedy field where smashed autos were arranged like some sort of modern art sculpture garden. I couldn't imagine any of these wrecks being capable of locomotion, least of all the old Plymouth Charley indicated. It looked like it had once been red or maroon in color, but it was so rusted and patched with Bondo, there was no way to be certain.

'Hal says a chipmunk has made the tailpipe his abode,' said Charley. 'Watch to see if he comes shooting out the backside when I start her up.'

'I hope for his sake he's out gathering nuts.' I tried to fasten my seat belt, but the strap had been sawn off below the buckle. I had to knot the loose ends instead.

The Plymouth coughed, shook, and died when Charley tried the ignition. He tried again, this time giving it a little gas, but with the same result. On the third attempt the car shivered itself awake and we were able to move forward. We turned left on Main Street in the direction of Dead River Plantation.

'Where are we going?'

'You'll see.'

Across the river, Bigelow Mountain rose four thousand feet into the sky, a dark and jagged shape. In the seventies a developer proposed building an enormous ski resort on the mountain's opposite slope, facing the existing resort at Sugarloaf. He said he wanted to turn the area into 'the Aspen of the East,' but activists organized a referendum to foil his plans. In the end, the State of Maine bought the mountain and established a preserve from the Carrabassett

River in the south to the Dead River in the north. Environmentalists considered it a huge victory, but it was hard to feel much joy about the situation now, given Wendigo's development plans for the surrounding region.

Charley turned south on Route 144, following the Dead River away from town. Farther along that dark forest road were a few houses and farms, a schoolhouse, the fish hatchery that had so recently been the command post for my father's manhunt, and of course the Natanis Trading Post, where Truman Dellis lived over the barn.

That was when I realized where we were headed.

＊I hadn't seen the Dead River Inn since the night I got my skull busted by those three bikers. Now the sight of the heavy wood sign, hanging beside the road, sent a chill through me. The inn was a rambling old hotel with dormer windows and gables and two massive granite chimneys. It had a veranda along the first floor with rocking chairs set up so visitors could gaze down the half-mile dirt drive that led back to the road.

We parked the Plymouth under some tall hemlocks and went around front to the porch. The screen door made a wheezy sound as Charley pulled it open, and then it snapped shut on my heels. I followed him into the dining room across the lobby from the tavern.

The inn's restaurant was an expansive, low-ceilinged space with pillars scattered among the heavy oak tables and captain's chairs. The wide pine floorboards needed a new coat of varnish. Framed black-and-white photos of the inn's employees from its postwar days to the present hung on the walls along with amateurish oil paintings of loons and moose. Along one wall, light was leaking inside through linen curtains the color of mummies' bandages.

Given the hour, we had the dining room more or less to ourselves. A family with three small children were the only other diners, and they were preparing to leave.

A thin, buck-toothed waitress, dressed in gingham, came over. 'Sorry, guys, we're closed,' she said. 'Oh, it's you, Charley!'

'Hello, Donna. Is Sally around this afternoon?'

'She went down to Skowhegan. But she should be back in a couple of hours.'

'So what's the soup du jour?'

'We just finished serving lunch. The cook's gone up to his room.'

'Oh, no,' Charley said with a disappointment that seemed out of proportion to the situation.

'But I could, maybe, rustle up some sandwiches.'

'Could you? We'd appreciate it. And could you bring us some coffee, too?'

'Of course!'

The waitress scurried off to make our lunches, trying without much success to get her thin hips to wiggle as she walked away.

'I think that waitress has a thing for you,' I said.

'She's just being polite to an old man.'

'No, I think she likes you. And I believe you were flirting with her just now.'

He removed his baseball hat and set it on the table. His grizzled hair stood up as if electrified.

'Who's this Sally?' I asked.

'Sally Reynolds. She owns the place. I haven't seen her since the night of the shootings, and I wanted to ask her how things have been going. It can't have helped her business.'

'So this is where Wendigo held the meeting — in this room?'

'People were packed in tighter than sardines. Hotter than hell, too.'

'You were here?'

'I was.'

It hadn't occurred to me that the old pilot might actually have been present at the meeting. 'Tell me about it.'

He pointed to the front of the room. 'Well, there was a table set up over there with that Jonathan Shipman from Wendigo sitting at it. He was dressed head-to-toe in brand-new clothes from L.L. Bean. Looked like a fashion model for their summer catalog. Anyway, he was seated beside Ted Rogers and Fud Davis, who both used to work for APP and took jobs with Wendigo. And that fool Newhall who represents this district in the state legislature. And a lady from the Forest Council — I forget her name, nice looking, though.'

'What happened?'

'First, Newhall spoke about how Shipman was a guest here and deserving of our courtesy and all that. Then the Forest Council lady got up and said a few words about how the new timber companies are committed to doing things the same as Atlantic Pulp & Paper to preserve public access. Then Rogers and Davis both said some more reassuring horseshit. Then Shipman got up.'

The waitress arrived with a coffeepot. Charley waited politely for her to fill our cups before he spoke again.

'Now this Shipman character,' he said. 'He was a piece of work. You could tell he was a lawyer, that denim shirt couldn't hide his true nature. It was the words he used — 'comprehensive reevaluation of holdings' and 'strategic non-timber operations.' I guess he figured he could pull the wool over our eyes if he used enough legalese.'

'Did he say anything about evicting people?'

'Oh, he didn't come out and say Wendigo was going to cancel the leases, but his meaning was clear enough.'

'What happened next?'

'People started shouting. They didn't even wait for him to finish. I was standing in the back of the peanut gallery — over there, next to Sally — and I could just about feel the thermostat go up ten degrees once people started yelling. I thought that numbskull Tripp's head might explode.'

'Did you see my father?'

'I didn't. Nor did I see Truman Dellis. Brenda Dean was drinking in the bar earlier — that's what Sally told me, anyway — but I didn't see her at the meeting. Russ Pelletier was here. I think it just about killed him to sit still for two hours without a cigarette. But he did it.'

'When did the meeting end?'

'Nine o'clock or thereabouts.'

'Did Shipman and Brodeur just get up and leave, or was there an altercation?'

'Tripp tried to get in his face, but Deputy Brodeur gave him the heave-ho. Or so I heard, anyhow. I'd gone home by that time. The original plan was for Shipman to stay overnight here at the inn, but I guess he had second thoughts. Not that I blame him. Brodeur was driving him over to Sugarloaf to escape whatever lynch mob might form.'

'You mean this was a last-minute change of plans?'

'More or less.'

'So whoever ambushed them must have known about the change. Did any of this go out over the police radio?'

'No.'

'So who knew about it?'

'Brodeur and Shipman, of course. Sally Reynolds. The sheriff and his deputies. And I guess I should add myself to the list.'

I pictured Twombley's cherub face. 'No one else?'

'Not that we know of,' said Charley. 'You're on the right track, though. Whoever shot Shipman and Brodeur did have the inside scoop. The killer knew they were driving over to Sugarloaf, and he knew exactly where to set up an ambush.'

'Then it couldn't be my dad,' I said. 'How would he have known any of this? Who would have told him?'

'Here comes our lunch' was Charley's only answer.

★ ★ ★

Donna had prepared tuna sandwiches with ripe tomatoes on thick slices of homemade bread. While we ate, Charley told me that his camp, where he and his wife lived from ice-out in April through deer season in November, was just across Flagstaff Pond from the public boat launch. I asked if his wife Ora flew, and he said he had tried to teach her once, but she didn't even enjoy going up as a passenger anymore. The subject seemed to make him melancholy, so I let it drop.

After we'd finished our sandwiches, Charley excused himself — to call his wife, I figured — and left me alone at the table. I sat in the empty room and listened to the afternoon sounds of the inn: the hum of a vacuum cleaner upstairs, the clatter of dishes being washed and stacked in the kitchen, the sharp *clack* of a screen door as someone carried out the trash. But in my mind I also heard a murmur of ghost voices that grew louder when I closed my eyes. With a little imagination I could place myself in this same room six nights earlier. I could sense the heat of close-packed bodies. The sour smell of sweat. The night air as electric as the seconds before a lightning strike.

I opened my eyes to see Charley Stevens coming through the door. A toothpick was tucked in the corner of his mouth. 'I thought we

249

might make a small detour.'

I rose to my feet. 'What kind of detour?'

He grinned like a mischievous boy. 'Since you came all the way up here, and we're just around the corner, so to speak, I figured you might like to see the scene of the crime.'

★ ★ ★

We went out to the car and somehow got it started again. But instead of heading back down the drive, which is what I expected, Charley drove us across a ragweed field that stretched from the south side of the property to a wall of distant evergreens. He followed two parallel grooves that had been worn into the sun-hardened dirt, like an ancient wagon trail on a prairie. Up ahead I saw a cut in the trees.

'This used to be a two-sled road,' said Charley.

'A two-sled road?'

'They'd haul logs out of here with a two-sled rig — like two bobsleds joined together. Runs all the way out to the main road, three miles. Except there's a gate on the other end now. Sally gets some mountain bikers using it these days. But mostly it's the partridge hunters who use it come fall.'

'Why did Brodeur go this way? Why not just drive back the way he came?'

'Tripp and some of the others were waiting out front of the inn with their trucks. Guess young Bill figured he'd slip out this way before they were wise to him.'

'What about the gate?'

'Most of the locals know the combination.'

The old logging road was dappled with what little late afternoon sunlight managed to make it through the pine boughs overhead. In the shadows beneath the trees I saw bracken ferns and wintergreen and the bone-white trunks of birches. I was reminded of the swamp road where I'd set my bear trap. The signs of recent traffic showed themselves more clearly here than in the sunbaked field near the inn. Tire marks from all the police vehicles rutted the soft dirt.

We came to a clearing in the woods where the bigger trees had recently been harvested and now thin popples and birches were coming up like green shoots after a wildfire. Yellow police tape hung in strips from some of the nearest trees. Pollen floated everywhere, catching the sunlight like thrown glitter.

Charley halted the car. The sudden quiet was like my heart stopping.

'This is it?' I asked.

But he didn't feel the need to answer such an obvious question. He just moved the toothpick from one side of his mouth to the other. We got out and stood in the hot open air. Charley pointed ahead to where the road reentered the forest.

'They drove into the clearing,' he said, 'and he was waiting for them on the other side in the dark. His truck was blocking the road, facing back this way across the clearing, and I figured he hit them with a spotlight to blind them. His first shot went through the windshield on the driver's side and straight on through Deputy

Brodeur's throat.' He tapped the hollow beneath his Adam's apple. 'The second one took the top of his head off as he was slumping forward over the wheel.'

'What about Shipman?'

'The third shot got him in the shoulder as he was trying to get out. He managed to get his door open and stagger back this way.' He led me to the edge of the clearing. 'But he didn't get but a few steps. Probably the killer shouted at him to stand still and he did, poor son of a bitch. The bullet that finished him was fired point-blank through the back of his head.'

He knelt down and touched three fingers to the ground. Nearly a week had passed, and I knew crime scene technicians had been over every inch of this clearing, taking samples, but I still thought the dirt looked darker there, as if Jonathan Shipman's blood had left a permanent stain on the earth.

'The one thing I can tell you for sure,' said Charley, straightening up, 'is that the man who did this is a poacher. He jacklighted those men just like deer.'

When he looked at me, there was a steeliness in his eyes I hadn't seen before.

No, that wasn't true. I *had* seen it before — eight years earlier, the night he stood on the dark stairs leading up to my father's camp. Behind the affable exterior was a knife-sharp intelligence. I wondered how many poachers had underestimated Charley Stevens and found themselves worse off for it.

'Why did you bring me to this place?'

His gaze was direct and piercing. 'Because you wanted me to.'

Suddenly the sun lost all its warmth, as if an invisible cloud had passed across its face. 'All right,' I said. 'I've seen it. Now can we go talk to Truman?'

He spat the toothpick on the ground. 'Whatever you say. I'm just the chauffeur here.'

23

We didn't talk for a while, just sat side by side, driving. The hot pine-needle smell of the forest floated in through the open windows. After a mile or so we emerged from the tree-clotted darkness into sunlight again. Between the logging road and Route 144 stood a rusted metal gate. Charley turned the numbers on a combination lock until he got it open.

'How about closing that gate for me?' he asked after we'd idled through.

I walked back behind the Plymouth and pushed the heavy gate shut and snapped the combination lock closed, giving the dials a spin for no good reason, as if I cared whether anyone got through here that wasn't supposed to.

Charley turned south in the direction of Dead River Plantation. Even in broad daylight, this was a desolate stretch of road. How much creepier it must've seemed to Jonathan Shipman. I could easily imagine his emotional state, sitting in the police cruiser, having faced down a crazed pack of Maine rednecks, the eagerness he must have felt to escape these dark woods and see the bright lights of the Sugarloaf Mountain Hotel — civilization and safety in the form of luxury condominiums and an eighteen-hole golf course.

But he never made it out. Neither did Bill Brodeur.

I thought of my sergeant, Kathy Frost,

speeding up here, propelled by anger. She was going to arrive at the Flagstaff town office and find Charley and me missing. Why was she so intent upon rescuing my doomed career? Didn't she understand it was too late?

We crested a hill where the roadside pines and maples fell away and you could see the verdant farms along the Dead River. At the very top of the rise was a wood-frame structure — like a false-fronted saloon out of the Wild West, complete with a porch gallery and a watering trough in which were planted a few struggling geraniums. A big sign fastened on the roof proclaimed: NATANIS TRADING POST. What caught my eye, though, was the wooden Indian about twelve feet tall, rough-carved and cartoon-ishly painted, that loomed at the edge of the parking lot.

'There's the FBI,' said Charley.

'FBI?'

'Fucking Big Indian.'

Natanis, I remembered, was the legendary Wabanaki Indian — the last of the massacred St. Francis tribe — who guided Benedict Arnold and his troops up the Chain of Ponds and across the Height of Land into Quebec.

Nice monument, I thought.

I searched for the barn behind the trading post and saw it standing off to one side, a chocolate-colored structure with a window where the hayloft should have been and a rickety external staircase going up to the top floor. There was no vehicle outside, though.

'Looks like Truman's not home,' said Charley.

'I guess we're out of luck.'

'I want to meet this Vernon Tripp.'

Charley gave me a long look. 'That might not be such a good idea.'

'I want to meet him.' I tugged loose my seat belt knot and opened the door.

'He's a volatile character.'

'Yeah? Well, people say I am, too.'

There were flyers posted on the door of the trading post, pieces of colored paper with angry words in big type — SPORTSMEN! PROTECT YOUR RIGHTS! RESIST CORPORATE TERRORISM! DON'T TREAD ON U.S.! No wonder Jonathan Shipman wanted a police escort.

The inside of the Natanis Trading Post looked like a parody of an old-time North Woods general store. Deer antlers and animal pelts hung from pegs along the walls. There were dusty racks of camping and trapping supplies mixed with lots of cheap souvenirs.

Mostly, though, there were guns. I saw rifles and shotguns locked into wall racks and an L-shaped glass counter containing handguns and spotting scopes and ivory-handled buck knives. Behind this counter a squat man with a scarred, shaved head and a dark goatee stood talking to a customer. He looked just the same as he had two years ago, when my dad spoke with him at the Dead River Inn.

'Hi there, Vernon!' said Charley.

Tripp's expression was none too friendly. 'What's this — a raid?'

'Good afternoon to you, too.'

'Government agents aren't welcome in my store.'

'You know I'm retired.'

The customer who had been talking to Tripp slipped out the door. I'd seen his eyes get all shifty as soon as he heard the words *government agent*. I hung back a little, trying to figure out just what Charley was up to.

'I believe you just cost me a sale, Officer,' said Tripp. He had a strangely affected way of speaking, sort of a talk radio host's grandiloquence and baritone. Not what I expected from the shaved and tattooed exterior.

'Doubtful,' said Charley. 'Now why are you in such a sour mood, anyhow? I'd thought you'd be the happiest man in Flagstaff these days.'

'And why's that?' He puffed his chest as he spoke and tucked his chin into his neck. I imagined him watching cable news in the dark and speechifying back at the set as if he were another pundit.

'With Jack Bowditch on the run, you're in the clear again. You should be celebrating.'

'Celebrating?' Tripp held up his hands, palms out. Raw marks encircled his wrists. 'Look at what that bunghole McKeen did to me. I should sue him for false arrest and brutality. All hail the mighty police state.'

'Brutality? You threatened Jonathan Shipman — '

'Please.'

'You threatened him. I heard you, and so did two hundred other folks. Then half an hour later,

257

you report a double homicide on your CB. The first cop on the scene finds you standing there with a loaded weapon in your pocket and three more in your truck. Now how do you expect him to react?'

'Point one, I have a concealed carry permit. And there were other people there, too.'

'But you were the first one on the scene, before anyone else — you said so yourself.'

'I'm a patriotic citizen who reported a crime. I deserved a medal, not shackles.'

'That's only because you were chasing them. You were still pissed off. You were waiting for Shipman and Brodeur to come out, and when they didn't, you realized they'd gone off the back way. So you gave chase.'

I stepped forward, unable to keep my mouth shut another second. 'You mean he found the bodies?'

Tripp glared at me. 'Who's the greenhorn?'

'Mike Bowditch,' I said.

'As in Jack Bowditch's son?'

'That's right.'

'Mike's with the Maine Warden Service,' explained Charley.

'Well, isn't that ironic?' To my surprise, Tripp suddenly laughed, revealing a mouth full of amalgam fillings. 'Jack the Poacher's son is a game warden. He sure kept that a secret.'

'He told me about you, though,' I said.

'Is that so?'

'We almost met before. Two years ago at the Dead River Inn. You were drinking with him at the bar when I came in. He called you a

258

paranoid militia freak.'

Tripp didn't take the bait. 'He's called me worse to my face.'

'You're saying there's no bad blood between you?'

'Your old man can be quite a bastard when he's smashed, but he's a hero, in my book. As far as I'm concerned he deserves a gold star for what he did to that worm Shipman.'

'You're forgetting a police officer was also killed,' said Charley.

'I'm not forgetting.'

'So why are you smiling?'

The humor was gone from Tripp's expression as fast as it appeared. He began stroking his goatee. 'It was unfortunate that deputy got shot. That shouldn't have happened.'

'We can see you're all broken up about it,' I said. 'So the police arrested you when they found you at the scene. How come that didn't make the papers?'

'Two reasons — one, they let me go without charging me, and two, they had no evidence against me.' Tripp backed up against a rack of guns and began squeezing his fists. 'What's with the third-rate third degree, Charley? You're not a warden anymore. You're just a lowly leaseholder like me. Last I heard, you were going to lose that nice camp. I'd think you'd be glad Wendigo got vamoosed.'

Something moved past the barred window at the side of the building. I heard an engine die and a door slam shut.

'Truman's home,' said Charley.

259

'What do you want with my tenant?' asked Tripp.

'Mike just wants a word.'

'Is that so?' Suddenly Tripp's eyes widened and a grin spread across his face. 'Wait a minute. I see what's going on here. You think maybe you can put the blame on someone else instead of your dear old dad.'

I felt my face warm with blood. 'My father didn't kill those men.'

He shook his head sorrowfully. 'Keep telling yourself that, greenie, if it makes you feel better.'

'Fuck you.'

'Come again?' He reached beneath the counter.

Charley touched the brim of his baseball cap. 'All right, Vernon, we've taken up enough of your precious time. Come on, Mike.'

But Vernon Tripp had the last word. 'Your old man did it, Mikey boy. It wasn't me, and it wasn't Truman. Don't try to pin it on somebody else.'

★ ★ ★

Outside, a logging truck passed along the road, carrying a load of timber to the dowel mill up the road. I waited for the noise to die down before confronting Charley. 'What the hell was that about? How come you didn't tell me the cops arrested Tripp the night of the murder?'

'Because they let him go. He couldn't have done it, Mike.'

'Well, maybe he helped someone else do it!'

260

Charley's eyes were as flat as coins. I couldn't tell if he was considering my suggestion or downwardly adjusting his estimation of my character. The more time I spent with the retired pilot, the harder he became for me to read. He affected this patient air, like he was indulging me for a few hours until he had to fly me back home. But he seemed just as eager as I was to grill Vernon Tripp. What kind of game was he playing? The weight of something the store owner said suddenly struck me. 'Did Tripp say your camp is on leased land?'

'That's right.'

'So you mean Wendigo is evicting you, too?'

'Yes.'

'Why didn't you tell me?'

'I thought you knew.' He smiled that big jack-o'-lantern grin of his. 'Does that make me a suspect, Warden? Seems like it should.'

'You're not high on my lists of suspects, Charley.'

'That's a relief, because I don't even have an alibi.'

'You don't?'

'Afraid not.'

I pointed at the barn behind the trading post. 'Well, let's see if Truman Dellis does.'

★   ★   ★

A fat-tired pickup truck, with an ATV crammed in the bed, was now parked beside the barn. Its engine was making that ticking sound hot engines make as they cool.

261

We climbed the external staircase to the top of the barn. Blankets hung over the door window, making it impossible to see what was inside. I found myself reflexively reaching down to touch my sidearm, but of course I wasn't wearing one. Charley rapped on the door. 'Truman? You in there?'

We listened to the traffic passing along the road. Charley gave me a shrug. I stepped forward and began pounding. 'Come on, Truman, open up.'

'Who is it?'

'Game warden,' I said.

'What do you want?'

'I want you to open the door. That's why I'm knocking like this.'

'Go away.'

Charley said, 'Come on now, Truman. Show some manners and open the damned door.'

The curtain parted for an instant and then quickly fell shut. The door opened and I saw a man I hadn't seen in eight years and probably wouldn't have recognized, anyway. The face was familiarly flat and round, but now a jagged red scar ran from the scalp through one sightless eye and down the cheek to a notched jawbone. Looking at that cruel scar I wondered what instrument of violence could have split a man open from skull to jaw and somehow left him alive.

'Do you remember me?' I asked.

'Yeah,' said Truman, 'I remember you.'

'You mind if we come inside?'

He moved to block the door with his heavy

body. 'What do you want?'

'I just want to ask you a few questions. About the homicides outside the Dead River Inn.'

'I already talked with the cops.'

'Well, now you can talk to me.'

Truman focused his good eye on me. 'I don't know where your old man is.'

'I know that.'

'Him and me don't hang around no more.'

'I know that, too.'

'Then what do you want?'

'It's about B.J.,' I said. 'She's been saying things about you.'

He ran his tongue over his cracked lower lip. 'Like what?'

'Let us in and I'll tell you.'

Truman let go of the doorknob and stepped carefully back into the room, still facing us. He wore a mustard-colored canvas shirt and stained green workpants and muddy boots. For the first time I saw that he was holding a rifle in the hand he'd kept hidden behind the door.

Charley looked at the rifle and smiled wide. 'Is that how you answer the door, Truman? What if it's the Publishers Clearinghouse come to give you a million dollars? You might shoot old Ed McMahon's head off before he even hands over your sweepstakes check!'

Truman's good eye blinked slowly. 'Ed McMahon's dead.'

'Why don't you put that gun away?' said Charley.

Truman lowered the barrel and stepped back into the apartment.

'I guess that's the best invite we're going to get,' Charley said to me.

I followed him into the room, leaving the door cracked open behind us. The apartment stank of stale cigarettes, dirty laundry, and dishes left to molder in the sink. I also detected what I hoped was the odor of a cat's litter box — although I saw no sign of a cat. The furnishings were Salvation Army surplus: ripped couch, painted metal table and chair in the kitchenette.

'What did B.J. say?'

I made my voice firm. 'How about setting that gun down first so we can have a conversation?'

'It's my house. What did B.J. say?'

'She calls herself Brenda now.' I kept an eye on the rifle in his hand, wishing like hell that Charley could talk him into putting it down. But the old game warden seemed surprisingly unconcerned. I remembered the night eight years ago when Truman had last pointed a loaded firearm in his direction. 'I just finished talking with her an hour ago,' I continued.

'So?'

'I guess you two had a falling-out. She didn't say why, but I'm figuring it was over my father. You didn't like her being his girlfriend, right?'

He didn't speak, just waited for me to continue, his good eye as blank as a cow's. There's a peculiar challenge that comes from interrogating a slow person — all the tics you try to pick up on aren't there half the time. Either their lies are so obvious they slap you in the face, or there's just this generalized confusion that makes the emotional state impossible to read.

Charley sensed it, too. 'If it were my friend messing around with my little girl, I'd sure as hell be pissed off.'

Truman rubbed his lips with his free hand. 'What did she say about me?'

I decided subtlety was going to be wasted on Truman Dellis.

'She said you and Russell Pelletier killed Jonathan Shipman and Deputy Brodeur.'

He shook his head so vigorously that his hair swung. 'No.'

'She said you killed those men and then tried to frame my father.'

'I didn't do nothing.'

'So why did she say those things?'

A sheen of sweat stood out along Truman's brow. 'I don't know.'

'She claimed she saw you out at Rum Pond the day before the shooting. Is that true?'

'No.'

'She said she saw you talking with Pelletier behind the boat-house.'

'I wasn't there!'

'So why is she saying these things about you?'

'I don't know.'

'Your own daughter is going around saying you're a murderer, Truman. Why is that?'

'Because she's a whore!' The barrel of the rifle began to shake in Truman's hands.

As wired as I was on adrenaline, I was beginning to have second thoughts about the wisdom of confronting him like this. 'All right,' I said, holding my hands up. 'Let's just calm down here.'

Charley didn't seem to hear me. 'Truman,' he said, 'what really happened to your face?'

The question seemed to catch him off guard. It certainly caught me off guard. He touched the stitched red line on his cheek. 'My face?'

'How'd you really get that scar?'

I had no idea what Charley was getting at. But I was afraid to look away from Truman.

'Chainsaw broke on me. Got me across the face.'

'I don't think that's what happened.'

'You calling me a liar?'

'Yes, I am.'

'Charley,' I said.

'This is my house!'

Charley didn't speak. He remained absolutely still.

Truman raised the barrel of the rifle until it was pointed at the old warden's sternum. 'Who the fuck are you, calling me a liar in my house!'

'We're leaving.' I took hold of Charley's biceps. The muscle felt like a steel cable. 'Come on.'

'You'd better be careful who you point a gun at,' said Charley in his quiet voice.

'You ain't a warden no more!' said Truman.

'No,' Charley said. 'But this man is.'

Truman glanced in my direction. The barrel of the rifle wobbled.

I said, 'Threatening an officer with a firearm is a felony. So why don't you put that gun down?'

The rifle stayed where it was. 'This is my house,' said Truman. 'You're trespassing. You get out of here.'

'All right,' said Charley finally.
'Go!'
I felt behind my back for the doorknob and got the door open. We backed through the lintel onto the staircase.

'We'll talk again,' I said. But it was an empty threat.

Truman just slammed the door.

★   ★   ★

My heart was beating hard as we made our way down the stairs and back to the car. A faint breeze was blowing from the west. I felt it through my perspiration-soaked shirt. The muscles in Charley's neck stood out like cords.

'What the hell was that?' I said.

'You're the one who wanted to interrogate him. Did you hear what you wanted to hear?'

It was a good question. More than anything I was just shocked at how quickly I'd forgotten everything I knew as a law officer about keeping a situation from escalating out of control. Maybe Kathy Frost was right: My judgment these days really was fucked. 'He might have shot us.'

'I don't think so.'

'What was that you were saying about his scar? You think my dad gave it to him.'

'I'm not sure it has anything to do with what happened last week.'

'It sounded like you thought Truman might've actually done it. Killed those men, I mean.'

'He's capable of murder.'

'So you think Brenda was telling the truth.'

'No,' he said, ending my half-second of hopefulness with a single word. 'Just because Truman's a dangerous man doesn't mean he's guilty of those particular crimes.'

We climbed back into the Plymouth, and Charley started the engine. I felt a growing heaviness in my limbs as the adrenaline left my bloodstream. 'I didn't like being in there without a pistol.'

'It would've been lots more dangerous if we'd been armed.'

'What do you mean?'

'Having the only firearm in that room made Truman feel like he was in control of the situation. I couldn't have pushed him like that if we were also armed. He might've got spooked.'

'You mean you deliberately tried to piss him off?'

'Of course,' Charley said, smiling as he settled his shoulders back in the seat. 'How was I supposed to learn anything useful otherwise?'

He turned the wheel, and we started back toward Flagstaff. The shadows of the trees had grown longer across the road. Dusk was coming fast.

'So what did you learn?'

He grinned. 'That I'd better not piss him off again.'

'Do you deliberately provoke everyone you meet?'

'Everyone? No, not everyone. Just ninety percent or so.'

24

It was still afternoon, but just barely. The sun was still shining, but as soon as it dipped behind the mountains I knew it would be fully dark. The few houses we passed along the road had turned on their porch lights in anticipation of dusk.

I'd had my little chat with Truman Dellis, and now what was I going to do? I didn't want to go home to Sennebec — and I certainly wasn't going to ask Charley to fly me back now — but what could I accomplish staying here? All day long my anger had kept despair at bay. Now the adrenaline was draining out of me, and I felt as purposeless as a man can feel. Kathy Frost would be hunting for me, too, and she was one person I couldn't bear to face.

'You can drop me at the inn,' I said.

'Say again?' Charley rolled up the window to hear me better.

'The Dead River Inn. I thought I'd get a room there for the night.'

'So you're planning on sticking around, then?'

In my memory I saw Sarah speeding away from our old house. I remembered the look on Lieutenant Malcomb's face at Brodeur's funeral and the anger in Kathy's voice on the phone. 'I've got nothing to get back to.'

'Why don't you stay over with us? The Boss is

a fine cook and I know she'd enjoy making your acquaintance.'

'I can't impose on you two like that.'

'It's no imposition.'

'Thanks, anyway.'

He nodded, but he seemed genuinely disappointed. 'The Dead River Inn it is. I've been wanting to talk with Sally Reynolds.'

★ ★ ★

The parking lot was already half-filled with pickups, most with ATVs parked in their truck-beds after the local custom. There were also a few boat-sized Buicks and Oldsmobiles representing the summer cottagers from nearby Spring Lake. The early birds had arrived for dinner.

I followed Charley into the dimly lit tavern across from the dinning room. Reflexively, I looked for the three bikers, but I didn't see their ugly mugs among the crowd of locals. Behind the bar a silver-haired woman, wearing a denim shirt with the sleeves rolled up over her tan arms, was pouring drinks. A lighted cigarette hung from her bottom lip in violation of Maine state law concerning smoking in bars and restaurants.

'Sally!' said Charley.

The woman glanced up at the sound of his voice. She had the weathered face of a person whose lifelong hobbies have been chain-smoking and sunbathing. Her hair was cut close, so it stood up like a wolf's pelt. Two years ago in this same room she'd pointed a shotgun at my father's head until the police came to arrest him.

'Charley Stevens,' she rasped. 'I heard you were in today for lunch.'

'Donna made us some sandwiches. She's a nice young woman.'

'She's got a crush on you, too. You want something to drink?'

'A cup of coffee — if it's not too much trouble.'

'What about your handsome young friend?'

'Jack Daniels.'

'Now there's a man after my own heart.' She ground out the stub of her cigarette in a heavy ceramic ashtray filled with the stubs of about twenty others. 'You look real familiar,' she said as she poured my shot. 'Yeah, I remember. You were in a fight here. That was the night your dad nearly cut a guy's throat.'

'I've still got a scar from that night.' I tapped my forehead at the hairline.

She fixed her eyes on mine, her gaze direct and unashamed. 'I guess your old man never worried that you were really his kid — looking like you do.'

'Mike's a game warden down on the midcoast. He's helping us with our investigation.'

She set down the liquor bottle in the well. '*Our* investigation? And just how exactly are you involved in this?'

Charley raised his eyes from his coffee mug. 'Oh, I'm just helping out. Doing a little flying for the state police. That sort of thing.'

'You're supposed to be retired, Charley.'

'You know me. I can't help sniffing around.'

'You should be home with that beautiful wife of yours instead of sniffing around here.'

'Home is the next stop.'

'Does Ora know what you're up to?'

'You know I can't put anything past that woman.'

'That's because she's smarter than you.'

'She is that.' He slid off his stool and winked at me. 'I'd better give her a call now that Sally's shamed me into it.'

I watched Charley disappear into the lobby in search of a pay phone. When I turned back, I found Sally staring at me hard with those icy blue eyes. She pointed a nail at my forehead. 'That's a honey of a scar.' There was an edge to her tone that hadn't been there a moment ago.

'It helps me remember a bad night.'

'I wouldn't let your old man in here after that fight. It was the last straw.' She lighted a cigarette with a silver Zippo lighter identical to the one my dad brought back from Vietnam. 'So how exactly are you helping the investigation?'

'The police wanted me to talk to someone here in Flagstaff. They thought she might know where my dad is.'

'Brenda Dean.'

My reaction gave me away.

She laughed, a parched, whiskey-voiced laugh. 'I bet you didn't have any luck, either. She must have loved talking with you, though.'

'Why's that?'

'She likes giving every guy she meets a hard-on. The good-looking ones especially.'

I let that comment go unremarked. 'I heard

she was here the night of the public meeting.'

'She was here. She comes in by herself sometimes. Sits at the bar and lets guys buy her drinks. She gets hammered and then drives all the way back to Rum Pond. How far is that — forty miles? I tell her she's lucky she hasn't lost her license by now or crashed into a moose or something. I guess some people have more luck than they deserve.'

'I think most people have less luck than they deserve.'

'Another barroom philosopher. Just what we need around here.' She raised her eyebrows as if she was about to say something, but at that second she was called away by a man at the other end of the room wanting to order a beer. When she'd poured it for him and taken his money, she returned to the spot in front of me and looked directly into my eyes again. 'You know that deputy your old man murdered?'

'I'm not so sure he murdered anyone, actually. But that's just my opinion.'

She bared her teeth in a smile. 'Let me guess, the real killer was a one-armed man.'

I kept my head down and sipped my drink. Where the hell was Charley?

'Let me tell you about that deputy,' she continued.

'I knew Bill,' I said quickly. I wasn't looking for a fight. 'We went to the academy together.'

'Then you knew he was a good kid. And a good cop. And he didn't deserve what happened to him.' She filled a shot glass for herself. 'If I

273

had somebody in the bar — your friend Brenda, for instance — who was too shit-faced to get behind the wheel, I'd give him a call so he could set up his cruiser at the end of the road. Some people might say I shouldn't do that to my own customers, but I say you don't have a right to kill yourself or anyone else.'

The words were out of my mouth before I could stop them: 'Maybe you should just tell your bartenders to stop serving drunks.'

'That's cute,' she said, giving me the blue glare again. 'Another thing about Bill Brodeur is that he volunteered to drive Shipman back to Sugarloaf. He didn't have to do that. He didn't like what Wendigo is planning on doing — evicting the leaseholders. But he believed the guy had a right to be safe, and when the sheriff asked for someone to drive this asshole, Bill volunteered. That tells you the kind of cop he was. He put his life on the line for someone he didn't even like.'

'He sounds like a good cop.' I meant the praise to sound sincere, but she didn't take it that way.

'He died in the line of duty. I'd say that made him a good cop.'

Charley, fortunately, picked that moment to return. He came, whistling, back to the bar as if all was right with the world.

Sally crossed her leathery arms. 'I was just about to tell your young friend here what I was doing in Skowhegan today.'

'What were you doing?' I asked, unable to stop myself from goading this woman who was so intent on goading me.

274

'Visiting my cousin in jail. Maybe you know the name — Wallace Bickford?'

'How is Wally?' Charley sensed something was amiss, I could tell from the caution in his voice.

'Scared, sick, confused. He doesn't even remember the night he was arrested. He just woke up in jail with the dt's. And now he's facing felony charges for firing a gun at police officers.' She was sneering at me now, not trying to hide her contempt anymore. 'And you know the saddest part? That sweet, brain-injured man still thinks Jack Bowditch is his friend. The jerk who got him into this trouble and nearly got him killed.'

I stood up suddenly. 'I've got to take a leak.'

In the bathroom I leaned against the wall over the urinal and wondered how this day could get worse. With my father on the run, I was the closest thing people had to a punching bag around here. Well, at least I was performing a public service.

One thing was certainly clear: No one appreciated my poking around the shootings. It was like something out of Agatha Christie. Maybe the whole damn town was in on Shipman's murder. I could almost picture the scenario: All of Dead River was involved in a conspiracy to drive off Wendigo Timber with Brodeur somehow getting shot in the crossfire. I laughed to myself at how fast the booze had gone to my imagination.

I found Charley waiting for me outside the door, hat on and ready to leave. I wasn't so eager to stick around myself. 'You'll have to forgive Sally,' he said.

'Why's that?'

'She sees your face, and all she thinks about is your dad.'

'That's not my fault.'

'It's not. But just so you know, it was her idea for Deputy Brodeur to drive his passenger out the back way from the inn. She feels responsible for what happened. She thinks they'd both be alive today if she'd never suggested the idea. And maybe she's right.' He put a hand on my shoulder. 'I just called Ora, and she said she'd be heartbroken if you didn't spend the night with us.'

'All right.' I couldn't imagine Sally Reynolds would ever rent me a room at this stage. And I dreaded the ride back south with Kathy Frost if my sergeant should ever find me.

'I thought you might reconsider.'

In the parking lot I saw two teenagers making out, and the truth came to me in one bright bolt. 'Sally and my dad had a thing, didn't they? That's one of the reasons she hates Brenda. That's why she's bothered by my face.'

Charley didn't say a word in response, but he didn't have to, either.

25

At the boat launch on Flagstaff Pond Kathy Frost was waiting for us. She was seated in her green patrol truck, watching the lights come on in the distant cottages across the lake. Tied to the dock where we'd left it, Charley's little floatplane bobbed on the darkening waves.

We'd just dropped the old Plymouth off at Flint's garage, and I was having second thoughts about imposing myself on Charley and Ora. The bourbon had left my insides feeling scorched. Or maybe it was just an aftereffect of all the confrontations I'd endured that day. Seeing the brittle expression on my sergeant's face didn't make me feel any better. She hitched her thumbs in her gunbelt — her usual tough-gal pose — and spat a wad of chewing gum into the dirt.

'Now, how in the hell did you find us, Sergeant?' Charley asked with a delighted smile.

'I called your wife. She told me you were headed back this way.'

'That's good detective work.'

My sergeant was in no mood for the old pilot's jauntiness. 'Jesus Christ, Charley. It's bad enough Mike's fucking up his career without your helping him. I told Malcomb I'd have him back to Sidney this afternoon. Where the hell were you two?'

'Mike wanted to see the scene of the crime.'

'So you decided to play tour guide? It's a

277

goddamned homicide investigation.'

'It's not his fault,' I said. 'I told him I wasn't going to wait around for you. He came along to keep an eye on me.'

She exhaled sharply and rubbed her nose, which was peeling from a recent sunburn. 'Well, it doesn't matter, at this point. It's probably too late, but maybe we can still salvage your job.' She gestured at her truck with her thumb as if hitchhiking a ride.

I stood still. 'I'm not going, Kath.'

'What?'

'I'm staying in Flagstaff.'

She looked from me to Charley, found whatever confirmation she needed in his sheepish expression, then swung back around on me. 'So you're just going to disobey Malcomb's order?'

'I guess so.'

'You *guess* so?' She gaped at me as if she had never truly seen my true self before. 'You ungrateful, turd-brained, son-of-a-bitch. You understand what this means?'

Her anger was creating an echo in me. You reach a point where you're just tired of people second-guessing even your worst decisions. 'Do you want my resignation?'

'No! But I'm not going to stand for this insubordinate bullshit, either. Forget second chances. You've already had your third and fourth.' She turned and paced away ten yards, trying to get a handle on her fury, than came back with fists clenched. 'I don't know what kind of rescue fantasy you've got playing in your head,' she went on, 'but it's seriously twisted. Your old man's a fucking cop killer. And all you're doing with this crap is taking yourself down with him.'

'Shut up, Kathy.'

'Sarah said you inherited your dad's self-destructive gene. I guess she was right.'

'Leave Sarah out of it. You had no business calling her, anyway.'

'She still cares about you, even though you treated her like shit. God knows why.' She stood close enough that I could smell the bug repellent on her — the familiar sweetness of Avon Skin So Soft. 'If you think throwing your life away is going to help your old man, then you're beyond hope. Give me your wallet.'

'My *what*?'

'Your wallet.'

I handed it to her without asking why. She removed my warden service identification card and stuck it in her breast pocket. 'You don't have your badge on you, I'm assuming. And I hope to God you weren't so stupid as to bring your sidearm up here?'

'Everything's at home,' I admitted.

'Lieutenant Malcomb will expect you to surrender the badge and pistol.'

'So you're accepting my resignation?' My surprise surfaced in my voice. I thought we both understood my offer was just another bluff.

'It sure looks that way,' she said. 'But if you're any kind of man, you'll have the balls to tell Malcomb in person.'

I stood there in disbelief as she got back into

279

the truck. The engine roared, and the pickup backed up abruptly, brake lights shining. But she must have thought of one more thing because she stopped suddenly and rolled down the window. 'It wasn't rabid, by the way.'

'What?'

'Your bear. The tests came back, and there was no sign of rabies. But I suppose you don't care about that anymore.'

Of all the things she'd said, that comment stung the most.

As we watched her taillights disappear through the trees, Charley said to me, 'I'm sorry that I contributed to this situation.'

Without a word to him, I turned and walked down to the end of the float and stared into the black water. I was thinking about the first time Kathy took me out to 'work' night hunters. She'd staked out a Jeep trail in Burkettville, where poachers were reportedly jacklighting deer. We set up an artificial deer decoy by the side of the road and hunkered down in some brush to wait. Then, just after nightfall, the skies opened up, and it began to pour. Kathy and I spent six hours crouched in the rain and never saw a single vehicle. The poachers had the good sense to remain indoors, but we were drenched to the skin. Afterward Kathy had only to say 'Bucketville' and we'd both crack up laughing.

Now I was no longer a game warden. The realization just wouldn't sink in.

Sarah had called me self-destructive. The label certainly seemed to fit. In the past few days I'd lost a last chance with my former girlfriend, my career, and a friend I hadn't truly appreciated. And what had I gained?

I felt the dock sway beneath Charley's feet. 'Are you all right?' he asked.

'You're sure Ora won't mind putting me up for the night?'

'When I was a game warden,' he said, putting his hand on my shoulder, 'I brought home injured coons, foxes, and bear cubs. If there's anything Ora's used to, it's me bringing home strays. As long as you don't start gnawing the furniture, we'll both be fine.'

⋆   ⋆   ⋆

The floatplane skipped across the water, ten feet above the waves. Charley lifted the nose just enough to become airborne and then brought us down with a ducklike splash on the opposite side of the lake.

As we taxied toward shore, I saw a log cottage with a shingled boathouse at the water's edge and windows glowing gold through the pines. I felt my heart lift at the sight, as if I were returning to a place I'd once visited in childhood and then forgotten. It was a surprising sensation considering how depressed I was.

Charley brought the Super Cub up against the dock beside the boathouse, opened the door, and jumped out. He fastened the floatplane to cleats on the dock. I stepped down onto the riveted metal pontoon, holding on to one of the struts to keep my balance.

A dog came bounding from the cottage, a

gray-and-brown German shorthaired pointer with a quick-wagging stub of a tail.

'Hey, Nimrod.' Charley fell to his knees and let the dog lick his face.

I ran my hand along his coarse back while he sniffed my legs. 'Good-looking dog.'

'Dumb as a post.' He slapped me on the back, trying to rouse some good cheer in me. 'Come on, let's see what the Boss has got cooking.'

A strip of rough tar paper ran down the center of the dock and led to a paved walkway that seemed out of place in such a rustic setting. The walk climbed in a switchback up the lawn to the cottage. A wooden ramp rose to the porch door.

The cottage was built partly of peeled fir and spruce logs and partly of beams and cedar shakes, and it had a red-shingled asphalt roof and a squat fieldstone chimney from which a wisp of smoke was rising. Yellow light streamed out through the windows onto the forest floor. I heard classical music playing softly from a stereo inside.

'Ora?' said Charley, pulling open the screen door. 'We've got company.'

The inside of the house smelled of a log fire and of meat cooking in an oven. There were vases with wildflowers in all the windows and books piled everywhere on tables and on the floor. On the walls hung innumerable deer and moose antlers and mounted trout and salmon trophies the length of my leg. The furniture all seemed too short somehow.

'Ora?'

'Hi, Charley. I'll be right out.'

He frowned at the crackling fireplace. 'Isn't it a little warm to have a fire going?'

'My bones were cold.'

Charley removed his green cap and hung it from a deer-foot coat peg beside the door. His thick gray-and-white hair stood up with the electricity even after he tried to smooth it. 'She'll be right out.'

I gestured at the taxidermy on the wall. 'Those are some impressive fish.'

'Ora caught that salmon there. She's a better fisher than me. Always has been. Of course, it's harder now for her to get out than it once was.'

I was about to ask why it was harder when the answer arrived in the person of Ora Stevens herself. She rolled into the room in a wheelchair, a handsome woman with deeply set green eyes, high Scandinavian cheekbones, and shoulder-length, snow-white hair swept back behind her ears. She wore a spearmint-colored sweater over a white T-shirt, khakis, and tennis shoes.

Charley knelt down to kiss her pale cheek. 'How you doing, Boss?'

'Boss! I wish he wouldn't call me that.' She held out a hand to me. 'Hello, Mike.'

The grip was firmer than I expected. 'It's nice to meet you, Mrs. Stevens.'

'Ora,' she corrected me.

'Mike has agreed to spend the night with us,' he said, not mentioning anything about what had just happened back at the boat launch.

'That's wonderful. I have a room already made up.'

'I hate to put you out this way.'

She waved a hand. 'It's no bother. We don't get enough company these days, as it is. Can I offer you something to drink, dear? We have lemonade, iced tea, beer.'

'A beer would be great.'

'I'll have iced tea,' said Charley. 'I guess I'll show Mike around in case he needs to use the facilities.'

With Nimrod trailing us at every step, Charley escorted me through the cottage. I realized now the reason for the paved walkway and the low furniture. Everything in the house had been arranged to be accessible to Ora Stevens in her wheelchair. The cottage was larger than it looked from outside and was cluttered with all sorts of woodsy knickknacks: animal skulls and hand-carved duck decoys, eye-catching rock specimens, and lots and lots of books. There were several framed photographs lined up along the top of a bureau. I noticed that two young women appeared in multiple pictures. 'Are those your daughters?'

Charley nodded. 'Anne and Stacey.'

The photo that looked to be the most recent showed Ora standing — no wheelchair in sight — with her arms around both young women. Her hair was darker, as was Charley's.

'Do they live in Maine?' The question was all I could do to maintain the semblance of good manners.

'Anne does, down to Augusta. I'm not sure where Stacey is these days. She moves around a lot.' He guided me back out into the cottage's great room.

'I'd love to have a place like this someday,' I said honestly. It was the kind of cabin in the woods I'd always dreamed about.

'We only live here April through November. But sometimes I come up on my own to do some ice-fishing in the winter. It gets damned cold, but if I sleep out in front of the fireplace with Nimrod and a few blankets, I'm all right.'

'How much land do you have here?'

'Twenty acres. Of course it belongs to Wendigo since we're on a lease.'

'And they're really going to evict you?'

Charley made a face. 'Oh, I expect they'll give us a chance to buy the land at a price five times what we can afford to pay. After we refuse, they'll make an offer on the buildings here, knowing we don't have the money to move them anywhere else. That's the way it happened when they went into Montana, from what I understand. Wendigo never evicts anybody. They just force you to sell out at their asking price.'

'How long have you been here?'

'Thirty-three years.'

Ora came rolling out with our drinks and a bowl of roasted pumpkin seeds on a tray on her lap. 'Dinner will be ready in half an hour,' she said. 'Why don't we go out onto the porch?'

Charley's mouth tightened. 'I thought you felt cold.'

'I'm warmer now,' she said with an unconvincing smile.

Charley and I sat down in wicker rocking chairs, facing the lake, while Ora positioned her wheelchair to one side.

'Supper smells great.'

She smiled. 'I hope you don't mind moose. Charley got about three hundred pounds of meat from a man in town who hit one with his car.'

'Totaled his Subaru,' he said. 'Lucky he wasn't killed.'

'The irony is the poor man is a vegetarian.' Ora gave a sad laugh.

'We'll be eating moose until it's coming out our ears,' said Charley. 'How many moose have you shot?'

'None, yet.' It was an embarrassing admission for a Maine game warden.

'You'll get one with brainworm or struck by a car before too long, and you'll have to put it down.' He was speaking as if I hadn't just resigned from the Warden Service. 'So I understand you shot a bear last week.'

'It was killing pigs. I was hoping to relocate it somewhere up this way, but a farmer wounded it, and I had to put it down.'

'How big a guy was he?' asked Charley.

'Two hundred pounds. But he looked twice that size.'

'Bears always look bigger than they are,' he said. 'That's the problem I have with baiting them during bear season. These dimwit hunters shoot the first bear that comes close to their tree stand. Half the time it's a yearling cub, thirty-five pounds or so. Then they're too embarrassed to haul the little thing back to camp, so they stash it behind a brush pile and try for a bigger one.'

'Charley.' Ora gave him a hard look.

286

'I'll shut up,' he said. 'Baiting just gets me steamed. I know the state's got to manage the bear population, but still — '

'Charley.'

'I'm finished.' He took a sip of iced tea.

We gazed out through the porch screen at the lake's dark chop, the lights of Flagstaff burning like yellow and red stars in the far distance. The purr of a motorboat carried across the water, a fisherman returning late to shore.

Then Ora said, 'Mike, I'm sorry about your father. This must be very difficult for you.'

'Thank you,' I said.

'Have you talked to anyone about this? A minister or counselor?'

'Ora,' said Charley.

She leaned forward and touched the arm of my rocking chair with two fingers. 'You can't save him, dear. Whatever happens is up to him. I hope you'll remember that.'

'Ora, that's enough.' Charley rose to his feet. 'My God, what a busybody you are. She loves to ask questions she has no business asking.'

She looked up at her husband, leaning back in her chair. 'Charley's right,' she said.

'You don't need to apologize.'

'Oh, yes she does.' He took hold of the rubber handles on the back of her wheelchair and pivoted her toward the door. 'We'll check on supper and let you finish your beer in peace.'

They left me alone on the porch.

★   ★   ★

Dinner was the best I'd had in ages. The roast was lean and tender with a stronger flavor than beef. There were new potatoes and onions from the Stevenses' big garden, and Ora steamed some sort of greens Charley plucked from the yard. On the table was a Mason jar of wild mushrooms pickled in cider vinegar and a crusty loaf of home-baked bread wrapped in a warm napkin.

It was the kind of meal my mother never made. I remembered all the nights I'd spent as a kid staring down at an orange lump of boxed macaroni and cheese. Even when my dad brought home deer meat she managed to burn all the taste out of it. She just never put any effort into cooking. And, of course, the TV was always going, background chatter to their arguments.

Charley and Ora drank glasses of cold milk they poured from a pitcher. But I stuck with beer. There were four empty bottles in front of me, and I was feeling woozy by the time Ora brought out the blackberry pie.

'Charley gathered these berries along the dirt road that leads out here from town,' she said. 'We grow or gather most of what we eat. Always have.'

'On a warden's pitiful salary, what else could we do?' he said. 'We're like that Ewell Gibbons feller from those old TV commercials? 'Did you ever eat a pine tree?' There's just so much to eat out there if you know what to look for — fiddleheads and frog's legs and mushrooms. Then there's the

288

usual game: moose, deer, rabbits, squirrels.'

Ora patted his hand. 'Charley has a stronger stomach than I do. I can do without rodents,' she said. 'I do love fish, though. Trout and salmon. Pan-fried perch and bullheads.'

'Of course, these days you can't eat fish like you used to,' said Charley. 'On account of the mercury. All that damned acid rain from the Midwest dropping down into our lakes and rivers, poisoning our fish and birds. That's another sad development from when I was a lad. But I guess every old fart says the world has gone to hell in his lifetime.'

'I think it really has,' I said.

Ora looked at me with concern. 'Why do you say that?'

'There's no wilderness left. There are roads everywhere now, and GPS receivers if you do get lost. You can make a cell-phone call from the top of a mountain or the bottom of a cave. You can go to the ends of the earth and if you look up, you'll still see a plane flying overhead.'

I hadn't realized how crocked I was until I'd opened my mouth. But the more time I spent with Ora and Charley, the angrier I became at Wendigo for threatening to take away this beautiful house and this life of theirs. I thought of that heated meeting at the Dead River Inn, and part of me felt a little murderous.

'It's just change,' said Charley with a big grin.

'Change for the worse.'

'Son,' he said, shaking his head with mock

sadness, 'you are the youngest old fart I've ever made the acquaintance of.'

★ ★ ★

After Charley had washed the dishes, he said, 'Let's call some owls.'

Outside it was dark. When we looked out through the windows all we could see were our reflections floating like ghosts on the glass. Charley lifted his green cap from its peg and put it on his head, and then Ora turned off the lights in the house, and we all went outside. In the darkness I could smell the lake and hear a rustle of breeze in the treetops. Crickets were chirping under the cabin.

'Do you speak Owl?' Charley asked me.

'Not fluently.' I could taste the beer on my breath.

'I'll teach you, then.'

He cupped his hands around his mouth and made a shrieking noise that sounded like *Who-cooks-for-you.* He repeated the noise a few times, modulating it so that it was always a little different.

'Barred owl,' I said.

'It's good to know they're teaching you something in warden school.' He repeated the noise again and then we waited.

Through the branches overhead stars were salted across the night sky.

Far away I heard a noise: *Who-cooks-for-you.*

'There he is,' said Charley. 'Let's see if I can draw him in.'

Back and forth Charley and the owl called to each other, the bird moving closer and closer until finally the answering hoots were coming from a tall evergreen directly overhead.

'Do you feel him watching us?' Charley whispered.

'Yes.'

'He's up there in that big spruce looking down at us wondering, 'Where's that son-of-a-gun owl who's poaching on my territory?' *Who-cooks-for-you!*'

'Charley, don't torture the poor bird,' said Ora.

'We're just having a conversation. Why don't you give it a try?'

I cupped my hands around my mouth and made a loud attempt.

No response.

'You get an A for effort,' said Charley softly, 'but an F for pronunciation. Try it again but garble the sounds together more. You're talking to an owl, not a person.'

'Charley's a regular Dr. Dolittle of the Maine woods,' said Ora.

I gave the call another attempt, focusing on the actual sounds the bird was making, not the human words they reminded me of.

This time the owl answered.

Charley clapped me on the back. 'There you go. You want to try some coyotes?' He pronounced the word *ki-otes*. 'We've got to drive a little ways, but it's not far. How about you, Boss? You up for a moonlight drive to Pokum Bog?'

'No, thanks,' she said. 'I want to get back to that book I'm reading. You two go.'

'We'll miss you.' Charley knelt down and kissed her on the lips. Then in the near dark we watched Ora wheel herself back up the ramp and into the house. A moment later the light flickered on in the hall window, and we saw her smiling face shining back at us.

★   ★   ★

We were riding along over a dirt logging road in Charley's pickup truck, the headlights cutting a path for us through the dark.

'Can I ask you a personal question?'

He laughed. 'You sound like my wife. Whenever she says those words, I get the hell out of the room. But go ahead.'

'Why is Ora in a wheelchair?'

He smiled, a tired smile. 'I knew I should have left the room.'

'I don't mean to pry.'

'It's all right. It's common knowledge. Hell, I thought everyone in the Warden Service knew.' He kept his eyes on the road while he spoke. 'We were in a plane crash six years ago, before I retired. I'd been nagging her to learn to fly for thirty-odd years and finally she gave in. I practically live in the air, so I figured she'd take to it the way I did.'

'What happened?'

'I had another plane back then. I showed her a few things on the ground, the instrument panel and how to use the stick, but

I didn't spend near enough time. Then the first couple times we went up together she did fine, better than I hoped, so I figured that was it. She was a natural, I thought.'

He rolled down the window, letting air rush in between us.

'Well, the third time we went up together the wind was really blowing and she panicked bringing us in to land. We came in at the wrong angle, and there was nothing I could do. The plane got crumpled down to half its size. It was a miracle we didn't both get killed. She broke her back, and I got off with a concussion and a busted flipper.' He lifted his right elbow. 'But then I've always been close to indestructible.'

We turned off the main dirt road down a narrow path. Tree branches brushed the sides of the truck as we blundered ahead.

'I'm sorry,' I said.

'Me too. And of course it was harder for me being the one relatively uninjured, although Ora never blamed me for what happened.'

'But your daughters blamed you.'

He glanced over at me, eyes narrowed. 'You're quite the perceptive young warden. I guess I'll have to watch what I say around you from now on.' He swerved slightly to avoid a toad in the road. 'Yes, Anne blamed me at first, but not anymore. Stacey, though . . . I think she blames us both. But me more.'

I didn't say anything else, and he didn't, either, until we'd finally come to a stop.

The path dead-ended at the edge of a small black pond in the hollow between wooded hills.

There was a dark cabin there half-hidden in the trees and the ruin of an old pier jutting out into the water. 'That's Jim Grindle's old cabin,' Charley said. 'He's living in a nursing home down in Waterville with Alzheimer's. I suppose it's just as well, given what's happening with Wendigo.'

He flicked off the highbeams and we got out of the truck and walked down to the waterline, letting our eyes adjust again to the darkness. In the weeds frogs were blowing like bagpipes. And the sky was an enormous black bowl overhead.

'How's your astronomy?' Charley asked.

'I know the Big and Little Dippers, of course, and there's Mars. Those are the Pleiades. I'm fairly certain that's an airplane. Or a UFO.'

In the starlight I could see Charley smiling at me. 'That's not so bad. My dad made us memorize all the different constellations, summer and winter. They say birds navigate by the stars.'

We stood there for a while breathing in the rich balsam smell of the forest and the algae smell of the pond.

'Let's see if I can get those dogs singing.'

He cupped his hands around his mouth, just as he did with the owl, but this time the sound he let loose was a thin, mournful howl.

Almost instantly there came a cry from across the pond, a high-pitched wail that sent shivers up my spine.

Charley called again, and the first coyote answered, and then a second coyote, off on one of the hills, joined in. Then a third and a fourth replied.

'This pond is the boundary between two family packs,' said Charley softly. 'I think they've got a feud going on over whose it is. Some nights it doesn't take much to get them worked up.'

Back and forth the coyotes called to one another, wailing like lost souls.

'Listen to them sing,' he said. 'Doesn't the sound of it do something strange to your heart?'

'Yes,' I said. 'It does.'

26

When I awoke the next morning, sunlight was streaming through the window beside my bed. I lay there a long time, breathing in the warm balsam smell of the forest that drifted through the screen.

Lying there, it was easy to fantasize about hiding out here from my life, enjoying Ora's home cooking and Charley's stories. But in my heart I knew it was a false dream. All I was doing in Flagstaff was interfering with a homicide investigation, making it less likely — not more — that the detectives would ever focus their attention on Truman Dellis, Russell Pelletier, Vern Tripp, or anybody else, for that matter. It was time I stopped playing Hardy Boys with Charley Stevens. My life back home was a mess and I needed to clean it up.

My father was somewhere far away, maybe in Canada, maybe not. He might be caught today or next week or never. My being here would make no difference. The thought that I might somehow be able to talk him into surrendering — if the opportunity ever arose — was laughable. We were strangers. We always had been. Ora Stevens was right: I couldn't save him.

I found her sitting in her wheelchair on the porch with a cup of tea, reading Jane Austen's *Emma*. She turned when she heard my footsteps and removed her bifocals and gave me a big smile.

'Did you sleep all right, dear?'

'Better than I have in a long time, actually.'

'I always sleep better in the woods myself. Charley's out with Nimrod, but he should be back soon. There are clean towels in the bathroom, and Charley left a T-shirt that should fit you.'

Charley was sitting at the kitchen table, drinking coffee, when I came out of the bathroom. 'There's the man of the hour,' he said.

I pretended to look over my shoulder. 'Where?'

'I hope you're hungry because I'm making my world-famous, four-grain waffles.'

'It's the only meal he cooks,' said Ora from the porch.

He gave a mock frown. 'My secret's out.'

I sat down at the kitchen table while Charley poured me a mug of coffee.

Ora rolled herself in from the porch. 'What did you see this morning, dear? Anything unusual?'

'Mostly thrushes and chickadees. There was a mourning warbler singing over by that new clear-cut. And Nimrod spooked a partridge.'

'There was a red-eyed vireo outside my window,' I said.

He raised his eyebrows.

'My girlfriend taught me a few things,' I said. 'Ex-girlfriend, I mean. She's a hardcore birder.'

'What's her name?'

'Sarah.'

'Pretty name.'

'She's prettier than her name.' I smiled at the memory.

'What's she do for a living, dear?' asked Ora.

'She's a teacher's aide, studying to be a teacher. But I think she has higher ambitions than that. She wants to change the educational system across the country.'

'And how long were you two together?'

'Off and on, four years. We met in college.'

'So why aren't you together anymore?'

'Ora,' warned Charley.

'It's OK,' I said. 'Sarah doesn't like what I do — what I did — for a living.' It was a simplification, a lie, basically, but I didn't want to get into all the things I'd done to alienate her.

Charley turned around from the stove. 'Why the hell not?'

'She doesn't think being a game warden is a real career. She called it 'a small boy's idea of a cool job.''

He laughed. 'Well, of course it is! What's wrong with that?'

*　★　★

As we ate I thought about how I'd bad-mouthed Sarah to the Stevens. Why was I always unfair to her that way? Maybe she did have some reservations about my job, and maybe she did worry too much about money, but she'd never actually asked me to quit being a warden. What the hell was wrong with the men in my family that we forced the women in our lives to leave us?

After breakfast, I asked to use the Stevenses' phone. I got Sarah's answering machine, and since she didn't believe in screening calls — she saw it as an act of impoliteness — I knew she wasn't home.

'Sarah,' I said. 'I owe you an apology. I've made a lot of mistakes lately — you have no idea — but the way I treated you is the worst. I'm up at Flagstaff now. Some things have happened. I might not be a warden for very much longer. I'm not going to ask for a second chance, because I don't deserve one. I just wanted to apologize one last time.'

When I came out of the bedroom, Ora was off somewhere and Charley was washing and drying the dishes with the police scanner going in the background. I asked him if he would fly me home to Sennebec. 'I appreciate the hospitality you and Ora have shown me,' I said, 'but I need to get back and face the music.'

'I understand,' he said, and I was surprised at the sadness in his voice. 'I'll go tell Ora.'

He disappeared down the hall. I stood looking out the windows at the smooth surface of the lake, a perfect mirror of the blue sky above. It was a beautiful sight, but it only made me feel more alone.

★　★　★

The phone rang. I heard Charley pick up in the bedroom, heard him say hello. Then he closed the door.

299

I waited, feeling my heart beginning to speed up.

Finally the bedroom door opened, and Charley came out. His expression was hard for me to decipher. 'That was Soctomah. He just got off the line with Brenda Dean. I guess Truman got stirred up last night after our visit. He called over to Rum Pond wanting to know why Brenda was telling the authorities he killed those men. She told Soctomah he threatened her. She says she wants police protection.'

'You mean she's still out there?' She'd told me she was just going to gather up her things yesterday and leave. If she really thought Russ Pelletier was a murderer, why did she spend the night? 'So what's Soctomah going to do?'

'He said he'd send a trooper out to Truman's place to chat with him. And I told him I'd fly over to Rum Pond to see what's up. That is, if you don't mind making a stopover on the way home.'

It seemed that I was going back to Rum Pond one way or the other.

★ ★ ★

Charley had already gassed up the plane, readying it for another day in the air. Ora wheeled herself down to the dock to watch us depart.

'Well, Boss,' he said, kneeling down to kiss her. 'We're off into the wild blue.'

'Be careful.'

'You know me.'

'That's why I'm saying be careful.'

'Thank you for everything, Ora,' I said.

'Please come back and see us again.' She took my hand in both of hers.

'I will.'

She smiled, but her eyes were full of doubt.

I climbed into the backseat while Charley gave the plane a shove away from shore, hopping after it again to land on the pontoon. He was as agile as a monkey getting in and out of that plane.

A minute later, after he'd strapped himself in and started the engine, we were skittering off across the lake. The air was dead still, but we rose as if swept aloft on a gust of wind. Charley turned so that we banked back over the cottage. I looked down and saw Ora wave at us from her wheelchair at the end of the dock. From this height she seemed so small and frail. And just like that, I felt a premonition that something very bad was about to happen.

★ ★ ★

The woods stretched out beneath us like a nubby green bedspread thrown over the hills. The glare of the sun, blazing white in the eastern sky, made it impossible to see far in that direction, but in the west I could clearly see the heavily forested mountains that marked the boundary with Canada, forty-some miles away.

Charley was uncharacteristically quiet. Every now and again he zigzagged the plane to pass over a clear-cut or to parallel a logging road for some distance. A couple of times he canted the plane completely onto its side to have a better look at something on the ground. I never saw anything but trees.

I tried to start a conversation over the intercom. 'You're awfully quiet.'

'Did you tell Brenda you'd talk to Truman?' he asked.

'No. Why?'

'I don't like this. It doesn't feel right.'

Between two mountains up ahead a body of brownish-blue water reflected the clouds. We came in directly over the forest gate that blocked the driveway leading from Wendigo's logging road to Rum Pond. The stand of old-growth pines was still there. But for how much longer? I wondered. The next thing I knew we were over the water, making a sharp U-turn to approach the camp from the south. I looked for my father's cabin on the eastern shore of the lake, but the pines hid it from view. We settled down with a splash on the water and began taxiing toward the compound of log buildings that was the sporting camp. I saw a motorboat moored at the dock and canoes drawn up on a beach, but there wasn't a soul in sight.

As we drew up to the dock, a door opened at the main lodge and Russ Pelletier stepped out into the sun. He wore blue jeans and a paint-spattered canvas workshirt that looked too hot for this weather. On his belt was a big knife in a sheath. He didn't raise his hand or greet us in any way, but remained standing there, smoking a cigarette on the doorstep, while the plane came to a stop.

'He doesn't look too happy to see us, now does he?' said Charley.

'Not really.'

We climbed out of the plane and Charley tied a rope to a cleat to keep it from floating off. Side by side we walked up to the main building.

'Morning!' said Charley.

Pelletier's mustache needed trimming, and his oil-black hair hung over his forehead in heavy bangs. 'Hello, Charley.'

'Where are all your guests?'

'Left this morning. Don't have any more until Friday. You always said I should probably close this place in August, given how little business I get.' He gave a smirk. The full sunlight showed the nicotine stains on his teeth. 'But I guess I won't have to worry about that problem soon, will I?'

'I guess not.'

He looked at me over Charley's shoulder. 'You're here about Brenda, right? She's over at Jack's cabin.'

'You fired her then,' I said.

'No, she quit. She did it in front of my guests last night. Classy as ever. She doesn't seem to be in any hurry to leave, though.'

'We'll talk with her,' said Charley pleasantly. 'But first maybe you'll invite us in for a cup of coffee.'

Pelletier exhaled a cloud of smoke. Was it really possible that he and Truman had set my dad up? I remembered the story Brenda had told about him — how he'd tried to rape her. At this

303

moment, he looked capable of all the bad things she'd claimed.

'Sure,' he said finally. 'Come on in.'

There wasn't a trace of welcome in his voice.

★ ★ ★

We sat at one of the long tables in the dining room, across from him. Through the big plate-glass window that made up the southern wall of the room I could see the aluminum canoes on the beach and Charley's plane moored at the dock.

'So I guess you're looking for a new cook,' I said.

'Why? You want a job?' Pelletier crushed the butt of a cigarette in an ashtray. 'Doreen said she'd help me out until I found someone.'

His hatchet-faced ex-wife didn't strike me as the charitable type. He must have promised her a mint in exchange for her help. 'It sounds like you won't miss Brenda,' I said.

'And she won't miss me. The only reason she stayed here the last couple years was Jack, the damned cradle-robber. What kind of fifty-something-year-old guy hooks up with a girl that young? It's disgusting, is what it is.'

'She was devoted to him?'

'That's not the word I'd use. They fought like cats and dogs, but she loved him. Women have always thrown themselves at the guy, for some reason. And I think he loved her, which was a rare thing for Jack. He's always had some woman in his bed, but he never gave a shit for any of

304

them.' Pelletier's red-veined eyes met mine. 'Except your mother.'

Charley took a sip of coffee and glanced out the window. 'Something's been bothering me, Russell, and I hope you can help me sort it out. You think Jack killed Jonathan Shipman and Bill Brodeur, right?'

'Don't you?'

Charley scratched his chin. 'That's the thing of it. If he did, I can't figure out why.'

'What do you mean?'

'Well, you're the one with the grudge against Wendigo, not Jack Bowditch.'

Pelletier leaned forward. 'Are you trying to imply something, Charley?'

'I'm just saying that Jack's motive doesn't seem all that strong to me.'

'You've been hanging around this kid too long. I think Jack had plenty of motive.'

'How so?'

'Wendigo is shutting me down. That means they're kicking him out, too. I think he got drunk and pissed off, and he decided he was going to do something about it. I think it was a stupid spur-of-the-moment thing to do — which is the story of Jack's life, if you ask me.'

I said, 'So how did my father know Brodeur was taking Shipman out the back way?'

Pelletier glared at me. 'What's that?'

'Whoever killed those men knew Brodeur was driving Shipman out that logging road. How did my dad know that? Who could've told him?'

'How should I know?' Pelletier asked. 'Charley, what the hell are you doing here? I understand why the kid cares about this, but why are you defending a son of a bitch poacher like Jack Bowditch?'

'I'm just trying to figure a few things out.'

'I already talked to that Indian detective about this.' He coughed into his hand. 'Frankly, I've got better things to do with my time than sit here playing a game of Clue. Jack Bowditch killed those two men. I don't know why, and I don't care. All I know is that I'm losing my business and my home and what happened last week won't change that.' He rose to his feet and loomed over us. 'If you want to talk to B.J., you know where she is. Now I've got a roof to fix.'

Listening to that imperious tone, I couldn't help remembering how he'd bossed me around eight summers ago — how he'd called me his 'serf' and made my life hell. I despised him all over again. He was halfway to the door when I called out, 'You tried to rape her.'

Pelletier spun around. 'What?'

'Brenda says you tried to rape her three years ago.'

'That's a fucking lie!'

'She said that after you and your wife split, you started coming on to her, and that my dad stopped you. She said he beat the shit out of you, and that you've been holding a grudge against him ever since.'

Pelletier advanced on me, hands balled into fists. 'Who the fuck do you think you are talking to me like that?'

I stood up. Charley jumped between us. 'Mike's just repeating what the girl said.'

306

'I never touched her!' said Pelletier.

I didn't care what he said. 'That's not all. She claims you and Truman Dellis conspired to murder Jonathan Shipman and blame it on my father.'

'She what?'

'She says she saw Truman out here the day of the shootings, talking with you behind the boathouse.'

'That's bullshit! I haven't seen that drunk since I fired his sorry ass.' Pelletier turned his attention from me back to Charley. 'You don't actually believe this crap?'

It took the old pilot a few moments to answer. When he did, his voice was soft. 'No, but I do believe there's a reason the girl hates you. Something happened between you two to make her this mad.'

Pelletier became quiet.

Charley's tone was measured. 'What happened, Russ? You can't deny it was something.'

Russell Pelletier ran his yellow-stained fingers through his greasy hair, looked away, and took a deep breath. 'It was after I fired Truman — for being drunk all the time. Doreen and I were having problems. One night Brenda and I were here alone. I thought she was sending these signals. You don't know this girl, Charley.'

Charley folded his arms. 'Go on.'

'We started kissing. It just happened. The next thing I knew, she started freaking out. She said I was disgusting. She called me all kinds of names, and she ran off, leaving me lying there on the couch. All I did was kiss her.'

'She was just a girl, Russell,' said Charley. He scowled. 'Tell that to Jack Bowditch.'

'What happened next?' I asked. All the contempt I felt for him came through in those three words.

He ignored me and focused on Charley. 'When I woke up, Jack was standing over me. She must have told him what she told you. We had a fight.' He fumbled in his shirt pocket for his cigarettes, found one, and lit it. 'He beat the crap out of me, basically. I told Doreen I fell down the stairs, but she didn't believe me.'

We watched him tuck the plastic lighter carefully back in his pants pocket. Again I noticed the knife sheathed on his belt.

Pelletier continued: 'She started going over to Jack's cabin after that. She'd go over there after dinner. She just seemed obsessed with him, and I wasn't going to get in the middle of it. I had my own troubles with Doreen, by that time.'

Charley nodded slowly. 'What do you think she's got against Truman?'

'He didn't mess with her, if that's what you're thinking. Or I never saw any sign of it, anyway. After Truman's wife died, all he cared about was getting drunk. Most of the time I think he forgot she even existed.'

Charley absorbed this information. Then he asked: 'You heard about Truman's accident?'

'With the chainsaw? Yeah, I wondered if Jack might have done it to him — whipped him across the face with the blade. Or the chain might have broken in the woods like he said.' He inhaled so deeply on his cigarette that an inch of it burned to ash before our eyes. 'I'm not proud of what happened that night with B.J. But I didn't rape that girl, and I didn't kill anyone, no matter what she says. She's a goddamned liar, Charley.'

My head was throbbing. I was worried that Charley might be swallowing Pelletier's story. 'She told the truth about my dad beating you up,' I said. 'She told the truth about your having a grudge against him.'

'Jesus Christ,' said Pelletier exhaustedly. 'She uses people. She used your old man, and now she's using you, kid.'

I heard an appliance humming softly in the kitchen, the only sound.

'I guess it's time I had a talk with the young woman,' Charley said at last.

27

We left Pelletier standing outside the main lodge, lighting yet another Marlboro.

A dirt road, scarcely more than a wheel-rutted path, led over to my father's cabin, but the most direct route was by water. Charley and I borrowed one of the camp's aluminum canoes and paddled across the cove to the gravel beach where, eight years ago, we'd first met. In the shallows minnows scattered under our paddles and the canoe made a metallic knocking noise as it struck bottom. Charley hopped out with a splash and hauled the bow up, scraping, onto the stony shore.

We stood together looking up the steep plank stairs that scaled the hillside to my father's cabin, both of us, I think, remembering that night when Truman Dellis had aimed a deer rifle at him from the darkness above.

Charley cupped his hands around his mouth, just like he did to call the coyotes. 'Brenda Dean! It's Charley Stevens and Mike Bowditch!'

There was no answer.

'We made enough racket with that damned aluminum canoe,' he said to me. 'You'd think she would have heard us.'

Along the stairs I noticed hanging shreds of yellow police tape that someone had ripped down. 'So much for this being a crime scene,' I said.

I hadn't seen the camp in eight years, but it looked no different. There were the same three separate log cabins angled onto the porch. All had rusty screen windows and screen doors that made the rooms hard to see into.

We checked the three cabins, but Brenda wasn't in any of them. I was struck by how clean everything looked. There were the same propane stove and fridge from when I was a kid, and even the same weathered topographic maps pinned to the log walls, but none of the mess I remembered. The floors had been swept. The beds had been made with clean sheets and blankets. Knowing the miracle Sarah had performed on my own home, I could only attribute the transformation to Brenda's woman's touch.

'Maybe she's up at the outhouse?' I suggested.

Charley nodded. 'Hate to disturb her there, but we should see.'

Behind the middle cabin, facing the hillside, was a stack of weathered firewood with a blue tarp thrown over it and a couple of storage sheds. The dirt road wound away through the trees in the direction of the sporting camp. Down it a little ways was my father's stinking two-seater outhouse.

She wasn't there, either.

Charley pushed up the brim of his cap and gave his forehead a scratch. 'Where the hell is that girl?'

'Right here.'

To our left Brenda stepped out from behind a shaggy hemlock along the road. She was wearing the same oil-spotted blue jeans she'd worn yesterday and a man's faded blue chambray shirt, and she was carrying over her shoulder an old single-barreled shotgun. Charley and I were both unarmed.

'What are you doing hiding in the woods?' Charley asked.

'Getting the drop on you, old man.' There was a shine in her eyes that didn't seem natural. Her smile showed her crooked teeth. 'I thought you guys were supposed to be game wardens.'

I could see the corded muscles in the pilot's neck standing out like braids in a brown rope. His eyes flicked from the shotgun back to her dilated pupils. 'You called Detective Soctomah,' he said. 'You said your father threatened you.'

Her face tightened. 'He said he'd kill me if I didn't shut up. He told me you came to see him.'

'What was I supposed to do?' I asked.

'Arrest him.'

'What else did Truman say to you on the phone?'

'He said he killed those men.'

'He did, did he?' Charley brushed a bug off his ear.

The ripe smell of the outhouse was all around us. The thought that Truman had spontaneously confessed to the murders was just too good to be true. Even if he did have a part in the killings, why admit it over the phone? Truman was dumb, but not that dumb. Which raised again the question: How far should we trust Brenda? I remembered the humiliation on Russell Pelletier's face as he told us about the night my dad

312

beat him up. Brenda had accused him of trying to rape her. My father had believed her story, but I couldn't shake my doubts.

'You don't believe me, do you?' she said.

Charley gave a slight smile.

She turned to me. 'I swear to God, it's the truth.'

'How about handing over that shotgun?' said Charley.

She gripped it tighter. 'What for?'

I put my hand out. 'Come on, B.J., give me the damned gun.'

'Don't call me that!'

This was the second time in two days I'd confronted an angry person with a firearm — like father, like daughter — and I was getting sick of that nervous flutter in my stomach. 'It's hard to have a friendly conversation with you holding a loaded shotgun,' I said.

'Fine.' She held out the gun for me. 'Here.'

It was an old New England Firearms one-shot: the kind you can buy for seventy-five bucks at a pawn shop. The safety had been switched off. I switched it back on. 'Why were you hiding from us?'

'I wasn't hiding from you. I was hiding from Truman. What's wrong with you people? Why won't you just arrest him?'

'Someone from the state police is talking with your father right now,' said Charley.

'Are they searching his place, checking his truck?'

'And why should they do that?' asked Charley.

'To find proof that he did it, that he killed those men.'

'What do you think they'll find?'

'I don't know, evidence.'

'The police already have evidence that Jack Bowditch killed those men.'

'It was a setup. I told you that. Truman said he did it.' Her hands were shaking, she was so upset. 'No one ever believes me!'

We watched her storm back to the middle cabin, yank open the screen door, and disappear inside. The door clattered shut behind her.

'What do you think?' he asked softly.

'She's lying about Pelletier,' I said, 'but I'm not sure why. And another thing, why does she want the police to search Truman's truck?'

'Good question. Let's see if we can get an answer.'

* * *

We found Brenda in the kitchen cabin, standing with the propane refrigerator open. She'd grabbed a can of Budweiser and was gulping it down right there, with the fridge ajar. It wasn't even ten o'clock.

'Isn't it a little early for that?' said Charley.

'I had a rough night.' She was breathing hard from drinking so fast.

'Why don't we sit down and have a talk.'

He gestured to the knife-scarred picnic table in the center of the cabin. It was the same table on which my father had butchered that deer he poached, the night I first met Charley Stevens.

314

Brenda sat down across from us. I set the shotgun carefully beside me on the floor.

'When did Truman call you?' asked Charley.

'Last night, late.'

'He called on the radio phone?' I asked.

'Yeah. We can't use a cell phone here on account of the mountains or something. You have to go five miles up the road to get a signal.'

'And he was calling for you and not Pelletier?'

'Maybe he was calling for Russell. I don't know. He got me instead.'

'Did Russ Pelletier hear your conversation?'

'No, he was asleep.'

'Pelletier said you'd moved over to this cabin after Jack Bowditch disappeared. What were you doing back over at the lodge?'

'Getting my stuff.'

'What stuff?' I asked.

'I don't know, boxes from when I was a kid, that sort of stuff. Jesus.' She took another sip of beer. 'I waited until he was asleep to go over there because I didn't want to see him — and that's when I heard the phone.'

'If you think Russell Pelletier conspired with Truman to murder those men, weren't you afraid to go over there?'

'I had my shotgun.'

Charley pulled on his chin in a reflective way. 'If Truman called you last night, why did you wait until this morning to contact Detective Soctomah?'

'Because they already arrested me once. Those cops think I'm a liar. I didn't think they'd do anything if I told them.'

315

'So why call them at all?' I asked.

'I don't know. I guess I wanted someone to know in case.'

'In case what?'

'In case something bad happened.' She gazed directly into my eyes. 'You should have heard him on the phone.'

Looking into her eyes, I was disturbed again by the animal reaction I had to her. It troubled me to be attracted to this woman. 'What exactly did Truman say?'

'He said, 'You goddamned bitch. What lies are you telling about me?' And I said, 'It's the truth. You killed those men, you and Russell.' And he said, 'I'll kill you, too, if you don't shut your fucking mouth.' Then I hung up.'

'So that was it?'

'Yeah.'

Charley leaned forward. 'How long did you know Bill Brodeur?'

She looked startled. 'Who?'

'Bill Brodeur, the sheriff's deputy who was murdered with Jonathan Shipman.'

'I didn't know him.'

'You never met him at the Dead River Inn?'

Suddenly, far off in the forest, we heard a horn honking, followed by the noise of an approaching truck engine. Brenda leaped to her feet and ran to the screen window looking out to the road. Charley kept his eyes on her as he rose.

'It's Pelletier,' she said.

Charley turned to Brenda. 'Why don't you stay here while we go see what he wants?'

'I don't want to talk to that asshole, anyway.'

316

I reached down and grabbed the shotgun. Then I followed Charley out the door and through the middle cabin.

Pelletier's new truck was coming down the road fast, bouncing over the sun-hardened ruts. It braked at the edge of the dooryard, and Pelletier poked his head out the window and shouted over the diesel engine, 'You got a call back at the camp.'

'Who from?'

'Soctomah. He needs your plane.'

I felt my stomach sink. 'What's going on?'

'Truman's disappeared. They need you to help search for his truck.'

'What the hell for?'

'He wouldn't tell me. Soctomah wants you to call him. Hop in and I'll drive you back to camp.'

Charley stepped close to me. 'This is strange,' he said in a whisper.

'What do you think is happening?'

'Maybe the state police found something at Truman's place.'

'What should we do?'

'Go talk to Soctomah, I guess.' He turned back to the window from which Brenda was watching us. 'You mind coming out here, Miss Dean?'

'What for?' came her voice.

'We're going to take a ride over to the camp.'

'No way!'

I looked at Charley. 'You want me to drag her out?'

'No,' he said. 'I'll go with Russell and talk with

317

Soctomah. You stay here with the girl.'

'Do you trust Pelletier?'

'Trust him? No, but I don't think he's a murderer. I may have to leave right away. If I do, I'll leave a message with him. You can call me over the radio — or call Soctomah and he'll tell you what's going on.' He took a step toward the idling truck.

'Wait,' I said. 'Why were you asking her about Brodeur?'

'Whoever killed those men knew Brodeur was planning on driving out the back way, down that logging road. How did they know? I'm guessing Brodeur told the shooter himself.'

'You think he was in on it? You think someone double-crossed him?'

'Charley!' Pelletier shouted. 'Soctomah said it's urgent.'

'Stay with her,' Charley said. 'Whatever you do, don't let her out of your sight. And hang on to that shotgun.'

I glanced back at the kitchen cabin and saw Brenda move behind the screen. 'I plan to.'

He patted me on the shoulder and gave me his big grin. 'I'll be back in no time. If you run into trouble, call me on the radio phone!'

If I was confused before, this turn of events left me completely bewildered. Was it possible that Brenda was telling the truth about Truman? And if so, what did that suggest about Pelletier's involvement? Charley didn't believe that Russ was a killer, but I was past the point of trusting my instincts.

I found Brenda in the kitchen cabin, sitting up

on the picnic table, smoking a cigarette, drinking a beer: the dictionary definition of a nervous wreck. 'What happened?'

'The police are searching for Truman. They need Charley's plane.'

'I told you he did it!'

'We don't know what's going on.' I remained in the doorway, the shotgun against my shoulder. 'It might be something else.'

'It isn't,' she said confidently. 'So why are you still here?'

'Charley thought I should stay.'

'I don't need a bodyguard.' The words were defiant, but the look on her face was playful.

'How about a babysitter?'

She jumped down from the table and took a step forward, coming face to chest with me. 'I want to sit on the porch — if it's all right with you.'

I stepped aside. She shoved open the screen door and plopped into one of the two Adirondack chairs my dad had built by hand. I leaned against the porch railing, gazing out at the water. The lake shined with a blue light through the trees.

There was a long silence between us that made me uncomfortable.

'You really cleaned up this place,' I said at last. 'I almost didn't recognize it.'

'Jack needs someone to take care of him. All men do.'

I smiled in spite of myself. 'You think we're all a bunch of slobs.'

'The one thing I know about — living here all my life — is men.'

I was still chewing over that remark when I heard the sputter of Charley's Super Cub coming to life. Then the plane came skimming by on its pontoons and I watched it lifted upward into the sky as if by an invisible hand. The sound it made — an insect-like hum — grew fainter and fainter until finally all I could hear were the real insects in the pines and the lake lapping against the shore.

'Well,' I said, mostly to myself. 'He's gone.'

'Good,' she said.

28

When I worked at Rum Pond, the only time Brenda and I ever spent together was in the kitchen. She'd be peeling potatoes for dinner while I scrubbed out the pots from lunch. I can't recall a single conversation we ever had. She was twelve, and I was sixteen, and, at the time, that was a pretty big gap.

My only real memory of actually conversing with her came one afternoon, just before I packed my bags and went home. I was mopping the pine floor in the dining room. After a while, I got the sense of someone watching me — that cold-breath feeling along the back of the neck. I looked up and she was standing in the kitchen door, this stick-figure girl, all braids and cheekbones, watching me with a weird expression. I can only describe it as hatred.

'I heard you're leaving,' she said.

'Tomorrow. I'm going back to Scarborough.'

'Why?'

'My dad doesn't really want me here. No one does.'

Her hands were balled into fists by her sides. 'I hope you get in an accident,' she said, and darted back into the kitchen.

Those were the last words she spoke to me. At the time I remember finding that interchange funny. I remember shaking my head and laughing. And then I forgot all about them — and her — for eight years.

'I never thought about what it was like for you growing up here,' I said now. 'Being the only female.'

'Doreen Pelletier was here until a few years ago, but you know how she was — the old witch. And there were always women guests. But puberty was no picnic, if that's what you mean. After a while, though, you get used to the itty-bitty-titty jokes.' She was slouched in her Adirondack chair, watching me with those animal-black eyes of hers. 'So now what?'

'We stay put.'

'For how long?'

'Until Charley comes back.'

'You mean we just sit here all day?'

'We don't have to sit,' I said. 'We can go over to Rum Pond and I can use the radio phone and find out what's going on.'

She folded her arms across her breasts. 'I told you I'm not going over there.'

'Then it looks like we're staying put.' I removed the single shotgun shell from the chamber and put it in my pocket.

'What are you doing that for? If Truman shows up, he'll kill us both.'

'If he shows up, I'll reload it.'

She shook her head in disbelief. 'You won't have time. You'll never hear him coming. The next thing you know you'll be looking down at your chest wondering how that bullet hole got there.'

'Thanks for the warning.'

She let out a big laugh. 'You're such an asshole.'

'I get called that a lot. It goes with my job.' Or at least it used to, I thought.

'It has nothing to do with your job,' she said with a cockeyed grin. 'You're just an asshole personally.'

I could see how this day was going to go.

'You used to be a nice guy,' she said. 'That summer you lived here, I really liked you, even though you never paid any attention to me. What happened to you?'

'Nothing happened to me.'

'Yeah, it did. How come you left that summer, anyway? It was only July and you were supposed to stay through August.'

'I was tired of being Russell's serf.'

'You never said good-bye to me.' She finished her beer and then shook the can to see if she had missed a drop. She hadn't. 'You didn't like me then, and you don't like me now. I think I make you nervous.'

The sun slid out from behind a cloud and suddenly it became very bright and hot again on the porch.

'You don't,' I said.

'It's the thought of me and your old man doing the nasty.' The beer had given her voice a raspy edge. 'It really bothers you, doesn't it?'

'We're not going to have a conversation about this.'

She smiled as if this was the exact response she'd hoped for. 'You get a picture in your head of us humping, and it freaks you out.'

'Enough, Brenda.'

'Or maybe,' she said, 'it turns you on. Yeah, that's what it is. It turns you on to think about us having sex.'

'End of conversation.'

She stood up from the Adirondack chair. 'I'm getting another beer. You want one?'

'No, thanks. And I don't think you should have one, either.'

'Yeah, well, you don't get a vote on what I put in my body.'

She opened the screen door and disappeared into the kitchen. Charley said to watch her — as if she might try something. Did he suspect Brenda of being the killer? And why had he asked her those questions about Brodeur? The suggestion was that she and my father might somehow have conspired with the deputy. Did Charley think they'd double-crossed him after he delivered Shipman to the ambush site?

And what the hell happened with Truman that the police were now searching for him so intently? Was it really possible he and Pelletier had set my dad up?

The door banged open, as if she'd kicked it, and she came out, holding two cans of beer. 'I brought you one, anyway.'

'I don't want it.'

She came over to me and set the beer down on the railing. Then she leaned forward on her elbows and gazed past me out at the lake. She was so close I could smell her sun-warmed hair. 'You really do look like him,' she said, without looking at me.

324

'Excuse me?'

'You look like Jack. Younger, though, and without the beard. Thinner, too.'

'What are you trying to do, Brenda?'

She gave me a look of wide-eyed innocence. 'What do you mean?'

'Why are you playing games with me?'

She didn't answer at first but turned back toward the water. 'I'm bored,' she said finally. 'I get bored easily.'

'Then find something to do.'

With that, she straightened up and gave me a huge smile. It was as if a beautiful idea had arrived in her head like a dove from heaven. 'I'm going swimming.'

'Swimming? You're not afraid Truman's going to show up?'

'If he does, you'll protect me.'

Don't be so sure, I wanted to say.

★ ★ ★

I waited outside the cabin for Brenda to put on her bathing suit. From moment to moment she seemed either much older or much younger than her actual age of twenty. She would look at me, and there would be a sad exhaustion in her eyes that reminded me of old people I'd seen in nursing homes. Then the next minute she would become this flirty teenager. Were these sudden shifts calculated or could she just not control herself?

Pelletier said that my father loved her as he hadn't loved anyone since my mother. The more

I thought about it, the more I believed that this was the truth. Brenda was definitely attractive, and her emotions were just as volatile as my mom's.

So why had he left her behind when he turned fugitive? If he truly loved her, as Pelletier said, why did he leave her behind at Rum Pond?

I was still trying to figure it out when the cabin door opened and she came out wearing a purple bikini top and cut-off blue jeans. Her arms and legs were tanned a deep brown and her skin was so tight across her stomach I could have traced the abdominal muscles with my finger. She had freed her black hair from its braid and now it spilled loose over her shoulders.

'Let's go swimming.' She grabbed a towel from the clothesline that hung between two of the pine trees nearest the porch and skipped down the stairs to the water's edge. I tucked the shotgun under my arm and followed.

She waded out until she was waist-deep, then dived headfirst into the water. I took a seat on a sun-heated granite boulder beside the canoe and waited for her to come up for air.

But she didn't.

Half a minute passed, and then a full minute. I knew she was playing with me, but it didn't seem to make a difference. I felt my pulse quicken in spite of myself.

Finally her head appeared, maybe fifty feet from shore. 'You should come in!'

I ignored her invitation and glanced instead over at the sporting camp across the cove. I saw Pelletier's truck parked beside the lodge door, but there was no other sign of him.

'Hey, asshole, I'm talking to you!'

Brenda began swimming toward me until she was in just over her head, treading water. For maybe a minute she was silent, her expression pure anger. Then out of nowhere a smile broke across her face. It was as if a switch got thrown somewhere.

'You're so uptight,' she said. 'What is it with you cop types?'

'Was Bill Brodeur uptight, too?'

In an instant the anger was back. 'Screw you,' she spat at me, before disappearing again beneath the surface.

★ ★ ★

She swam for a while longer. Then she emerged, dried off, spread the towel across a flat patch of pebble beach, and lay down in the sun. All without a word to me.

The lake was utterly still. Not a trace of a breeze ruffled the surface. The sky between the mountains was such a deep blue I would have believed the earth's atmosphere was burning away with each advancing hour.

Brenda rolled over onto her stomach. Her back was slick with perspiration.

'You're going to get burned,' I said.

'You already are.'

She was right. I hadn't used sunscreen this morning, and the skin of my face was beginning to feel tight as a mask. I tried moving back into the shade of the pines, but it was only a little less bright and just as hot. A cicada whined in the tree above me, the sound jabbing through my eardrums.

'I want to go over to the sporting camp,' I said. She opened her eyes. 'What for?'

'I want to call Charley. I'd like to know what's happening with Truman.'

'Pelletier would've come over if there was anything to report.'

'I'm not so sure about that.'

She propped herself up on her elbows. 'I'm not going.'

I rose to my feet. 'I'm not asking you, Brenda. We're going, both of us.'

She climbed to her feet. There were little dents in her knees from the gravel on the beach. 'I want to put some clothes on.'

'What the hell for?'

'It'll just take a second.'

Before I could respond she was running up the stairs.

⋆ ⋆ ⋆

A few minutes passed, and she didn't reappear. I looked up at the camp, half-hidden amid the trees on the hillside. What the hell was she up to? Did she have another firearm up there?

'Shit,' I said aloud.

I removed the single shell from my pocket and slid it into the chamber of the shotgun. Slowly I climbed the plank steps, feeling certain that she was watching me from behind one of the darkened window screens.

As my head came level with the porch I said,
'Brenda?'

'In here.'

Her voice came from the cabin on the left
— the one where my father slept. With the sun
shining directly against the side of the building, I
couldn't see inside.

'What's the holdup?'

'It's all right, you can come in.'

I gripped the door handle and pulled. A beam
of dusty sunlight shined ahead of me. In it I saw
a chest of drawers and my father's big iron bed,
but I didn't see Brenda. I stepped inside.

She was standing naked in the near corner of
the room.

'Jesus.' I turned my head away, tried to back
up, missed the door. 'Put some clothes on!'

'I saw how you were looking at me.'

'You're crazy.' I kept my head turned but I
could still see her out of the corner of one eye.
She took a step closer.

'I could see what you wanted to do to me.'

'I'll be outside.' I spun away and reached for
the door.

She grabbed me from behind, her arms
closing around my waist. Through my T-shirt I
felt her breasts against my back. 'I was in love
with you first.'

'Brenda,' I said, reaching down to peel her
hands away.

'I want you to fuck me, Mike.'

'Stop,' I said. 'Stop.'

Her breath was heavy with alcohol. 'Please.'

I closed my hand about her wrist and yanked

it away. The force made her cry out with pain, and when I turned around her eyes were fierce and her mouth was open, and I could see her teeth.

'No.' I squeezed her wrist. 'It's not going to happen.'

'Jack likes it rough, too.'

I pushed her away. She was surprised and nearly fell back onto the bed. She knew I meant it now and her mouth curled up on one side. 'What's wrong with you? You afraid you can't get it up?'

'Put some clothes on,' I said, turning my back to her.

'Jack was right,' she called after me. 'You are a faggot.'

★　★　★

The unopened can of beer she'd brought me before was still on the railing. It was warm, but I opened it and drank it down.

How many beers had she had, anyway? Sally Reynolds had said she was a regular at the bar at the Dead River Inn. I could easily believe it. With each drink she seemed to grow more aggressive: conversationally, physically, sexually. Back in Flagstaff she'd seemed so helpless, so much in need of my protection. Now all that tamped-down anger inside her was coming out.

I heard the door open behind me.

She'd put on a T-shirt and the same damp cut-off denims she'd worn on the beach. The look she gave me when our eyes met showed nothing but disdain.

'Let's go,' I said.

She didn't budge. She shook a cigarette out of a pack and put it between her lips and tried to light it, but the lighter wouldn't flame. 'Shit.'

Just then, I heard a single, sharp, cracking noise in the distance.

'That sounded like a gunshot.'

'It's Pelletier hammering again. He's been doing it all day.'

'I don't think so.' The truth was I had been distracted and wasn't sure what I'd heard. But I had a bad feeling. 'Come on, let's go.'

She gestured toward the kitchen. 'I need to get a match.'

I removed the cigarette from her lips and dropped it on the porch. This time, she didn't fight me.

29

Brenda refused to paddle. She sat in the front of the canoe with her arms crossed and her back rigid as a wall. When we reached the opposite shore of the cove, she surprised me by jumping into the shallows and hauling us up onto the beach beside Pelletier's other boats.

'I thought you were going to stay in the canoe,' I said.

For an answer she gave me a stone-faced look. I swapped the paddle for the shotgun and followed her up the dirt path. The plate-glass windows of the main lodge were mirrors reflecting a backward image of the lake and the mountains. The sky had been neon blue all morning, but now I saw tall, cumulus clouds piling up to the west of Holeb Mountain. I didn't like the look of them. I didn't like how deserted the sporting camp felt, either.

We paused outside the screen door. 'Russell?'

There was no answer.

Again, Brenda startled me by forging ahead. Inside, a bitter smell hung in the air. In the dining room the blackened coffeepot was beginning to smoke. I switched the machine off and followed her through the kitchen and pantry. Pelletier was nowhere to be found.

We backtracked out to the great room and tried a different hall. The door to the camp office was ajar and I peered in. The radio phone sat on a shelf beneath the only window.

'I wonder where he is,' I said.

'Probably jerking off in his cabin.'

Not an image I cared to have in my head. 'Maybe he went into town.'

'He's probably in his cabin.' Brenda took a step in the direction of the kitchen door. When I didn't move, she said, 'Come on.'

'I'm going to call Charley.' I entered the office and sat down behind the desk.

She hung in the doorway as if a spell prevented her from entering the room. 'Pelletier doesn't like people in his office.'

I ignored the warning and dialed Charley's cell-phone number. He answered almost immediately: 'Charley Stevens!'

'It's Mike.'

He spoke loudly above the noise of his plane: 'I tried calling Rum Pond a while ago but didn't get any answer.'

'I don't know where Pelletier is. I'm here with Brenda and we can't find him.'

'That's queer,' he said.

'He was hammering before, but I haven't heard him for a while.' I glanced out the window, but the office faced the lake, not the cabins. 'He'll probably turn up. What's going on?'

'The detective got an anonymous tip this morning to check Truman's apartment. When they showed up they found he'd vamoosed. The door was open, though, so they had a peek inside. I can't tell you what they found, but it's changed their minds about a few things.'

So Truman had vanished, too. What the hell

333

had Soctomah found in his apartment? 'If they're looking for Truman now, what does that mean for my dad?'

'He's still a fugitive . . . ' His voice trailed off. 'Listen, I want you to ask the girl something for me.'

My eyes flicked from the window back to the doorway. Brenda was no longer there. 'She's gone.'

'What?'

'She was just standing here. I looked away for a second and she disappeared.'

'You need to find her.'

A door slammed inside the lodge. I closed my hand around the shotgun resting on the desk before me. Suddenly Brenda appeared in the door again. Her chest was rising and falling. 'Come quick!'

'What is it?'

'Pelletier!' She dashed back down the hall without waiting for me.

'What's going on?' Charley asked.

'I don't know, but it's something to do with Pelletier. She wants me to follow her.'

'Do you still have that shotgun?'

'Yes.'

'Hold on to it. I'm going to head over your way. Should I get a patrol car out there?'

'I don't know,' I said. 'I'll call you right back.'

'All right, but don't let her out of your sight.'

'She already is.'

'Be careful, son.'

★ ★ ★

334

I reloaded the shell and switched off the safety. Then I moved cautiously down the hall and out the back door. I wasn't sure which way she'd gone, but Pelletier's truck was parked behind his private cabin, so that was where I started.

When I came around the corner of the building I saw the door standing open. I saw something else, too: a trail of blood that led from the porch into the undergrowth at the edge of the forest.

'Brenda?'

I found her standing just inside the door, holding both hands over her mouth.

On the floor lay Russell Pelletier.

He was lying on his back with his arms out. His head rested on a big bearskin rug in front of the fireplace. A pool of blood spread out beneath him like red wings. Near one hand lay a hunting knife with a bloody blade. Both of his eyes stared up at the rafters.

I knelt down and checked his pulse with two fingers, but I felt nothing. The body was still warm, but the skin had begun to take on a waxy look and a faint grayish color around the lips.

Don't touch anything is the first lesson you learn about crime scenes. Brenda's bare feet had left bloody smears along the floorboards. Her toes were painted red with it. But there were other tracks as well — the prints of a man's heavy boots. Not Pelletier's.

I scanned the floor. The shell casing from the murder weapon had rolled partway under the paw of the bearskin rug. The brass came from a rifle, but not being free to pick it up, I couldn't say what caliber.

'There's no sign of a knife wound,' I said aloud. 'Which means the blood on the knife isn't his. Before he died, he must have stabbed the person who shot him.'

'Truman,' she said, speaking slowly and softly. 'Truman did this.'

I rose to my feet and closed my hand around her bare arm, trying to move her toward the door. But her whole body was dead weight. 'We have to call the police.'

'But he's still out there.'

'I think he's wounded. He won't get far.'

'You have to find him — before he kills us.'

'We'll sit tight and wait for help. We'll be fine.'

'What was that?' She turned her head sharply in the direction of the open door. 'I heard a noise!' She pulled loose of me and darted outside.

'Brenda!'

I saw her sprint around the corner of the cabin, headed for the main lodge. Then, taking a step into the open, I heard a sharp metal-on-metal sound come from somewhere in the trees. The noise put me in mind of a car door slamming. The killer was still here. And I was letting him escape.

The blood trail showed brightly in the sunlight, a wet red path leading into the bushes. When Pelletier stabbed his murderer, he must have severed an artery, there was such a spray of it. A man couldn't bleed like that and live, not without medical attention. My heart was seized with a perverse hope: It was Truman trying to get away, Truman dying from loss of blood. But what if it wasn't him? What if it was my father? I couldn't leave him to die in the forest. I had to know for certain.

I took the first few steps without realizing what I was doing. Then a cloud drifted across the sun and fear hit me. I entered the woods, following the blood trail.

I put my feet down softly, as I had learned stalking deer, heel first and then toe, avoiding dry leaves and fallen branches where I could, pausing every few steps to listen. Young birches and poplars had sprouted up along the forest edge, and the green of their leaves showed the red of the fallen blood.

The trail could have been made by a drunken man. It staggered left and right, leading first deeper into the woods and then veering back toward the camp road. Here and there, shafts of sunlight pierced through the canopy to the pine-needle floor of the forest. In those sunlit patches the blood drops were bright as rubies.

Sweat rolled down into my eyes and stung like acid. I thought of the stories my father had told me of trailing gut-shot deer for miles, how often the deer ended up circling back because, even mortally wounded, they feared to leave the safety of their home territories, as if anything worse could happen to them. And I wondered whether the man I was tracking had circled back behind me and was even now aiming a rifle at me from some secret place in the trees.

The trail angled sharply to the right. Up ahead

a green wall of raspberry bushes grew along the shoulder of the camp road, blocking it from view. The bushes were very thick, and I knew I would have to bust my way through them to get to the road. When I stepped out into the sun, I would be an easy target for a man with a rifle.

I paused beside a big pine and scanned left and right, looking for a way through the tangle of bushes.

That was when I caught sight of the truck. It was parked up the road from the camp, thirty or so yards from me. All I could make out was a metallic flash of blue amid the forest-green. But I knew.

It was a blue Chevy with an ATV in the bed. Truman's truck.

I felt a giddy, lifting sensation in my heart, as if I'd just taken a strong drink. It was Truman after all. He had killed Pelletier, he had killed Shipman and Brodeur. Charley had been wrong about my father. Everyone had been wrong.

But where was Truman? Maybe he had made it to the truck and passed out. Maybe he was sprawled in the road, dead. Or maybe he had heard me coming and was waiting in ambush to shoot me even as his blood drained away.

If he was waiting for me, it made sense that he was watching the road in the direction of the camp. He would expect me to come that way. In which case, the best bet would be to come around him from behind. I would need to circle a dense stand of firs to do that. The balsams were no taller than big Christmas trees, but they grew together so closely I couldn't easily slip through them. I followed the outer edge of the stand deeper into the forest, stepping carefully over fallen trees whose branches rose into the air like spikes. The ground was very dry, and no matter how slowly I stepped, twigs snapped. I felt as stealthy as a freight train.

A bend in the road hid the truck from view. My scratched and sweaty arms were powdered with dust, and my T-shirt was smeared red with raspberries. I wiped the perspiration from my hands on my pants and did my best to dry the shotgun grip with my shirttail. Then I filled my lungs full of air.

I moved along the side of the road, staying in shadows as much as possible. Soon I could see the rear end of the truck. The bed was open. Truman was nowhere in sight. I crossed to the other side of the road to have a look at the driver's side.

Truman was slumped against the door, his legs out in front of him, holding both hands over his stomach as if he'd eaten too much. He wasn't moving. Even from a distance of twenty yards I could see the puddle of blood under his legs. The rifle lay in the dirt a few feet away.

I trained the shotgun on him and edged forward. 'Truman Dellis!'

He didn't move.

I drew closer, keeping the shotgun aimed at his chest. I'd seen so much death in my job, I thought I could always recognize it. But now I wasn't sure what I was seeing.

Truman's eyes were closed and his head lolled to one side, motionless. I saw the slash where

Pelletier had stabbed him in the gut. His shirt bore the red handprints he'd made trying to keep the life from draining out of himself. The blood lay in a viscous puddle at my feet. I kicked the rifle away from his hand. He didn't even twitch.

I wedged the butt of the shotgun in the crook of my right arm to hold it one-handed, and then I knelt down to feel for a pulse in his throat. And as I did, Truman grabbed me.

30

I lurched backward, but his grip was too strong to break. Wild eyed, panting hard, with blood smeared across his teeth, he yanked with his free hand at the barrel of the shotgun. I tried to bring the butt up against his jawbone, but he threw his weight, and we both fell over onto the bloody ground.

My breath exploded out of me with the impact, and it was all I could do to keep hold of the gun. He had the barrel by both hands now, trying to wrench it away. I brought a knee up between us, wedging us apart, pushing against his wounded gut.

He let out a howl and punched me hard in the nose. Lights flashed in my eyes. He was fighting for his life, struggling for control of the gun. I drew my knees up again, but he just kept coming.

Hands slick with blood, I felt myself losing my grip.

I don't know which one of us pulled the trigger.

It all happened in a millisecond. The recoil drove the shotgun hard into my stomach. Through a blue haze that burned my eyes I saw him jerk back, as if in super-fast motion, and in that same instant I was splattered with blood.

The smell of cordite hung in the air. My eardrums ached.

Oh, God, I thought.

Somehow I was on my feet, breathing hard, pointing the empty, shaking shotgun at his motionless body. Half of his head was gone. Above the jaw there was nothing I recognized as a human face, just blood and tissue and scraps of skull.

I had to brace myself against the truck bed to keep from collapsing, trying to swallow down the taste of vomit. How had this happened?

Truman's hunting rifle lay in the dirt near the front tire of the truck. I stared at it dumbly. Why didn't he just shoot me as I came up on him? Why had he played dead? None of this made sense.

His shirt had rolled up and I could see the clean stab wound through his soft gut. With a gash like that, he'd been bleeding to death even before I shot him. As if that absolved me.

I knelt down beside the man I'd killed.

I'm not sure how long it took me to notice the bruises. Five minutes might have passed before the wounds around Truman's wrists caught my eye. Then it came to me what the raw-looking marks were, and the recognition had the force of someone stomping on my chest.

I grabbed Truman's rifle and ejected the magazine.

The rifle was a bolt-action Remington 30-06 — the same caliber that Soctomah claimed had been used to kill Shipman and Brodeur. I was almost certain this rifle had also been used to kill

Pelletier less than half an hour ago. From the smell alone I knew it had just been fired.

But there were no bullets in it now. Pelletier had been killed by a single gunshot to the chest. It didn't make any sense that Truman's rifle should be unloaded. And why were there rope burns on his wrists?

★   ★   ★

The sun was playing hide-and-seek behind dark clouds as I sprinted back to Pelletier's cabin. The air had become heavier, and a breeze now stirred the leaves along the road.

Outside and inside the cabin I searched frantically for clues I might have missed the first time. The story told itself in blood: Truman Dellis and Russell Pelletier had an altercation in the cabin. Pelletier stabbed Truman with a hunting knife, and Truman, somehow, improbably shot Pelletier through the chest, using the same rifle with which he'd killed Jonathan Shipman and Bill Brodeur. The co-conspirators had eliminated each other. There was no apparent explanation for their quarrel, but it offered a tidy resolution to the murder investigation with only one question left unanswered: Where was my father?

I needed to call the police.

★   ★   ★

When I came around the corner of Pelletier's cabin, I found Brenda standing in the lodge

343

doorway, holding a long-barreled Ruger revolver in one hand. I stopped in my tracks.

'What happened?' she asked, gaping at the blood on my skin and clothes. 'I heard a shot.'

'It was Truman,' I said.

'Is he dead?'

I nodded. 'I'm sorry.'

'I'm not.' Her mouth tightened into a sneering smile that scared the hell out of me — even more than the Ruger.

I was out in the open with nothing to hide behind and no shells left in my shotgun. 'Where did you get that pistol?'

'Pelletier's safe. I know the combination.'

I took a step toward the door. 'I need to call the police.'

'They're on their way,' she said quickly.

'You called them?' I tried to hide the disbelief in my voice.

'Yeah.'

'I should talk to Detective Soctomah myself.'

She refused to move aside. 'What are you going to tell him?'

I kept my eyes on the revolver. If it was the gun Russell had showed me once, it was chambered with a .44 Magnum round for bear hunting. 'Pelletier and Truman killed Shipman and Brodeur. I don't know why. Maybe they thought they could scare off Wendigo, make them change their plans for Rum Pond. They framed my father. Then they killed each other.'

'I told you they did it! I told you Jack was innocent!'

'Yes, you did.'

She narrowed her eyes. 'You don't sound convinced.'

'It's what happened.'

'Did Truman say that?'

'We didn't have a conversation. He grabbed the shotgun and it went off.'

She didn't smile exactly, but there was a look of glee in her eyes that shocked me. I had no idea how much she'd hated him.

'What the hell did he do to you?' I asked.

She bared her teeth. 'He killed my mom.'

'What?'

'They were walking home from a bar one night, shit-faced. She fell down into a ditch. He let her freeze to death, he was so drunk. He just came home and crawled into bed, and he never remembered a thing. They found her the next morning lying in a snow bank. I was seven years old. We came to Rum Pond after that. So, yeah, I'm glad he's dead.'

I looked at her, stunned into silence for the longest time. Then I took another step forward. 'I need to call Soctomah.'

The Ruger came up, pointed at my chest. 'Something's wrong with you.'

'I just killed a man.' I lifted the barrel of the shotgun slightly. 'Now I need to call the police. So why don't you put the gun down and get the fuck out of the way.'

It was the wrong thing to say.

The first shot from the Ruger tore through the air centimeters from my head. I heard the .44 slug smack into the cabin wall behind me as I hit the ground.

'Don't move!' she said.

She fired the second and third shots into the air.

When I raised my head, she shouted again, 'Don't fucking move!'

I pressed my forehead to the dirt. 'Take it easy.'

She advanced on me until I could glimpse her dusty bare feet, the barbed-wire tattoo around one slender ankle. I had a jackknife in my pocket, but that was all by way of a weapon.

'Shut up! Just shut up. Lie there and don't do anything stupid.'

So we waited, me with my hands folded behind my head, my heart drumming against the ground. Overhead, I heard the wind rising in the pine boughs and felt the shadow of clouds creep across the sky. Rain was coming.

'What did Truman tell you?' she asked.

'Nothing.'

'He told you something.'

'He didn't have to.'

'What do you mean?'

But before I could answer, I heard another voice, a baritone: 'What happened? Why did you signal me?'

I raised my head a little and saw a tall man materialize, as if from nowhere, out of the bushes across the road. He was dressed completely in breakup camouflage, the brown-and-gray pattern used by turkey hunters. His pants were mud-spattered and tucked into rubber boots, and he carried a deer rifle on a sling over his shoulder. He wore gloves and a camouflage hat with a thin mask that hung over the face like a brown veil.

'He knows!' Brenda said. 'Truman must have told him.'

The man pulled the mask loose, and for the first time in two years I saw my father's face.

31

You cannot describe betrayal. To someone who has never suffered it, there is no adequate way to communicate the sudden loss of balance that comes when you discover you've been played for a fool. Especially when the person who has betrayed you is someone you love. In a single heartbeat, betrayal throws everything else in your life into doubt. If this was false, what else is? Shame and second-guessing set in immediately. The signs were there all along, so how did you miss them? Sometimes the humiliation of being betrayed is so powerful you retreat back into disbelief. Denial, after all, is a pretty strong narcotic.

But for me there was no escape back into self-delusion. When I discovered the marks around Truman's wrists and found his rifle to be unloaded, it sent a surge of panic through me. Instinctually, I knew what these things meant, but I didn't allow myself to acknowledge the full implications of what I was seeing. Now there was no looking away from the terrible truth.

My father's eyes seared me with the consequences of my folly.

His face was deeply tanned with blue hollows beneath the eyes and more gray in the beard than I remembered — my face in twenty-five years, maybe, if I lived that long. He looked big, barrel-chested, and broad-shouldered in his camouflage shirt, but not as big as he had once seemed to me.

'Truman must have told him,' Brenda said.

'No,' said my father. 'Mike shot him before he could say anything.'

She looked confused, frantic. 'How did he know then?'

'The ropes,' I said from the ground.

He swung the rifle off his shoulder and tucked the stock under one arm casually so that he could fire it with one hand if he needed to. 'Get up, Mike. Slowly. This situation has already gotten too far out of hand. And I know you're prone to stupid heroics.'

I pushed myself up on my knees. I felt as though I'd had the wind knocked out of me.

'That's far enough.'

'You wouldn't shoot me,' I said with all the confidence I could muster.

'I would!' Brenda, her face flushed with anger and alcohol, waved the .44 in my face. 'What's he talking about? What ropes?'

'You wanted to frame them,' I said. 'Pelletier and Truman — you wanted to frame them for those murders. That's why you came back here.'

He scratched his beard as if waiting for me to continue.

'You kidnapped Truman back in town and drove him out here in his truck. Then you shot Pelletier. You stabbed Truman with Russell's knife, and cut him loose so he would run. You wanted him to bleed to death. You wanted to make it look like they killed each other, but you messed up. The ropes you tied him with left cuts

349

and burns around his wrists.'

'What else?' Like any failed trapper, he wanted to know how he'd given himself away.

'Truman's rifle,' I said. 'It didn't make sense it was unloaded. You planted that rifle there to incriminate him.'

'How'd you figure it all out?'

'I remembered something you told me when I was a kid. You said the secret to trapping is covering your own tracks.'

He smiled a rueful smile. 'I taught you a good lesson.'

'You didn't teach me a damned thing.'

The smile went away. 'You got your mother's smart mouth, that's for sure.'

I thought of my mom. We had both believed in him, both argued on his behalf against Neil. Now my father was bad-mouthing her. 'How'd you know I'd come out here?' I asked. 'You couldn't have planned that. There's no way.'

'We didn't,' he said.

Brenda jumped in. 'We just wanted the cops to go to Truman's place again so they would start looking for him. Then, after Jack took care of things, I was going to call in them two killing each other. We never figured that old fart would fly you out here.'

The mention of Charley gave me a fleeting sensation of hope. He should be here soon, I thought. But was he bringing the police with him? Either way, I needed to stall them.

I looked my father hard in the eye. 'So what did you plant at Truman's apartment to make the cops think he was the killer? It couldn't have been the murder weapon since you brought that here.'

'My boots, the ones I wore that night. I left them on the porch for the cops to find.'

'Not too subtle.'

'Yeah, well, Truman was an idiot. He'd do something that dumb.'

In my mind's eye I saw the headless body again. 'Everyone thinks you're in Canada.'

'I know.'

'That's why you called Mom from across the border,' I said.

'What's he talking about?' said Brenda, slurring her words.

'I called Marie,' he said.

The muscles in her shoulders tightened. 'You didn't tell me that.'

'I wanted them to keep looking for me in Canada.'

Her eyes blazed. 'Now what are we supposed to do?'

My father reached into the pack on his belt. I saw Brenda flinch as if she half-expected him to produce a handgun to shoot her. But he only drew out a tangle of bloody rope.

'I'm sorry about this, Mike,' he said. 'But until we can talk this out, it's the only way.'

He tied my arms behind me with the same red-stained cord he'd used to bind Truman. I thought of resisting, but then decided not to. I'd seen what he'd done to Pelletier and Truman and Shipman and Brodeur — four men dead at his hands. But even now, I couldn't believe he was really capable of killing me. Brenda, however, was another story. Adrenaline and alcohol had given her eyes a big-pupiled glassiness that worried the hell out of me.

Gently, my father directed me inside the lodge. He guided me back to the dining room, with its long tables and its view of the lake through plate-glass windows. Clouds darkened the sky above Holeb Mountain. 'Sit down,' he said.

The smell of burnt coffee hung in the air.

Brenda perched across from me, sitting on a tabletop with her dirty feet on the bench and her denim-covered crotch level with my eyes, resting the heavy handgun on her knees.

My father found a bottle of whiskey in a cabinet and brought it out. He took a slug.

'I want some of that,' she said.

He splashed a little whiskey in a coffee mug and handed it to her. 'You want a drink, Mike?'

'No.'

Brenda wiped her mouth. 'So what do we do now?'

'That's up to Mike.' He softened his voice. 'I know this is hard for you, son. Hell, it's hard for me. I never wanted any of this to happen, but it did, and now my neck's on the chopping block. You think I could actually surrender without some pissed-off cop popping me first?'

My voice broke. 'I believed you. I told everyone you were innocent. I came up here to prove it.'

'I appreciate that, and I'm sorry I had to mislead you. But I needed your help. I still do.'

'I'm not going to lie for you, if that's what you're asking.'

He shook his head, sadly. 'You don't understand.'

'What's to understand? You killed four men — one a police officer and three others just to cover your own tracks.'

He raised three fingers. 'I killed three men. You killed Truman.'

'After you stabbed him.'

'But you were the one who shot him. Do you think the police are going to believe your story? They're going to think you were part of this from the start, the way you ran around trying to pin the shootings on Truman and Pelletier. How do you think it's going to look to them when we tell them you killed Truman.'

I felt like I'd been spat upon. 'So now you're trying to blackmail me?'

'I'm just laying out the situation so you see what's in all of our best interest.'

'I'm not to going to keep quiet. I'll tell the state police what I know. I don't care how the hell it looks. And if you run, I'll do everything I can to help them catch you.'

My father took his hat off and set it down on the table and ran his hand through his gray-flecked hair. I saw the exhaustion in the slump of his shoulders, the shadowed sockets around his eyes. Maybe I could capitalize on that exhaustion until help arrived.

'What I want is to know is why you did it,' I said.

'What does it matter?'

'It matters to Jonathan Shipman's children.'

'Who?'

At first I thought he was joking. Then it came to me. 'It was never about Wendigo. All this time everyone thought Shipman was the target. They assumed the deputy just happened to be in the wrong place at the wrong time. But it was the other way around. It was Brodeur you were after.'

He stood at the broad window with his back to us, the rifle slung over his shoulder, holding the liquor bottle and gazing out at the chop blowing across the lake. Gray, watery light streamed around his bulky silhouette.

'But why?' I asked. 'Why'd you do it?'

'You wouldn't understand.'

Brenda gulped down the rest of her bourbon.

'It was because of you, wasn't it?' I said to her.

'Screw you.'

'Did you fuck Brodeur — is that it?'

My father turned around, his face dark with warning.

'That pig raped me,' she said.

'Just like Russell Pelletier tried to do?'

'Shut your mouth, Mike,' my father said.

'She's lying.'

'I am not,' she said. 'He raped me and he got what he deserved.'

'No,' I said. 'I don't think that's what happened. I think that's what you *said* happened when my dad found out about you two.'

'You're full of shit.'

I spoke past her to my father. I knew I had his full attention. 'She told you Brodeur stopped her

354

one night driving back from the Dead River Inn, right? Sally Reynolds said she used to drive drunk all the time, and Brodeur used to stake out the inn. I bet she said he forced himself on her.'

'He did!' she said.

'No, I think what happened is you made a deal with him. He was going to arrest you for driving under the influence, so you offered to have sex with him. Maybe it became a regular thing after that for you two.' I glanced over her shoulder at my father's dark silhouette. 'Is that how you found out, Dad? You came home and found the deputy here and wondered what was going on. You were suspicious and angry and you scared her and that's when she told you about the rape.'

He put down the whiskey bottle and studied the back of her head for a long time before speaking. 'She said he wouldn't leave her alone.'

'Don't listen to him, Jack.' She slid off the table and approached him, holding the .44 loose in one hand. 'He's just trying to confuse you. That's why he's saying these things.'

'You said that cop was stalking you.'

'He was!' She pressed herself against his chest and gazed up into his eyes. 'Why would I help you kill him after that meeting? Why would I tell you where to ambush him if I didn't want him dead?'

'Because you were afraid,' I said. 'You knew what my dad would do to you if he found out the truth about you and Brodeur.'

'Screw you!'

'She set you up, Dad. You killed those men

355

because of a lie she told you, and now you've killed two more. All because of her. She's played you, and she played me.'

She pressed one hand flat at the base of his throat. 'Don't listen to him.'

'She tried to seduce me, too,' I said.

He shook his head as if he hadn't heard me clearly. 'What?'

'Less than an hour ago in your cabin. She took her clothes off.'

She spun around and aimed the handgun square between my eyes. 'I swear to God I'm going to shoot you if you don't shut your mouth.'

Reaching out, faster than I could have imagined possible, my father jerked the Ruger from her hands. I was surprised it didn't go off as he pulled it loose.

He leaned his face close to hers. 'Is that true?'

'No! He's lying again.'

'I'm not,' I said. 'I swear.'

'You little bitch.' He raised his hand as if to pistol-whip her.

'It wasn't like that! I just wanted to keep him from coming over here until you had a chance to do what we said.'

'So you spread your legs for him?' he said, his hand still poised to strike.

'I'm sorry, I'm sorry. You know I love you.'

'You don't!'

'I do. I do. Please, Jack. I'll be good, if you let me go. I'll be a good girl for you. Please.'

For an instant I thought he might punch the pistol grip into her face. But instead he tossed her down to the ground. She collapsed in a ball at his feet.

My father and mother had fought like this. I remembered how many nights the threat of violence had hung in the air of our rented trailer. But, unlike Brenda, my mother had never been a drunk. There is no desperation like that of two alcoholics clinging to each other even as they drive each other to madness. I felt as if I was witnessing something between them that no third party ever should. Was this why he came back for her — because she shared his particular insanity?

His eyes were wet with tears. 'Why do you do this to me?'

She shook her head and sobbed. 'I don't know.'

I had been trying to wriggle my arms free, but it was no use. The ropes only tightened. The nerves in my hands began to tingle as the blood flow dammed up.

He tucked the .44 into his belt. 'Get up,' he commanded her.

She crawled to the nearest bench and pulled herself up to a sitting position. She hung her head so that her dark hair hid her face and she rubbed her wrist with her good hand. 'I'm sorry,' she repeated. 'I don't know what's wrong with me.'

My father stood over her, breathing heavily. 'I don't, either.'

Brenda raised her head suddenly. 'What's that noise?'

At first I heard nothing but the refrigerator

whirring in the kitchen, then I became aware of a faint drone, almost a whine, growing louder. I'd forgotten about Charley in all that was going on.

'It's that old game warden!' she said. 'They were on the phone before.'

'You didn't tell me he was coming back.'

'I didn't know.'

'It's not just Charley Stevens,' I said. 'The police are on their way, too.'

The plane was approaching fast. Through the plate-glass window we saw it zip suddenly into view, headed down the lake away from us — white and red against a smoke-gray sky. In a few seconds Charley would circle around to bring the plane down on the water, facing the camp.

'Please, Dad,' I said. 'You've got to give yourself up. It's not too late.'

My father twisted around, his mouth tight with rage. It was not the expression of a man about to surrender. I felt a shudder ride up my spine. Then he slid the hunting rifle off his shoulder and shoved aside the door.

'No!' I said, rising to my feet.

Brenda rushed to the window and pressed both palms to the glass.

As Charley turned the Super Cub toward the camp I saw my father, standing with his back to the window, legs planted apart, lift the semiautomatic rifle and aim it carefully at the cockpit of the plane. The shots were sharp, percussive, and evenly spaced — one after the other after the other — and the plane gave a sudden jerk, like a flying bird wounded on the

358

wing, and rolled to one side. I saw the exposed white belly of the plane and thought it might spin completely over, but instead it righted itself briefly and turned away again, steadying.

But already my father was taking aim again. More shots rang out. The plane began to wobble as it retreated farther and farther down the lake. Charley couldn't hold the wings level.

The plane hit the water first with its pontoons but it bounced up again and when it hit the second time, it came down at an angle. One wing knifed the surface and broke apart. Far down the lake, half a mile or more, too far for me to see anything clearly, I watched the wing fly off and the aircraft go sharply down. With a tremendous, soundless splash it came to rest, floating, no longer a plane, just a white and red wreck. It was gone in less than a minute. I stumbled backward, knocking against a table.

My father loomed in the door. He had the face of a stone statue.

I couldn't answer, couldn't speak.

My heart was as big as the room.

32

For the longest time I couldn't will myself to move. Then rage began welling up inside of me, and the numbness went away. I struggled against the straitjacket of knots.

'You son of a bitch!'

'You should have told me he was coming back.' He lifted the whiskey bottle from the table and drank as if to quench a desperate thirst.

'You don't know what you've done,' I said.

He wiped his mouth and shook his head as if he felt sorry for me. He knew exactly what he had done.

'You're a goddamned coward,' I said.

'Shut up, Mike.'

'Fucking coward!'

The punch he gave me across the chin felt like a glancing blow from a sledgehammer. It snapped my head around, and I lost my balance and fell backward across a table. I tried to get up, but he grabbed me around the throat with one hand, thumb and forefinger digging into the nerve bundles beneath the jawbone, and he held me down with his weight until fireworks exploded across my retinas.

'I told him to call the police,' I gasped. 'They're coming right now.'

He brought his face close to mine. He stank of whiskey and sweat-drenched clothes and long hours spent wading through rotting peat bogs.

For a moment he stared into my eyes — so similar to his own in color and shape — and I knew he was trying to gauge my truthfulness by looking for the telltale signs of deceit in himself. What he saw, I don't know, but he let go of me, making a noise almost like a growl, and I slumped back onto the table.

From across the room Brenda said, 'Maybe we could use him as a hostage.'

My father stood above me, one hand gripping the butt of the .44 in his belt. Dusk was hours away, but a dark haze had come in through the windows. I saw a greasy smear of raindrops on the pane. A storm front was rolling out of Quebec.

'Jack?' she said.

'Let me think!'

Wind hissed through the chinks between the log walls of the cabin.

He removed the Ruger from his belt and waved it at me. 'Get up.'

I slid off the table, stumbled sideways a few steps, and straightened up. My jaw ached, my arms were numb.

Brenda put her hand on his forearm, but he shook it off as if he didn't like the feel of her flesh.

'What do we do?' she asked.

'Pack some food. We're getting out of here.'

*   *   *

Rain clattered on the metal roof, the first rain I'd heard since the night at Bud Thompson's farm when the bear had killed his pig. Had it only been a week? That night seemed a lifetime ago.

'Why did you call me?' I asked hoarsely.

'What?' He stood staring out the window, but the glass was so fogged with humidity he couldn't have seen a thing, not even his own reflection.

'The night you killed those men, you left a message on my answering machine.'

'I thought you could help me with the cops.'

So that was it. Even in the first hours following the murders he'd been looking for a way to cover his tracks. Among the alibis, excuses, and lies he might use to cover himself he had remembered his son, the game warden. Why was I so shocked to realize that his only thought of me was as a means of hiding his guilt?

'They'll find you,' I said to him. 'You can't escape.'

'You're coming with us.'

'I won't be your hostage.'

Brenda appeared in the dining room. She had found an olive-drab poncho which she'd pulled on over her T-shirt. She was lugging an overloaded rucksack with both hands. 'You want me to put this in the truck?'

'No. The canoe.'

'What?'

'We're going across the lake. They'll be looking for us on the road. I know places we can hide until we can cross over to Canada.'

She let the rucksack drop. 'I'm not going to hide in some wet hole.'

'Then stay here and go to jail for the rest of your life.'

'Why should I? I didn't kill anybody.'

He turned on her. 'What did you just say?'

'You killed those men, not me.'

He put his hand on the .44 in his belt. 'You want to stay here? I can arrange it.'

She gnawed at her lip but didn't answer.

'What'll it be?' he said.

She reached down and lifted the rucksack again. He nodded. Then he said to me, 'Get up, Mike.'

'No.'

He pulled the pistol loose from his belt and held it by his side. 'I said get up.'

'You won't shoot me.'

He pushed the muzzle of the gun against my sternum. I could see the calculations going on behind his eyes. Dead, I would be easier to manage and just as useful a hostage, as long as Soctomah believed I might still be alive. It made sense to shoot me. In his situation, it was the rational thing to do.

But, for whatever reason, he couldn't do it. He jammed the Ruger back in his belt and grabbed the ropes binding my arms and began to twist them. Pain shot up my arms like white-hot wires shoved under the skin. I tried to remain standing, but he kicked my legs out from under me.

He dragged me outside into the rain and mud. Exhausted as he was, his strength was still incredible for a man his age. My shoulders seemed about to pop loose from their sockets, and I bit my tongue from the pain. He dropped me in the sand beside the longest of Pelletier's battered aluminum canoes. I rolled onto my side. Wet sand stuck to one side of my face. Rain slid into my eyes and down my cheeks.

'Get in the canoe.' In his ragged breathing I heard what his exertions had cost him.

I didn't move.

He kicked me in the small of my back. 'I said, get in the fucking canoe!'

I tried to get to my knees, but with my arms roped behind me, it was nearly impossible. I had to roll onto my stomach and lift my ass in the air to get my knees under me.

He had me sit in the bow, facing backward. Then he pushed us off into the open water.

The wind was blowing a chop along the lake. Gray-green waves knocked the hull of the canoe and splashed over the gunwales. My T-shirt and jeans were already soaked through from the rain.

This time Brenda paddled — she had no choice. My father stared right through me as if I were a ghost. Raindrops danced off the brim of his camouflage cap.

Over their shoulders I watched the lodge and cabins grow smaller and smaller. All the windows were dark. Behind the sporting camp the old-growth pines made a jagged edge, like a dark saw blade, against the lowering sky. I listened, hoping to hear the wail of sirens, but all I heard was the slosh of water, the whistle of rising wind.

He was steering us down the lake, staying close to the shore. Eventually we would pass the spot where Charley had crashed.

364

What, I wondered, would we find floating there?

★   ★   ★

The chop bucked the canoe up and down, but my father kept us moving in a straight line. His strokes were deft and seemingly effortless, pulling the canoe forward rather than pushing it along as amateur paddlers try to do.

The summer I'd stayed at Rum Pond I'd asked him to teach me to paddle the way he did. He said he would, but he never did. And so I had spent hours alone, after dusk when all the dishes were washed, teaching myself to paddle — maybe in this same canoe. Now I remembered the balsam-scented dusk descending on the lake and the bats skimming low over the surface, feeding, and everywhere the trout rising, making ever-expanding, intersecting circles in the water. But mostly what I remembered was looking up at my father's cabin, hearing his laughter and Truman's through the trees, and feeling unspeakably alone.

★   ★   ★

A styrofoam cup floated past, then a sheet of waterlogged paper. Afloat in the distance I saw one of the paddles Charley had kept lashed to the struts of the plane. It was broken like a bone. Farther still, I saw the Super Cub, upside down, its cockpit swamped full of water, a hundred or so feet to one side of us. Maybe it rested on the shallow gravel bottom of the lake. A faded orange life jacket bobbed in the waves without a person in it.

In my mind I saw Ora sitting in her wheelchair at the end of the dock as we had taken off this morning. She had waved at us, waved good-bye to her husband. She would never see him alive again.

My father didn't even give the plane a glance. He kept paddling.

Brenda was smirking at me. My pain, apparently, amused her. A few hours earlier, I had felt sorry for this lonely girl raised by men, but now I just wanted to wipe that smirk off that cruel face. I had no other motivation, no other thought as I stood up in the canoe.

The smirk vanished. Disbelief widened her eyes. My father started to speak, but no words came out of his open mouth. There was an instant when I stood above them, calm and perfectly balanced, and we were still gliding forward. Then, just like that, the canoe tipped over, and we were all in the water.

★ ★ ★

I went in headfirst, upside down and unable to right myself without the use of my arms. I scissored my legs and twisted. I felt thrashing movements around me. Bodies in the water. My foot kicked something hard. For a split second, my head broke the surface, but I couldn't stay afloat, and I slipped back under the chop. Water rushed up my nose and into my lungs. Water burned my sinuses like acid inhaled.

Then my feet touched bottom. It was the gravel floor of the lake. I pushed off with both feet. Again my head broke the surface and again I slid back. But this time I didn't slide completely under. The water was shallower. I felt rocks under me. I could stand.

Behind me I heard splashing. I didn't pause to look. I struggled into the shallows. The water felt like quicksand holding me back, pulling me down. My legs had no bones in them. All I could think about was making it to the trees.

And I almost did.

My father tackled me at the water's edge. He lunged forward out of the shallows and got me around the knees and I went down, chest first, onto the rocks. My breath exploded out of me. I rolled onto my side. He was on his knees in the water, pawing at my legs. I drove my boot into his face. He'd lost his hat and his rifle, but the .44, I could see, was still somehow tucked in his belt. He spit blood into the lake and rose up onto his feet. He stood over me, red-faced, hair plastered in a weird way across his forehead, looking like someone I had never seen before. A complete stranger.

Suddenly the Ruger was in his hand.

I waited for it. There was nothing else I could do.

Then the surf washed a canoe paddle past his legs. He must have seen the movement out of the corner of his eye because he paused and looked over his shoulder. Brenda was nowhere in sight. The canoe had drifted against the shore. It looked almost jaunty as it bounced along on the waves.

'Brenda?' he called.

There was no answer. Rain was coming down in sheets.

'Brenda?'

And, just like that, he forgot me. Calling her name, he waded back into the depths, trying to find her. He pushed at the water as if it were sand he could clear away with his hands, but it just flooded back. He dove beneath the surface and vanished for the longest time.

I remained seated on the cold stones. My heart was galloping in my chest. It didn't occur to me to run. I wanted to see him come up with her. In spite of everything, it was what I wanted.

Finally he broke the surface.

He had her in his arms, but her head was back and her mouth was open and she wasn't moving.

I watched him carry her out of the lake and lay her down on the hard stones. He knelt over her, with his back to me.

There was a deep red gash on her forehead above her eye. Her skin looked bleached. Her black hair spread beneath her head like a dark tangle.

He started kissing her open mouth, trying to make her breathe. Then he began pounding on her chest. I had never seen him frantic before. I had seen him angry and happy, drunk and sober, but never, visibly, afraid. Her body jerked, and her head lolled toward me, but I knew it was just the force of his hands making her move. His strength pushed water out of her lungs and up her throat, but she wouldn't breathe. She hadn't been underwater for more than a few minutes, but she was dead.

I leaned my back against a boulder and used the leverage to get to my feet. Wind-driven rain smacked the surface of the lake. If he was crying, I couldn't hear him, but his shoulders were shaking.

He had come back for her. He could have stayed in Canada and might even have eluded the police there, traveling north and west, becoming in time one of those nameless men you see pumping gas in small towns or working behind the counter of roadside convenience stores, anonymous men living always one step ahead of their past. But instead he had risked capture and death to come back for her — this unbalanced, alcoholic girl who had already betrayed him at least once.

'Dad?'

He gave no indication of hearing me. Motionless as he was, he could have been another of the glacial boulders scattered along the lakeshore. When he finally arose, he never gave me a glance, just staggered off into the forest, clutching the Ruger to his chest. He crashed through the undergrowth like a wild animal and was gone, leaving me with nothing but questions.

Would the police run him to ground before he reached the Canadian border? Or, like the escaped German POW he'd told me about, would he disappear without a trace into the Maine woods, never to be seen again?

My answer arrived in the form of a single gunshot that came booming through the trees. I'd always thought of my father as the ultimate survivor. But in that, too, I was mistaken.

★   ★   ★

I cut myself loose with my jackknife.

I had a hard time pulling it from my pants pocket, but eventually I was able to get my numb fingers to grip the handle and slide it out. I dropped the knife a few times before I was finally able to saw through the cords that bound my wrist. As the circulation returned to my forearms and hands I felt first a tingling and then a dull throbbing ache.

Leaving the bodies for the police, I picked up the paddle that had washed onto the shore and then waded out to where the canoe had come to rest amid the branches of a half-sunk birch tree. I pulled the canoe onto the gravel and flipped it over to get the water out of the bottom. Then I dragged it back into the shallows and climbed in.

The wind had subsided and the rain seemed to be lightening — at least the sky was no longer so dark.

I paddled out to the Super Cub.

The pontoons of the wrecked plane jutted above the surface of the lake. Even with the breeze blowing, a diesel smell hung in the air, and floating streamers of iridescent oil showed the currents that usually moved unseen through the lake.

Up close I could see that the plane was

balanced on several submerged boulders. I counted three bullet holes just in the fuselage. Peering into the water I could make out the pilot's door hanging open, but I couldn't see into the cockpit.

I set the paddle down in the canoe and prepared myself to dive over the side. But dread of what I would find in the cockpit froze me in place. Rain fell into my eyes, blurring my vision. I tried to wipe them clear, but it was no use. I took a deep breath and watched a seat cushion float past the bow.

That was when I noticed the little island. It was just a clump of boulders, really, that rose up from a sandbar maybe fifty yards away — between the wreckage and the opposite shore. I hadn't noticed it before.

Something green seemed to be wedged between two of the rocks.

I lifted the paddle again and began to chop at the water. In less than a minute I had drawn close enough to the boulders to see that the shape was a man wearing a green shirt. He didn't appear to be moving.

'Charley?'

The canoe glided closer as if pulled by a magnet. I saw the back of his head, one suntanned arm thrown over a boulder, hanging on.

'Charley?'

The wet head turned. A swollen eye opened.

'There you are,' he said, as if he had been expecting me.

33

He looked like hell. He had been shot in the left arm and leg. The wound to his arm was just a bloody groove where the bullet had grazed the triceps. The leg wound was something worse. The bullet had burrowed like a worm into the meat of his thigh. It had missed the femoral artery, but even so, he was losing blood at an alarming rate. The skin of his face, beneath the red-and-violet bruises, was drained of color. His pulse was weak, his breath fluttery.

'I thought you were dead.'

I'd pulled him up onto the rocks and was now trying to stanch the flow from his leg by applying pressure with both hands. Dark-looking blood leaked between my fingers.

He winced. 'Don't speak too soon.'

'I'm going to get you out of here, Charley.'

He smiled, but his eyes were full of doubt. 'I think I'm going into shock.'

'You're a tough old geezer. You'll make it.'

I made a pressure bandage out of my T-shirt and wrapped it tight around his leg. Then I went to fetch the canoe. I'd kicked it away leaping into the water and had to swim out to retrieve it. Getting Charley into the canoe without overturning it wasn't easy. He passed out from the pain of being lifted up, and I had to shake him to bring him around again. He looked me full in the eyes.

Flecks of spittle clung to his lips. 'What happened?'

'You passed out.'

'Shit.'

I pushed off with the paddle and turned the canoe in the direction of the sporting camp, a mile up the lake.

He tried to clear his throat, but his voice was still faint and strained. 'Where's your dad?'

'He killed himself.'

'I thought I heard a shot before. What about the girl?'

'Drowned.'

He nodded as if this explained everything. 'If I pass out again and don't come around, tell Ora I'm sorry.'

'You can tell her yourself.' The rain had stopped, but I hadn't noticed until I'd begun paddling again. The wind had died down and a mist was rising off the slick surface of the lake. 'You're the one who told me you were indestructible.'

'Told you a bunch of lies.' He smiled and closed his eyes and folded his hands on his chest. But he was restless and couldn't keep his fingers and feet from twitching.

'Stay with me,' I said.

'I'm not going anywhere.'

I tried to keep my strokes calm and controlled. My arms and shoulders ached as if I had done a hundred pull-ups, but I never stopped, not even for a second.

The lakeshore slid along the side of the boat, an endless wall of dripping pines and birches. We passed beneath the tumbling, talus cliffs of Holeb Mountain, its bald summit dissolving into clouds. Up ahead I saw the sporting camp take shape out of the mist. First the dock, then the lodge.

Blue lights were flashing behind the buildings. It took me forever to realize what those lights were.

★ ★ ★

Before Charley had broken off his search for Truman Dellis, he put in a call to the state police. The first trooper had arrived at Rum Pond only minutes after my father and Brenda made me step into the canoe. Now there were troopers, deputy sheriffs, and game wardens all over the scene. Wearily I watched them carry Charley away, making a stretcher of their interlocking arms. I tried to follow, but hands restrained me. I turned my head. It was Soctomah. He was wearing a navy Windbreaker over a bulletproof vest. He wanted to know what had happened. Where, he wanted to know, was Brenda Dean?

I pointed down the lake.

For an instant the detective followed the invisible line that extended from my fingertip as if the mists would part and bring her into view. Then, just as quickly, he turned back to me, his face dark with confusion and impatience. 'What happened?' he asked again.

'It was my father,' I said. 'He killed them all.'

★ ★ ★

Someone found a shirt for me. Someone else brought me a paper cup with black coffee in it.

After Soctomah and Menario were reassured that there was no longer any present danger — that my father had no armed accomplice lurking in the woods — they sent a boat down to the other end of the lake to find the bodies. Then they sat me down at a wet picnic table and made me describe what had happened from the moment Charley and I arrived this morning at Rum Pond. They wanted to know about my discovery of Russ Pelletier's body and how much I had disturbed the crime scene, and they wanted to know the exact sequence of events that resulted in my shooting Truman Dellis. The entire camp was being cordoned off, they said, and the state police evidence recovery team needed to know every step I had taken and what I had touched and what I'd left alone.

'You were describing how you stood up in the canoe,' said Detective Menario, pushing a little tape recorder across the table at me. 'Why'd you do that?'

'I don't know. I guess it was the look on her face.'

'What look?'

'She couldn't stop grinning. It made me mad.'

'So the canoe overturned?'

'That's right.'

'And she never came up?'

'She hit her head on something underwater. It might have been a rock or maybe she came up under the canoe. I remember kicking something pretty hard when I went under. It might have been her head.'

Menario gave me an incredulous smile. 'And your father was so grief-stricken he shot himself.'

'She was the reason he came back.'

'I thought you said he came back to frame Pelletier and Dellis.'

'The real reason was Brenda. After she drowned, he had nothing else to live for.'

'A real romantic.'

My coffee had grown cold. I poured it onto the ground. Dusk had begun to fall. Out on the lake I saw trout rising as insects hatched out onto the surface. Soon the bats would come out to feed in the dark. 'I'd like to go to Skowhegan. I'd like to wait with Ora at the hospital.'

The tape recorder clicked off on its own. Menario reached into his Windbreaker for a new microcassette. 'Let's go over this again,' he said.

'It can wait,' Soctomah said to his partner. 'Why don't you go find a ride for Mike.'

Menario looked at him sourly. Then he stuffed the recorder in his pocket and walked off.

'He's a good detective,' said Soctomah, watching him go.

'I'll take your word for it.'

'The A.G. is going to have to take a look at what happened with Truman Dellis. Your shooting him, I mean.'

I shrugged. 'It doesn't matter what happens to me.'

A boat motored up to the dock. We watched the state police unload two body bags, carrying them up the hill to a waiting ambulance.

I stood up. My joints felt a hundred years old. 'I'd really like to get going, if it's OK with you.'

'I understand,' he said.

★   ★   ★

My last view of Rum Pond Sporting Camps was in the mirror of Deputy Twombley's patrol car. Once again he had been designated my private chauffeur. Lit up by the blue strobes of police cruisers and the lights brought in by crime scene investigators, the camp receded into the darkening forest. I wondered if I'd ever see it again.

Probably not. Pelletier didn't have any children, that I knew of, no heirs except maybe his ex-wife, but it wouldn't matter if he'd left behind a family of ten since there was no way in hell Jonathan Shipman's murder would stop Wendigo Timber from developing this land. There was never any chance of that happening, no matter what Vernon Tripp and the others might have hoped. The leaseholders would be evicted from their camps throughout the region and this hundred-year-old sporting camp would be sold to some hedge fund millionaire to turn into a private lakeside retreat to be used two weeks every summer.

Which meant Charley and Ora would also lose their home of thirty years on Flagstaff Pond. What would they do then? What would Ora do if he never returned from the hospital?

Twombley didn't say a word during the drive. His puffy face was lit up by the dashboard, but I couldn't read his expression. I rolled down the automatic window, letting the air rush in around my head, and closed my eyes.

He woke me sometime later. We had arrived at Redington-Fairview General Hospital in Skowhegan and were idling beside the ambulance bay. I started to get out, but he called after me. 'Bowditch.'

'Yeah?'

He stared at me for a long time, then shook his head and said: 'Never mind.'

I went inside to start my vigil.

Kathy Frost was already there in the brightly lit waiting room, talking with a forest ranger I didn't recognize. She took one look at my bruised and bloodied face and all the toughness went out of her. For half a second I thought she might actually hug me, but instead she shook my hand hard enough to crush bones. 'I'm really sorry, Mike.'

'Me too. About everything.' My throat was so dry my voice was just a rasp.

'Don't beat yourself up.'

'You were right about my dad. I don't know why I couldn't see it when it was so clear to everyone else.'

'You were too close to the situation.'

'That's what you kept telling me.'

'It's my eternal curse not to be believed, Grasshopper.' It was the best she could do for a joke under the circumstances, but I appreciated it. She stuck her thumbs in her gunbelt, a question obviously weighing on her mind. 'So what the hell happened up there?'

378

I could have told her about the murder of Russell Pelletier, and my fight with Truman Dellis, and the part I played in the drowning of Brenda Dean, but I was too tired. Rather than say anything more, I cut to the heart of the matter. 'He shot himself.'

She would have to get the rest of the story from someone else. I glanced toward the admitting desk. 'Do you know anything about Charley?'

'They've got him in the ICU. He has some internal injuries, and they're worried about his heart.'

'He lost a lot of blood out on the lake.'

'You did what you could.' She reached into her pocket and handed me something. In my palm was a Warden Service I.D. card. 'I guess I forgot to give this to Malcomb. Oops.'

Just then, as if summoned by the sound of his name, the lieutenant came hurrying through the emergency room door. He always looked so stone-faced, but tonight there was real fear in his eyes. He had just lost his wife last year to cancer, and now his close friend was also near death.

'How is he?' he asked Kathy in his gravel voice.

She told him what she knew.

He listened intently without even a glance in my direction. If he was concerned about me, he didn't show it. But after Kathy finished, he turned and stared into my eyes and, after a long silence, said, 'It sounds like you saved his life, Warden.'

Hearing him call me 'Warden' was a surprise

after everything that had happened, but I wasn't getting my hopes up. 'It was my fault he was injured.'

'I doubt Charley would agree with you.' He removed a pack of cigarettes from his pocket, then remembered where he was and stashed them back. 'He's a tough old bird. He's walked away from crashes before.'

I got the impression that Malcomb was trying to convince himself of this. 'So now what do we do?' I asked.

'We find a doctor to check you over. And then we wait.'

'Would you mind if I borrowed your cell phone first? I have someone to call.'

★   ★   ★

'Michael?' said my mother. I'd reached her at the home of Neil's daughter in Long Beach, California, where they were staying until my father could be brought to justice. 'Michael, what is it?'

'He's dead, Mom.'

She caught her breath, loud enough for me to hear. 'What — ? What happened?'

'He shot himself. It's true what the police said. He was the one who killed those men.'

'No.'

'He was guilty all along, but we were too blind to see it.'

'No.' Her voice was shaky. She was close to sobbing. 'Why? Why would he do such a thing?'

I didn't intend to be cruel to her. The truth

was brutal enough. But who was I to shield her from it now? 'It was all over a woman that he loved. But she's dead now, too. He came back to Rum Pond for her, and when she died, he must have decided that he couldn't go on without her.'

'Who was she?'

'Just a girl.'

'I always thought — ' She was crying openly now, no longer holding anything back. 'I always thought it would be me.'

So there it was. Fifteen years ago, after her divorce, she had expected a similar phone call, but it never came. Was it my imagination, or was she jealous that in the end he had loved another woman more?

'Michael?' It was Neil. He had taken the phone from her. 'Your mother is — she's very upset. My God, it's horrible news.'

Holding the phone to my head, I put a hand to my other ear to cover the clamor of the hospital. What more was there to say, at this point? 'You were right, Neil. You were right, about him, and we were wrong. We should have listened to you.'

He paused. 'You weren't thinking clearly — neither of you were.' He paused, and I could hear her sobbing in the background. 'What's going to happen? What are people saying up there?'

Why was I surprised that neither of them had asked about me? 'I'm sure it'll be front-page news tomorrow. If you're worried about the media, you might want to stay out there for a few more days.' Across the room I saw more wardens streaming into the waiting room. Charley

Stevens had friends beyond counting. 'Neil, I have to go. Tell my mom that I love her.'

After I hung up, I took a step toward the gathering wardens, then looked down at the cell phone in my hand. Finally, I got up the nerve to call Sarah.

'I've been so worried about you,' she said.

I'd wanted so much to hear her voice, but then when she answered, I found that I could barely speak. 'Thanks.'

'Kathy called me on her way to the hospital. She told me what happened. It's so horrible.'

'You don't know the whole story.' My voice broke as I said this.

She must have sensed something about my emotional state because she paused a long time before she spoke. 'Mike, did he hurt you?'

'No,' I lied.

'Can you tell me what happened?'

I could feel something inside myself starting to give way. I don't know whether it was the long day catching up with me at last or hearing Sarah's voice again. But I feared that I might break down in the hospital corridor if I continued this conversation.

'I can't,' I said. 'I will when I get back, OK?'

'I'll be here,' she said, and I knew it was a promise.

*   *   *

At 11:45 the following morning, Charley opened his eyes. It seemed like half the members of the Maine Warden Service had come by during the night, as well as assorted other law enforcement officers and citizens of Flagstaff and Dead River. Sally Reynolds was there, and so was Donna, the mousy waitress from the Dead River Inn. Most everyone left me alone. I was dozing in a corner of the waiting room when Charley woke up. He asked to see me almost immediately.

He smiled weakly at me when I came around the movable screen.

Ora sat beside the bed, as did their oldest daughter, Anne. She was an attractive brunette, about thirty, with her mother's high cheekbones and her father's strong jaw. She had a cup of ice chips she was feeding him to quench his thirst.

'They won't give me water,' he told me.

'The bastards,' I deadpanned.

He grinned again, and I saw some of the old impishness in him return. 'You look like shit.'

'I guess no one's shown you a mirror.'

'They did, but darned if it didn't crack.'

'How's the leg?'

'Still attached to the rest of me.'

'That's something.'

'Yes, it is.'

'He's going to need a lot of physical therapy,' said Anne.

Charley rolled his eyes.

'I'm so sorry about your father,' Ora said to me.

I was too stunned to respond. My father was the man who had shot her husband, who had brought us all to this place of fear and

383

waiting for death, and here she was expressing her condolences to me over his selfish and cowardly suicide.

People disappoint you so often. I hardly knew how to react when they surpassed all your hopes.

We do hope that you have enjoyed reading this large print book.

Did you know that all of our titles are available for purchase?

We publish a wide range of high quality large print books including:
Romances, Mysteries, Classics
General Fiction
Non Fiction and Westerns

Special interest titles available in large print are:
The Little Oxford Dictionary
Music Book
Song Book
Hymn Book
Service Book

Also available from us courtesy of Oxford University Press:
Young Readers' Dictionary
(large print edition)
Young Readers' Thesaurus
(large print edition)

For further information or a free brochure, please contact us at:
Ulverscroft Large Print Books Ltd.,
The Green, Bradgate Road, Anstey,
Leicester, LE7 7FU, England.
Tel: (00 44) 0116 236 4325
Fax: (00 44) 0116 234 0205

Other titles published by
The House of Ulverscroft:

THE LOST

Claire McGowan

When two teenage girls go missing along the Irish border, forensic psychologist Paula Maguire has to return to the home town she left years before. Swirling with rumours and secrets, the town is gripped with the fear of a serial killer. But the truth could be even darker. Surrounded by people and places she tried to forget, Paula digs into the cases as the truth twists further away. What's the link with two other disappearances from 1985? And why does everything lead back to the town's dark past — including the reasons her own mother went missing years before? As the shocking truth is revealed, Paula learns that sometimes it's better not to find what you've lost.

PAGANINI'S GHOST

Paul Adam

It's the most exciting concert Cremona has seen in years. The headliner is a brilliant young Russian playing a violin once owned by the 19th century master, Nicolo Paganini. But the triumphal performance is immediately overshadowed by the murder of one of its sponsors. Solving the murder will require a journey into musical history — and to make that journey, Cremona's police chief will require the assistance of Gianni Castiglione, elderly charmer and only mildly larcenous expert in violins.

EYE CONTACT

Fergus McNeill

From the outside, Robert Naysmith is a successful businessman, handsome and charming. But for years he's been playing a deadly game. He doesn't choose his victims. Each is selected at random — the first person to make eye contact after he begins 'the game' will not have long to live. Their fate is sealed. When the body of a young woman is found on Severn Beach, Detective Inspector Harland is assigned the case. It's only when he links it to an unsolved murder in Oxford that the police begin to guess at the awful scale of the crimes. But how do you find a killer who strikes without motive?